To Andrew McCall

Contents

∘◯∘

Acknowledgements and Thanks

°☺°

Diana Athill
Simon Michael Bessie
Desmond Briggs
James Oliver Brown
Catherine Carver
Lionel Davidson
Eckhart Maunchly*
Michael Elkins
Lt Col Dov Eshkol
the Gavron family, Jerusalem
Gen 'Motta' Gur
Sir Michael Hadow
Major Gen Amos Horev
Jeremiah Kaplan
Nadder Khirrish

Kibbutz Ayelet Hashachar
Rabbi Abraham Levy
Q Love
Robin Miller
 ex Grenadier Guards
Anwar el Nuseibeh
Tim O'Keefe
Simon Raven
Tony Rudd
Leon Shalit
David Susman, ex Palmach
Professor Hugh Thomas
Graham Watson
Professor Yigael Yadin
Professor Yaron

* The author hopes his other mentors in electronics will condone, in the impossibly early year of 1948, Ezra's demonstration of a model of the printed circuit.

The Sterling Family

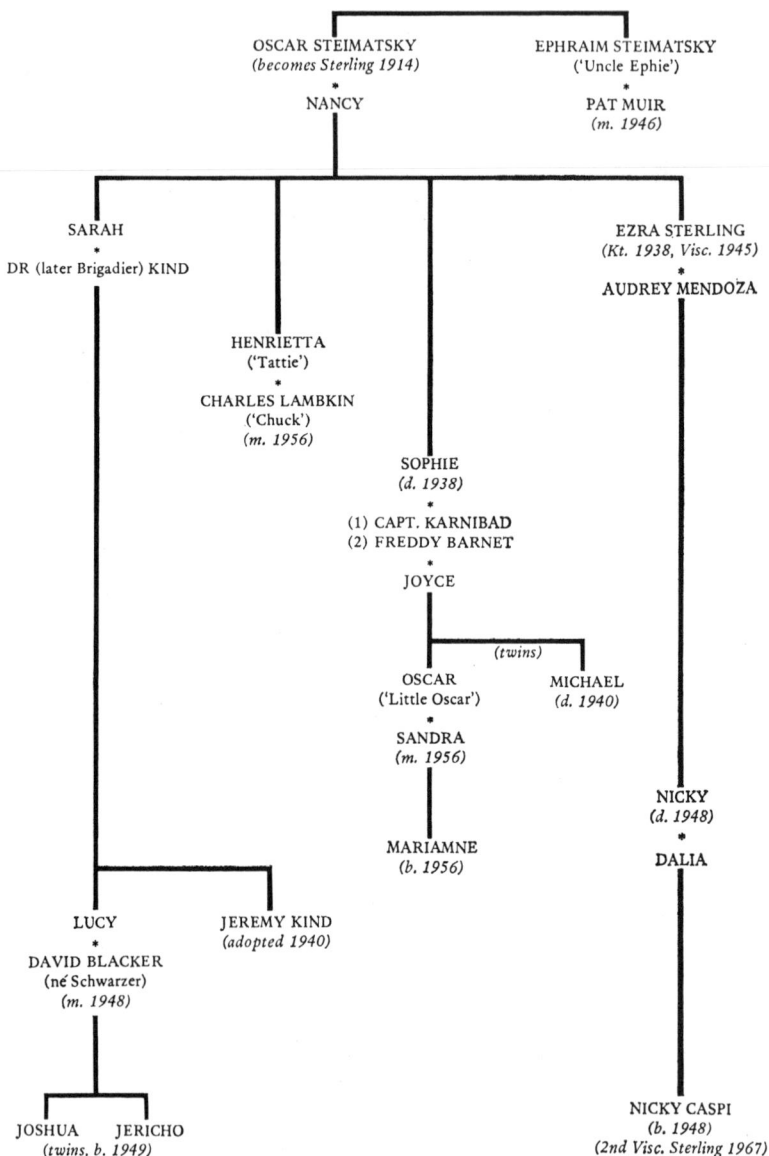

OSCAR STEIMATSKY
(becomes Sterling 1914)
*
NANCY

EPHRAIM STEIMATSKY
('Uncle Ephie')
*
PAT MUIR
(m. 1946)

SARAH
*
DR (later Brigadier) KIND

EZRA STERLING
(Kt. 1938, Visc. 1945)
*
AUDREY MENDOZA

HENRIETTA
('Tattie')
*
CHARLES LAMBKIN
('Chuck')
(m. 1956)

SOPHIE
(d. 1938)
*
(1) CAPT. KARNIBAD
(2) FREDDY BARNET
*
JOYCE

(twins)

OSCAR
('Little Oscar')
*
SANDRA
(m. 1956)

MICHAEL
(d. 1940)

NICKY
(d. 1948)
*
DALIA

MARIAMNE
(b. 1956)

LUCY
*
DAVID BLACKER
(né Schwarzer)
(m. 1948)

JEREMY KIND
(adopted 1940)

JOSHUA   JERICHO
(twins, b. 1949)

NICKY CASPI
(b. 1948)
(2nd Visc. Sterling 1967)

x

Prologue: 1881

◦◉◦

'Next!'

He didn't look like a Jew boy. He was tall with wide-apart grey eyes, slightly hollow-chested perhaps, but then none of them had much flesh on them.

'*Name?*'

'Steimatsky.'

'First name?' (The immigration officer at Hull had quickly learnt not to ask for their Christian names.)

'Oscar.'

'*Haben Sie Geld.*'

The boy pulled a leather purse from under his belt and tipped out on to the desk three gold rings held together by a piece of wire.

The immigration officer sniffed. 'You need the address of a jeweller in the town.' He wrote something on a piece of paper which the boy studied calmly, but he did not move. 'And here's something to get you a meal,' and he gave the boy a florin.

The boy took it and turned it over. He then handed the piece of paper back to the officer saying: '*Ihr Name, bitte!*'

The immigration officer was surprised.

Bernard Blond the jeweller offered him ten pounds for the gold rings, which would last him at least a month if he were careful. Blond's wife, Rachel, was not a pretty woman but she had a sweet smile and she looked up the trains to Leeds in her Bradshaw and wrote the times and changes on a large piece of paper and underneath his time of arrival put the letters 'G.W.W.P.': God willing weather permitting.

He stayed the night with the jeweller and Rachel hoped her son – she was with child – would grow up so good.

The next afternoon Oscar Steimatsky stood in the office – if you could call it that – of Mr Gordon who came from his town, Grodnow. He had climbed up some rickety stairs at the end of a warehouse full of broken bicycles, cash registers, chicken wire, buckets and sewing machines. Mr Gordon was distraught. 'There are too many of you. Business is bad. Why don't you go to New York? When you write home tell them to stop sending me people!' The boy regarded him with concern, even compassion.

Mr Gordon felt guilty. He fumbled with a cash box and eventually opened the lid. There was nothing in the top compartment. He sighed. It was the sound of a good man who read the Talmud every morning and tried to act out its injunctions. 'Visiting the sick . . . acts of charity.'

'Look,' he said, 'this is a crown, a whole crown. Now go away . . . *Please.*'

The boy handled the coin. He had never seen such a big one. It looked like a medal. He walked back down the stairs.

A few minutes later Mr Gordon heard noises. He went to investigate. The boy had taken off his coat and was fiddling with a dismembered cash register. He must have his own tools.

'Hey! I thought I told you to go away.'

The boy looked up, smiled and went on tinkering, whistling through his teeth as he did so. Mr Gordon shrugged his shoulders. He'd never repair *that* one.

Twenty minutes later the boy returned carrying the cash register. There was no room to put it down on Mr Gordon's desk. Gently he removed some papers, cleared a space and set the machine down. He pointed to it.

Fascinated, Mr Gordon pressed the red NO SALE button. (It indicated his mood.) The machine emitted a dispirited *ping* and the drawer shot out revealing the crown piece.

The boy shook his finger, walked round the desk, stared at the machine and leaning over Mr Gordon's shrunken back, quickly pressed six buttons. The bell rang out clear and proud, like a young church, and up shot £99 19s 11d – the most it could do.

The boy laughed triumphantly.

He is ambitious, thought Mr Gordon, but is he ambitious for me? And that is how the family started the business.

PART ONE

1936, 1940

1936

◦◯◦

'But you can't go tomorrow. You can't drive on Shabat.'

'Uncle Ephie, those days are over. In America the Jews play golf. . . .'

'They said that two thousand years ago,' Ephie interrupted his ambitious nephew with his favourite remark.

'I think he wants to show me his swimming pool. He has a house in Sussex.'

'Swimming. Who swims on Shabat? God forbid.'

'Uncle Ephie,' said the younger man patiently, 'how many times have you been to the Far East? I need to know for the prospectus. That's why I'm telephoning.'

The sound of an ancient throat being cleared and cheerful wheeze. It was the sort of question Ephie Steimatsky liked to answer. Ezra Sterling had his gold fountain pen poised over a blank in the sentence: 'Mr Ephraim Steimatsky, Director in Charge of Overseas Sales, has visited the Far East —— times on behalf of Sterling Brothers.'

'My last trip was my last trip, I can tell you. This morning . . .'

'You said that two thousand years ago,' said Ezra coolly.

'This morning I looked in the mirror,' Ephie continued, 'and I thought I was shaving the face of a dead man.'

'How many times, Uncle Ephie?'

The older man sighed. Ezra frightened him. His poor dead brother had sent him to America and America had turned him mass-production mad. Who needed to expand? He had enough money surely. He'd made a good *shiddach* with that toffee-nosed Audrey Mendoza, a beautiful Rolls-Royce, a lovely boy. . . .

'Three times before the war, and thirteen times since. But I warn you, that was my last. . . .'

'Thank you, Uncle Ephie,' said Ezra, replacing the receiver, and inking in the figure 16.

The stockbroker's house, one of Henry VIII's innumerable hunting lodges, had been enlarged in the time of Edward VII to accommodate the lady's maids and valets of its many guests. It had indeed been recently embellished by a swimming pool and a formidable stainless-steel diving contraption, which glittered angrily in the sun. As Jenkins, Ezra's chauffeur, drove past, he had uttered the immemorial sound, 'Coo-er.'

The stockbroker was like a Bateman caricature of a war profiteer. He wore an eyeglass, an oversize carnation and he smoked a cigar. 'Well done!' he said. 'You're just in time for a glass of wine.' He glanced admiringly at the gleaming bonnet of Ezra's Phantom III Rolls-Royce. The Jew had style.

'Yes, if you could see that my chauffeur . . .'

'Certainly, I'll see your man gets fed and watered. The servants' hall is there.' He pointed to what seemed to Jenkins a distant building. Jenkins plodded off.

'You didn't bring Arthur with you?'

'No,' said Ezra. Sir Arthur Coleport's function as a non-family director – 'the Sabbath goy,' Ephie called him – was to make the introductions.

The iron-studded oak door, massively battened, was opened by a butler and Ezra glanced up at the hammer-beam roof of the great hall.

'May I wash my hands?'

'Of course, dear boy, how thoughtless of me.' He beamed. 'Sinnockson will show you and then you'll join me on the terrace.'

'This way, sir, if you please.'

Ezra noticed an organ and a conductor's stand at the far end of the hall.

'So you have concerts here?'

Sinnockson sniggered. 'Well, not exactly, sir. Mr Anderson likes to conduct and I play – the gramophone.'

In the cloakroom Ezra was impressed by the two wash basins,

the rows of clean wellington boots, and by a huge Chinese jar full of shooting and other sticks. On the walls were framed photographs of the stockbroker's schooldays, depicting him as beagler, cricketer, and possibly head of house. There were also photographs of prize bulls basking in the solicitude of their white-overalled attendants.

The place glowed with wealth and solidity. Ezra understood why his visit had been insisted upon. In the City Anderson had a reputation for being lucky, but also slightly 'hot'.

Sinnockson was waiting for him. In the hall Ezra paused, digesting the sounds of summer through the opened lattice windows.

'How nice to have a place in the country.'

'I'd much rather a place in town, sir,' said Sinnockson. 'It's dull down here during the week.'

Ezra looked at the man. He seemed presentable.

'When you want a change, telephone my secretary. Mr Anderson will give you the number.'

'Thank you, sir,' said Sinnockson with feeling.

'I have your list for the pink forms,' said the stockbroker. 'I assume they're mainly friends, relations and customers. There's bound to be a premium on them because we may have pitched the issue a little low. Quite handsome. You realize you're making a lot of presents?'

'To customers and our agents. Why not?'

'No friends or relations?'

Ezra shook his head.

The stockbroker poured him out another glass of champagne which he called, mysteriously, 'boy'.

'You don't believe in mixing business with friendship?'

'Very nice, this champagne,' said Ezra.

'Krug. I'll send you a case on Monday.'

'You don't think that's, er . . . premature?'

The stockbroker leant back in the hammock which creaked easily and waved to his wife who was deadheading roses in the garden below.

'Not with these profits. You've got everything going for you. You're still young. Anything electric is good news. If rearmament gets under way you're geared for that. By the way, what do these initials mean?'

He leant forward and pointed to an item in the prospectus.

'It's a sort of early-warning system we do, with others, of course, for the Air Ministry. On the secret list, fairly advanced stuff.'

'Ah. A result of your father's connection with the War Office.'

'Yes,' said Ezra. 'He was a great patriot,' and he allowed himself a bleak smile. 'You see Father could make anything and Ephie could sell anything. Father could make anything work and Ephie could sell things which didn't exist.' Ezra laughed and drank his champagne. 'He once came back from Hong Kong with an order for electric clocks. So Father designed one and suddenly we're in the electric clock business!'

'Any good?' asked the stockbroker.

'No,' said Ezra. 'I killed it; they never wear out and what happens when there's a power failure? People go mad.'

'But the office equipment division is far the most profitable side of Sterling Brothers.' The stockbroker leant forward and pointed to some figures. 'Look – in relation to capital invested.'

Ezra did not look.

'There is no capital invested,' he said impatiently. 'We're really sub-contractors on no risk. It's an old-fashioned system. High mark-up, expensive agents. No stock, manufacture to order. Good as far as it goes . . . but isn't it better to have a slice of fruit cake than the whole of a penny bun?'

The stockbroker was not sure and grunted.

'No,' said Ezra. 'Big profits come by selling quality at quantity prices. Take this glass. An American wouldn't say, as we do, how much can I make on it? He'd say, "What happens when I manufacture enough to get the price down to a dollar?"'

The stockbroker winced. He was proud of his Waterford.

'These Army contracts – I know it's all hush-hush but my pals among the jobbers are going to telephone me and . . . well, it's a sentimental place, the Stock Exchange, and they appreciate an indiscretion – some inside dope, as they say.'

'Yes,' said Ezra. 'How about this? The Army think a lot of Colonel Sterling, Royal Engineers, formerly Sergeant-Major

Steimatsky, right? Like I told you, he can repair anything. His English isn't too good but they want him to organize training manuals. They want him to stay on after the war. But he's no fool and Ephie won't let him. He told me if he hadn't been so good with his hands, he'd have been a general.'

The stockbroker felt obliged to make a gesture of protest.

'No, it's true, the English despise experts. He realized that. Said he'd spank me if he found me mending a fuse. That's why I went to Harvard.'

'Hmm, yes . . . Have we got that, I wonder.' The stockbroker rustled his papers. 'Good; "graduate of the Harvard School of Business". Tell me, if I may be personal . . .'

'Personal in English means rude, doesn't it?' Ezra smiled to take away the hurt. 'Sure, go ahead. Shoot, as we Harvard boys say.'

'Do you benefit, or rather did you, from the, er, fact that Hore-Belisha at the War Office . . .'

'. . . Is a Jew? No, if anything the reverse. Besides, Leslie's more interested in the soldiers having clean socks than clean rifles. That canard about his really being called Horeb-Elisha . . .' Ezra shrugged. 'Audrey knows one of his aunts. They come from Mogadir in Morocco and their name is Belisha. His stepfather was Sir something Hore and adopted him, so – Hore-Belisha.'

'Ah, I didn't know that,' said the stockbroker slowly. The canard, as Ezra called it, was accepted in the City.

'It's no secret. But as Nicky told me the other day, "Prejudice is not just based on ignorance, it depends on it." '

The stockbroker looked puzzled.

'Nicky? That's my son. He's at prep school and much given to aphorisms. But there was no prejudice against my father. Big Oscar, they called him. Tall, strong, clean, brave, loyal, he was everybody's home-made Jew. The original of "Some of my best friends" – you know?'

'Certainly the business has an excellent reputation in Leeds.' Anderson did not add that the Stock Exchange was not unimpressed by the City connections of Ezra's wife, Audrey Mendoza. (Arthur Coleport had told him how the couple had met – on the maiden voyage of the *Queen Mary*. The next morning Audrey had *not* said,

'In the circles I move in, sleeping with a woman does not constitute an introduction,' as advised by her haughty mama, and they had been married in Bevis Marks, Audrey's family synagogue, 'under the top-hatted stare of the high-caste Jews.')

'Leeds!' said Ezra. It wasn't Leeds that mattered. It was Whitehall. 'Big Oscar knew the Ministry of Munitions like his own backyard. And he was the first Jew to be president of a British Legion branch, the first to get a Territorial Decoration – isn't that what deputy Lord Lieutenants get for meeting the royal train?'

'Yes, exactly, very respectable.'

'Then we must put it in the prospectus. The Stock Exchange likes respectability.'

'Right,' said the stockbroker briskly. 'So we are offering half a million pounds, at five per cent loan stock, and a million A shares at ten bob each. . . .'

'And no voting shares,' said Ezra.

'No, they stay with the family.'

'Good.'

'And I bet you that within three days of the prospectus being forged, the whole lot will have been taken up. There'll be heavy stagging and you'll be my youngest millionaire.'

Ezra managed a more endearing smile.

'By the way, Arthur told me of a little trouble you had getting into some golf club.'

Ezra coloured. 'Did he?'

'He meant well,' said the stockbroker gently. 'And I saw this advertised in *Country Life*. I thought it would interest you.'

It was a large house between High Wycombe and Oxford, with a nine-hole golf course in the park.

'Quite a size,' said Ezra.

'Well,' said the stockbroker easily, 'so are you.'

They both laughed.

'Just one thing before we join the others, Ezra. With your range of products, have you never thought of having your own label?'

'Label?'

'On gramophone records. A friend of mine, Ted Lewis at Decca . . .'

'No,' said Ezra. 'Too vulnerable. When I was in the States I saw a lot of record companies go broke. I don't ever want a brand name. I prefer to make the bits. Rather have my labels on guns. Much safer.'

The stockbroker was right. Six weeks later the jobbers jammed the elevators in his office building, the share price leapt from 10s. to nearly £2 and the family among them were suddenly worth £3 million, on paper at least.

Ezra entered into negotiations for the purchase of a property known as Turners, a desirable country residence with the added attraction of its own private golf course, and he paid £1500 for an ill-favoured rectory near Lingfield which smelt of Irish stew and linoleum and would be suitable for housing Jewish refugees.

1940

∘◯∘

I

A soft swishing noise, then a clomp and a sort of groan which Mrs Eirene heard through the open door of her office. She replaced the top of the fountain pen which she had used since she was a schoolgirl in Berlin, stood up, dusted her skirts and walked with the authority of a matron down the corridor. She was a short, bossy woman with a whisper of a moustache on her upper lip and rather good legs. First she was annoyed that the floor of the restroom was being cleaned, not on her instructions, then her eye was caught by a heap of jewels, a tiny treasure, in a Craven A ashtray on a table by the door. They could only belong to Miss Tattie, the eldest, possibly the richest, because the only unmarried one of the family. Then she saw Miss Tattie all of a heap on the floor. Had she fainted or, on that hot day, with her enormous weight . . . Mrs Eirene dwelt flickeringly on the rings, loot of twenty years' shopping at Cartier's, coagulating, tenantless, in the ashtray, but she threw the thought right out of her proud German heart and bent down to minister to Miss Tattie, pushing her head forward between her knees, massaging her neck and loosening her frilly and far too tight brassière. This simple drill seemed to work.

'What happened, what happened?' groaned Miss Tattie. 'Am I dying?'

'No, my dear, you only fainted,' said Mrs Eirene.

'Oh, really I'm most grateful, most grateful to you, you may have saved my life,' she murmured.

'You only fainted, Miss Tattie,' said Mrs Eirene.

'Well, I am most grateful to you, Mrs Schwarzer,' said Miss Tattie in her normal voice.

Now upright as Queen Victoria on the restroom's one iron bed, Miss Tattie majestically stirred the nice cup of tea which had been provided, watched by Eirene Schwarzer and by Miss Shapiro, the sort of dithery lady attached to all institutions who turns up sensing disaster – the greater the quicker – but who had, at least, made the tea.

Miss Tattie's unintentional use of Mrs Eirene's (as she was generally known) proper name had reminded that lady of her position in relation to the family, which supported the Jewish refugee office where she worked and which paid the school fees of her son David Blacker, currently in his first year at St Paul's and whose needs must therefore be attended to with dispatch and, thought Mrs Eirene, with some zeal. Her instant compassion – she was the daughter of a Berlin gynaecologist who had never believed *he* would be hauled off in the middle of the night – for the collapsed heap of clothes which had contained Miss Tattie was quickly changed to a practical concern to render service to a family famous, like all good dynasties, for generosity to those who helped them.

It would have been possible to put Miss Tattie into a cab, there were still plenty around, but it was not possible to put Miss Tattie into a cab because the family preferred not to use taxis. They were all driven around by chauffeurs in Rollses – subdued, not as grand as they could have been, but Rollses. Sir Ezra had one, a rather large one; Lady Sterling had two, one being kept in the country. Sarah Kind, Sir Ezra's other sister, had one and Freddy Barnet, who had married poor Sophie the *meshugana*, had been made to have one; and then Uncle Ephie had an old one down in Margate which followed him at three miles an hour to *shul*.

Mrs Eirene had this crucial information – such as that for some reason Miss Tattie used her brother's car in town but never her sister-in-law's – through her son David, who had been taken up in quite a big way by the family when the Schwarzers, highly recommended by the Sterling agent in Hamburg, came to England from Berlin in 1936. David in turn had lapped up this family lore from Sir Ezra's only child Nicky, with whom it had become David's habit and privilege to spend the school holidays at Turners.

Standing now before Miss Tattie, who was raising a thoroughly stirred and slightly chipped cup of tea to her round little mouth,

Mrs Eirene knew exactly the form. She should telephone Miss Tattie's companion, who would ring Mrs Winterbourne, Sir Ezra's secretary, who would procure Sir Ezra's chauffeur to fetch Miss Tattie and take her to Park Lane where they both lived. The family preferred that instructions concerning themselves should involve, inform and inconvenience as many people as possible. In this way, provided they were well served, and they usually were, their wishes gained momentum as they travelled down the line.

Mrs Eirene therefore said to her charge, 'I think I'd better call Miss Attlee for you.'

Miss Tattie made a gesture both of deprecation and approval. Then it reminded her of something: 'My rings,' she muttered, pointing across the room. Mrs Eirene stood her ground but Miss Shapiro followed the direction and went to fetch them. She held them out to Miss Tattie in the Craven A ashtray as if it were an offering. Neither woman could stop herself from watching the rings disappear into their owner's fat hands and both wondered, 'Couldn't she have given us just one each?'

'I think,' said Mrs Eirene, 'we must find you some war work more suited.'

(This phrase mimicked in Frau Schwarzer's gauleiter voice by Miss Tattie at dinner at Audrey's joined the treasury of official family anecdotes. Audrey commented, 'I do believe that woman would enjoy the war a great deal if we were on the other side.') Actually she was quite right. Mrs Eirene before making her important telephone call had returned to her office and poured out a glass from a warm half-bottle of Moselle which she kept in her desk and had said to herself, 'That woman! Those awful, awful rings! These English with their frozen pipes in winter, no ice in summer, how do they think they can win this war, against *us*?' – and with some force she banged her clenched fist against her right thigh, a gesture habitual with her when crossed, which she often was.

2

That evening, Sir Ezra returned home in a foul mood. He'd been let in by Charles, the butler – the footman having been called up only that day – and he beckoned him into the bedroom. He sat on the bed with a moan and tried to get his shoes off. He looked crumpled and rather piqued, thought Charles, and he bent to help him, but his submission and the implication that the effort was too much annoyed Sir Ezra who brushed him aside. 'Bring me some slippers and a drink, will you?' he said. Charles hesitated and decided first to go and get the drink.

Sir Ezra padded into his dressing room holding the offending shoes by their laces and threw them out of the window. Then an idea seized him, he started on the rest of the footwear and by the time Charles was back with his drink – whisky, water and no ice – Sir Ezra was shouting, 'Bloody things, bloody things,' and throwing them out of the dressing-room window into the well of the courtyard below.

'Don't do that, Ezra, someone might get hurt.' Audrey had appeared and stood by the aghast manservant. It was true; a size 10 shoe, built by Lobb to last for a lifetime and complete with a tree in three parts, could, if it landed on an unfortunate porter, cause a lot of damage.

'You'd better go and get them back, Charles,' said Audrey.

'I don't want the bloody things back, they hurt – give me my drink,' Sir Ezra said to Charles, who was clutching the whisky, water and no ice as if for support. 'And you can keep them,' he added as Charles trotted down the corridor on his errand. 'They might fit you, Sinnockson, they certainly don't fit me.'

Charles almost broke into a canter; there was a place in the Pimlico Road which paid well for gentlemen's handmade shoes in good nick, but usually, he reflected, one had to wait for *dead* gentlemen's shoes.

Purged, Sir Ezra sat on his bed gripping the heavy cut-glass tumbler as if it were a hand grenade. It was well wrought, English, in excellent taste, like Audrey, his wife. He looked up at her just before an expression of some tenderness had time to leave her beautifully made-up face. Holding the whisky in his right hand, he drank it down in two gulps and patted the bed beside him with his left. Audrey put the glass on a silver coaster and went to fetch her husband a pair of slippers, making a clucking noise when she saw the mess in his dressing room; she found the slippers and placed them gently by the side of Sir Ezra's huge feet, then sat down on the bed beside him.

Sir Ezra stared at the slippers as if they too had offended him and then moved his head to kiss his wife on the nose. Audrey's classic oval Sephardic face was made remarkable by her eyes, sometimes purple, sometimes green. She maintained her face carefully and, often to Ezra's irritation, in the fashion of the thirties, in public. But his was a gesture of ancient affection. Normally Audrey would have snapped open her powder compact to repair the damage, now she sat waiting for him to begin.

Sir Ezra started in the more familiar, controlled, soft voice which the family adopted for a certain sort of tale. 'So,' said Sir Ezra, 'I say to myself I'm a new boy, not *grafpetochky* like at the office, I mustn't say anything until I am spoken to, I sit at the back of the class where teacher can't see me and I can't see teacher and I turn up on time, right? Three o'clock they tell me, after luncheon they tell me, three o'clock at the Treasury, Room so-and-so. But where is the Treasury?' He spread his arms out. 'Do you know where is the Treasury, do I know where is the Treasury?'

Audrey was silent as intended.

'Does Mr Peter bloody Jenkins know – that *pots* my chauffeur? Finally, we've been up and down Whitehall three times and I get hold of a bobby. Officer, I say, can you please help me. I have an engagement at the Treasury and I don't know where it is. So what does he do? Bright lad, very bright lad, he points across the road. We'd passed it three times, Jenkins and I. And Jenkins, the *schmuck*, sits there, he just sits there. The bobby stops the traffic with one hand and moves us across Whitehall with the other.'

Sir Ezra stood up in his stocking feet and imitated the policeman's gesture. 'Like that. So he walks over and before that Jenkins has time to stop the motor he's handed me out of the car. So there I am, seven and a half minutes late for my first committee meeting at the Treasury. So I give him a quid.'

'A pound for that?' After all her years of marriage Audrey was still slightly shocked at the little spectacles the family liked to make of themselves.

'Bright lad,' murmured Sir Ezra. 'Dickinson, something like that, no, Police Constable Nickson 427, attached to Bow Street.'

(In fact Sir Ezra had done more than just remember the policeman's name, he'd told the young man to come and see him after the war, which meant of course giving him a job. PC Nickson then said that he hadn't much education, to which Sir Ezra answered – which was quite untrue – that *he* had had none. If the boy, thought Sir Ezra, turned up at the office, that would be proof enough of his intelligence. This exchange, which PC Nickson was to remember, had lasted all of ten seconds.)

'We've got to the Treasury,' Audrey reminded him. 'By the way, Ezra, how long does this go on for, I've got a masseur coming at . . .'

'Never mind, dear, I don't know, but we should be over in time. All right, so now I'm inside the Treasury and a fellow in a sort of cashier's glass box has asked my business and he wants me to fill out a form and I'm beginning to think, Let's pack the whole bloody thing in and then some little *nebs* who's been sent down for me takes me to a lift. He presses the button, I press the button, the lift – nothing. I notice a notice, the notice says *Lift out of order*, oh England, and so we walk up a great big staircase which we could have walked up easily in the first place and then down corridors and corridors and corridors and then outside the committee room thirteen minutes late, dammit, thirteen minutes late,' Sir Ezra almost hissed.

In order better to work out his next instalment he began to pace up and down the room.

'For God's sake, Ezra, sit down, you're not at the Zoo.'

Sir Ezra pressed the bell and stared at his wife gloomily until Charles appeared.

'Drink,' grunted Sir Ezra, handing him his glass.

'And while you are about it, Charles, could you please mix me a martini cocktail,' said Audrey.

Although there was a war on, Charles wished they would remember he was a valet and not a butler. 'I'm not s-sure, my lady,' he stammered, shaken thoroughly by the dishevelled appearance of his employer.

'Oh, it's not difficult, Charles, gin, ice, just not too much vermouth and don't bruise it,' said Audrey.

Charles left, shutting the bedroom door discreetly behind him.

'And now he'll really know what to do,' said Ezra. 'What do you mean, don't bruise it? You know, Audrey, what von Moltke said? He said that if possible instructions will always be misunderstood. Poor Sinnockson,' Sir Ezra chuckled. 'Don't bruise it indeed! . . . Where was I?' he asked.

'You were thirteen minutes late,' said Audrey.

'All right then, there I am in this big room, chandeliers, oil paintings of fellows in wigs, not one of them any good, we've better at Turners. Walpole *schmalpole*' – Sir Ezra mocked his own erudition – 'and God help me they're waiting for me, just *schmoozing*, waiting for me, not what I wanted at all, making me feel even later shows lack of respect, quite an important committee, an honour to be on it and so on. I made my curtsy, apologies, mumble-mumble, and sat next to a man called Bowyer.' Sir Ezra the second-generation immigrant sometimes had difficulty with English names.

'Bowyer,' said Audrey primly. 'A man who makes bows.'

'And bows and arrows and pitchforks are about what we've got,' said Sir Ezra, voice up a note or two. 'And tell me something, what do you think Mr Bowyer from the Min. of Ag. and Fish, as he calls it, is doing on a committee to raise a British Government war loan on Wall Street?'

So that's what it is all about. The Sterling business in America, thought Audrey, but she said in her same voice, 'You must remember, Ezra, in wars the English lose every battle except the last.'

'Not in this one they won't. Not with wooden tanks! We need dollars for real tanks not tanks you can light with a match. You don't know, my love, you don't know how bad it is.' He patted his wife's thigh and continued. 'Anyhow, there I sit and they start talking loans, interest, bank rate, Government brokers, but I'm the new boy so I sit *stumm* and I sit there for fifty minutes, sharpening my pencil which doesn't need sharpening. . . . Oh, I've brought it for you, a little souvenir,' and he dropped the small item stolen from the Treasury in two pieces in her lap.

'And?' asked Audrey.

'Well,' continued Sir Ezra, 'there's the Min. of this and the Min. of that, all with their little labels in front of them and a don from Oxford, something to do with economics – bright lad – and then there's this fool of an Ambassador they've *schlepped* up from his old-age pension in Andover.'

(Andover was a key place in family lore, it was Nazareth; nothing good could ever come out of Andover and anybody who was no good came from there. Poor mad Sophie, Ezra's sister, had finally died in an asylum in Andover.)

'And this *pots*,' continued Ezra, 'our American expert, you understand, is going on for the third time around about "our" – that's the British – "our" friends in the State Department and it was just about then that I managed to catch the chairman's eye, as they call it.

' "With the greatest respect, Mr Chairman –" I begin quietly "we have heard about our friends in the State Department, I think we should be more concerned with our enemies in the State Department." And then I told them.'

Audrey had a brother, David Mendoza, a retiring, selfish sort of man who, when not touring the Near East in search of carpets for his bachelor apartment in Ryder Street off St James's, played piquet in the St James's Club. Ezra disliked him, giving no reason, and called him 'that overcultivated gentleman, your brother', or simply, which of course stuck, 'St James'. David Mendoza, whose invitations to Sir Ezra to luncheon at the club, with a few friends, Mrs Winterbourne had standing orders to refuse, once complained to Audrey of Ezra's boorishness, adding that really it was a shame since his brother-in-law was, in his view, quite *sortable*, and yet was never seen anywhere. This was true.

Even after the successful Sterling flotation of the thirties, which had brought the family into some sort of recognition, at least as millionaires, they made no overtures to English society, never risked stubbing their toes on any closed doors. In *Who's Who*, where the chairman of the Treasury committee had looked him up, Sir Ezra listed golf as his recreation, and had his own nine-hole course at Turners; taking their lead from him, the family, Audrey excepted, entertained mainly each other, each other's friends, each other's mistresses, connections and hangers-on. Though their names were high on every subscription list in London they paid, rather than belonged. They gave, as they put it, but never of themselves, and they were seen in neutral places like the Carlton at Cannes, the Normandie in Deauville, the Ritz in Paris, and at the Captain's table of the *Queens*. There they were seen, but never known, and they consistently avoided places where objection could be made or taken to the fact that they were Jews.

For Audrey there was no such restriction, in or outside her mind. The wealth – and occasional style – of her family had for generations back woven them silkily into the fabric of English society, and they belonged to the same clubs and regiments as the gentile upper classes, attended the same schools and moved on to shared firms of brokers and banks. This connection was one of Ezra's reasons for wishing to marry Audrey and the main reason for the match being opposed, on paper. However, Ezra's presence, his ability, his success, and his knighthood 'for services to medicine' had won them over; when St James announced that Ezra was quite *sortable* he spoke for them all. As mistress of Turners, Audrey had established, in a few years, a place in *her* family tradition, of entertaining the influential and the distinguished who might, coincidentally, have been her friends. Though these occasions were in the deepest sense political – much is decided in England at country-house parties – they did not include the middle echelon of the civil service.

So no one in that committee room on the first floor of the Treasury in May 1940 had ever met Sir Ezra, though the chairman remembered seeing his photograph, then plain Mr Sterling, once in the *Financial Times* and then again (it had been the same one) later in *The Times*, when he'd got his knighthood – a hospital or something – but this did not seem to be the same man. The chairman had expected a little dark chap with a big nose and a funny accent of the kind which echoes in Bournemouth and from persons slamming the doors of their Jaguar motor cars. The photograph had not shown Sir Ezra's great grey eyes, his hammer-like nose, his full silvering hair, nor the size of the man, which was twice what one would expect; nor did it tell anything of his voice, a voice one leaned towards it was so gentle and sure, as they were listening now.

He did not presume, Sir Ezra began, being a simple man of business, to give a history lesson before so many learned men, but he had some practical knowledge of America which perhaps could be the reason for his presence there that afternoon. He had in fact, as a young man, spent a year at an American university and had observed that in the United States the sons of the ruling classes, brought up on John Quincy Adams, were instructed in attitudes of suspicion towards the British Empire and that their natural bent was to engineer its downfall and rejoice in its misfortune. Of course it didn't apply to Mr Cordell Hull, who was the principal ally of President Roosevelt in his policy of intervention, but to those sophomores whom he had known at that time and were now in the State Department and whose cousins were bankers in New York. 'Some of them are not necessarily,' said Sir Ezra, smiling at the man he had interrupted, 'our friends.'

Just then the clock, commemorating the victories of Marlborough, began to strike four, and Sir Ezra waited. But nobody spoke.

'They speak our language, of course,' he went on, 'but that doesn't imply any special sympathy for the British Empire now. There are many Americans with British names, but there are ones with names like Kennedy and McCormick who are saying and writing things about England which friends don't say of each other.' The man from the Foreign Office, who had to read the American newspapers, nodded as if his head would fall off, and the don from the Ministry of Information, for whom the reference to John Quincy Adams had been intended, tugged his woollen tie appreciatively.

Ezra looked at the two rows of men with their eyes on him; the chairman was studying the ceiling.

These were Americans, continued Sir Ezra, with enough influence to sabotage any British war loan, and we could not afford that, we could not even risk it. Neutral powers would draw their own conclusions from the failure of a British Government war loan on Wall Street. No, until the dollar assets of British capitalists had been transferred to the pockets of American businessmen, £1,000 million, £2,000 million – he didn't know how much – the Govern-

ment would not be able to raise a penny on Wall Street. The
committee was, of course, aware of the extent of those assets
possessed by firms like Lever Brothers, the Daimler Car Company
or Courtaulds. Why, his own small business earned in sales and
royalties one-third of its total revenue from the United States of
America. . . . All this must go, and on terms beneficial to the
American businessman. 'We cannot win this war without dollars,
gentlemen,' concluded Sir Ezra. 'We need a lot of them and we
need them quickly. How we dispose of our assets I leave to you.
That is all I have to say.'

Then Sir Ezra, unused perhaps to the ways of committees, had
stood up, bowed to the chairman, and left the room, divided into
those who had risen to their feet at his departure and those who had
not.

Sir Ezra had finished that part of his saga and stood staring gloomily
at his stockinged feet.

'Well,' said Audrey, 'that seems to have gone off all right. Put
on your slippers, dear.'

Sir Ezra groaned.

'I still don't understand what's got you into such a terrible state.'

Sir Ezra groaned again as he did what he was told.

'So,' he said, in a changed voice, 'I'd said my party piece, so I
went down to the car. Jenkins was asleep in the back seat. I woke
him up and got him to drive me to the Ministry. At least he knows
where that one is.'

'Which Ministry?' asked Audrey.

'Oh, you know. Where your friend – the Minister of Economics,
or whatever he is.'

At this moment, Sinnockson announced the arrival of the masseur.
Sir Ezra wanted to dismiss him but he was finally asked by Audrey
to wait.

Audrey thought it a bad sign that the Minister in question, whom
she vaguely remembered having to entertain at Turners because of
some Government contract, had suddenly become *her* friend, and
she sensed that Ezra had reached that part of his story where things
had obviously gone wrong, and sensed that his account of it would

be brief. Her husband, she considered, hadn't enjoyed power or money long enough to relish the occasional disaster.

'He wouldn't see me. I had sent a note: "Subject: Winning the war." I got an answer back from some *schmuck* of an assistant principal, Pray, would Sir Ezra be more specific? Praying, that's all they think about.'

'Oh, it's just that they're all trying to imitate Winston,' said Audrey, who knew about such matters. 'I'd better go now, dear, and see Mr Edmunds.' And Audrey got up, taking Sir Ezra's empty tumbler with her.

'So,' muttered Sir Ezra, 'Ephie can go to New York.'

'What?' Audrey almost shrieked, stopping in her course. 'Uncle Ephie, that poor old man? You'll kill him. Why New York, for heaven's sake?'

'I'll tell you, if you listen. Look, New York raises half the money for the Democratic Party, right? And two-thirds of that comes from the Jews, two million of them. And poor, well, let's say rich, old Uncle Ephie knows them. He's got lines on them, the Senators, the *schmotter* trade, the lot. He can talk to them; they're friends of Father's. Ephie doesn't know much but he knows about money. He can talk to them in Yiddish. The banks are no good in this business. He can talk to the Jews, and he can also do something for me.'

Audrey stood still.

'Now, off you go, Audrey. It doesn't do to keep Mr Edmunds waiting. Most inconsiderate,' mumbled Sir Ezra happily, as he reached for the telephone; but as he did so it rang.

3

The members of the family always said of themselves that they only understood three forms of communication – telephone, telegram and Tell Hélène, Ezra's not quite discarded mistress. Hélène was a faithful gossip, a source of information and, as the war grew less agreeable, of butter, petrol and clothing coupons.

The family did not believe in letters and post-cards, said thank you with flowers sent before rather than after the event, when they could be seen and be of use, and detested any more elegant form of gratitude. Letters took time to post, a day or two to arrive; telegrams were quick, expensive and worked.

So, despite the good news it contained, Sarah Kind looked disapprovingly at the letter on her breakfast tray. Why, the poor child might have been in that terrible home for weeks. She knew what it was like, that home; the family paid for it. A Victorian rectory with all aspects facing north, cold and smelly. It had been hurriedly electrified for the reception of Jewish children smuggled out of Europe in the vanguard of Nazi hostility and finally of an advancing German army, from ports stretching from Portugal to Norway. It did them well enough, but it wasn't right for her son, thought Sarah.

Sarah was an open woman, so it was no secret that she longed for a boy, but so far, despite the efforts of her husband, the Doctor, of his kind and expensive gynaecological friends and their clinics throughout Europe, she had only produced one daughter, Lucy – and it had not helped being told that it was really her fault, and that there could be no more children. Nor was it anything to do, as Uncle Ephie warned her, with the will of God. She knew these things could be arranged. She could have adopted a child, of course, but not through the intervention of her sister-in-law, Joyce, she of the good works, who was all for her finding a foundling. The sight of those rows of rickety children with runny noses in Joyce's institutions appalled Sarah, and she would not endure again the business of bringing up a child which had to have a nursery and a nursery maid and another bossy, rustling Norland nanny with eyes, as the Doctor had said when he dismissed her, like a pickaxe. (Little Lucy had been found howling longer than usual with a safety pin stuck through her nappy *and* through her little tummy.) No, Sarah had told René one tipsy evening at Deauville, she wouldn't go through all that again. She wanted a son grown-up enough to talk to, and René agreed.

René Shalom was the Sterling agent in Paris, and usually contrived to be in Deauville at the same time as the family. He was a shambling ox of a man, but daintily shod, and useful to the family which he had met through poor, mad, extravagant Sophie on one of her Paris sprees. When it had emerged that René's mother had been a friend of old grandmother Nancy Sterling in her retirement, this had offset an otherwise suspect connection and he had been taken by the family as their agent in France for some business and for all private affairs. René's visits to London provoked a torrent of dinner parties among the family who all received him gladly, only Audrey taking care to seat him a long way away from Sir Ezra, who teased all obvious homosexuals. When any of the family went to Paris, René introduced them to the couturiers and in his apartment in the Avenue Matignon gave parties for them well covered by the commissions he had earned. He arranged their suites in the Ritz or the Crillon, and it was rumoured attended to their every need. He had certainly arranged at the boy's earnest request the defloration of young Oscar, Sophie's son. There was no family confidence too minute for René and when Sarah, Ezra's most well-beloved sister, spoke to him of her hopes and frustrations, which he had already known, it was in his interest, and probably his inclination, to help her.

'*Ça va, chérie. Je vais vous trouver un fils, un heir,*' he had said, wagging a finger. '*Dites-moi, est-ce qu'il doit être totalement* Jewish?'

'Not at all,' Sarah had said. 'I don't like ugly little boys.'

'Half Jewish?' asked René, making a funny little gesture, like turning off a tap. '*Moitié juif?*' (René's French was very much his own.)

'Yes,' said Sarah, '*moitié juif,*' and she had laughed.

Well, René had been as good as his word. Enclosed in a letter from the matron of the Lingfield home was a note, hardly readable it was so crushed, from René on his private writing paper, addressed simply to Sarah Sterling (not, she noticed, to Sarah Kind, her married name), 14 Maddison Place, Kensington. It read:

Chérie,
     Veuillez soigner ce petit, pendant la duration, explication plus tard.

Still pinned to the piece of letter was a thousand-franc note. (It occurred to Sarah much later that the French for 'duration' could not possibly be *duration.*)

No member of the family was noted for indecisiveness; Sarah pressed the button of the intercommunication gadget which the business had installed in all their houses and heard the voice of her husband in the dining room, surprised, querulous and bored all in one note. 'Eh?' said the Doctor.

'Sorry, dear, wrong number. I've got a son,' she added as she switched him off – it was perfectly safe, he wouldn't have heard.

She pressed the right button and asked Keegan to get the office for her. In the language of the women of the family this meant Mrs Schwarzer, that awkward adjutant for their work on behalf of Jewish refugees.

Mrs Schwarzer took her time to come to the telephone.

'This little boy, Mrs Schwarzer.'

'Yes, I know. The Greek boy.'

'Greek?' Sarah drew on her fifth Du Maurier of the day, and coughed.

Mrs Schwarzer waited.

'Yes, Matron wrote to me about him, and I told her to write to you direct.' There was a silence as Mrs Schwarzer rustled some papers. 'Moise Sousis.'

'You mean to say she wrote? She couldn't pick up the telephone?'

'In Lingfield there is no telephone,' replied Mrs Schwarzer in her best British voice, 'to pick up.' She had wanted to add, 'Don't you know there's a war on,' but seeing no direct connection between these two situations had not done so.

'How old is he? How long has he been there? Is he all right?'

Matron's letter had simply said that the boy had arrived at Southampton on a Polish boat from Bordeaux.

'Can you get him up for me?' pursued Sarah, in a more begging voice.

Mrs Schwarzer gripped the receiver very hard.

'We have a lot of children arriving in all sorts of conditions from many lands, these days,' she said. 'We cannot keep track of any one individual child. He will be looked after just like the others.' She paused. 'All I can tell you, Mrs Kind, is that this child arrived with a lot of new clothes' (good old René, thought Sarah) 'which Matron said came in very useful, and that he carried no infectious disease. I am sure you may visit him whenever you like.'

'Thank you, Mrs Schwarzer,' said Sarah, almost meekly, 'for your help,' but as she stubbed out her cigarette she muttered, '*Rortzer!*' of that persistently awkward person.

Then she thought a little, but not for long. Lingfield, where was that? In the south-east where Uncle Ephie lived – Margate. He had a car and a chauffeur neither of which did anything if it wasn't Saturday, and it wasn't Saturday, was it. Keegan would know.

The butler, who had never been summoned to his mistress's bedroom before, arrived in a green apron for which he apologized, taking in the unusual sight of Mrs Kind in bed in some disarray, hairnet, cold cream and an almost exposed bust. She looks a sight, thought Keegan (they were Jewish people and Keegan was RC), but she's all right. The nicest lady anyone could ask for, and his face, which he thought expressionless, showed affection and alarm.

'Keegan, is it Saturday?'

'No 'm.'

'Is Lingfield in the south-east?'

'Yes 'm. Sort of.'

'And Margate's in Kent?'

'Yes 'm.'

'Then I want you to telephone Miss Pat in Margate. I want to talk to her right away.' And with that, Sarah bounded out of bed, cigarette holder in her teeth, shot into the bathroom and shut the door.

'Here, 'm?' queried the desperate Keegan. But as the sounds from within of joyous slooshing continued, he withdrew and like an actor at an audition, addressed the empty air, in a firm voice:

'Best to put you through from the pantry, 'm.'

Since the only reply was an impolite noise, and not wishing to see his mistress again in so excited a state, Keegan hurried out of the bedroom down to his own territory.

'Who's that?'

'It's me, Mrs Sarah.'

'Yes, I know, Mrs Sarah. It's me, Pat, Miss Muir.'

'How is he?'

'He's asleep.'

'Good. How is he when he's not asleep?'

'Terrible. He hates it. The war, I mean. If it isn't being bombed, it's being shelled, and then it's being invaded. He says we should ask Mr Hitler for peace, and let him keep France if he wants it. And anyway, he wants to go to America. And he's quarrelled with all his friends, even the Schulzes won't talk to him, which makes him worse because he hasn't got any card games, and he gets so bored and . . .'

'Pat, will you do something for me?'

'Oh, yes, Mrs Sarah.'

'You've still got Sandys and the car?'

'Yes, but what for I'm not sure. He should be driving a tank.'

'And petrol?'

'Oh, yes. We get coupons for going to *shul* and he knows some people in the black market. I know where he keeps them.'

'Good. Will you get a pencil and paper?'

'Yes, Mrs Sarah.'

'The boy's name is Moise, M-o-i-s-e, Moise –'

'Hold on, Mrs Sarah. I think I'll get a pen.'

State Registered Nurse Pat Muir had mousy hair, done up in a bun at the back, and freckles, and little blue eyes, which showed sometimes glee, sometimes malice. She'd been with Uncle Ephie since she'd first come to nurse him via Audrey, who'd found her for little Oscar's diphtheria, and had stayed with him because there had seemed nothing better for a spinster with a large unexploited bosom and no prospects to do. And also in the hope of a legacy from her frail but strangely vital employer. (She needn't have bothered; it had all been arranged. Ten years with the family was worth a lifetime in other people's employment.) Though a chatter-box she was quite trustworthy, and being a sort of emergency nurse for the family, knew them all and was known by them.

Pat Muir followed Sarah's instructions, but also left a long note for Mrs Sandys about her employer's diet. And so, only a few hours later, Uncle Ephie's plain, old-fashioned black Rolls stopped outside 14 Maddison Place. Sandys, the chauffeur, extinguished his Woodbine between thumb and forefinger, put on his chauffeur's cap, and tightened his tie.

Out of the back seat popped a little dark boy, dressed in continental fashion with short trousers, followed by Miss Pat, who took his hand. The little boy ran up the stairs, pulling the nurse behind him.

All this was watched by Sarah and the Doctor from the deep, long windows of the drawing room.

'You don't mind, do you? I've always wanted a boy.'

'When, my love, have I ever minded anything you did?' said her husband, who appeared to be crying. 'I'll be in the study if you want me,' and he shuffled out.

Sarah stood still – the Sterlings never cried – waiting for the front doorbell to be answered, and puffed on her cigarette.

'Miss Pat and the little boy, 'm,' announced Keegan.

And that was how Jeremy first saw her – through a cloud of cigarette smoke, smiling, and with her head turned slightly askew as was her habit when concentrating. They stared at each other.

'He's been sick,' said Miss Pat approvingly.

'Has he had anything to eat?' asked Sarah, screwing up her face.

'Only a whole carton of banana ice cream. We found a Wall's depot in Croydon.'

'No wonder he was sick.'

'No, it's that stupid car.' It was clear on whose side Miss Pat was. 'I'm always at him to get a new one,' she went on.

That the little boy found this dialogue incomprehensible was clear by his asking, 'Mama?'

'I think he's worried about his mother,' said Miss Pat, a trifle unnecessarily.

'Papa?' asked the little boy.

Oh dear, thought Sarah, this is the worst bit.

'And he can only speak Greek, they say. Poor little lamb.'

A sudden private softness in the nurse's usually jolly voice must have released in the child a sense of desolation suppressed by the excitement of his first boat trip and the briskness of the institution where he had spent some motherless weeks with other refugees, for he moved to the nurse's side and there, on that friendly bosom, cried and cried and cried.

Keegan, still standing like an unhappy setter uncertainly at the door, asked if he should have a meal prepared for Miss Pat and the little boy in the nursery. Sarah said, 'No, no, Keegan, bring something in here on a tray like we used to do for Miss Lucy when she wasn't well.'

'Right away, 'm.'

Miss Pat subsided in the nearest armchair, produced with her free hand from a large brown ostrich-skin handbag, a present from one of the family, a handkerchief, blew her own nose on it, and then his.

'I think we both need a gin and something,' said Sarah, moving towards the cocktail cabinet.

'Gin and orange for me, please, Mrs Sarah,' snuffled Miss Pat as she stroked the little boy's head.

The sobbing declined. He watched Sarah with large eyes as she walked across the white carpet towards a corner cupboard, and when this opened to a blaze of light and mirror, he ran across and contemplated the rows of coloured bottles. Sarah gave him a cassis with water.

'*Vissinada*,' he said, sniffing it.

'You like it?' asked Sarah.

He turned and surveyed the room. 'Like it,' he said, and smiled. Sarah bent and kissed him.

'You see, he can speak a bit of English. You'd better take him to Harrods and get him some clothes.'

'Oh, yes, Mrs Sarah. He did have some but they took them all away.'

'Did you have any trouble getting him out of that place?'

'Well, yes,' said Miss Pat, taking a deep breath and bracing herself for a description of her triumph. But she interrupted herself when she saw that the little boy, who had meanwhile been shutting and opening the cocktail cabinet, had found a complicated sort of electric cigarette lighter which looked like one of Sir Ezra's gadgets.

'Don't play with that, dear. You'll break it. ... Then I told Matron he was going to stay with you.'

'Quite,' said Sarah, gulping her drink. After all, the family did pay for the bloody place.

'She said it was irregular, but she'd send on the papers.'

'Adoption papers?'

Miss Pat's little blue eyes grew littler. This was a piece of news, and she was the first to know.

'We must think of a proper name for him,' Sarah said as the little boy opened and shut the cocktail cabinet for the umpteenth time.

'Yes, he has a very funny foreign name, I must say. What does it mean, Mrs Sarah?'

'Moise? Moise Sousis? Moses, I suppose.'

At the sound of his name, the little boy looked up and stopped playing with the cupboard.

Sarah rummaged in her handbag and found what she wanted: a crumpled piece of paper, with a French banknote pinned to it, which she slowly unfolded.

'Moise Sousis,' she said again, and held it out to the boy who rushed forward to take it.

'Oh, yes, Mrs Sarah, that must be – the piece of paper he wouldn't let go of. They had to take it from him when he was asleep. He held it so hard that the pin stuck in his hand.'

Sarah gave the money to the boy, and kept the piece of paper.

'*Polla kremeta*,' said Moise.

Yes, thought Miss Pat, savouring her stall seat at this family highlight, and there's plenty more where that came from, you lucky little boy, Master Kind. And because she was not without compassion she thought of all the other little boys and girls who weren't so lucky and who were still in that place near Ashford, and she began to feel all sniffly again.

'You'd better take him upstairs and unpack yourself. I have to talk to Sir Ezra.'

At the mention of that name – why, even Mr Steimatsky was frightened of his nephew – Miss Pat flinched, but she did have the courage to say that she couldn't possibly unpack because she hadn't known she was staying and had brought nothing with her, and what would Mr Steimatsky, who was after all her employer, and did need her, and so on, and oh dear . . .

All Sarah said, as she took out a note from her wallet, was, 'You'll need something to buy some clothes for London. Here.'

And she handed Miss Pat some banknotes. She unfolded them and gasped.

'Fifty pounds, Mrs Sarah?'

'Well, the war might go on for some time. Hurry up, my dear, clothes might be rationed by tomorrow. And ask Keegan to ask the Doctor if I can borrow *the Times*, will you, just for a moment?'

'Yes, Mrs Sarah.' And the nurse and her new charge tripped out of the room.

'Algernon! How can people still call themselves Algernon?'

Sarah had put on her reading spectacles, and was searching the birth columns of *The Times* with Keegan standing by as ordered ('Don't go, Keegan, you'll do. I want you to help me'). It was, after all, too important a matter for the Doctor to be consulted. Hadn't he even suggested if they had a son he could be called Syphilis? A shepherd boy, he said.

'Think of something that goes with Kind,' Sarah said. 'It must be dum-diddy Kind.'

'Elijah,' said Keegan hopefully, not at ease, but unwilling to leave.

'No, no, that's de-dumdy. Anyway, Elijah's Jewish and I'm rather bored by Jews.'

'Christopher,' suggested Keegan, moving to the other end of the scale.

'No, no. Oh, here's one. What about Timothy? Isn't it extraordinary how people go on being born with a war on and everything?'

'Timothy,' repeated Keegan, rolling the word round his tongue as if at a wine-tasting.

'A bit sissy, isn't it,' said Keegan, 'for a little boy?'

There were more inane exchanges between mistress and servant, both enjoying themselves, according to licence, until Sarah decided on Jeremy. It was a gentle and thoroughly English name. Keegan liked it. Besides he wanted to get on with his work.

'Master Jeremy,' he said. 'A nice addition to the family, if I may say so, 'm.'

Sir Ezra's private line at the flat was connected to only one instrument, which stood on a table between his and his wife's bed, and was more or less reserved for the family and Mr Wilson, his man at the office. Monopolized by Audrey in the morning for her outgoing breakfast-in-bed calls, this instrument was tacitly reserved for Sir Ezra in the evening up to eight o'clock, when it automatically cut itself off.

Sarah of course didn't know that Ezra had been about to make a telephone call himself, and so her conversation had begun badly. Ezra was brisk on the telephone except with those of Audrey's callers whom he disliked. Courtesy was applied in inverse ratio to concern.

'Yes?' Sir Ezra had asked.

'Ez,' said Sarah.

'Yes, Sarah, what do you want?'

This now forgotten but once familiar use by Sarah of his childhood name was a signal between them; it really meant 'really' from Sarah: Now I don't often ask you for anything, do I? But this I want.

It would therefore be something difficult and expensive that only he, Ezra, could arrange, like the Kind clinic for ... well, never mind. His Knight Bachelordom could have been connected with Sterling philanthropy in such an unfavoured area of medical research.

'Sarah, it's yours. Now tell me what it is.'

Sarah told him, and at first there was not much he liked about his sister's tale. First, the Greek boy's provenance, as Audrey would have said. René Shalom, for God's sake, that flabby old pansy. How old was the boy anyway? he asked apprehensively. Sarah didn't know – no papers: about seven or eight.

'Ah.' And then this business of adoption. Wasn't it almost as bad as marrying 'out'? Mind you, the business could always use nice boys, he supposed. And Sarah needed a bit of an interest there. . . . And what, by the way, did the Doctor think?

'He was,' said Sarah carefully, 'moved.'

And they both laughed, for the Doctor's easily turned on tears were an asset at the funerals of managers and agents throughout the world.

Sir Ezra had already committed himself to helping his sister, so on with the battle. He would have to get on to the Home Office, or rather to get Arthur – their connection – to get on to the Home Office. Arthur, the family's Sabbath goy, was equipped to arrange the adoption and the naturalization of Sarah's new son. Moise Sousis – that was his name, wasn't it – could become, Sir Ezra supposed, Jeremy Kind, a member of the family. Not quite yet, depending on how he turns out. Not perhaps a fully paid-up member, because that would mean more shares, but a sort of country member, Ezra thought to himself.

But when Sarah mentioned how the little boy had arrived earlier that afternoon in Ephie's old Rolls, driven by Sandys and accompanied by Ephie's nurse, Pat, Ezra, who like many successful men of business, always put the divinity into his calculations, saw Jeremy's arrival as inspired. If the boy needed a nanny, Ephie would lose a nurse. So now he *had* to go to America. It was good, therefore, that Sarah had telephoned. God was behind his people.

'Ez, where do you think the boy comes from? René wouldn't have sent us anybody, you know.'

'It'll be something to do with the business, I suppose,' said Sir Ezra. 'René's still in Paris. God, I don't know what's going to happen to him. Sarah, hasn't he got a Swiss passport or something? Wait a minute, I think I've got it. The boy's Greek, you say. We had an agent in Hamburg. He was Greek, a Greek Jew, but he wasn't called Sousis. He was called' – Sir Ezra flicked through his mind – 'Mizrachi. May be a relation. God knows what's happened to him either. Hamburg used to be a good place, but now . . . Do you want me to try and do something for them, the father and mother, I mean?'

Even in 1940 there was still a way, if there were the money, of ransoming Jews from the Nazis. The route was via Vienna and Zurich. The Rothschilds had done it and so, earlier, had members of the family. But it had become expensive and difficult, and again very expensive.

'No, Ez,' said his elder sister, 'I think you'll have done enough.'

Sarah Kind wanted her son without parents.

4

'Sheernasty we call it,' said little Oscar.

'What?'

'Sheerness. This place we sit on. It's a sort of pile.'

'What happens there?' asked Sir Ezra, not very interested.

'Oh, great big guns which never go off, and poker.'

He looks new, thought Ezra, new Sam Browne, new uniform, a little too well-cut perhaps, and a new pip which he keeps on checking to see if it's still there, and then his new watch from Cartier, which Audrey had given him when he got his commission.

Little Oscar, under Sir Ezra's stare, returned his favourite-nephew grin.

'Where's he now?' asked Sir Ezra sharply.

Little Oscar jerked his big head in the direction of Claridge's.

'You got him in there all right?'

(The business kept a room at Claridge's for visiting agents, but it was occasionally nowadays commandeered by the management, with many apologies, for a high-ranking Pole or some such.)

'Yes, I said it was for Mr Ephraim *Sterling*. They seemed to know the name,' added little Oscar drily.

He was not a fool, this son of mad Sophie, thought Sir Ezra.

'How was he, I mean, how was he?'

'Oh, very funny,' said the young man. 'Really very funny.'

'You can tell me about it if you like,' said Sir Ezra.

Uncle Ephie was not at ease with the telephone and it was useless to communicate with him in this way because if anything disagreeable had to be said he would instantly go deaf, or hold the receiver the wrong way round. So, as a solution to the problem of getting through to his uncle, Sir Ezra had thought of *his* nephew, Second Lieutenant Oscar Barnet, RA, staying on his first leave as an officer with Joyce, his stepmother, and bound that night for the Café de Paris with some *shicksa*, no doubt. Sir Ezra had been right on both counts, but it also happened that little Oscar had to be back with his unit at o-nine-hundred hours, as he put it, so, reluctantly, he couldn't oblige his uncle this time.

The war, Sir Ezra had countered, could last another day, and besides he would cause a telegram to be sent to Oscar's unit from the Ministry. He didn't believe that this would be Oscar's first brush with the authorities. The young man did not yet know of any officer in the British Army as commanding as his uncle, and the reference to the business of the steward at Oxford, whose daughter he had put in the family way, was only too well taken. On that occasion Sir Ezra had truly and expensively settled mother and child, apparently without little Oscar's stepfather or Joyce ever knowing and without the college sending him down. And then, too, they had been conspirators.

So now the young man agreed to his uncle's plan. And with a light heart at dawn the next day, having extracted the Phantom III from the somnolent mews inhabited by Jenkins behind South Audley Street, little Oscar thundered down to Margate, touching eighty, as he would later recount to an admiring mess, on the new Ashford bypass.

Uncle Ephie had been fully dressed, down to a straw hat with a ribbon and a cane, sitting on his veranda in a rocking chair from which, at the sight of his great-nephew, he made a not too serious effort to rise.

Little Oscar bent down to kiss the old gentleman on his rheumy cheek.

'Ah, *shalom*,' Uncle Ephie had said, looking at the uniform. 'I thought you were the police.' He looked again at his impatient nephew. 'A cup of coffee?' he asked. And then, in a far from infirm voice, he bellowed, 'Mrs Sandys!'

'Sir?' That good woman appeared immediately.

'You remember little Oscar, don't you, Mrs S? Poor Sophie's boy. Look at him now. Isn't he beautiful?'

Mrs Sandys did remember and also knew the urgency of the occasion and was loyal to it.

'I've packed his bags, Mr Oscar, as best I could without Miss Pat's being here, but I can't manage to lift them all. Sandys isn't back yet.'

'Bags? What's all this about bags? What's going on?' Uncle Ephie banged his cane.

'Surely, Uncle, you got the telegram?'

Uncle Ephie looked blank. He was going to deny everything.

'Couldn't Ezra have picked up the telephone? Look, my boy, they steal my car, they steal my chauffeur, they steal my nurse. Those *gonefs*.' Uncle Ephie was beginning to enjoy himself. 'Without which I am paralysed, paralysed. All without so much as a by-your-leave. And leave me – He flung up his arms and dropped his cane. 'Pick that up, will you, dear boy? I need all the support I can get.'

'And didn't I make you a lovely cold rice pudding?' said Mrs Sandys. To Oscar, 'He's not supposed to eat starch, you know.'

At this point, Sir Ezra, who enjoyed listening to family stories as much as he liked telling them, couldn't resist an interruption. 'You know,' he said to little Oscar, 'he only eats the skin.'

And with a cackle and a bound he lumbered across the little study to the bookshelves from which he extracted a bottle of champagne. 'Have a glass of wine,' he said.

To hell with the Eighty-Fifth Heavy Ack-Ack, thought Oscar, as the iced champagne crept through his veins. This is much better.

'Well,' said little Oscar, 'we get him into the car and then he's forgotten something.'

'His smoked salmon and his rotten bananas,' supplied Sir Ezra.

'Uncle Ezra, you know everything.'

'No, but I know Ephie. Do you know what that old man did? He damn near ruined us.'

Sir Ezra leant back in his chair, elbows on the arms, his big hands carving the air.

'You should know this now, I think, little Oscar, you're old enough.'

Oscar blushed in expectation of a confidence from Sir Ezra. And as they both sipped their champagne, he leant back in his chair too.

'Well, you know when I floated the business, the shares were oversubscribed? About nine times?'

'Right,' said little Oscar, who knew this bit.

'Well, they come on the market well over par, right? So, I sell a bit, but they go on going up. I sell. I sell some for the family and the charities. Your aunt needs a clinic, and so forth and so forth. But the family's all right by now. A lot of cash and worth a million each, dammit. But still the shares go up. Well, anything electric's fashionable. And then I say, well enough. Stop. *Schluss.* Nobody in the family sells any more. The shares go on going up. The accounts are good – why shouldn't they? And then three months later – *kerplunk.*'

Sir Ezra let his hands fall to the floor.

'The broker rings me up one morning and asks me if I've seen the *Financial Times.* No, I haven't seen the *Financial Times.* Why, I ask. Sterlings have dropped from eighteen to twelve bob in one afternoon. The broker says they were all A shares, voting shares, being unloaded. Now, who had that many A shares, I wonder.'

At that moment, a bell rang.

'Shut the door, will you, Oscar?'

Little Oscar did as he was told and turned round to see his uncle leaning forward expectantly.

'Uncle Ephie?' he whispered.

Sir Ezra nodded many times.

'Why?'

'Look, Oscar, he's an old man. He sees a profit, a very big profit, he thinks. And he takes it. Mind you, he's a bit of a *rortzer*, too. Know what I mean?'

Oscar didn't quite. They hadn't taught him Yiddish at Stowe.

'Well, Uncle Ephie didn't like what I'd done in the business. . . .'

And at that moment, as if to make Sir Ezra's point, Audrey's voice crackled into the room over the Sterling intercom.

'Ezra, come out of there. We're waiting for you.'

'All right, all right,' he mumbled, and he crossed the floor and switched off the apparatus and poured out two more glasses of champagne.

'You see what I mean?' And he jerked his head towards the amplifier. 'That sort of thing. Ephie hated electricity. He liked mechanical calculating machines, filing cabinets, office machinery, you know. Anyway . . .'

Sir Ezra settled himself back in his chair and lit a cigar.

'The shares. Where are they now? Twenty-seven, twenty-seven and three. The old fool would have had twice as much if he had stayed with me. Mind you, we only took two years to recover.

Uncle Ephie was the rat, and in 1936, 1937, 1938, 1939, up, up, up and now the war.'

'Yes, what about the war, Uncle?'

'It'll be the same. Just like the last one, only better, I'm afraid. Last time it was field telephones; now it will be stuff for aircraft. Our problem will be excess profits and possibly capital taxation.'

'Yes, but the war. Do you think, I mean, what do you think of it?' asked the young man.

'Oh, we'll win it, if that's what you're worrying about. Your Aunt Audrey is sure of that. Come on, we'd better go, or we'll be in the doghouse. She wants to see you about something.'

And he walked out of the room.

Sitting down with his hat on, helping Sinnockson to put cream into his coffee – 'That's enough, steady, no, all right, just a little more' – was Uncle Ephie.

'We met in the lift,' said Audrey.

'Ah,' said Ephie, without looking up. 'My young kidnapper and the master-mind itself. Morning, Ezra. I brought you some smoked salmon, the proper stuff a friend of mine gets in Margate, not like the *dreck* they give you at Claridge's.' And Ephie pointed to a packet on the table.

Little Oscar noticed how much it had diminished since yesterday.

'Sleep well, Ephie? Bed all right? Bananas all right?' asked Sir Ezra.

'Do you know, Ezra, Audrey and little Oscar, let me tell you something.'

Uncle Ephie leant forward and said in a walls-have-ears voice, 'Claridge's have the deepest shelter in London, deeper even than Buckingham Palace. I know because the hall porter told me. You can spend the war there in perfect comfort. I can put Pat upstairs in a maid's room. ... And such interesting people, very high-up people, kings and things. I had quite a nice *schmooze* with a German officer in the breakfast room, and he told me ...'

'A German?' said Audrey.

'He spoke German,' replied Uncle Ephie. 'I spoke German.'

'Your great-uncle,' said Sir Ezra, by way of explanation to little Oscar, 'speaks Yiddish in all languages.'

'So he was Dutch,' continued Uncle Ephie. 'Anyway, he told me that we have these aluminium frying pans in Dover or . . .'

'Audrey!' Sir Ezra had already had enough. It was, of course, only a stratagem and it was good that the old man could still play a hand; encouraging, considering the assignment he was about to propose. But the thought of Ephie conducting the war in his straw hat from Claridge's . . .

'. . . Somewhere like that. And when the Germans land . . .'

'Audrey, have you something for Oscar?'

'Yes, I'm sure Uncle Ephie would like to see it. Oscar, go and ask Sinnockson for that parcel from Finnegans. Just wait, Ephie, this is a real family occasion.'

'*Pouf*,' said Ephie. 'They all became *pommes frites*. What family occasion?' he added balefully after a pause.

'Just you wait,' said Audrey as little Oscar came back with a long box. 'Now, Oscar, I thought officers weren't supposed to wear their Sam Brownes in ladies' drawing rooms.'

'My God, I believe they're not. But actually, Audrey, I have to go. There's a train at twelve twenty from Victoria which I really must get.'

'Ectually, I haif to go,' mimicked Uncle Ephie, cross that his secret information had not impressed.

'Do as your aunt says,' ordered Sir Ezra cheerfully. Little Oscar with some difficulty did so, and deposited his Sam Browne on the floor.

'Now open the box.'

Inside the box and swathed in purple tissue paper was another Sam Browne belt, but as it emerged an old one, almost black with shine and affection, as shiny as only an ex-sergeant-major would see that his Sam Browne was shiny.

'Grandfather's?' asked the young man.

They nodded. Uncle Ephie blew his nose, and was the first to recover.

'I don't know why we kept it all these years. Of course it dosen't fit you, it wouldn't have fit you, it was far too big, your grandfather was a huge man.'

'You bear his name,' said Sir Ezra heavily.

'The silly *schmock*,' said Uncle Ephie, 'volunteering like that.

What sensible Jewish boy ever volunteered. And he was far too old.
I told him he would get killed.'

'But he didn't,' said Sir Ezra.

'Yes, but he might have been. And then where would I have been?
Leaving me to run the business like that.'

'Come on, Uncle Ephie, say goodbye to Oscar.' She had seen
the young man fretting for his train.

'Oh, goodbye then,' said the old man and screwed up his eyes
for a kiss.

Little Oscar, even handsomer now in big Oscar's old Sam
Browne, embraced his uncle and aunt in the same way, and gave a
half-military salute.

'Oscar!' Sir Ezra rapped out.

'Sir?'

'Oscar,' said Sir Ezra softly, 'I daresay that some of your former
colleagues at that officer cadet school aren't quite as well off as you,
are they? They might appreciate a new Sam Browne.'

Blushing, little Oscar retrieved his belt.

'You needn't have spoken like that, Ezra,' said Audrey when he
had gone. 'He's a good boy.'

'And that will make him a better boy,' replied Sir Ezra. 'Now,
Ephie, I want you to listen to me.' And he turned his back on his wife.

Ephie easily understood Ezra's thinking. The equation went: New
York equals Jews, equals money, equals the Democratic Party,
equals F.D.R. for a third term and America coming into the war.
There were two million Jews in New York. But what about *them*,
the other ones – the ones who ran the elevators and, more regrettably,
City Hall, the advertising agencies, the stock market and the banks?
No Jews there, were there? Ephie didn't think he was up to playing
politics at this sort of level, and he wouldn't get very far if he tried.
And this brought him to another point. Who was paying for his
outing? Ezra knew he always stayed at the St Regis?

'Ah,' said Ezra, 'I'm coming to that. I want you to sell the
business, and this is for why.' And he explained.

Ephie Steimatsky listened. The plan was tortuous and neat. He
liked it.

'You mean,' he said, 'you want me to sell the business and you don't want to sell the business?'

Ezra nodded.

'Nominees? Ah ha, make it legal, Mrs Segal! You mean that?'

'I mean that,' said Ezra.

And they both smiled at their cleverness.

'What about my commission? How much is the Corporation worth in America, Ezra?'

Ezra named a figure, two per cent of which in commission would have seen Ephie out.

'Two and a half,' said Ephie, 'plus expenses. And I'll probably be torpedoed, so it won't cost you. If you think it's going to be easy to sell the business to nominees you can *trust*, you're *meshugana*.'

'Uncle Ephie, you have a point. All right, there'll be a board meeting this afternoon. I'll send you all the papers.'

'Hey, what about my nurse? I can't be without Pat, you know. I need a lot of medical attention in my condition. You're doing everything you can to kill me, Ezra.'

At that moment, the old man looked immortal.

'She can join you later when things are easier. And don't worry about medical attention. Those ships have everything. They even have lifeboats.'

According to the family, and never denied by Sir Ezra, Uncle Ephie left England on one of the *Queens* in the early part of the war because he couldn't find any bananas. His passion for rotten, or as he called them 'delikvessens', bananas dated from a business trip to China before the First World War. He had met in Shanghai in 1908 or thereabouts a co-religionist from Baghdad who appeared to be in control of the local race course and the local stock exchange, from whom he had learnt the joys of rotten – deliquescent – bananas. They were best kept, as chambermaids from New York to Hamburg had learnt to their dismay, in a dry, warm place, like an airing cupboard, until they had grown black all over. Then the tops were cut off with a sharp knife, and with a long, slim, special spoon, for it was important not to break their now tender skins, the contents delved out. Delicious.

The family's belief that Uncle Ephie's trans-Atlantic dash in 1940

– his wartime mission, as it were – had been in pursuit of bananas confirmed their version of his private-spiritedness and emphasized Ezra's influence in procuring him a berth. And later in the war, when Uncle Ephie read reports in the papers of doctors in England appealing for bananas to save the life of some child dying from a digestive disease, he always brought up the question with the Miami branch of the Bundles for Britain Campaign, of which he was chairman; not that he understood quite how bananas could cure the disease, it was simply that the thought of anybody wanting bananas and not getting them, really moved him.

5

Joyce's parties were dreadful and for no one was their prospect more full of apprehension than the hostess herself, a big woman who, Sir Ezra said, looked like a camel when she didn't look like a horse. Why Freddy had married her was quite clear; Joyce was the opposite of Sophie – poor, mad, chic, nymphomaniac, drunken, suicidal and now, finally, in-Andover-deceased Sophie. Freddy Barnet, a just-articled solicitor in a small family firm, had only once lost his head and that had been over Sophie. Sophie had laughed when Freddy, many years younger, had suggested marriage. She had laughed and laughed. 'I don't marry any more,' she had gurgled, 'I fuck.' Shocked, Freddy had persisted, but it was Sir Ezra who had arranged the match, seeing in the solemn if youthful Freddy someone who could protect his crazy sister from herself and from other predators. And indeed, Freddy, in his secret doting – doting but, to Sophie, in an oh-so-maddening – way had tried; he had found a succession of nurses for the twins, Sophie's sons by the absconded Karnibad, and gave them his name, and he found a brain specialist for their mother in the face of her dwindling sanity, until he had himself collapsed finally of nervous exhaustion. Sophie had been removed by Sir Ezra to that place in Andover, the twins taken to Turners, and Joyce, some sort of *mishpocher*, had moved in to housekeep. No one in the family was surprised or particularly pleased when, only a month after Sophie's death, the two were married in the new Reform synagogue opposite Lord's. A silver-framed photograph on the piano in the drawing room – they had music in common – showed the embarrassment to Joyce even of this event. She was seen gripping her husband with one arm, and her bouquet with the other, looking out of the side of her eyes at her newly acquired stepsons, the twins, who were dressed in their best grey flannel suits, with buttonholes, nonchalant, spotty and bored. Opposite this photograph, above the mantelpiece, was a huge painting by de Laszlo of the first Mrs Barnet in her court dress complete with ostrich feathers and tiara. It always seemed to those who knew Sophie and loved her despite everything, on looking at the portrait, that Sophie was amused at what was happening in the white-on-white drawing room she had once so prettily presided over – at least early in the evening.

Sophie's annual official party for the family had always been given on the eve of her departure for Deauville to attend the *Bal des Petits Lits Blancs*, for which endless fittings had been arranged and cancelled. Not that the next morning, Sophie, snoring ginnily in the arms of someone she had seduced to her bed, had always been able to rise in time to get the plane from Croydon – 'Madame has a migraine' had been the code for this sort of behaviour. Nevertheless the party had become a fixture and a mammoth one.

Joyce's family had for generations been lawyers and solicitors. They had risen to positions of trust in a society which grew to respect their diligence and skill. The family had maintained its Judaism but diluted it to compromise with attitudes of the middle-class Victorian world, whose opinions they had to satisfy if they were to prosper. The children's scholarships had led them steadily through Clifton or St Paul's to Oxford and the Bar; Joyce, whose family had always voted Liberal but who had herself studied at the London School of Economics and was a socialist, Joyce had hoped on marrying her second cousin that neither of them would have to behave as ostentatiously, as she put it, as the rest of the family – and now with the war on? Did Freddy really think, asked Joyce, her earrings quivering, when Hurricanes and Messerschmitts were tearing each other up in the sky, that this was quite the right moment to continue having Sophie's pre-Deauville party? Freddy pointed out that Sophie's party had become a sort of tradition, that the family rather enjoyed the few traditions it had acquired, and it was now expected of them to continue. Was it not a small price to pay? You couldn't have your *bagel* (Joyce winced) and eat it, as Sir Ezra would say, now could you?

Both of them knew the party was inevitable. For Audrey had sent a case of Krug (Sir Ezra's particular mark) with a note saying how much they were both looking forward, etc. (The fact that the invitations had not gone out was trivial.) Sir Ezra had determined, in fact, that the show must go on, and that was enough.

'And,' added Freddy, 'you know he hates earrings, so you can't wear them. And now, let's check the list.'

Joyce did not move.

'Now, come on, Joyce. Be sensible. Without the family where would we be? You wouldn't like me to go back to conveyancing, would you? We've got patents, royalties, lovely lawsuits all over the world, and now with the war – *whoof!* – business booms. We've just got a contract, by the way, from the Ministry of Defence for a new kind of . . . well, never mind. What I mean is, we're happy, aren't we? Well, I am. And without the family what would you be doing? What about your work in the East End? All those poor little brats? What about taking Mother and Father to Covent Garden?' (Joyce's mother and father, of course.) 'And afterwards to the Savoy? What about Bayreuth? And that cruise we were going to have in the Greek islands?'

Joyce nodded. It was all terribly true. She had never heard Freddy spell out their condition before. Perhaps it needed a war for people to tell the truth.

'But it's all so hypocritical. . . .'

'Quite. Okay, and what is hypocrisy? *L'hommage que le vice rend à la vertu.* Which makes you a virtuous woman, my love.'

'La Rochefoucauld,' said Joyce dutifully.

She's a good girl, thought Freddy, as he watched her blow her attenuated and now reddening nose. And of course she's right.

Joyce brightened at the thought of a bit of organizing and wondered whether she could wear her FANY uniform at the party, which would indicate that she had dodged Sir Ezra's decree concerning earrings. She got out a piece of writing paper and wrote down, with her gold Parker pen, a Christmas issue from Audrey, a list which was headed: 'Us (2).'

'Father and Mother,' echoed Freddy.

'The boys – two,' said Joyce, scratching away. 'If they can get forty-eight hours, that is. Mind you, it is the weekend. Oscar will probably bring some bit, won't he?' asked Joyce disapprovingly. 'I always thought it an act of absolute madness to give that boy, to let an undergraduate have all that money. Five hundred pounds a year – ridiculous.'

'Why?' asked Freddy quickly, for in fact Oscar on going to war had confided to him, but he hoped not to Joyce, that he had fathered a child.

'Just too much money for one young man.'

'Well, he's got to get used to it, one day. It's his, or rather Sophie's.'

'All right. Let's put Oscar plus one, query.'

It takes a very poor-spirited person not to enjoy drawing up a party list and Joyce was not like that, so soon she was happy, but since this was a family occasion the list more or less wrote itself.

The family enjoyed entertaining, believed in parties as a matter of policy, and when Tattie had been through the menopause and was considered safe to be let out of her kosher boarding house in north London she spent some of the money, which had accumulated so monstrously in her confinement, on parties which were the talk of London. Despite Ezra's distaste she had been known to ask to supper at the Savoy the entire cast of a revue. Alone of the family she recruited the transient personnel for her entertainments from outside the approved circuit.

Admittedly, theatrical people were safe. They were self-obsessed, gay, tolerant of Jews and almost anything else. And finally too stupid to take advantage of the family. Sir Ezra was fond of remarking that it wasn't by chance that the French Revolution had enfranchised everybody save servants and actors, but it was well known that he himself was partial to the odd actress, and one or two film stars had returned to New York with her cabin trunk stuffed with a mink coat, a present from Sir Ezra, for services rendered.

The family, Audrey excepted, was really only at ease surrounded by the people and things it had bought; its guests were connected by an invisible thread, that of dependence. If that thread were ever broken the guests would surely all fall down. Lesser members of the family could and did risk introducing a new person into this circle but it was rather like taking a 'chance' card at Monopoly. You could as it were 'advance to go' and 'collect' or be landed with a thumping bill for the repair of your houses. Yes indeed, producing a new face, even at her own party, Joyce knew to be a pretty dicey proposition.

None the less, she decided to invite, with Freddy's approval, Richard Poll, an Oxford don she had known as a student at LSE; he was fashionably of the left, more than a shade common and would therefore go down well with Sir Ezra who was emotionally disinclined to enjoy the company of the English ruling class. Husband and wife had the same solemn thoughts as Richard Poll's name went on to the party list. There was no such thing as a trivial introduction and they knew they were taking a risk.

Sir Ezra was the source of all punishments and all rewards. Both were on a grand scale, unexpected until they happened and then if one subscribed to the ethic, they appeared to be logical and even fair. Minor offences like the wearing of earrings or the driving of Jaguars, both for some reason distasteful to Sir Ezra, were punished with a frown. Major offences, like the selling of shares in the business, for which of course Uncle Ephie had been banished, could come more expensive.

'There is always money kept in the bank in case,' as Sir Ezra wearily explained, 'anyone should need it.' Little Oscar had 'needed' it, to bail himself out of that Oxford adventure. And the same fund had provided a hat shop in Knightsbridge for the almost discarded Hélène.

All anybody (in the family) had to do, Sir Ezra would continue, was to ask. This wasn't quite true. In fact, checks arrived usually unasked for, with a single note from the family's banker, 'Jolly' Jack Webster, saying that ... well, take the case of little Oscar's twin, on the occasion of his third-class honours degree in history: 'Your account has been credited with £5,000.' So the administration of this fund, thought to be quite unnecessarily large, and referred to in the family as 'the dole', was apparently haphazard but, like everything else controlled by Sir Ezra, equitable. For indeed this was exactly the sum, as little Oscar's brother Michael later discovered, that the steward's daughter had been paid for having his brother's bastard.

Jolly Jack Webster was on the list of course. So were the family's doctors Maurice and Eva, ridiculously named Krapf. He a gentle man, a bit of a *schlemiel*, but was alleged to know all the best specialists; she a lesbian, brilliant and inquisitive. From the office, Mrs Schwarzer there had to be, and her boy David, but he would come up from Turners with Nicky. From the business Sir Arthur, Chaimy Hassan who had invented the electric cigarette lighter and installed the intercoms in the family houses and the automatic gates at Turners, and who wore a beard, rode a bicycle, was a Communist, innocent and much loved. And then there was that little rat Wilson. 'And Mrs Wilson,' piped up Freddy.

'Is there one? I didn't know.'

'Oh yes, Harry Wilson's only mistake. He keeps pretty quiet about her, but she turns up at times like this.'

'And then there are the warrant holders.'

'Eh?'

Freddy looked at his wife as if she were an insubordinate recruit. Jokes about the family had to be the right kind of jokes.

'Oh come, Freddy, don't be so . . . disingenuous.' Very much a Left Book Club and *New Statesman* girl, this was one of Joyce's words. 'Everybody calls them that.'

Freddy wondered quite who 'everybody' might be but not for long.

'I mean,' said Joyce icily, 'Miss Tattie's osteopath, for instance. What's his name, David?'

'Davies.'

'Yes. And Audrey's decorator and the antique dealer and the gallery man and their band leader and her trainer – and her brother.'

'Oh yes. St James. I rather like him. A stylish bird. We'll have to ask them all. I wonder how he's enjoying the war. I don't see *him* in a gas mask.'

At the time of Joyce's party the phoney war and some of the sickly panic of late '39 was in the past; cockney sparrows bored by country life were homing in on a London which was still intact. Narvik had been forgotten. Dunkirk converted into a folkloric victory. The fall of France shrugged off. People were wont to say to each other, 'Now we know where we stand.' There were plenty of strawberries that summer, and cream, delivered by errand boys who whistled *We'll Gather Lilacs in the Spring Again* as they pedalled along the cosy sunlit avenues of St John's Wood. Everybody was heartened by that song in August 1940, and by the speeches of Churchill and by the score – 37 Messerschmitts, 14 Hurricanes, or so it said on the six o'clock news. It all showed we were winning the battle in the air and proved that we British were best alone, backs to the wall and defending as we had for nearly a thousand years a sceptr'd isle, and better without the embarrassment of Allies. And besides, the weather was marvellous; day after day, as the aeroplanes ripped the sky apart, the sun shone.

Nevertheless, the people who knew the real score – that the Germans would not be deterred by the pitchforks of the Local Defence Volunteers or stories of the Straits of Dover ready to be ignited, nor impressed by the campaigns to convert aluminium pots and pans into Hurricanes – these people, like the Deputy Prime Minister, who was known to fear the worst, or like the publisher Sarah had once met who carried poison against the knock-knock-knock of the Gestapo at the door, all these were prepared for an invasion we could not possibly resist, and had only one question in their minds: it was that question which Richard Poll was asking of Victor Bridleton, an American college friend of Sir Ezra's from the Embassy, as they both stood, champagne in hand, in Joyce's St John's Wood garden.

'Well, what *would* bring you into the war?'

The American transferred a green cigar from one side of his mouth to the other, scratched his ear, contemplated the young don, smiled at Sir Ezra, who stood there, head cocked, approving the audacity of the question, and replied in the Southern accent so pleasing to the English ear:

'Well, Ezra knows my feelings and I believe you know Sir Ezra's.

You gotta remember that I work for the U.S.A., and our Ambassador . . .'

At that moment, Joyce, spotting the three of them so successfully in conversation, lolloped through the crowd in her FANY uniform, brandishing a bottle of champagne in each hand like a pair of dumb-bells, and with a hoot of 'Don't let the skylight in, as Thomas Love Peacock would say,' filled Bridleton's empty glass.

This effectively destroyed (as it was not intended to do) their little conversation, but unlike lesser men wanting to remove themselves from unpromising social scenes, Sir Ezra did not ever feel the need to mumble an excuse. He simply walked away, sparing the eager hostess not even a nod. Joyce looked stumped.

'Good heavens, Joyce,' remarked the don. 'You look as if you were going to win the war single-handed. What are you? An admiral or something?'

In her uniform, Joyce looked formidable.

'Well,' she said, seeing that Sir Ezra was safely removed and now sitting between his sisters on the (only) garden bench, 'strictly speaking, I am on duty. But my boss knows Audrey or rather Audrey knows my boss if you know what I mean. You know Lady C——?'

'I don't,' replied the young don drily, 'but I can imagine.'

Snubbing Joyce was apparently contagious, and he turned to pursue his conversation with the interesting and possibly important American.

A little boy wearing a Mickey Mouse gas mask and a Harrods grey flannel suit ran up to Sir Ezra, saying, 'Guess who I am?' Sir Ezra lifted up the flap of the rubber of the boy's mask. 'You're Hermann Goering.' The gas mask shook from side to side. 'Benito Mussolini?' Again. 'The Aga Khan?' No. 'Franklin D. Roosevelt Jones?' 'I give up.'

With difficulty the boy removed the mask. 'I'm Jeremy Kind,' he said, all red-faced.

'And you put that gas mask back in its case where it belongs, Master Kind,' spoke up Miss Pat, and did so.

'My God, my very own nephew, Jeremy Kind, and I never recognized him,' said Sir Ezra. 'Congratulations, by the way, on becoming a British citizen.' He turned to Sarah. 'I meant to tell you, Sarah, it's all all right. I got a call this morning from the Home Office. They'll be sending you some forms to fill in.'

'*Now* you tell me, Ez,' said Sarah, reaching up to pat his cheek.

'Come on, let's talk to some of these people.' Sir Ezra stood up and took Jeremy's hand.

'I'd rather not. I'd rather stay here with you and Mummy. Besides, I've talked to them all already,' said Jeremy dismissively.

'Oh, the little *grafpetoch*,' said Sir Ezra.

'What's that?' asked the little boy.

'Stuck up, grand,' put in Tattie. 'You go with Ezra, there's a good boy.'

'Don't you think it's a good idea?' asked Sarah of her sister as they watched Sir Ezra amble off.

'As long as you're happy, that's what I say.'

'Is that what you say?' said Sarah.

The sisters were cold together, like two planets. They circled in the same system but they did not touch.

'You'd never think he wasn't a little English boy,' said Miss Tattie to her sister, meaning well.

'He is a little English boy. He's almost forgotten how to speak anything else. Didn't you hear Ezra say so? He thinks of me as his mother. Don't you think I could be?'

'Not really, Sarah. Different kind of skin.' But Miss Tattie's mind was elsewhere. Unwilling to wear spectacles her little damp blue eyes were screwed up trying to follow her brother's progress around the darkening garden. She hardly noticed that Madame Ooh-la-la had sat down between them, gasping.

'Fancy you two *schmoozing* together. I'm coming to *kibitz*.' Like many in the family circle who were not of the faith she was apt to exceed in Yiddish.

Ezra moved through Joyce's guests like a prince at a levee, smiling, gripping the shoulders of the men, remembering their names, their wives' names, the names even of absent mistresses and always holding hard on to Jeremy's hand, presenting him to everyone, explaining him, delighting in him. Nicky, his friend David and Chaimy the inventor were arguing by the long white linen-covered table which served as a bar by the fruitless espaliered tree, watched with half an eye by a gently swaying Sir Arthur, the other eye being fixed on the bottom of a young waiter.

'We never really trusted Churchill, y'know,' Sir Arthur contributed.

Nicky rounded on him with the ferocity and *audace* peculiar to a schoolboy. 'That's an intelligent thing for you to say, Sir Arthur. You're right, of course, he's a dangerous inebriate, and treacherous too, like his ancestor, the first Duke, who deserted his own army in the middle of the night. . . .'

'*Comment?*' Hélène had joined the conversation.

'Yes. 1688. He stole away like a thief in the night and I quote the *Encyclopaedia Britannica*!' said Nicky triumphantly. 'How can the British proletariat trust a man who wanted to set troops on the miners, who . . .'

'Any more of this, my boy, and you'll end up in jail under Eighteen B,' interrupted Sir Arthur amiably, wondering how such vituperation could flow from such pretty lips.

'Possibly,' said Nicky coolly. 'But I think I may be too young.'

'Can't you stop him talking like this?' asked Hélène of Chaimy. 'I know it upsets his father.'

Chaimy contemplated her with his fine melancholy eyes. 'What a nice woman you are,' he said, and kissed her full on the mouth.

When Sir Ezra advanced on this group, Nicky was in the middle of some thesis about the Russians' indifference to a capitalist war. When he saw his father he rather obviously walked away.

Finally, and it seemed to Tattie that it would never happen, he did acknowledge the presence at the party of her beloved. They came face to face. She could see that they were shaking hands and little Jeremy had been released at the same time.

'Ezra Sterling. You are Pilot Officer Lambkin.'

'Yes, sir. Most people call me Chuck.'

Sir Ezra tilted his head back the better to examine the man and breathed in slowly. It was the stance of a bull elephant.

'From?'

'The South, as you can probably tell, Sir Ezra.'

'And you know Victor?'

'Only because he's at the Embassy of the United States where I am registered. It's through him that I have the acquaintance of your charming sister, Miss Tattie.' At this moment the fellow actually had the cheek to give that lady in question a sort of long-distance cowboy wave. 'A most civilizing experience for a hick like myself.'

'I've been to some civilized places in the South.'

The American interrupted: 'I doubt, Sir Ezra, whether you are familiar with St Francisville, Louisiana. It is, as we say, a one-horse town. One bank, two insurance companies, one guy in the crop-spraying business – that's me, that's how I come to know a little about flying, you see,' and he flicked with his hand at the wings stitched on to his RAF tunic.

'Well,' said Sir Ezra, 'you must get Tattie to . . .'

Again Sir Ezra did not finish because a lady standing in a darkened window on the first floor back of the house facing Joyce and Freddy's garden shouted out in a wobbly but clearly upper-class voice:

'Isn't it about time you bloody Jews remembered there's a war on?'

She must have been standing at that window for some time unnoticed and drinking, watching the rich Jews' party to which she had never been asked. Perhaps her rage had gained some animus from the bee-like buzz of cheerful German voices below the stairs where had congregated Dr Feinberg, a German refugee saved from the maw of Defence Regulation 18B by Sir Ezra; Yolande, Joyce's Viennese refugee, 1938 vintage; and of course Mrs Schwarzer, rejoicing a little too loudly in the opportunity of expressing herself in her native tongue. Nor was the lady's remark all that fair. Joyce was in uniform, of a kind, and so was the Doctor, now attached to the War House, as he called it, on a crucial but not much talked about aspect of military hygiene. There was little Oscar in his grandfather's Sam Browne, Michael with the white flashes of an officer cadet, there was of course that pilot officer of Tattie's. And most of the others were women, or too old, or children and they were too young. It *was* unfair. They didn't even look, people thought to themselves, particularly Jewish. (Who looks Jewish in uniform?) Thought Sir Ezra, no children from *his* family had been sent off to America. He did not have to inspect the origin of this bombshell as the others had done, but stood absolutely stiffly looking at Pilot Officer Lambkin. He was almost able to feel a smirk in the darkness from the lady in the house opposite, at the effect she had had, and he was, like the others, dumbstruck. Two thousand years of history forbade a quick retort. It was the young waiter, possibly drunk but brave, who broke the horrid silence with a clear cockney voice:

'And innit about time, lovey, you went to bed?'

The lady replied by sharply pulling down the blind. She must have withdrawn into the room and switched on the light, for seconds later to the joy of the party the blind snapped up again and the light flooded out. There were cries of 'Light! Black-out!' and little Oscar bawled bull-neckedly across the garden wall. 'Didn't you know there was a war on?' But it was all rather feeble and an atmosphere of quiet prevailed, not helped by the Germans who went on buzzing, obviously not aware of the horror above stairs.

'I'm afraid it's Mrs Carson-Boothe - on the bottle again,' said Joyce.

'Can't you get Dimmi to turn those Germans down a bit, for Chrissake?' said little Oscar angrily.

Dimmi, beloved Czech major-domo to the family, was doing exactly that, and suddenly with the buzz from below silenced the garden party grew cold, sober and uneasy. Sir Ezra beckoned to Dimmi as he walked majestically up the stairs of the garden.

'Now what's going on?' said Joyce to Freddy who had moved to her side.

'I should think Ezra's had enough and wants to go home or . . . wait a minute. Oh, I think we're in for a sermon.'

'My God, why can't he tell me? After all, I *am* the hostess,' said Joyce, and so she advanced.

'Ah, Joyce, my dear, you have done us well. Dimmi and I were saying how wonderful it would be if we could possibly go on inside. I see you've managed a coal fire in the drawing room,' and so saying Sir Ezra took Joyce's arm, a real honour. 'Perhaps if you said something, Joyce, they might go upstairs.'

'As it's getting a bit cold,' announced Joyce in a strained FANY

voice, 'I think we'd better go inside where there's lots more . . .'
She was going to say 'champagne', but with the echo of the
denunciation still in the air, she couldn't finish, and just said,
'There's lots more of everything.'

Some of the guests were wondering, with the black-out and
everything, whether the party wasn't really over now, but a buzz
was fomented by Dimmi, walking delicately among them, to the
effect that the nannies and children were to go home but it was
hoped that everybody else would stay on as – 'My God, I know,'
interrupted Nicky. 'Father's going to give us one of his pep talks.'

In Sophie's time, at this hour, the nannies and children would
have shuffled off but the grown-ups would be treated to some quite
serious roulette and the party could go on till dawn with her smart
friends dropping in. It used to be a marvellous party, the band
leader would telephone a band, the director would know some girls
who might amuse the twins and their friends, and Sophie would
pass out, recover, and so on.

But there was, as the lady opposite had reminded them, a war on,
and so now Miss Tattie huffed dutifully to her feet, and helped
noticeably by Pilot Officer Lambkin was propelled up the circular
iron staircase, laddering her stockings on the roses there thought-
lessly entwined. There was a slight jam at the top of the stairs
because David Mendoza had arrived in an excited state and wanted
to join the party below. He was late, he was sorry, he had been to
have drinks in Belgrave Square and couldn't find a cab. His news
was that they – the Messerschmitts – had been coming over like
snipe but we had bagged 22 of them that afternoon. He waved his
matching Sulka handkerchief like a schoolboy as he announced this
and there was some cheerful clapping. Audrey motioned to him to
go back inside with his friend, some backgammon-playing back
bench MP from the Club who had been a well-known supporter of
Chamberlain. Collecting the clan and its dithering supporters from
the garden into the white drawing room was a slow business, like
getting toothpaste back into a tube, but they made it in the end and
nobody attempted to leave as what appeared to be a fresh lot of
Dimmi's waiters – or had they just changed their coats? – poured
yet more champagne into clean glasses.

Richard Poll was anxious to be off but could not find his mackin-tosh, and was hunting for it with that air of distress usually reserved for the loss of an heirloom. He asked after it of Dimmi.

'I'll see you have it, sir, when the time comes.'

'But the time has come,' said the petulant don. 'I've got a train to catch, I've got to get back to Oxford.'

'We'll get you to your train, sir. I think Sir Ezra has something to say to all of us.'

What on earth did this Slav headwaiter think he was doing? Poll seethed. And what did he have to do with this jumped-up lot of German Jews anyway? And who was going to stop him leaving a party when he wanted to? Dimmi's eye gently flickered over the angry man's face, half friendly, half pleading, but there was so much authority in the way he stood between Poll and the front door that the don had to yield. He snorted and, followed by Dimmi, returned to the drawing room where Sir Ezra stood in front of the fire, flanked by his sisters in armchairs, with the Doctor and the Pilot Officer beside them in a parody of a royal family portrait. The rest of them took up their positions, Freddy and Joyce and little Oscar, with his slightly sloshed Veronica Lake-like girl, and Oscar's twin, and only Nicky not participating, but lolling against the back of the wall opposite smoking – but it was all right because he had been Bar-Mitzvahed – a youthful cigarette. The servants had disappeared, but Dr Feinberg and Chaimy had come up from below stairs together with Yolande and Mrs Schwarzer. Audrey sat on the other mammoth white sofa between her brother and the befuddled but ready-for-anything MP. Sir Arthur was up in front, facing Sir Ezra, his large frame squeezed in a smallish chair, wondering whether if he lit a cigar this might spoil the pleasure he planned for later that evening. Harry Wilson stood with his wife looking know-ing next to Jolly Jack Webster, who was trying to compose a frown on his sunny countenance. Madame Ooh-la-la was silent for once, staring to her front like a good pupil, and the rest of the clientele looked peeved, bored, embarrassed or benign depending on their dispositions and on the effect of the champagne.

'First I would like to thank Joyce for her hospitality: it is good of her to make these arrangements in such difficult times; then I would like to welcome the friends of the family, old and new. . . .' Did Sir Ezra flick a fairly contemptuous finger at David Mendoza's Munich friend? Anyway, the Conservative Member stirred in his chair. 'They are welcome at all our gatherings. I don't know where we'd be without them.' Sir Ezra stared at the ash gathering on his cigar. 'Always welcome,' he mumbled. He looked as if he were going to fall asleep. He woke up.

'What the lady said over the garden wall is quite apropos of what I want to say to you. We Jews have always been blamed when anything goes wrong with a nation. We are supposed to be part of an international conspiracy, at least that's what Herr Hitler says, and there are still people in this country who believe him. Nobody has ever asked me to join an international conspiracy!' There was, as they say in Hansard, some laughter. 'All I know is,' and Sir Ezra stretched out his arms as if to hug the whole drawing room, 'that you are my friends, and all I know is that the people who have persecuted my people have become undone. Look at Ferdinand and Isabella. . . .'

Oh good heavens, thought Audrey, and noisily reached for her powder compact. Sir Ezra looked at his wife, but Audrey remained unquelled as only Audrey could. Nicky looked across the room at his mother, and Sir Ezra looked at Nicky. Their glances met and they both, magically, smiled, as Audrey placidly dusted her cheeks. It was only a tiny exchange but in that room full of flickering eyes, it was observed and some thought that Audrey had stumped Sir Ezra, that he would have to wind up and they could all go home.

But no.

'God', intoned Sir Ezra, looking hard and with a different expression at his son, 'has not made us heathens or slaves, has set upon us the obligations of being men, to which I will add the obligations of being Jews.'

(Tattie stirred. She didn't understand what Ezra was saying about Ferdinand and Isabella, but during her long exclusion from the world she had had recourse to religion, and she had recognized the reference to the morning prayer in which she remembered that her own particular condition, that of being a woman, was not very flatteringly referred to – which was one of the reasons why, when she had got out of that dreadful place, she had gone Reform.)

'There is nothing in our religion,' continued Sir Ezra, 'to prevent us fighting our enemies, and remember our enemies are this country's enemies. We are English Jews, first English and then Jews. My father understood that when he joined up in the last war, over age, as a volunteer. Both my nephews have joined up. Our old Uncle Ephie has risked his life to cross the Atlantic to try and persuade our friends there to come in with us –' (They were too polite to do anything but believe Sir Ezra at this point.) 'And there is evidence in this room of the fellow-feeling which some Americans have for us. . . . I hope, sir, that you are the first of many swallows,' said Sir Ezra looking at Chuck, and he paused while Chuck, who had not taken his eyes off the speaker since the beginning, removed the cigar from his mouth and acknowledged the remark with a short un-smiling nod.

'And one thing more I must say,' Sir Ezra went on. 'Money can't buy everything but it can still buy a lot even during a war. I am sure that no member of this family will be seen to abuse that factor. We must all tighten our belts, and if others who are privileged don't, *we* must. We Jews must be seen to know that there *is* a bloody war on. And now,' said Sir Ezra, looking at his watch, 'if I don't take our friend to the station, he'll miss his train.' And without a glance at anybody, he bounded across the room, grabbed the little don's arm, and was gone, leaving the company flat, but suddenly garru-lous.

'I didn't understand what he was on about, did you? He didn't seem to make much sense,' remarked David Mendoza to his friend. 'He did to me,' replied the Conservative Member. 'You see, in politics it doesn't matter what you say, but it does matter who you are.'

'I never realized you lot were so bellicose,' said Richard Poll as the Rolls nudged its way through the black-out, the great headlamps crippled by regulation black masks. There was a silence. Had he gone too far? Sir Ezra seemed to be thinking.

'Oh yes, we can even fight on the Sabbath. Have you never felt the urge?'

'To fight, you mean? Certainly not, I'm a coward. And besides, my legs are too short. I think I'm probably a pacifist. I rather subscribe to Morgan Forster's view of patriotism.'

As Sir Ezra did not know it, the don informed him.

'But didn't the Spanish Civil War bother you at all? I imagine you are not in faovur of fascism.'

'Surely. And it bothers the Duchess of Athol. And of course in 1936, being a very poor undergraduate, a lot of my friends were Communists and some of them even went to Spain. But it was a mess, and I hate mess.'

'*Very* poor you don't sound,' said Sir Ezra.

'Oh, I know. I like to be taken for a smart young don from a smart old college, but in fact I come from a mining village in Durham. My father broke his leg when he was quite young, thank God, otherwise he would have died of silicosis. But even so, the poor fellow spent the rest of his life moaning because he couldn't go down that bloody pit again, while my mother scrubbed other people's floors as well as ours. We weren't just very poor, Sir Ezra, we were starving.'

'And you never thought of becoming a Communist? My son . . .'

'Oh, I know. I talked to him. Very fiery stuff, I must say, but you must realize it's only a pose. It'll pass, it's just done to annoy you.'

'Eh?'

'Yes, I mean, haven't you read Dostoevsky? The strongest human emotion is between father and son. You know.'

'What should I read?'

'Oh, I can't remember now. I think I must have had too much of your champagne. Or Joyce's rather. It's good of you to give me a lift.'

But Sir Ezra was interested. 'Have you ever thought of a political career? You were the only person to make any sense at that meeting the other day at the Treasury.'

'No, I wasn't, Sir Ezra. There were two of us. Yes, and I shall probably try and find a constituency, perhaps after the war. There's not much going on now. In the Labour Party, of course.' He sounded a touch defiant.

'If the occasion should ever arise,' said Sir Ezra slowly, 'when you need any help, I would be most interested.'

'Help? How's that?'

It being dark in the back of the Rolls, Sir Ezra had to lean over and take his companion's right hand and rub his right thumb gently across the palm. 'I know of no situation when the possession of ample funds can be a serious disadvantage. Not even in the Labour Party.'

Only when Poll had waddled off into the steamy cavern of Paddington Station did Sir Ezra remember that he had been too much intrigued by the conversation to ask after the committee where they had first met. It was good of Joyce – how did she know? – to arrange their second introduction. They must all come down for the weekend.

The boys' taxi ride to the Bag o' Nails had not been so happy. Little Oscar's *shicksa* had been sick over his service dress, a model of its kind by Kilgour, St James's tailor, and a present from that elegant fellow his uncle, who felt strongly about such matters and shared the view of little Oscar's OCTU instructor that 'it is a tradition of the regiment that you go to a rattling good tailor.'

So it had been decided that little Oscar's brother should take the girl back to the night club, and maybe swap her for a better one, while little Oscar would take the cab on to, oh God, where? It was silly to go back to Freddy's, as the boys called their stepfather, as they'd all be in a flap about tidying up and Joyce would be all toffee-nosed. No, the best place would be Tattie's flat. She never went to bed and would never tell on anybody.

To Oscar's surprise, but after all, why not, the door was opened not by Miss Tattie or by Miss Attlee who lived in and who stayed up with Miss Tattie when she was alone, but by the American. Chuck was at his ease, in his braces, more than slightly drunk and smoking his usual cigar.

'Why!' he drawled. 'You've thrown up all over your tunic. Well, that's no crime in America. Come in, boy, and we'll soon have you fixed up. Say hello to yer aunt.' And he jerked a finger in the direction of the salon and swayed off down the corridor, in search of water and a bowl.

Little Oscar stood in that most expensive drawing room, fearful of spoiling the Aubusson, but he needn't have worried for Tattie was (once again) on her knees at the end of the room, where the carpet had been rolled back, in an obviously happy condition.

'Hello, Oscar, do you want to learn how to shoot crap?'

'No thanks, Tattie,' said Oscar, noticing the pound notes scattered around. 'Boy,' he said much later when he told the story, 'I don't think I can afford to.'

At the house in Maddison Place, Jeremy fell asleep as Miss Pat was undressing him. She was folding away his grey flannel jacket when she felt a paper rustling in the pocket. It was a brand new, beautifully engraved £10 note, the kind which Sir Ezra stuffed into little boys' pockets when they weren't looking. She decided to retain it for safekeeping.

Joyce and Freddy lay naked on Sophie's great bed which they couldn't get out of the house – God knows how it got in – had they tried, and watching through the open window the searchlights as they anxiously inspected the sky.

'I thought it all went off rather well. Well done, my love.'

'I don't think I had all that much to do with it, really. That poor Mrs Carson-Boothe.'

'She should be locked up.'

'Not really. She told me a dreadful story. She's convinced I'm not Jewish, by the way. Her husband was swindled out of his money in India. Somebody called Levi or Cohen, of course. So now she loathes Jews, really loathes them.'

'Us,' said Freddy. 'I don't think Ezra's speech was up to his usual standard.'

'I think he really was more put out by Mrs Carson-Boothe than he let on. Still, apart from that, it did go off quite well. And everybody found taxis in the end. I suppose you'd booked every cab rank in St John's Wood.'

'Not me,' said Freddy. 'Somebody in the office, Dimmi, I suppose.'

'Ouch, steady, Freddy.'

'Yes?'

'Freddy, I believe you have a cockstand.'

'I believe I have, my love. Thank you for . . . pointing it out.'

PART TWO

1948

It was hot, even in the shade of the cemetery, even for a South African. The captain looked down disgustedly at his sweat-stained khaki shorts, a relic of the last proper war, when overpolite black men washed, pressed and returned one's kit. This is a terrible business, not even a war, just a mess, he thought; but it had looked from the headlines which he and his friends clucked over by the swimming pool in Houghton such a noble, even a holy, adventure, and an interesting change from talk about the Stock Exchange and playing golf with other Jo'burg Jews. So suddenly after a few high-balls in the bar of the Houghton Club, all eight of them had agreed to come to the Holy Land loaded with stolen Lugers, compasses, maps and binoculars. Not just for these items but for their ex-perience of war – some of them had been at Tobruk, okay they had surrendered but still, it had been a war – and also because they were intelligent, brown-legged and confident, they were all given com-mands in the Palmach.

The captain considered his platoon sprawled round the cemetery. A good place to conceal men, he thought. Some were playing poker on the tombstones, one was reading a Penguin Homer. And another was actually *dovenning*. They were worthless, the East End Chassids – spindly, spotty and short-sighted, either lunaticly bold and dis-orderly or terrified and equally disobedient, and he was rather frightened of the light he sometimes saw in their eyes. 'Jesus Christ, what a shower!'

The captain looked from the parapet which separated the cemetery from the glary white dirt track below, wiped the sweat out of his eyes with his sleeve and took out a khaki handkerchief, thoughtfully provided by his mother who liked everything to be correct, and wiped the eyepieces of his binoculars. He examined the hillside opposite. It was difficult to see much because of the sun. Even the sun was in the wrong bloody place: wasn't God supposed to be on *their* side?

The fighting, if there were to be any, had not strictly speaking begun. But then Palestine, in these early days of May 1948, was not a strict place. The new state was due to be born on the 14th, the date when the British mandate over Palestine was to expire, but could it survive? The Arabs had sworn to push it into the sea, and it was just possible that the Arab Legion, armed and officered by the British and led by Glubb Pasha, a sort of fatherly Lawrence of Arabia, was competent and well-organized enough to do this. The Legion was thought to have British 25-pounders ready to shell the new city of Jerusalem, but how many and where? The general objective was the defence of Kfar Elion, between Hebron and Jerusalem, and it was the job of the captain's platoon to draw the Legion's fire, to get a map reference and do nothing more. Beyond the hill below him was country held by Arabs which he could not see, but judging by the contours of his map the view from the top of the hill of where the Legion might have hidden their artillery could be extensive. So he had sent a section forward under Corporal Steimatsky – eleven trembling Cockneys, one from the art department of an advertising agency who claimed he could bring back a sketch of the landscape, another a bumbling fellow called Schiff who carried the field telephone, the idea being that if anything were to happen to the section they could communicate their reconnaissance with the captain, who in turn could relay back to his headquarters. Wally Schiff adored Nicky, as everybody called the corporal, a kibbutznik from Beth Alpha in Galilee, followed him around like a dog. Come to that, they all did. The corporal taught them Hebrew, instruction they would not take from the Chassids. He was an unusual boy, passionate, cool and gay all at once, but distant to him, the captain. Why the hell wouldn't he take a commission? He was obviously, to use that British phrase, an officer and a gentleman. But in the one long conversation to which the captain had been treated, the corporal had explained that war was an extension of capitalism and his duty was to stay in the ranks, just as it had been to change his name from Sterling back to Steimatsky. . . . Pretentious little twerp. Still, the crazy fellow was halfway up that hill and where he led the section would surely follow. The captain was right to have chosen him, though perhaps he should have waited till a little later in the day when the sun would have been behind them. But they had enough water, enough food . . . if only they remembered to keep their heads down.

The thing came over the hill out of the sun – black, large and noisy considering it was only an elderly Taylor Craft. The captain had just time to yell 'Heads down!' to his men and to notice a white arm waved by one of the men on the hill. It was incredible, didn't they know? But of course they knew nothing. As the bi-plane tottered over their heads and away, the captain half-marched, half-ran, furiously to the field telephone and cranked violently. Schiff answered with an unmilitary ''Allo.'

'Give me the corporal,' he snapped. 'Corporal?'

'Sir?'

'That was one of Glubb's planes. Recce. They may have seen you and they may not.'

'I thought it was one of ours.'

'Christ, man, we don't have any. At least not like that.'

'Sir –' (different tone), 'what do we do now?'

'Continue as before, only for Chrissake keep them spread out and as to this man of yours who waved, tell him I'll have his bollocks off when he comes back. Make them put more dirt on their faces and arms and keep their heads down!'

Nicky looked up at the blue sky, down at Wally's anxious Airedale face and across at a tethered nanny-goat which had been abandoned by an Arab villager and was having trouble nudging off the attentions of her obviously teenage kids. 'They should be beyond that sort of thing by now,' he thought. He felt pretty silly himself, like the day he'd resigned from the Boy Scouts because the patrol leader wouldn't let him bake the potatoes *his* way. The whole thing was so childish.

'Come on, Wally,' he said, 'on and up.'

To the captain on his seventh cigarette, from a Player's tin marked *H.M. Ships Only*, the section seemed to be moving quite well up the hill. Two minutes ago the Taylor Craft had returned and this time his men, both on the hill and in the cemetery, had taken the proper action – faces to the ground. Then through the binoculars he saw the section pause, stop and huddle together under a boulder. He got to the field telephone.

This time it was the corporal. 'Sir ?'

'Corporal, I told you to keep the men spread out.'

'Yes, I know, but Wally thinks he's broken his leg, and he's fallen on top of me, and we can't move him.'

'Christ! Tell them . . .' He was interrupted by the arrival of a shell. It soared over the hill like a well-hit shot with a Number 8 iron, quite slowly, to the astonishment of the platoon who had never seen a shell fired in their lives. It fell about a hundred yards below the section to the right. The captain cranked desperately at the field telephone and as if in response to unheard orders, a number of figures detached themselves from the boulder and started running down the hill. They stopped and lay dutifully still with their heads down when they heard the drone of the persistent Taylor Craft.

'Good boys,' thought the captain. 'They're learning.'

The second shell was also wide, but fell above the two men, locked together in what seemed to be a loving embrace. The third killed a goat and the captain saw quite clearly two kids sucking greedily at their dead mother, oblivious of the explosions.

The fourth was nearer.

'Bracketing,' muttered the captain.

His runner came up to him. 'Sir, we can hear them talking.'

The captain ran over to the radio operator who handed him the earphones. There was just a lot of crackling. The radio operator nodded to him to be patient.

'Ah yes, there they are.' A clear English public-school voice. 'Left three degrees, four five hundred, charge one, fire!'

'What a bloody waste of ammunition,' thought the captain. All this for a couple of Jews and a goat.

On queue, the fifth shell – or was it the sixth? – was lobbed over the hill and fell twenty-five yards to the right of the boulder where cuddled the two men. His men. The shrapnel must have got them. It was too near.

There was nothing he could do – yet.

To try and rescue them, or what was left of them, would reveal to that bloody Taylor Craft, due over any moment to radio the effect of the last shell, the position of the rest of the platoon. The captain decided to wait for what was left of the section, then they could say *Kaddish* for Nicky whatever-his-name-is. Or was, for from looking through the binoculars, he'd clearly had it. Though it was difficult to see what had happened to the other chap. Then he'd have to write a report and consider the alternatives for future action. The men were now silent, frightened and attentive.

And so, more or less, it was. The Taylor Craft came over low, this time from left to right, and this time the pilot must have seen the two bodies no longer in the shadow of the boulder. The rest of the section had rejoined the platoon, intelligently by a roundabout route, and as happens in these situations, a leader had naturally emerged. It was the copywriter who came up to him and asked, 'Sir, is Nicky, I mean Corporal Steimatsky, all right?'

'Didn't you see?'

'No, we were . . . We kept our heads down when we heard the shell coming, and then I'm afraid we just ran. Nicky told us to scarper. That's just what he said, sir. You see, he wouldn't leave Wally. He said, "Now, the rest of you scarper." '

The captain did not reply directly but handed the boy his binoculars, and as he walked away, said over his shoulder, 'And by the way, you'd better take over from him as section leader.'

'*Oi*,' muttered the copywriter as he focused the lenses on the body of his predecessor. 'What a way to get a promotion.'

The captain walked back to what had already been nicknamed the Light Programme and picked up the earphones. It was the same well-bred voice:

'Observation, report two enemy dead on Hill Sixty-seven. No sign of the rest of them. I think it was just a recce patrol. There were no mortars so I don't think they'll give us any trouble. Can you send a quad to pick them up? That shouldn't take you more than half an hour, so I'll be over the field hospital by, say o-one-

thirty hours. Intelligence will want me to identify them. Over.'
The reply was inaudible.

It was helpful of them to advertise their intentions so clearly on
the air, thought the captain. They probably didn't think we had a
radio; the *chutzpah* of the bastard. He sounded like he was ringing
up Harrods.

The men had heard the news and quickly began to make plans;
for each Jew a different plan. They were going to mine the road,
shove a Molotov cocktail into the turret of a tank, they were going
to get Nicky and Wally and bury them according to the law, they
were going to get that gun whatever.

The captain, patting his head three times in the correct military
manner, summoned them to his side. They respected the signal and
gathered round. 'Now, listen,' began the captain in his clipped
South African voice down almost to a whisper. 'This is what we're
going to do. We must not attract their attention in any way. We
can't attack the quad, which you should know is a light armoured
vehicle for towing twenty-five pounders. We will say *Kaddish*.'

At this point one of the Chassids produced his yarmulke and
made as if to pray. But the captain cut him off with a gesture. 'Later!
We've lost two men but we have achieved something.' They looked
at him disbelievingly.

'Remember our orders are to locate Glubb's artillery. We've
done that. There is one twenty-five pounder. It is forty-five
hundred yards from that big stone, in that direction. You saw the
shell, didn't you?'

They nodded – it had been a sight and sound they would not
forget.

'Well, if there's one twenty-five pounder, there's probably a troop.
Tomorrow I'll send the map reference with a runner to HQ and
if they can rustle up an aircraft we can knock them out. Field guns
have no defence against aircraft, remember. From now on until
that quad has turned up and gone home I want you to be as quiet
as mice. No smoking, no talking, and when the sun goes down there
is something we can do.' He paused. 'I want two volunteers.' There
was silence. Thirty pairs of Jewish eyes looked at him warily.

'Put it another way,' said the captain, smiling for the first time that day. 'Is there a butcher in the house?' One man put up his hand.

'Yes?'

'Sir, my uncle is a *schochet* and he used to . . .'

'Fine. Now, any one who can see in the dark?'

The butcher's nephew nudged his buddy. 'Chaimy, you can see in the dark, can't you, Chaimy?'

'Right. You two can go up that hill after dark and liberate those two little goats. They'll still be there. The two Cohens, you two, can light a fire inside one of those bloody mausoleums, but inside, man, because I want no fire, only smoke. We're lucky, tonight there's no moon, so we should be safe. We will dine, gentlemen, on roast kid.' He paused. 'Very delicious and –' the captain glanced at the Chassid – 'and quite kosher.'

This raised a slight laugh and the platoon looked almost admiringly at their leader.

'And now we'll say quietly to ourselves *Kaddish.*'

They all stood and yarmulkes or handkerchiefs of one kind or another were produced from tunic pockets. Some could say it in Hebrew, some in English and some, to be honest, didn't know what was going on. The captain found his prayer book, another thoughtful inclusion by his mother, and read to himself 'Magnified and sanctified be his great name (Amen) in the world. . . .' What an extraordinary religion, thought the captain. A man dies and you thank God.

The lieutenant's jeep came to a theatrical halt and almost blinded with dust the bedouin with a rifle between his knees squatting outside the field hospital tent. The man rose to his feet and saluted gravely. He held up two fingers. 'Engleesh,' he said.

'English? Oh my God.' The lieutenant hurried into the tent and his driver undid his *kufir* and lit a cigarette. The tent was open at both ends to allow the air to move but it was still oppressively hot. Luckily, there was no smell – yet. Only two of the neat camp beds were occupied, at opposite ends of the tent, a sensible arrangement since the first man's body was completely covered except for his feet by a grey army blanket, and was obviously dead, while, from the groans coming from the other end, the second was obviously alive.

The lieutenant contemplated the shape under the blanket and bent down to read the label tied to its big toe. It was a buff card of the kind used by matrons on schoolboys' luggage. It read STEIMATSKY, N.

'That was the best I could do, sir,' a voice said in English. A British medical orderly had replaced the bedouin as his escort.

'But he said they were English. Doesn't sound English to me.'

'Oh yes, sir. They've got volunteers from England, mostly from the East End. East End yids. Wait till you see the other one. Proper kike, that one.' And then, to make a different point and with the air of one with something to display, he pulled back the blanket to reveal a face unmarked by war.

'I cleaned him up a bit,' he said.

The lieutenant gasped and started back as if he had been hit.

Now, now, thought the orderly, he must have seen a dead man before in his life. And there's nothing to get upset about with this one. 'You all right, sir?' he asked.

'Er, yes. Show me the other one, will you?' And he turned quickly to the other end of the tent.

SCHIFF, W., for that was the name on the label, was not a pretty sight. With his fleshy nose, crinkly hair, puckered forehead, pendulous ears and thick lips, Wally's features combined unkindly into a Nazi caricature made worse because his face was puffy and swollen with tears. Answering the lieutenant's questioning glance, the orderly said, 'No, sir, he's not in any pain. I've pumped him full of morphine anyway. It's a simple leg fracture, no wounds. He's just a bloody cry-baby, if you ask me. "Nicky, Nicky, Nicky",' mimicked the orderly.

'Schiff, shut up,' said the lieutenant as if to both of them.

Wally rubbed his eyes and his stubbly chin and stared at the officer, a man perhaps half his age. 'One of them bloody Arabs tried to pull my leg off.'

'You'll be all right now, Schiff. You're with the Arab Legion, a perfectly civilized army,' he said icily, 'which subscribes to the Geneva Convention.'

'Oh yes,' said Wally.

'And you aren't even wounded. You've just broken your bloody leg, as you put it.'

Wally was silent, but gazed at the lieutenant with a new approving look, but at the orderly with distaste. ''Ave you got a proper hospital, then?'

'Oh yes, all that. And now I want you to tell me ... Do you think you could leave me with this man for a moment? I want to ask him a few questions. Intelligence.'

The orderly looked displeased, but left.

'Now, Schiff, tell me.'

'Well, sir, I'm in Nicky's section, that's Steimatsky, but we all called him Nicky, we're halfway up this bloody hill and you know me, I'm a big fella, and I've got this effing field telephone strapped to me back ...'

'Field telephone?' But something flashed in the lieutenant's mind to make him change his tactic. 'Look, Schiff,' he said gently, 'technically you're a prisoner of war, and you don't have to answer my questions, only give me your name and number. Got it?'

Wally looked at him glumly.

'But you can tell me more about this Nicky, if you like.'

Wally's eyes misted and it looked as if more tears were on the way, but instead he raised himself up on his elbow and spoke in a confessional whisper to the lieutentant squatting by his side.

'He was a lovely boy, sir, and just before they started that firing I felt scared, and I ran towards him and I must have tripped and I fell on him and they couldn't move me and then he said to the lads, "Get back to the ..."'

'Yes, yes,' said the lieutenant, 'but where did he come from? Who was he, this Nicky?'

Wally ignored him.

'And we just lay there, for hours it seemed, and he tried to comfort me, as if I was his little boy and me old enough to be his father, and he told me funny stories.'

'Who was he, Schiff?'

'Oh, he wasn't like the rest of the lads. He was a comfortable boy. His dad was a toff, you could tell he was from a good family.' The doubt in the lieutenant's mind grew to certainty like a great weight upon his chest as Schiff babbled on: 'He should have been an officer. He was too good. That bit of shell should have been for me. But he got it and I got nothing. You see, I loved him and I got him killed, didn't I? If you'd have known him, sir . . .'

The lieutenant stood up. 'I did,' he interrupted. He straightened himself. 'He was the most incompetent fag I ever had,' he mumbled. 'Remember, Schiff, name and number and nothing else. Good luck.'

And praying he could control his tears, but knowing he could not, he stumbled out into the hard Palestinian sun. He stood still, his hands clenched over his eyes, breathing in the aromatic air, so hot that it hurt his nostrils, and said to himself, Please God, don't let me cry, not just yet. Conduct unbecoming and all that. It was his duty to inform the family. The lieutenant felt a spasm of grief almost like a movement of his bowels. He stumbled towards the jeep doing up his *kufir* so that only his eyes could be seen. He almost fell into his seat next to his sergeant and gestured him to move off.

As soon as they were out of sight the sergeant stopped and turned to the younger man whose head was turned away from him. 'If you don't mind a personal remark, sir, you look as if you've received something of a blow.' He took a cloth-covered bottle, unscrewed the cap, and said, 'Here, take a swig of this.' The kindness, the lilt of the Welsh voice and the familiar pedantic manner was too much for the lieutenant, who burst into tears. Only the sergeant's arm firmly extending the British Army water bottle barred him from collapse.

'Wow!' The shock of the alcohol for the moment blotted out any other feelings. 'What on earth?'

'Irish whiskey, you can't get Scotch,' said the sergeant placidly.

'Wow,' he said again, quietly, and wiped his lips with his hand. 'Well,' he said in a calm voice, as if rehearsing for later audiences, 'one of those two back there is somebody I knew at school. He's dead. The tricky thing is that his father is rather important. A lord, I think. A Jew, but a lord. And maybe something to do with the Government.'

'A scion of the Jewish nobility in that mob?'

'Uh huh. He was a crazy boy.'

'So?'

'We'll have to tell the authorities. I mean, the British authorities.'

The sergeant nodded. 'If we go on down this road we'll come to one of those road blocks the Guards have put up.'

'Guards?'

'King's Company Grenadier Guards,' echoed the sergeant, as he slammed the gear lever forward.

'Don't you think, Taffy,' shouted the lieutenant over the roar of the engine, and half hoping he wouldn't be heard, 'that if there is going to be a real fight out here we might be on the wrong side?'

The sergeant said nothing for a moment, then, 'You stick to your funny ideas, sir, and I to my pension.'

Mr Jonathan Barber was not enjoying himself. He was bored, and in the words of a recent musical, it was 'too darned hot'. Recently commissioned into the Guards, he had been sent from Wellington Barracks at the start of the season, to Palestine where the battalion's main duty, it seemed to him, was to watch while Jewish terrorists booby-trapped their jeeps and murdered Arab villagers. Of course the whole Palestine business was hellish but the bloody Government had no business to put the Army, and especially the Brigade, into such a situation. Jonathan Barber liked the Arabs. They had good manners, some were quite handsome, they giggled and entertained charmingly; the Jews he had seen had thick hairy legs and were quite appallingly keen.

He saw an Arab Legion jeep coming towards the road block, two men muffled in their *kufirs*. Oh God, they looked good, and as for the Trans-Jordanian frontier force with their Persian lamb headgear and those shiny boots ... Jonathan looked down at his uncovered knees and to restore his sang-froid lit a cigarette, put it in his holder as the chap from the Legion picked his way towards him through the coils of barbed wire.

'Morning.'

'Morning.'

The young Englishmen looked at each other, embarrassed. There seemed nothing else to do but to shake hands, there being no great difference of rank between them.

'Could I have a word with you?'

'Of course.'

They moved away from the men.

When the lieutenant had finished his tale, Jonathan Barber was incredulous. 'And you say he was at school with you. My God! An old Westminsterian, or whatever you call yourselves, in the Palmach.' Jonathan Barber spoke as an old Etonian.

The lieutenant let it go. 'I told you he was my fag.'

'Yes, I quite see something has to be done. You'd better see my company commander. Charmin' fellow.'

Twenty minutes after Jonathan had spoken to Tommy, as they called each other over the wireless, the lieutenant found himself in a Nissen hut furnished with just a camp bed, two folding chairs, a table on which was a bottle of whisky which Captain Tommy had insisted his servant procure before he would even speak. With equal considerateness, Sergeant Davis had been led off to another Nissen hut neatly labelled *Sergeants' Mess*. The lieutenant was beginning to appreciate the Guards' style. Captain Tommy, the charmin' fellow, was a symphony in blue – eyes, silk scarf, linen shirt and trousers and even suede shoes were all blue. But there was something about the eyes which suggested more than a trace of competence. And this emerged at what in 'current affairs' discussions was called the summing-up.

'So in an action the rights or wrongs of which neither of us is here to discuss, the son of a British peer was killed by a shell from an Arab Legion twenty-five pounder. The incident, or shall we say accident, may have been forgotten by tomorrow, or it may not. In any case, you were quite right as a British officer to pass this information on to us.' The lieutenant nodded gratefully. 'You see we live in an age of propaganda, and either side could blow this up in the papers. Or, as I said before, nothing might happen at all. I'll tell Colonel Billy, my colonel, who will . . . Oh well, never mind. You've done your bit. Would you like a drink?'

'No, thank you, sir.'

There was no reason for a full lieutenant to call a captain 'sir'.

2

One of the few dinner tables in London that night where the problem of Palestine was not discussed must have been Audrey's. And that was due to the absence, it seemed now forever, of her son, Nicky. When Westminster School had finished with him, he had left the country illegally – after all, he was subject to British military conscription – and had equally illegally joined one of the older commune-inspired kibbutz on the shores of Lake Galilee, calling himself Naphtali Steimatsky. Ezra knew this through the Jewish Agency who were happy that the first Viscount Sterling, a known anti-Zionist who had represented the British position unofficially in Washington and at UNO, should hear through them the whereabouts of his son. All he or Audrey had heard from Nicky himself had come in the form of a black-and-white snap of him holding hands with a short and very dark girl with a Fordson tractor in the background. 'You could smell her armpits and, my God she needed a shave,' said little Oscar when he saw it. It was considerate of Nicky to have communicated on the occasion of his father's elevation to the House of Lords, one of many institutions he despised.

Written in pencil on the back of the photograph were the words 'Congratulations. Love.' And then – it looked like an afterthought – 'to you both.' (Ezra had been pathetically grateful for that.) Perhaps Nicky had forgiven him. But for what, thought Ezra angrily, stabbing at a *goujonette* of sole. The boy should be here at this table with his family. He didn't have to wear a dinner jacket. Nobody minded his being a Communist. They were expected to rebel, the young. And anyway, *his* son could be anything he wanted. But not living in that unholy land which gave everybody so much *surus*. And, God forbid, in danger of his life. Nicky's place was here, being tutted over by Tattie and envied for his money by his cousins and annoying everybody with his silly left-wing talk. He could have been back in New College by midnight, in his nice little MG which lay rotting in a garage at Turners. Okay, he might be a bit *shikkeh*, but Nicky'd make it.

Ezra came out of his dream and offered a glass of wine from his own decanter – it was a family affectation that gentlemen had one each – to the lady on his right.

'Come, Eirene. A little Gewürztraminer. I got it specially for you. It's the only wine you can recognize with your eyes shut. You like it or you don't.'

'I like it,' said Eirene Schwarzer. 'I like it, Ezra, thank you.' In fact, she did not: to her it tasted of dung, but since her David was marrying into the family this was not a moment for honesty.

For the family and the business it had been a good war. Most of the aircraft destroying German cities had done so with the help of radio components manufactured and even invented by Sterlings. They prospered with decorum, indeed one of Ezra's earlier decrees had been to dismiss any accountant found taking advantage of the cost-plus system of a Government contract. This announcement had done the business no harm in the eyes of the commerically innocent Ministry of Aircraft Production. By the end of the war, with the growth of Bomber Command, Sterlings had increased their business more than three times over and had acquired a brand-new factory in South Wales almost as a present from the Government. As for making money, well, they paid excess-profits tax on their excess profits, but with no tax at all on capital gains, there was no point worrying. Every time Ezra did a tot the family was worth another couple of million quid.

He looked round the table. There was no setting for little Oscar's twin (why had he gone by no other name?) because he was not there to fill it. Michael had been a dull boy, given only to amusing himself. Still, as St James had remarked, it had been a chic bomb, the one which fell on the Café de Paris in 1940. This was not good enough. Boys were needed in the family, dull or otherwise. Ezra clenched his fists. There can be no more deaths. All of them with their children and, with God's help, their children's children, were or would be millionaires. And at next week's annual general meeting he was going to be happy to announce another bonus issue. No wonder the City loved him; it was a far cry from . . .

'Ezra! Ez!' It was Sarah. 'A *stiever* for your thoughts. Seriously, for a moment you looked happy.'

Ezra smiled. 'I was thinking about the sins of the fathers.

Descending unto the third and fourth generation, that's not good. I was just hoping your grandchildren would inherit some of my sins.'

'Don't you worry about that, Ezra,' declared Mrs Schwarzer. 'They will, I'm sure they will. I'll drink to that,' and bravely she nudged down a dollop of that revolting wine.

Prosperity – for it was a rule in the family that no one should join unendowed – had improved Eirene Schwarzer into being, she felt, and everybody else eventually felt, human. With the rump of her fashionable Berlin doctor father's collection of porcelain in a cabinet in her new Hampstead home, the good legs she had always had in nylons supplied by American officers who had convalesced at Turners, so you could see them properly, and her upper lip attended to (that morning) by Helena Rubinstein, she looked, as Ezra would have put it, like a *mensch*. She had in fact not been so much taken over as taken in. Her new appearance suited her and she had responded with an untapped gaiety and grace which had been hibernating beneath her office clothes.

Putting down her glass, she raised her hand to her eyes and said with a girlish mock-gulp, 'Frankly, Ezra, I don't think I like this wine after all.'

'The shipper shall be shot, Eirene,' replied Ezra solemnly. 'Sinnockson!'

'M'lud?'

'Would you be so kind as to open a bottle of that white burgundy from the case Mr Shalom sent us. I think Mrs Eirene would enjoy it.'

As if the *roi soleil* had impetuously handed the order of the Saint-Esprit to an ambitious subject in front of the whole court, the point was taken. This was a signal favour in three respects: the acceptance of her rejection, the ordering of a new bottle and Ezra's use of the appellation 'Mrs Eirene'. The newly honoured lady understood and smiled. Little Oscar at the other end of the table understood and flushed.

As Sarah's heir, Lucy's holding of Sterling ordinary shares was bigger than little Oscar's who had shared Sophie's mildly dissipated fortune with his brother. There had also been arranged a marriage settlement for Lucy's husband to which the family, especially Tattie, had had to contribute. So that the young couple's fortune was, after his own, Audrey's, Sarah's and Tattie's, the biggest in the family. If there were to be a struggle later – much later, please God, thought Ezra, and he patted his heart – for control of the business, this would tell. There were no other contestants; Sarah's Jeremy was, what? Sixteen or seventeen? More artistic than ambitious and anyway, he was only adopted. And then with Nicky in Palestine . . . but then perhaps Nicky would come back. My, the slaughter of fatted calves. Ah. Dreams.

Ezra surfaced from his cosy imaginings. Apart from shareholdings which could always be adjusted in little Oscar's favour, the two were matched as evenly as a pair of expensive gladiators. Both would fight to win, David Blacker with the net and foil and little Oscar, naked and unprotected, with a short broadsword. Ezra was pleased with this analogy, only Audrey would not approve because she liked spoiling little Oscar and also because she disapproved of 'unpleasantness', as she put it.

Both boys had been lucky and had enjoyed good wars. David Blacker, né Schwarzer, after a comic few months in the Pioneer Corps had been commissioned into the Rifle Brigade, joined the Commandos, survived the Dieppe raid, and had been wounded at Caen while carrying a senior officer to safety. It happened to be a Lord so David woke up in hospital at Southampton to find he had been awarded the Military Cross.

Little Oscar, rescued by a friend of Audrey's in the War Office from his Heavy Ack-Ack battery at Sheerness, was transferred to the Royal Horse Artillery and had reduced to handicap 2 at the Gezira Club in Cairo; he had married a NAAFI manageress called Sally, who had been relatively cheaply disposed of, been spotted by Montgomery, and as a brigade major had enjoyed himself as town major of Porto Ercole.

Ezra knew, in a roundabout way, that little Oscar had been frustrated in his ambition to command a battalion before he was thirty because he had failed the final test for potential colonels. On the last night of the course, when they all thought it was over, there was a party at which the mess stewards were instructed to keep everybody's glass tanked up, the idea apparently being to see how the candidates behaved when drunk. Passing out, vomiting, singing hymns were all permissible, apparently, but it was considered ruinous if in this frequently obtainable condition a commanding officer were to start, as Oscar did, a fight. Ezra chuckled to himself. Perhaps, he thought, someone had called Oscar a bloody Jew! Ezra smiled at his nephew now trying to stir his Aunt Tattie (who couldn't bring her American to the dinner party tonight) into life. Little Oscar had his weaknesses, he was reckless with money and reckless with women, guided more by his cock than his heart. That indiscretion at Oxford (when was that, '37, '38?), the Cairo incident (why marry the girl?). Then there'd been an Australian girl in Rome, whom he'd set up in Arlington Street after the war and was planning to discard only she wasn't having any, and there was a whiff of breach of promise in the air. Oh dear, oh dear, little Oscar did have his weaknesses, didn't he. But he had the strength and courage of a lion and the determination of an ice-cracker, for there was Tattie, beginning to smile and taking a second helping of chips.

'Where do you suppose they are now, our young lovers?' It was Audrey from the top of the table trying to make the conversation general, and referring also to what should, after all, be the matter in hand. She'd raised her voice because the table could seat sixteen, and though it could be folded up, it somehow never was, so there the nine of them were, grouped around it like islands.

'They're in bed,' said Tattie unexpectedly, and stuffed some more chips into her mouth before she could be asked to explain.

'They are,' said Eirene Schwarzer in her new authoritative voice, 'having dinner at the Hungaria, and then going on to the Four Hundred.'

'Usual routine,' said Joyce, bitterly. She was taking the Labour Government's peace as seriously as she had taken the war.

'The trivial round and common task doth furnish all we need to ask,' hummed Freddy, 'or doth it. Apparently not.'

Sarah and Ezra, who had not been exposed to Anglican hymns, looked blank.

Ezra saw David Blacker dancing with his niece Lucy, to the firm beat of Bert Ambrose at the Four Hundred. He would be slightly bored, his sharp blue eyes noticing what could be seen in the occasionally brightened darkness, but giving enough of his slight body to the already possessive and matronly girl to maintain her confidence and delight, for Lucy had always wanted David, since she was a little girl. Sarah had told Ezra she had photographs of David in her bedroom, had written to him every Sunday throughout the war and sometimes daily. First amazed and then amused, but always cool, David had replied, not at great length, but enough to provide evidence in Lucy's mind that he loved her too, and when he came back from Germany with ribbons on his black and green Rifle Brigade uniform, the girlish infatuation had become a twenty-year-old's passion. Frustrated by his taking up a mining job in Canada, she had gone into what used to be called a decline, but had a grand name now, like anorexia. And which the Doctor, her father, had anxiously described to Ezra as a serious condition, which could be fatal. Straining a faint but ancient acquaintance with Hochschild, the nickel king, with difficulty Ezra had procured the boy's posting to London.

And then it hadn't been over, for David Blacker was a cool one. Only once had he lost his temper, it was reported, when as a field security officer in Germany he'd found an SS general in a forester's hut, and had almost beaten him to death with a piece of wood. 'That's the sort of thing little Oscar would have done,' Audrey had commented.

There was Lucy, spoiled, selfish, rich and blinkered, the terror of her father and the bane of her mother, crazy to marry David.

'What do you think I am,' Ezra had said to Sarah, 'a pimp?'

Sarah hadn't replied directly.

'He'd be an asset to the business,' she said.

And so he would be, of course. Poor, ambitious, brave. The interview took place in the board room; Ezra refused to have an office of his own, preferred wandering around and sitting on other people's desks. It had been short and at the outset, for Ezra, bitter.

If he did marry Lucy, and he wasn't sure that he wanted to settle down yet, they'd probably go and live in Canada. This had been David's first shot; knowingly or not the young man could not have produced a bigger trump as his first card. The prospect of a member of the family leaving the country, and therefore the business, was to Ezra like the amputation of a limb. He'd been about to remind the young Schwarzer of what he, Ezra, had done for *him* and his mother since they were refugees, but all he said was, 'Why?'

'Well, Canada, you know. Easy life. I like skiing and in a year or two they'll make me a VP of the nickel division.'

'I know Hochschild's very fond of you,' replied Ezra, and the memory of having had to ask a favour of a greater man added to his pain, 'but you could be a director here tomorrow.'

The young man cocked his head and gave him a brief smile. 'Not tomorrow, tomorrow's Saturday, Shabat.'

'All right then, Monday,' said Ezra as calmly as he could.

There was a pause. 'What about the Brigadier, the Doctor?' David Blacker knew that Ezra never had added to his board of directors; there were never additions, only replacements.

'The Doctor wants to resign,' Ezra had replied (he didn't, but he would), thankful to be back in his own court. 'He'll be happy for you to represent the family interest, and with that and Lucy's trust and your own marriage settlement, you'll . . . have quite a lot to look after.'

There was a long pause. David had not expected to get what Ezra had not expected to give. 'What is little Oscar going to say?'

'Little Oscar and you get along, don't you? There's room for both of you in Sterlings, plenty of room. Now what do you say?'

The young man was silent, examining his own hands as if he had not noticed before how beautifully kept they were. 'Okay,' he said eventually, avoiding Ezra's blazing eyes, 'I'll think about it.'

This was too much for the first Viscount Sterling, he had suffered too much, something snapped. He stood up and slapping the edge of the board room table, he roared, 'You'll do no such thing, you'll say yes and you'll say yes now.' And he banged the table with a force which rattled the teacups of the secretaries in the adjoining offices, and made them fear for the safety of the good-looking young man they had glimpsed on his way to see 'the Lord'. David Blacker stopped looking at his hands and turned his face to Ezra's white and terrifying close face with a really sunny smile.

'Okay, Uncle, you win.'

Defeated, Ezra slumped back into his chairman's chair and allowed himself the comfort of a groan.

'Shouldn't we tell Oscar the good news?' asked David.

'Yes,' said Ezra, 'and tell them to bring some champagne.'

When both had arrived through opposite mahogany doors, Ezra felt better. Little Oscar hugged his new cousin with real joy and proposed lunch at Manetta's, a serious black market restaurant in Half Moon Street, where a coal fire burned away irrespective of seasonal regulations. They moved from discussing the new alliance, and details like the dinner to be given by Audrey for the new mother-in-law, to talk about the business. They ate hugely and happily and as the vintages summoned by little Oscar rolled down their throats they talked about expansion. The home market was soft, Sterlings could sell anything they wanted, but what about America or Europe where they still had agencies?

'What about Germany?' suggested David. It didn't exist at the moment, but it would. Soon Germany would be reconstructed and join NATO. 'Did Sterlings ever do any business there before the war?'

'A little,' Ezra had explained. 'Mostly equipment for radio stations.'

'Well,' said David, 'the occupying powers have bagged most of the medium-wave frequencies, so the Germans will have to go on to short wave. Which means lots of little radio stations, doesn't it?'

'If you think that good, David, you'll be worth your director-ship.'

David blushed, but little Oscar nearly choked on his brandy. 'Ah,' he said. 'I didn't know. Congratulations.'

It was decided that Ezra should go to New York, little Oscar to Paris, where René was still drawing a salary, and David to Hamburg, where there was no agent.

'Hamburg, isn't that where Jeremy . . .'

'Where Jeremy what? Did he tell you?' asked Ezra.

'Yes.'

'Was he concerned?'

'Not really.'

'Well, we can forget it. The whole of that family was sent to Oranienburg. You know what that meant.'

There was a silence.

David grasped the balloon as if it were a hand grenade any (more of this stuff and the clouds would vanish in the amiable fumes of a great Armagnac.)

No one with such a light head for liquor could be that tough, Ezra thought, as he and little Oscar carted David out of the restaurant, into a waiting taxi to the Athenaeum Court. They laid him out on his bed, taking off his shoes, loosening his collar and tie. He looked young and defenceless, not at all the ex-Commando who had just won a fortune that very morning. There was nothing revealing about David's belongings which Ezra and little Oscar, in tacit conspiracy, examined on the pretext of looking for a dressing gown, watched curiously by the porter who had brought them up. A set of old ivory hair brushes and a manicure case, both initialled, presumably his father's, a relic from Berlin. A pair of onyx and diamond cufflinks, and studs to match. A silver-framed photograph of Eirene when young, with starry eyes and a white dress, looking like Lady Diana Cooper only Jewish; and in the wardrobe, four almost identical chalk-striped, dark blue suits, with shoes to match. The uniform of a young executive on the make. And Ezra wished he had not noticed a rather dirty jock strap. On the sofa table was a copy of *The Economist* and the Business Diary. Ezra looked at little Oscar, clicked his teeth and nodded in the direction of the porter. Little Oscar extracted a clean five-pound note and then wrote on it with a gold pencil.

'Oh, he'll be all right, sir, I'll look after him. He'll sleep like that till morning.'

'When Captain Blacker wakes up,' said little Oscar, as he wrote on the folded India paper, 'will you telephone me at this number?' He handed the porter the note. It was a typical Sterling gesture. Ten bob would have done it, but a fiver made the porter their man, for life. Uncle and nephew walked to the lift and smiled to each other over the earnest face of the porter.

They stood in the spring sunshine by the still waiting cab. 'Bloody hot in that restaurant,' said little Oscar, kindly, helpfully, but Ezra wasn't listening. He prodded little Oscar in the ribs. 'Do you know what I'm going to do? I'm going to have me a *stauss*,' and he put his finger to his lips. Little Oscar's expression of wonder then had astonished the passers-by, and made Ezra laugh out loud now.

'That was a funny noise, Ez,' said Sarah. The Viscount sighed happily and turned to Eirene.

'How's the house coming along, Eirene?'

It was a subject which interested them all because Lucy and David had decided on a house in Chelsea, unknown territory as far as the family were concerned and therefore not totally approved of.

'All right,' said Eirene, addressing the company at large as if she shared their doubts. 'Only they can't get a telephone.'

At the other end of the table the Doctor cleared his throat. 'Ezra,' he said, 'couldn't you drop a line to the PMG?'

It was an intervention typical of the Doctor these days, for since the war his language had grown totally official. With millions of men under arms and away from home, his peacetime devotion to the spirochetes of the gonococchal family had really paid off and he had become a brigadier in the Royal Army Medical Corps and had cured a general in Rome of clap: he was dosed with penicillin, it was thought for the first time. The Doctor flew around Europe in an aircraft allocated to him alone and had also acquired one of Ezra's better inventions, a new title in the family: the Brigonorrhoea.

Sinnockson entered the dining room with a strange, creepy gait as if wishing to be unobserved, sidled up to Audrey and whispered to her. In the silence which followed, the whisper was deafening:

'Mr Mendoza is on the telephone.'

'I'll call him back.'

'He says it's urgent.'

'I'll still call him back.'

'It is,' hissed Sinnockson in desperation, 'something to do with Master Nicholas.'

The Palestine problem which had been kept away from Audrey's dinner party had entered and broken it. Audrey rose and, with the exception of Tattie who could not easily, so did everybody else. She walked towards the door held open for her by the butler, looking straight ahead, and paused only to brush an imaginary crumb from the shoulder of Ezra's velvet smoking jacket. They all sat down and nobody spoke while Sinnockson, helped by a waiter from the office, cleared away the débris of the last course and replaced that with bowls of crystallized fruit from South Africa, chocolates from Belgium and other goodies which could be found on tables of the rich in postwar England; nobody helped themselves, not even Tattie.

Audrey returned, her face white beneath her make-up. It was clear that something terrible had happened and that she did not wish to say what it was.

'Eirene, I'm sorry our little dinner party for you has finished up like this, but . . .'

'My dear,' said Eirene, and again, 'my dear. Now,' she said, looking at the other guests, 'we should go.'

And so saying, she stood up with her handbag and walked towards the still open door. A woman well acquainted with grief, she knew that when very fresh it is best left alone. The family followed Eirene out of the dining room, pressing Audrey's hand or kissing her cheek as they passed, but not daring to acknowledge Ezra whose dilated eyes appeared fixed on two Meissen cherubs delicately balancing on upstretched winsome arms a bowl of fruit just in front of him. When Tattie had edged out of the door, followed by the Doctor who half mumbled something in Hebrew as he went out, and the door had been shut, Audrey said, 'I think I shall have a little brandy.'

She moved to the sideboard and still standing, drank it down, poured herself another glass and returned to her end of the table.

'He's dead,' said Ezra quietly.

'Killed.'

'Can you tell me, Audrey,' said Ezra in the same far-away voice, 'why you should receive this information from your brother?'

'As far as I could gather, he was speaking from the Club. It was a private message from the Foreign Office. He'd just been asked to pass it on. They're very worried apparently, they don't want anything to go wrong. . . .' Audrey's voice faded away.

'Wrong?' asked Ezra very quietly.

'They're trying to be tactful and helpful, I think.'

But the damage was done.

'This damn thing's in the way, I can't even see you,' muttered Ezra and standing up, he seized the Meissen fruit bowl, so that the oranges and bananas and the pineapple fell about the still cluttered dining room table, and hurled it at a gilded Chippendale mirror.

'Wrong!' bellowed Ezra over the crash of china, wood and glass. 'My son is dead. What more can go wrong?' And he fumbled in his trousers for his shirt which he tore savagely. He sank back in his chair, let his arms drop to his sides; with his head back, he stared at the ceiling as if in a trance.

The sight and sound of her Meissen fruit bowl used to destroy one of her equally pretty but not quite so rare Chippendale mirrors did not unnerve Audrey. She had expected something like that. It had been quick, like thunder overhead, and it would soon pass. She pressed two switches which had been installed many years before but which she had never used. One automatically locked the door to the kitchen and the other the dining room door to the hall. The servants were still up and they could do their oohing and aahing in the morning.

She waited. Finally, 'Ezra,' she said. 'Ezra, wake up, and remember who you are!'

Her husband raised his arms towards her as if to embrace her and smiled. 'Who am I? I am a man without a son and what am I without you . . . nothing. Come here, my love, and talk to me. You can sit on my knee if you like.'

'Oh, don't be so silly, Ezra,' said Audrey, for some reason quite light-headed. 'But no more scenes, please.'

Ezra surveyed the dining room with a far from dismal air. 'I say,' he said. 'Coo-er. I'd better trot along and see that expensive Mr Weinberg and get you something to put in its place. I never liked those conceited little cupids.'

'No, you won't,' interrupted Audrey. 'I'll go and see Mr Weinberg and Mr Partridge,' she added, looking at her shattered mirror. 'We can't have a bull like you in the Antique Porcelain Company. Oh my God, Ezra, you are a mess.' She started to fix his bow tie and button up his waist. 'There is a man from the Foreign Office coming to see you about . . .'

'We're supposed, when we're told about the death of . . ., to tear our raiment,' said Ezra on the verge of tears.

'Yes, yes, yes,' said Audrey hurriedly as she fiddled with the buttons of his shirt. 'Plenty of time for all that later, and I would like you to remember . . .' – and so that he should not see her face, she bent down under the dining room table to pick up one of her husband's dress studs – 'that he is my son, too. Ah, there it is,' and she stood up, smiling. 'In the meantime, there is a lot to arrange about the burial which I gather is why this chap from the Foreign Office wants to talk to you.'

'In the middle of the night?'

'You know that in a few days we'll have to be out of that country. And what could we do?' Audrey identified herself naturally with the mandatory power.

'They could fly him, Nicky, the body, back to London.'

'They could, but I don't think it would be right.'

'Now,' said Ezra angrily, 'I'm not allowed to bury my own son? With my own hands?'

Audrey looked at him evenly.

'Okay, so our son with our hands,' said Ezra.

'That's not the point, Ezra. First of all, he was not at all . . .' She was about to say 'pious', but when applied to Nicky it sounded so absurd. 'He was not at all as you would say *fromm*. Remember the row about being Bar-Mitzvahed?'

'He's just like all those Communists,' said Ezra. In his indignation at the memory of another lost battle with his son, Ezra forgot that he was dead.

'Secondly,' said Audrey, 'he was a romantic and he wouldn't like that depressing place in Golders Green where I suppose we shall end up.'

Ezra nodded his agreement.

'And thirdly –' Audrey paused, bisecting the air in front of her with an index finger in unconscious imitation of Ezra's own habit – 'thirdly, there might be somebody who knew Nicky over there with ideas of their own. Or, Ezra, to be precise, of her own.'

'Like who, for instance?' Ezra was not with her at all.

'Ezra,' Audrey sighed. 'Don't you remember the photograph

Nicky sent? Yes, you do, because you took it to the business. Remember the girl? Hadn't it occurred to you, Ezra, that that was probably his wife?'

Ezra massaged the back of his neck with his hand.

'Nicky was like you, Ezra, he never did anything . . . casually. Don't you see? Look,' she went on, 'it's his first communication to us for nearly a year. He sends,' – in her excitement or to make her points, Lady Sterling had lapsed into the Yiddish present tense – 'he sends a picture of himself and a girl, his wife, it must have been his wife.'

'A sabra? A kibbutznik? I thought those people didn't believe in marriage. Free love and all that – everybody looks after everybody else's children and nobody knows which is which.' Ezra snorted.

'Nonsense,' said Audrey.

'Nicky certainly didn't believe in marriage. I remember a school essay he wrote; I've got a copy of it in the file. "Marriage is an institution presented by God to Mammon . . ." – or is it the other way round? No, that's right, by God to Mammon – "for the maintenance of the property of the rich and the preserving of the poverty of the poor." Not bad really for a boy of fifteen,' and Ezra's eyes began to mist again.

'I daresay he didn't believe in marriage,' continued Audrey implacably, 'but it is possible that she *did*. So, Nicky will be buried there, that's what she'd want and I shall see to it.'

'Yes, they killed him, they can bury him,' Ezra said quietly, almost to himself.

'What do you mean, "they"? Who?'

'It was the Zionists who did it. Zionists who killed him. What does it matter what bullet out of what gun. They're all made in Birmingham or Czechoslovakia, aren't they, and what does it matter which half of it, which *meshugana* pulled the trigger, Arab or Jew or . . .'

'British?' suggested Audrey.

'Exactly,' said Ezra. 'Which is why the Foreign Office is worried. I should have thought of it.' He stood up and began walking up and down the dining room as if rehearsing a speech.

'It has never been proved to me that Zionism is any sort of a solution, and now I know it is a folly which killed my son. There is no Jewish problem here, or not much of one, I am proud of that and proof of it. If only they'd had the sense to settle down quietly with the Arabs, buying the land from them and living under the British who had been administering a quarter of the globe with perfect efficiency for over a hundred years, there wouldn't have been all this trouble.' He turned on Audrey. 'And your son would be alive if he'd listened to me,' and he banged his chest. 'No one can deny that the British are the most tolerant and the most just people . . .'

'Yes, yes, Ezra, I quite agree. None of us have ever been Zionists, but you're not in the House of Lords now.'

'And none of us ever will be Zionists,' interrupted her husband. 'I think the family understand that. They will never get a penny out of me, nor from any member of the family.'

Ezra had paused by the fireplace and was staring at an ormulu clock which, Audrey noticed with apprehension, was supported by two modelled putti.

'Ezra, you go and change, you still look a mess, while I try and clear this up.'

'No, my love, I'll help you,' and Ezra pottered around the dining room righting what he had upset. 'Look at this, from the British Radio and Electrical Manufacturers Association on the occasion of my . . .' He stooped to read. 'Surely it should be at the business. Surely.'

'It was, but you insisted on bringing it here when you won it, or whatever they say. Ezra?'

'Hm?'

'Did you hear what I said about going to Palestine for Nicky's burial?'

'But Audrey, how will you get there? And the law is that he should be buried as soon, as soon as possible, our law, Jewish law.'

'I don't think you realize, it's all so silly,' and now it was she who looked distraught. 'He was only killed, he only died a few hours ago, and I was trying to tell you' – she swallowed and continued more calmly – 'that David had been told to tell me, that they'll fly Nicky back to London if we want. But we don't want that; that's what we've decided, haven't we?'

Ezra nodded.

'So that if they can bring him *here*, they can take me *there*, can't they. And I want you to persuade them. That's just what I want you to do. You know you can.' They faced each other, Audrey, her eyes now full of tears, her expression childlike but her confidence in her husband so frightening that for a second he felt fear, too.

He kissed her on the lips. 'I'll try, my love,' and he turned to the door. 'Dammit, Audrey, this door's locked.'

Normally at this hour, thought Ezra, Audrey and he would be playing bridge with the Doctor and Sarah. Little Oscar would have escorted Tattie round the corner to her drunken American and then would have joined up with Lucy and David at the Four Hundred, while Freddy and Joyce dropped off Mrs Eirene at her home, possibly asking her in for a drink and a *schmooze* at their house on the way. How death dislocated people! This modest arrangement had been broken and Ezra, who disliked surprises and delays unless he had arranged them, was moving towards a condition of ordinary bad temper as he fumbled with the telephone in his study. His fingers were too big for the little holes and anyway, he was not used to dialling. He had now exchanged his velvet dinner jacket for a heavy enveloping black silk dressing gown, emblazoned with yellow dragons, which Ephie had brought him back from China and which he had almost never worn. Audrey, with her maid, June, had started to pack – to emphasize her determination, he supposed, and Sinnockson had refused to go to bed. ('At a time like this, my lord, we all need support,' he had said severely.) And still, at twenty past eleven, the man from the Foreign Office had not shown up.

Finally, after three false attempts, Ezra got through to Freddy, who intoned to a background of booming Beethoven, 'Hampstead 7423, good evening.'

'Good evening, 7423.'

'Ah, Ezra, I thought . . . Could you turn that down a little, Joyce dear? Yes, thank you.'

'What are you doing?' asked Ezra for want of anything better to say. 'I have been trying to get you all evening. . . .' Ezra could make the most trivial enquiries sound like an inquisition.

'Well, we took Eirene home afterwards and she showed us round her house. Very nice, too, I must say.'

'So it should be,' said Ezra.

'Then we played this concert on the BBC. We've got this new automatic recording machine.'

'Oh, you're trying that?'

'It works, Ezra, it works,' said Freddy enthusiastically. (Freddy was the sort who smiled every time his car started.) 'It has a great future as a product, I think.'

'*Do* you?' said Ezra. 'I think it's ingenious and irrelevant. How many people would need a thing like that?'

Freddy was silent. He knew Ezra's common sense had prevented the business from losing money on many a new toy.

'Um, yes. Tell me, Ezra, are you all right? Is Audrey?'

'Fine, fine. Now, Freddy, there is something you can do for me.' At this moment a coloured light went on indicating that there was someone at the front door. 'I want you to tell the family to keep this to themselves if they can.'

'Indeed,' said Freddy, 'we thought of that. Or, to be honest, Oscar thought of it' – Freddy *was* honest – 'and he'll tell Lucy and David.'

'Good. But the point is, Freddy, that walls have ears, as we used to say in the war, and bad news –' Ezra gulped a bit – 'bad news travels fast and sooner or later the gentlemen of the press . . . Oh, hold on, Freddy, will you, for a moment.'

The door opened and Sinnockson was about to announce a visitor, but when he saw that his master was on the telephone he waited respectfully. With one gesture and a welcoming smile, Ezra dismissed the servant and motioned the young man to a chair, leaving the telephone unattended. The visitor, who was quite young, sat down and carefully folded his legs. Though not tall, he already walked with an apologetic official stoop and now sat, arms across his breast, fingers touching, eyes raised, unaware of, or trying to avoid, Ezra's scrutiny. The telephone said something.

'Ah, sorry, Freddy, someone's just come in. But I wanted to say that when the press rings up' – Ezra could not resist a glance in the young man's direction – 'there is nothing to report. When they get on to you or anybody in the business or in the family, nobody knows anything. Okay? Not "no comment", that means you do know something; just try not to talk to them,' and he replaced the receiver.

Both men stood up. Ezra in his barely anglicized kimono, dragons billowing, was a daunting sight, whereas the young man, in an ancient, almost green dinner jacket with sloping shoulders and a shirt with a wing collar and a double-breasted waistcoat, was not. A cartoonist would have enjoyed the encounter.

'Tom Brooker,' said the young man, extending an arm and bowing curtly. He then hiccuped.

'Well now, Mr Brooker, what can I offer you to drink? Brandy?'

'No, thank you, sir.'

'Champagne? There is some ready.'

Tom Brooker had no doubt that there was. He hiccuped again.

'Coffee?'

'No, but if I might trouble you for a glass of water.'

'Ah, water.' Ezra walked towards what Brooker had assumed was a set of Dickens or Scott, or Gibbon or something, which slid apart to reveal a bar, mercifully, thought the young man, without mirrors, and after a pause called out from behind his back, 'Vichy? Evian? Or Vittel?'

Pretending to consider this Rothschildian choice, the young man paused before saying, 'Vittel would be very nice,' but he spoilt the effect with another hiccup.

Ezra put the water by the visitor's table and returned to his own chair. 'The thing to do, they say, is to lean over and drink from the other side of the glass.'

The young man took a sip of water but not in the manner just prescribed.

'Tell me,' said Ezra easily, as if interviewing somebody for a job, 'a little about yourself. You went to which school?'

'Eton.'

'Uh huh. University?'

'Oxford, New College.' Tom Brooker thought he saw a look of pure hate flash in Lord Sterling's eyes.

'Then national service?'

'No, straight to the office, the Foreign Office, where I was recently lent to the Middle East Desk, which is really why I am here tonight. Strictly speaking, my boss, that is the Assistant Principal, he's the man you should have been talking to, but he's got the 'flu.'

'Nothing trivial, I hope,' said Ezra.

The young man was about to reply but a hiccup interrupted him. He ignored the remark. 'First,' he continued, 'I am here to convey our distress at having to be the bearers of such bad news.' He looked up at Ezra who faintly inclined his head.

'Secondly,' he went on, 'to tell you as much as we know, exactly what happened, and thirdly, to accept your instructions for the burial of your son who is presently in British military hands.'

All this he had rattled off efficiently without a single hiccup, but at the end there was a loud burp. Ezra had still not decided whether the affliction of the young man was temporary or chronic.

'Of course, I want to hear what you have to tell me,' said Ezra quite humbly. 'My wife and I are grateful to you and to your department for your concern. But first, I'd be interested to know your own views on the situation.'

'In Palestine, you mean? Well, sir, my own view, well, it's typical, isn't it? We British are being screamed out by both sides, following to my mind a completely impossible and apolitical decision by the UN. We have to lay down our mandate, hand over a small part of the Middle East to a tribe of fanatics without experience of government and surrounded by millions of infuriated Arabs who will push the whole lot into the sea.'

'I wouldn't mind if they did,' said Ezra.

The young man looked at Ezra, but it was clear that he meant what he said. 'Quite, and it's the Jews that are causing all the trouble. I was there last year and bloody nearly blown up in my hotel. It makes them rather unattractive, don't you think, sir?' There was another conclusive hiccup.

'You were going to tell me,' said Ezra.

'Yes, of course,' said the young man, and he unfolded a piece of paper from his inside pocket. 'Lord Sterling, do you know a Captain Nickson in the Palestine Police?'

Ezra thought and shook his head.

'No matter, but I think he knows you. At the end of a very long dispatch,' hiccup, 'he sends his deepest sympathy and asks to be remembered to you.'

'Oh, I'd like to see that dispatch.'

'I'm afraid you can't, sir, it has some political . . . and anyway it's classified,' hiccup. It was Tom Brooker's first mistake. He read in Lord Sterling's face a message which said, 'People like you don't say no to people like me.' He went on hurriedly. 'But perhaps I'd better work backwards. This dispatch from Captain Nickson, well, I might as well tell you everything. He's in the Special Investigation Branch of the Palestine Police, that's like our MI6,' hiccup, 'and they passed it on to us. It was based on information from a British army unit which in turn,' hiccup, 'had that information from a British officer seconded to the Arab Legion, which had been firing off shells, one of which I'm afraid killed your son.' He hiccuped. He made it sound as if the boy had sprained his ankle. He hurried on. 'An extraordinary story, sir, really, because this officer recognized your son in the field hospital' – his voice trailed away – 'even though he was under an assumed name.'

Ezra interrupted. 'What assumed name?'

Tom Brooker picked up his memorandum to himself. 'Naphtali Steimatsky,' he said slowly.

'Yes, I know,' said Ezra. 'Dear boy, that is his name, or would be his original name. We changed it in the last war, 1916.'

'Well, sir, I didn't know that. I always thought of you as Lord Sterling. We are very anxious to help,' he continued, 'and the moment you say so the,' hiccup, 'body will be coming back to England by aircraft.'

'They're pretty full up?' asked Ezra.

'Well, yes, because they're trying to fly out all the kit and personnel by the fifteenth. They'll never do it.'

'And going the other way?' Ezra.

'Oh, from here to Palestine? Well, I should imagine they're fairly empty, just the diplomatic bag and booze for the High Commission. Why?'

Ezra sighed. 'Look, why don't you let me get you a proper drink?

That Vittel doesn't seem to have helped you.'

Tom Brooker wanted to say no, but damnably a hiccup intervened, which Ezra chose to interpret as assent. So he consoled himself by pulling out his grandfather's gold watch from his uncle's waistcoat and studying it as if it held the answer.

'So,' said Ezra, his back to the young man as he poured out some brandy, speaking very slowly, 'you could say that my son Nicky who is English was killed by a shell, I think you said, fired by the Arab Legion which is officered by Englishmen.'

'Yes, you could say that,' said the young man, looking directly up at Ezra who was before him holding a balloon of brandy. 'But we would be most disappointed if you did.'

'I shan't,' said Ezra. 'As I told my wife, I am making no trouble for you out of this incident, which is all it is,' and he put the brandy down next to the glass of water and returned to his chair. 'But what about the Jewish Agency? You have considered that, I'm sure. You'll have considered the political capital they could make out of this, as I said, incident.'

Tom Brooker nodded.

'If my son's body is buried here, there won't be just a paragraph in the *Jewish Chronicle*, right? The Beaverbrook people will not be very sympathetic, or what about *The Times*, the *Telegraph*, the *New York Times* and the *New York Herald Tribune*?'

The young man from the Foreign Office almost shivered.

'But, if he's buried there, and my wife is anxious to be present herself, there would be much less interest. People are killed there every day.'

'Yes,' said the young man, 'but that won't stop the Jewish Agency saying . . .'

'They can say what they like,' interrupted Ezra impatiently. 'Only you and I know that what they say could be true. I take it that whoever spoke to Mr Mendoza at the St James's Club was not explicit?'

'Oh, yes, I'm sorry about that, we were just . . .' Hell, thought Tom Brooker, what were they trying to do? From the vigorous approach of this Jewish lord to the problems created by the death of his son, the efforts on the part of the office to be helpful had been, to say the least (and a use for one of his favourite words emerged), supererogatory.

'Quite,' said Ezra. 'So as far as anybody knows, that is to say anybody that matters, Nicholas Sterling had a fatal accident in Palestine and through the good offices of His Majesty's Government, his mother has been enabled to attend the burial service. You can turn it that way round, can't you?' and Ezra drew an imaginary circle in the air with his finger. '*Schluss*,' he added for emphasis.

There was a silence. It was certainly quite neat, thought Tom. He had obviously been working it out.

'So you want me to arrange for Lady Sterling to fly out to Palestine?'

'Yes.'

'We cannot guarantee her safety there.'

'She will understand that.'

'Nor, possibly, her early return to this country.'

'She can go to Cairo. We've got an agent there, and many friends.'

'Yes, I suppose so.' The young man hesitated.

'You are going to tell me the whole idea is most irregular?'

'No,' said the young man. 'I hope I can think of something more original than that, sir. It's simply that I have not the authority . . .'

'How long will you take to get it?' snapped Ezra.

Tom Brooker took a gulp of his brandy and sighed. His hiccups appeared to have vanished. 'May I use your telephone, sir?' Ezra made a gesture. 'I'd rather speak privately if I might.'

'Obviously. I wasn't thinking.' Ezra turned his head to the book-shelves, pressed one of the volumes and said in his normal voice, 'Sinnockson, could you come here for a moment?'

The reply was an indecipherable but obedient crackle.

'Do you have any books in this library, Lord Sterling?' asked Tom Brooker, determined to keep his end up.

Ezra contemplated the ranks of green leather-bound monuments to Jewish wisdom, the Torah, the Zohar and the Mishnah, their spines faded except for the glitter of a spanking new crest in doubtful taste. 'They're mostly for decoration, Mr Brooker. We Jews are philistine, you know. Ah, Sinnockson, could you show Mr Brooker to a telephone where he can talk privately.'

'Of course, my lord, I'll show the gentleman,' said Sinnockson, with the trace of a smile.

The cloakroom was spectacularly lush with yellow and brown striped flock wallpaper, rosewood dressing table, and on it a mammoth bottle of Guerlain toilet water. There were watercolours in heavy gilt frames which could have been Hogarth and looked faintly obscene, a pair of marble washbasins, but . . . no telephone. Sinnockson opened a smaller door to reveal a w.c. and by its side, a telephone. Brooker stood contemplating these two objects for a moment, gave the servant a little nod and waited for the man to withdraw. He then had a pee, flushed the loo noisily (he hoped) and sat down on the lavatory seat – there was no other way – dialled 'o' and asked for Uxbridge 206.

Seven minutes later Tom Brooker returned to the open study. which Ezra had clearly been pacing. He was now puffing a cigar. He turned round and his face was taut. With no expression on his face Brooker said, 'I shall need Lady Sterling's passport.'

Ezra smiled. 'Good boy, well done!' and lightly he asked, 'Did you notice the Hogarth watercolours in the cloakroom?'

'Yes, they are very fine.'

'The interesting thing,' said Ezra, puffing, jabbing his cigar in the air, 'is that, being slightly naughty, they must have been kept in a portfolio for about two hundred years and had hardly ever seen the light of day until I bought them. Then we had them framed and as it's the only room in the flat which gets no sunlight, we put them in there. Interesting, isn't it?'

'Yes.'

'Ah, now, let's go and get Audrey. You stay there.'

He came back and the two stood uneasily in the middle of the room waiting.

'My boss,' said Tom Brooker, to break the silence, 'was impressed by the force of our argument and the business about the political reaction, and I told him I had your word and presumably Lady Sterling's.'

Her only child was dead. Audrey lay stiffly on her bed, waiting for grief. It would not come. She wondered why; later, perhaps.

She heard Ezra shouting, 'Audrey, Audrey, come here, my love, and bring your passport.' She rose eagerly and went to her safe.

When she joined them she had taken off her jewels but had made up her face.

'You – you wanted this.' Smiling, she handed Brooker her passport.

'Ah, Audrey, this is Tom Brooker of the Foreign Office. He's made all the arrangements.'

'So quickly, too. How frightfully kind of you. We are most terribly grateful. Won't you two sit down and, Ezra, you can get Mr Brooker a drink. Look, he's got an empty glass.'

Tom Brooker sat down, happy at the warmth of this pretty woman's good manners. He appreciated insincerity and found it refreshingly agreeable after his session with Lady Sterling's powerful and bristly husband with whom every remark, every gesture seemed to be a battle to be won or lost. Tom understood what a Jewish friend at Oxford had said to him about the sensitivity of his race: 'You see for us nothing is trivial. If I cut my hand opening a tin of sardines, it's a pogrom.'

'Tell me,' said Audrey to Brooker when Ezra produced another brandy and retreated to his usual place. 'Tell me. What happens now?'

'Well,' said Brooker, adopting his previous position, legs folded, fingers touching, 'tomorrow, I hope tomorrow but I will be able to confirm this to you later this very night, you will board an aircraft from RAF Transport Command, rather early I'm afraid, at Blackbushe airport. Your passport will be in order and you will have it back with the appropriate documents, and a sort of To Whom It May Concern letter from the Foreign Office. But you shouldn't need that because the authorities concerned at the Commissioner of Police will know of your arrival and you will be met.'

'Isn't it awful,' said Audrey, 'but do you know I feel quite excited?'

Tom Brooker allowed himself a fatherly smile. 'I warn you, Lady Sterling, it will be very hot in Palestine, so you'd better take some light clothes. And it will be very cold in the aircraft, so you had better take a rug. Now,' he said, 'I'd better get on with it,' and he stood up. Ezra had led him out into the corridor when Sinnockson appeared, a little too quickly.

'We can't thank you enough, you've been so helpful,' said Audrey. 'Ezra, Jenkins can take him where he wants to go, can't he?'

'You sent him home, my lord,' said Sinnockson.

'Oh, damn the fellow.'

'Never mind. I'll take a cab,' said Tom.

The Sterlings handed the young man his clothes.

'My,' said Audrey, 'you do dress up at the Foreign Office.'

Then Tom Brooker made his second mistake. 'As a matter of fact, I slipped out to dine with Harold Nicolson at the Beefsteak. Of course I left my number.'

So, thought Ezra, he's been playing hookey and he's drunk. He thought Harold Nicolson only liked pretty young men.

When the gates of the elevator had shut on Brooker, Ezra turned to his wife.

'And now, wife, to bed.'

They discovered that they needed each other in every way that night, the night of the death of their son. Ezra was surprised and excited at the time, but later, recounting the experience to a doctor, he learnt that his reaction had been quite normal.

3

'It's a converted Lancaster, quite safe. I've just been having a *schmooze* with the pilot,' said little Oscar, as if, now, nothing could go wrong. He removed his bowler hat and pecked his aunt on the cheek. 'And I've got some things for you. Here are the cables I've sent: Jerusalem, Haifa, Tel Aviv and Cairo. It's quite a small country, Palestine, and you never know.'

'You have been busy,' said Audrey, reaching up to pat his cheek, freshly shaved and ruddy in the early morning.

'Hold on, more to come. Brandy,' and he handed Audrey an Asprey flask she remembered giving him. 'Ear plugs and Dramamine.'

'Thank you, but I've just taken some. I feel my tummy's still in Park Lane.'

'Good, you'll be all right. They know who you are and the aeroplane's full of Sterling equipment. They'll probably let you drive it.'

'My God,' said Audrey, and she looked at the aeroplane which reminded her of a flying coffin.

An RAF officer with the appropriate moustache and the blue and white diagonal ribbon of the Distinguished Flying Cross saluted and gestured towards the aeroplane. They had somehow found a ladder into the hatch, but Lancaster bombers are not designed to accommodate peeresses, so Audrey, in her hat and veil, with a huge crocodile-skin handbag which she was determined to manage for herself, was a delicate cargo to load. Then one of the engines, after a heave, broke into a heavy smoker's cough. Soon it was roaring away with determination and then its twin burst into cacophonic concert. Aboard the aircraft, a member of the crew guided Audrey tenderly through a maze of cables and throbbing metal to a bucket seat, strapped her in, tucked her up in her rug and thoughtfully handed her a large brown paper bag.

Audrey had brought *The Eustace Diamonds* by Anthony Trollope in the hope that absorption in Victorian trickery might distract her, but the print was too small to read in the juddery aircraft and the other books, detective stories by Agatha Christie and Dorothy Sayers, seemed so feeble and so irrelevant to her state of mind that she fell into recollections of her son, turning the pages of his life through her mind as from a family album. One photograph would not go away – the last one. She had to find that girl.

Half of a Nissen hut at Gibraltar was the RAF officers' mess, and entering on the flight lieutenant's arm she saw a small, dark young man wearing a large Homburg. He was, he had to be, a rabbi (Already? thought Audrey). Who else would wear a hat like that. He advanced, beaming.

'Lady Sterling?'

The buzzing in Audrey's ears was so heavy that she didn't know how to speak. She nodded.

He turned out to be a bright young man, friendly and inquisitive, like a mole. He wanted to tell Audrey about the Jewish community in Gibraltar. There weren't many left, he explained, most had gone to South America or to England or, of course, to Israel. Audrey had never heard Palestine described so directly, without explanation, in that way, and she felt on that not quite alien rock a sort of Zionist tug on her sleeve. At her expression the rabbi expressed his sympathy and apologized for being such a chatterbox, but it was most unusual for him to have the opportunity of talking to a Sephardi lady from England, especially to a Mendoza.

Numbed by the quickly changing scenes of the last few hours, Audrey had not stopped to think about the reasons for the rabbi's turning up at a RAF mess in Gibraltar, but now she understood. David had decided to inform his connections. He must have found out her movements. How awful of them not to have telephoned him back, but there hadn't been time. And he must have got on to the people at Bevis Marks to arrange this meeting.

'Oh, do tell me more about the community.'

'With pleasure, Lady Sterling. But first, you must tell me your son's full name. We would like to say a prayer for him this Shabat. Naphtali Steimatsky?' The rabbi made a note. 'Look, before you go, Lady Sterling. . . .' The flight lieutenant had reappeared. 'Your son should be buried according to our rites and I have taken the liberty of writing down the address of a friend of mine in Jerusalem who would perform the ceremony.'

'I'm sorry to interrupt, padre, but we have to leave in just a few minutes.' Turning to Audrey, the officer added, 'Well, like the old stage mail we rattle in, change horses, dump the letters and rattle off. Not much time for sightseeing, I'm afraid.'

'*Shalom*,' said the rabbi and shook hands solemnly with Audrey. 'And goodbye, Captain,' one professional to another.

The flight lieutenant gave a half-salute.

Escorting Audrey back to the aircraft, again holding her firmly by the arm, the flight lieutenant tugged his moustache with his free hand and said, 'Forgive me asking, Lady Sterling, but we don't often get passengers on this run and I've been wondering why you want to go to Palestine. I gather it's pretty rough out there just now.'

'Nobody told you?'

'There's no reason why they should. We just drive the thing.'

'I'm going to bury my son.'

'Oh dear, I'm so sorry, I never should have asked. In the services, was he? Bloody . . .' But he thought better of it.

'No,' said Audrey, 'but he was killed accidentally,' and she patted the flight lieutenant's hand. 'I'm glad you asked me.'

In the aircraft Audrey returned to her now familiar seat like a dog to its basket, and was touched to see that her rug had been neatly folded and her books tidied up. Though between them Ezra and little Oscar had provided for every emergency, it hadn't occurred to anybody that Audrey might be hungry, and the crew were delighted to see her ladyship tuck into a hunky tinned salmon sandwich and apricot pie, washed down with a hot viscose liquid which tasted somewhere between coffee and tea.

'Here you are, m'lady, a rosy leigh and a row on the lake.'

When Audrey realized that she must have eaten their rations, she felt ashamed and powerless. She had nothing to thank them with. Her thousand pounds in cash and her flask of brandy seemed suddenly useless.

At Malta she sat with the flight lieutenant and consumed a sort of high tea for which she had no appetite. But she did drink a glass of appalling local wine. Back in the Lancaster she struggled again with *The Eustace Diamonds*, but not for long, because the next thing she remembered was a gentle tugging on her sleeve.

'Where am I?' she asked, blearily.

'In twenty minutes we should be there, at Lydda,' said the airman.

'Heavens, what happened to Cyprus?'

'You fell asleep, m'lady,' (his mother had been in service so he knew and relished this form of address) 'and the skipper said to leave you.'

'How marvellous, and I haven't even taken a pill. Did I snore?'

'You do what you like, m'lady, and you can wipe your face with this.' He offered her a tea towel clearly stamped W/D. 'I lifted it from the NAAFI in Cyprus. There were some lumps of ice in it. It hasn't all melted; it's not very dainty, I'm afraid.'

'Anyway, though you won't be as comfortable as in a hotel, you'll be a lot safer and there won't be any reporters sniffing about. We had booked a suite for you at the King David – in the name of Mrs Silvermark.'

The police officer paused and looked at Audrey who, drained in mind and body, overlooked the subtlety and stared out at the astonishingly ordinary landscape as it flashed past the car window.

'I'm sorry about all this cloak-and-dagger stuff, Lady Sterling, but these are not normal times.'

What on earth, wondered Captain Nickson of the Special Investigation Branch of the Palestine Police, had induced the powers-that-be to let this delicate creature come to this most unholy land a few days before the end of the mandate, when it would have been simple enough to send a coffin to London – if that's what she *had* come about.

'The Commissioner's Office felt, and I agree with them, that you'd be better off in a private house. It's rather a nice place, actually. I moved into another officer's married quarters, it's Turkish, complete with a Hamam, you know, with nice tiles and all that.'

'You are most awfully kind,' said Audrey absently, and as this sounded a little cold, she turned towards her companion, looked at him closely and asked, 'Tell me, officer, is your full name Geoffrey Wriotheseley Nickson?'

The captain looked delighted, slapped his thigh and laughed. 'Your husband? He remembered? How marvellous. I never thought he would.'

'He never forgets anything; especially people's names.' She did not explain, as Ezra often did, that this faculty was more useful as a weapon than as a courtesy.

'Well, I am amazed,' said the captain with schoolboy enthusiasm. 'I certainly remember. I was a copper on the beat in Whitehall just at the beginning of the war, 1939 or '40. All I did was show Sir Ezra, as he then was,' added the policeman punctiliously, 'to the Treasury. And he gave me a quid!' And he laughed again. 'Quite a lot of money in those days, when a policeman's pay was three pounds something a week.'

'And then you joined up?'

'Yes. The military police, of course, got commissioned, had a good war, mostly in this part of the world. I'm rather fond of Palestine. I didn't feel like going back, so I joined this mob.' He looked out of the window. 'Sorrowful duty,' he said.

'Oh?' queried Audrey, charmed by the phrase.

'Well, I don't like it. A lot of us don't believe in it. That is, the more . . .'

'Sensitive?' suggested Audrey.

The policeman blushed. 'Trying to stop people coming to a place they have been dreaming about in concentration camps is just not on, is it?'

'There is a quota,' said Audrey firmly.

'Quota,' said Captain Nickson crossly. 'Do you think they'd take any notice of that? Nor would you if you were . . .' He stopped himself. 'Roberts?'

The driver turned round. 'Sir?'

'We stop somewhere here, don't we, to show Lady Sterling . . .'

The driver nodded knowingly and the Humber pulled into the side of the road just before the crest of a hill. Captain Nickson opened the car door for Audrey and led her to the top of the hill. 'There it is,' said the Captain. 'Lady Sterling, Jerusalem.'

Audrey removed the dark glasses which she had been wearing to hide the ravages of emotion and travel. She had hoped that as a Jewess, her heart might have missed a beat, but all she felt, as a Jewess, was irritation at the profile of so many Anglican-looking churches among the pines and olive groves.

'I took a Jewish Member of Parliament here the other day and he tore his shirt when I showed him this view.' He looked inquiringly at Audrey.

'Yes,' she said, 'men are supposed to do that, and also when they hear of the death of someone . . .' Audrey turned away and put her dark glasses back on.

In the car Audrey asked about the funeral arrangements for her son and showed Captain Nickson the address she had been given in Gibraltar. In reply she was handed a small, beautifully engraved visiting card in the English fashion, bearing the name of Solomon Lemnis with an address in Cairo on one side and that of Sterlings in London on the other.

'That's Mr Fixit, Lady Sterling, he's your agent in Cairo and he's arranged everything. We had to move quite quickly. It's something to do with the heat . . .,' and he bit his tongue because it sounded so callous.

Solomon Lemnis himself was almost round; dressed in a yellow linen suit and fanning himself with a panama hat circled with a big floppy black crepe band. He was sipping Turkish coffee and talking in Arabic to a servant girl, and he looked more like a host than a guest in Captain Nickson's salon. He rose to greet Audrey with a flourish. His eyes, crinkling with concern, respect and happiness, never left her face as he bowed over her hand. He stood back and contemplated her, the same expressions alternating on his face like a silent movie actor, and said something briskly in Arabic to the girl.

'You see I took the liberty of making myself at home.' He turned to the captain and his gesture took in a vast and vulgar arrangement of flowers which would not have disgraced the foyer of the Dorchester Hotel.

'Shall we sit down?' said the captain hesitantly.

'If I could just go and powder my nose.'

'How thoughtless of me. I'm sorry. I'll show you to your room. My driver will bring up your things.'

'Excuse *me*, Mr Lemnis.' The round gentleman bowed as if complimented.

In her bathroom, bars of expensive soap still unwrapped, demonstrated the solicitude of a bachelor expecting a lady visitor. Audrey was beginning to enjoy her expedition.

The funeral, Solomon Lemnis explained, would take place early in the morning. 'It will,' he sighed, 'be a fairly simple affair, but in view of these terrible times . . .' Audrey nodded. Lady Sterling would agree that as long as the proper rites were observed . . .

Audrey remembered the injunction of the Gibraltar rabbi and wondered whether she should refer to it, but from the deep Levantine looks of Mr Lemnis she imagined that the procedure would be nothing if not Oriental. The ceremony would be over in time for them to catch an aeroplane to Cairo on which they had – another sigh of self-congratulation – reserved places. Another sigh of relief.

'I'm afraid that's not possible, Mr Lemnis,' said the captain. 'Lady Sterling wishes to visit her son's kibbutz before she leaves Palestine. It's in Galilee.'

Solomon Lemnis gaped in horror. 'Kibbutz,' he muttered. 'In Kenneret? I feel it my duty to explain the danger ... How will you get there?'

'Oh, just four hours by car. Just a few road blocks,' answered the captain coolly.

The maid arrived with two more cups of coffee. Solomon Lemnis rummaged with one hand in an enormous leather sack while mopping his brow with the other. He extracted a flask of brandy and trembling, poured a little into each of the tiny cups, spilling a lot as he did so.

'She, that is Lady Sterling, you will almost certainly be assassinated. I cannot lightly agree to such an impetuous ...'

'Mr Lemnis,' the captain interrupted, 'Lady Sterling's safety is my responsibility and she's under the protection of His Majesty's Government.'

Since this was not exactly what the cautious Tom Brooker had told her in London, and later confirmed in writing from the Foreign Office, Audrey marvelled that a man with such clear blue eyes could lie so convincingly. Or had he thought of a way to secure her visit?

'Naturally,' said Audrey soothingly, 'there is no need for you, Mr Lemnis, to wait for me here. I can imagine it must be very difficult to get seats on aeroplanes.'

Solomon Lemnis sighed. 'Indeed.'

'It's enough,' continued Audrey, 'that you managed to get here so quickly yourself, and I believe I must thank you for making all the arrangements and I think it best that you get back to your er ... wife and family, who must be worrying about you.'

Mr Lemnis nodded briefly. 'If those are your wishes, Lady Sterling, it is not for me to disobey,' and he rose. 'Now I have business to attend to. I must settle with the *lavadores*.' He turned to the captain. 'The people who prepare the body ...' and he made a wrapping-up gesture with his left hand.

Audrey, at the mention of money, reached for her handbag, but

Solomon Lemnis stopped her with a movement of his fat imperial palm.

'No, Lady Sterling, there is no way in which you, Lady Sterling, could owe Solomon Lemnis any money. I have made all the arrangements.' And picking up his panama hat, his capacious leather bag, he bowed deeply to her, nodded to the captain and swept out. They smiled at each other.

'Extraordinary chap; mind you, bloody efficient. We were getting nowhere fast until he showed up. Then, click, click, click, the body was whisked away. . . . Oh, I am sorry, Lady Sterling.'

'No, no, please go on.'

'Do tell me, who are the lava – whatever you call them?'

'Oh, the *lavadores*. They are the people who lay out the body, and then, of course, he has to get what I believe is called a *minyan*; that is, ten men without whom you can't have any kind of service. I wish I knew more about it all, but I'm afraid I wasn't very well brought up.' She sighed.

'Now, Lady Sterling, I think you must be feeling tired. Why don't you take a rest?'

'No, not a bit tired. I just feel funny and rather . . . excited. I suppose the whole thing hasn't sunk in yet.'

'Funny?'

'Yes, the whole business is so funny, funny peculiar *and* funny ha ha, if you want to know. I feel I've known you for a long time and I want to talk to you. I don't know, perhaps it's the effect of the aeroplane. And by the way, please stop calling me Lady Sterling. My name's Audrey and yours I know is Geoffrey. So, Geoffrey . . .'

Captain Nickson looked really pleased. 'Yes?'

'Get me a drink, will you, a proper drink.' She had not touched her coffee.

'With pleasure, Audrey,' he said distinctly. 'I can give you some real Scotch, one of the few benefits of being a policeman in this country.'

'You must admit Mr Lemnis is funny – the sort of person one would never meet normally.'

The captain nodded and smiled as he handed her the glass.

'And what has been funny "peculiar" about these last twenty-four hours is what I've learnt about myself, about my husband even.' She broke off. 'I'm sorry to rattle on like this. I suppose you must think I'm a hysterical woman or something.'

The captain, still standing in front of her, squeezed her hand, blushed and sat down opposite her. 'No, Audrey, you just go on.'

'It's as if I'd never been born before. You see, I knew we'd never see Nicky again, though of course Ezra never gave up hope, he never, never gives up anything.' She paused. 'I knew he was lost to us years ago whether he died or not. He didn't . . .' She paused. 'He didn't approve of us, I'm afraid. Jews are rather like that. It often happens in families like ours. I mean his uncle, my brother, is the reverse. He's *plus anglais que les anglais*. He plays bridge every day at the St James's Club. Ridiculous!' Audrey paused to reflect that she had never thought it ridiculous before.

The captain said nothing, sensing that he was meant just to listen.

'Then, did I tell you what happened to me in Gibraltar? Well, let me explain that in my life so far I have not suffered in any way from being Jewish. I haven't even had to give it any thought. I was popular at school, a prefect and that sort of thing, and none of my friends were Jewish. I just thought of myself as coming from a well-established English family, some of whom, all right, had long noses and dark hair. Then suddenly my son, a Communist and a Zionist, is killed by the British.'

The captain put up his hand. 'Come on, Lady Sterling, I mean Audrey, not quite.'

'Oh well, near enough, you must admit. Anyway, this is the point of what I am trying to tell you. This is what happened at Gibraltar. A dear little rabbi met me and assumes I must be a Zionist because I'm a Jew and he is going to say a prayer for Nicky in the synagogue. And then the nice pilot of the aeroplane assumes because I'm Lady Sterling, which is all *he* knows, that Nicky was a British Army officer killed by bloody Jewish terrorists. . . .'

'But, Audrey, they're both right, don't you see?'

'I suppose so, but it is all a little confusing.'

'By the way, you know, Audrey, that you're expected at the High Commission tonight. But I'm sure they'll understand.'

'I'm sure you can get me out of that one, can't you? And maybe we could just have dinner somewhere quietly.'

'Maybe we could, but I think it would be safer . . .' He paused. He was about to say more discreet but he decided to say, 'much safer if we had something to eat here.'

The captain prepared, for him, quite an elaborate supper. His cook had left a cold chicken in the larder which he carved tenderly – the breast for Lady Sterling and the red meat for himself. He made a salad of tomatoes, having first removed the skins by popping them in boiling water for a second or two. He made a vinaigrette adding a dash of curry powder for interest. He put out some candles, but did not light them – the effect was corny - and waited for his guest. There was no sign or sound of her. Finally he knocked on the bed-room door. No answer. Gently, he opened the door. Audrey was asleep.

The first person Audrey saw was the flight lieutenant in full service dress, he even wore a sash and sword. He explained excitedly that he'd never been to Jerusalem, that he had 72 hours leave and that a friend had offered him a lift and that he could kill two birds with one stone (oh dear) and that he'd thought Lady Sterling might need a little moral support and by the way, he wanted to take this oppor-tunity of thanking her for the presents she had given to the crew (£5 each) but not of course because of that, because anyway they had wanted to come but he had thought that she didn't need too much of a crowd, did she? Nerves had destroyed the fighter pilot's normal reserve. He backed away in the middle of the sentence, and then Captain Nickson introduced her to a damp-handed man from the High Commission. Apart from the *minyan*, which consisted of five very old gentlemen and five white-faced spotty youths with ringlets and spectacles, that was that. Solomon Lemnis, dressed now in slightly deeper yellow suit with an enormous black crepe armband, took her by the hand and led her into a circular chamber in the middle of which lay a bare box on what looked like an Edwardian perambulator with big penny-farthing spoked wheels. At one end stood the rabbi wearing a black Homburg hat and with barely a nod he gestured to Solomon Lemnis who had taken on the role of the nearest male relative – perhaps because he spoke Hebrew. A dialogue ensued between the two of them and then in twenty minutes they were all in the open air, processing after the perambulator behind the chanting rabbi.

By a new grave was a pile of earth, some spades and on the other side in neat ranks was an almost vulgar collection of flowers which Solomon Lemnis led her to inspect. Every member of the family was represented at Nicky's funeral by what a local newspaper would have accurately described as a floral contribution. On each was a card (My God, Mr Lemnis must have bought up the shop, thought Audrey), with the name written in what must have been Solomon Lemnis's hand of every member of the family, Father, Sarah, the Brigadier, Freddy, Joyce, Henrietta (Tattie?), Eirene, Oscar, all of them, not forgetting David and Lucy. This inclusive array told the story of little Oscar's taste for organization and Mr Lemnis's for ostentation. Set apart from these mammoth offerings were three smaller efforts, one a wreath from the High Commissioner, one from Captain G. W. Nickson, Palestine Police, and the last, another tiny bouquet which made Audrey fumble for her dark glasses, for stuck clumsily to it was a piece of paper bearing the RAF crest and the motto *Per Ardua ad Astra*. She picked it up, crumpled one of its bay leaves in her hand and dropped it into the oh, so deep pit. As if that were a signal, the rabbi took a spade and shovelled a clod of earth into the grave and handed the implement to Solomon Lemnis. It was something they all understood, ashes to ashes, dust to dust, and even the man from the High Commissioner's office gingerly performed his stint. When all had done, the earth barely covered the coffin. The mourners stood around hesitantly. Solomon Lemnis approached Audrey.

'They have asked me what you want done with the flowers,' he whispered. 'They could be sent to a hospital.'

Audrey thought, damn the hospital. She gestured that they should be put into the pit. Solomon nodded and everyone picked up a bundle of flowers and threw them cheerfully into the grave. They returned to the building, washed their hands at a tap on an outside wall and dried them on a dirty towel. Audrey said goodbye to each and everyone, and it was over.

Most people, despite the attentions of history, contrive to die in bed without having heard a shot fired in anger, and even when whole nations are turned upside down, most people still rise up day after day to a happy and peaceful life. On that journey to Galilee Audrey wondered what all the fuss had been about. No machine-gun fire, no Molotov cocktails, the countryside was peaceful, perhaps it was everybody's day off? The regular road blocks manned by courteous British soldiery and the jeep in front of her police Humber with the sergeant cradling a sten gun reminded her that she was in dangerous country, but she suffered only from the dust and the loss of her scarf which must have floated out of the open car window while she dozed.

She woke up when the rhythm of the car changed as it followed the jeep off the main road, down a dirt track. She thought she caught a glimpse of water through the olive trees. They halted in a little concrete square which she supposed was the centre of the kibbutz. When the drivers had turned off their engines the silence was immense. At first Audrey thought the place had been abandoned, that the kibbutzniks had fled, but surely it was the Arabs who were leaving *their* villages? The buildings were simple and ugly. She could see the lake not quite clearly through the trees and she could hear a hum of children's voices chanting in rhythm; she noticed steam coming from a chimney and when a grey-haired lady emerged from a doorway, screwing up her face against the sun and putting on her spectacles which dangled down her front, Audrey reached for her handbag and waited for the driver to open the car door.

The older woman hesitated, looked quizzically, but not nervously at the jeep and advanced towards Audrey in a manner which reminded her of Eirene Schwarzer. She did not hold out her hand. Audrey moved towards her. The older woman's first remark was somewhat odd.

'I've been dreaming you were coming.' She spoke slowly with a strong German accent. 'I know it must be the mother. It is? So, you come quick, very quick. We were only told yesterday. You are his mother, of course.'

'Yes, of course.'

'And I am Irma Spiegelberg, welfare and laundry.' She smiled and held out her hand.

From her grip Audrey realized that both items would be kept in pretty good shape. She felt the curiosity of the three soldiers. 'How do you do?' Audrey managed.

Welfare and laundry looked her slowly up and down. However simply Audrey dressed, and for this occasion she had tried, it was difficult for her in that utilitarian setting not to look exotic in a simple linen *tailleur*, which she had buttoned up to conceal a mildly frilly silk blouse, her pearls which she always wore, her oval curved Cartier watch, and finally that enormous handbag with its hooped handle of pale tortoise-shell. The grey-haired lady with the bun and slippers was digesting it all.

'The children must see you, they will like it,' and she smiled. 'But first you will see Dalia.' And she took Audrey's arm and led her towards the building where steam had been issuing from a chimney.

'Dalia is cross. She cries a lot. Remember she only heard yesterday and maybe she is seeing . . .' The grey-haired lady gestured towards the Humber and jeep. 'And that will not please her at all.'

'My husband and I were told only a few hours after Nicky . . .'

'Just so, *protexia* – influence. Your husband is a big shot, I think, in England, a *grafpetoch*, no?'

There could be no answer.

'Where is he now, your son, where is the body?'

'We buried him yesterday, in Jerusalem.'

Irma Spiegelberg stopped in her tracks and turned on Audrey, hand on hip. 'We?' she asked.

'Yes, we buried him properly, according to our law.'

'In Jerusalem,' repeated the older woman. 'That is good, but Dalia will not like it. It was not possible, I know, but she wanted to bury him herself.'

Her voice was kinder now. 'Come,' she said. The two entered what must have been a laundry, for in one corner was a gigantic bubbling cauldron containing bloated sheets, pounded by a wooden paddle.

'Some kibbutzim don't have sheets. We are fortunate.'

The girl did not look up from her task. Irma Spiegelberg said something to her in Hebrew. She gave a quick glance, then turned away.

The older woman tried again, with more appeal in her voice, but it was no use, the girl turned further away as if wanting to obliterate herself. Audrey moved towards her but Dalia almost shrank into the wall, dropping the long wooden paddle she'd been using to stir the tub. Curiosity had restored Audrey's confidence and she looked hard into the shadows at the girl, who suddenly turned to face her unhesitatingly. She was little more than a child, seventeen or eighteen perhaps. She had been pretty and would be again when she stopped crying, and had her baby. Slowly Audrey pulled off her topaz ring and held it out to the girl, humbly, but she made no move to take it. Audrey put it down on a draining board overlapping the tub. The girl looked at the jewel for a moment and then, with a quick movement of her hand, flicked it into the grey-white frothy mess, seized the wooden paddle and began pummelling the sheets.

Audrey felt a tap on her shoulder. The interview had ended.

Outside the men had found a football and were kicking it around, but stopped as soon as the two women emerged from the laundry. The sergeant went up to Audrey who said to him, 'Is it all right if I just have a word with this lady, Sergeant, is that all right with you?'

'Quite all right, ma'am, we have a bit of time.'

'Tell me,' said Audrey, turning to Mrs Spiegelberg as they walked away towards her office, 'were they married?'

'Naturally, here we are not so *fromm* but *bei mir gibt es kein Mommser*' (with me there are no bastards). 'Naturally they were married,' said Mrs Spiegelberg quite fiercely. 'Why not?'

'Why not, indeed,' said Audrey. 'Can we talk about it?'

'Here is private, but you want to sit down maybe?' Once in her own room Irma Spiegelberg unbuttoned enough to accept a cigarette from Audrey, which made her choke, then laugh and splutter. There was some coffee on a primus stove with a row of enamel cups. Everything was neat. There was a poster on the wall of two businessmen carrying briefcases, having their faces slapped by a thick-thighed young man in shorts. There was an elderly Remington on the desk.

'Ah,' said Mrs Spiegelberg, 'you are noticing our poster. Let me explain: it says just "Speak Hebrew." '

'But why?' started Audrey.

'You see, in the 1930s before I came here, they would slap your face in the streets if they heard you speaking German or Russian or Yiddish even. Very serious people. Dalia's father was such a man, he was one of the founders of this kibbutz and *his* father came from Russia, from Baku where he had an oil well, until it was decided that Jews could not own oil wells. He could have become a Christian but he didn't want to, so he came here; so Dalia's second-generation sabra. This is her world, you must understand, and you' – and with an extra gesture of her hand, Mrs Spiegelberg included the military waiting outside – 'you are the enemy. I'm sorry,' she added and smiled.

'As a matter of fact, Mrs Spiegelberg,' said Audrey, 'that's what I wanted to talk to you about, because clearly Dalia will not talk to me, and I wanted to give you this.' Audrey swiftly dropped a fat white envelope which did not quite fit its contents and was crinkled by two elastic bands, on Mrs Spiegelberg's desk. 'Some money for the children.'

Mrs Spiegelberg looked at the packet as if it had spoilt her day.

'Lady Sterling, I am not of the finance committee, I cannot accept money. Maybe they . . .'

'Look,' said Audrey, 'they can use it how they like,' and she stood up.

'Maybe they will try to buy guns, Lady Sterling.'

'Couldn't they do something for the children?'

'No guns, no children perhaps? Come on, I'll show you, the children are all right,' and they walked out into the courtyard. There was the sharp crack of a door flung open too hard and suddenly the place was full of the sound of young voices tumbling over each other in a disorganized carillon. When the two women stepped out of the shadows, the gleeful shrieks had subsided and the children were milling round the jeep and fingering the sergeant's sten gun, from which he had removed the clip of ammunition, with awe. They were all chubby, pretty and clean, a thousand years away from the seedy *minyan* at Nicky's funeral. One started to pull at Audrey's skirt. The pupils of his eyes were like flakes of dark emerald, but they were riveted into a permanent squint. Audrey knelt down and hugged him, then looked enquiringly at Mrs Spiegelberg.

'Yes, Abba, we think he was one of those before whom the gas-chamber door shut. You know, at the end of the day, they had to stop work like everyone else. He was saved, but . . .' She shrugged. 'The shock.'

Abba looked into Audrey's face, sniffed and smiled. He muttered something in Hebrew. Mrs Spiegelberg laughed. 'He's reciting the blessing for a new smell,' she explained. 'The education committee doesn't like the children to learn blessings, but the children love them. They like to show off, especially this one, he's a clever one.' She took Abba from Audrey. 'And he's a bit spoilt. Now they will dance for you.'

She clapped her hands and said, '*Hora!*'

At this the children grouped themselves into a circle, patted and shoved into place by their teacher, an almost square dark girl with huge breasts and steel-rimmed spectacles, and began to sing and dance round a doubly embarrassed Audrey and a beaming Mrs Spiegelberg. In order to cover her confusion, Audrey handed Mrs Spiegelberg her card.

'You will write to me, won't you? And tell me about the child?'

'I will write to you, Lady Sterling.'

'And also if you want anything, anything,' repeated Audrey.

'Don't be fright, Lady Sterling, you have done a good thing today, coming to see us.'

Audrey was sure that this remark had nothing to do with the money she had left.

'You see, this is how we turn your soldiers into Zionists,' said Mrs Spiegelberg.

The children went on clapping and waving until they were out of sight. Audrey had asked to sit in the front seat of the Humber for the return journey. She turned round and waved and fancied she saw Dalia, at the door of the laundry, slightly move her hand, but maybe it was what in the war was called wishful thinking on her part.

'Geoffrey, it was terribly sweet of you to lay all that on.'

They were dancing to the tune of *La vie en rose* in his apartment. 'I'm sure that man with the damp hands from the High Commission didn't approve.'

'If he ever even finds out, I'm for the high jump.'

'Do you mean to say I shouldn't really have gone?'

'My dear Audrey, my orders are not to let you out of my sight, which is why I'm here now.'

In amazement Audrey pushed Geoffrey away from her and looked up at him. She forgot the absurdity and the joy of dancing with this man, a policeman in Jerusalem, to the sound of Edith Piaf's voice just the day after her son's funeral.

'You wanted to go, didn't you?' he asked.

'Yes, very much. You know I did.'

'Well, then.'

'Hadn't you taken an awful risk?'

'Look, it's so chaotic here, they need never find out. And if they did, what could they do, fire me?'

'Then Ezra can give you a job. He said he would.'

'He just said come and see me after the war. And that was ten years ago.'

'That's what he means. He'll give you a job.'

Geoffrey took her in his arms again. 'You don't think this will make any difference,' and he held her quite tightly.

'Geoffrey, the gramophone has stopped and you need a new needle.'

'Oh, I didn't notice. It's so nice just standing here holding you,' and he kissed her.

It was a welcome and not unexpected kiss, and the thought of leaving him perhaps forever that very night made him more attractive. But, oh God, thought Audrey, I mustn't, and this time she quite firmly disengaged herself and sat down.

'I'm sorry.'

'Oh, don't be sorry,' said Audrey. 'I can't tell you how wonderful it is for me to be thought, well, interesting, by a man like you. You've made me very happy and I'm behaving hysterically.'

'You were behaving quite naturally and quite beautifully.'

'Oh, do you think so? Tottering on the verge of adultery with the first attractive man I meet, the moment my husband's back's turned, and my poor Nicky hardly cold in his grave.'

'That all happened a long time ago.'

Audrey looked at him steadily. 'Yes, I suppose you're right. I must say I feel I've known you for ages, but for heaven's sake don't think I always behave like this. It must be all the excitement or something. Do you know, I've been faithful to my husband all these years?'

'And he?'

'Ezra? Ezra takes what he wants when he wants it, actresses usually. You know, he likes pretty women and they get a present from Cartier's on *his* birthday . . . you know what I mean?'

Geoffrey didn't know and he asked, 'So he can't really object?'

Audrey was about to say something, but the memory of the last night she and Ezra had spent together floated over her and she paused.

'He can't really object,' repeated Geoffrey.

'Of course he can, but I really don't know whether he would. He likes me to be admired, likes me to dress well. My God, now that I think of it, I've got nothing in black at all. I know he'd like you, you'd fit in. When you come back to England, you'd better come down for the weekend. We've plenty of beds.'

'There's a bed here,' said Geoffrey.

Audrey grew thoughtful, her mood had changed. 'Yes, Geoffrey, one for you and one for me, but there's no time and this is not the place.'

'Oh, all right. You don't blame me for trying? You do like me, don't you?'

'Yes, very, very much. Now tell me, Geoffrey, how do you manage to speak such good French?'

'Oh, in the war. Everything happened to me in the war, you know. But now it's finished and so I suppose in a way am I. There's nothing . . .'

'Oh, nonsense,' interrupted Audrey. 'You talk well, you dance well, you organize well.'

'But I've no qualifications.'

'You don't need any qualifications. Do you think my husband can mend a fuse?'

'Lord Sterling never had to mend a fuse,' said Geoffrey sharply.

'There's really nothing I can do except push stupid coppers around,' and he looked suddenly almost desperate and rather sweet, she thought. She wondered after all if she should let him kiss her again.

She smiled at him. 'Cheer up. Isn't there something called personnel?'

4

'Ezra, what does "IRA" mean?' interrupted Hélène.

She had been quiet, even depressed, in the back of the cumbersome new Humber on the grey way from La Guardia to New York, but perked up in Manhattan. On recognizing the Empire State Building, where a desultory group smoking on the sidewalk were holding placards with legends like *Don't Let Irish Rot in British Jails*, she had asked a question.

Ezra knew, but nodded at the eager, polite man from the British Information Services who had been their guide so far.

'Well, exactly, Mrs, er . . .'

'Hélène. Everybody calls me Hélène.'

'Well, if I may say, it's typical of what's happening in New York and it doesn't make our job any easier. This city is in the grip of Anglophobia, so that even the Irish have got on the bandwagon and parade with these old slogans from way back. The Trade Commissioner's office is in that building, so maybe . . .'

'What is your job?' asked Hélène without much interest, for she had spotted a windowful of fur coats.

'I'm one of the chaps here trying to sell British, and Sir Ezra, I mean Lord Sterling, who is on the Dollar Export Council, will surely appreciate the problems . . .'

'Well, you won't get far in this *bagnole* – how do you say – tub?' Mme Ooh-la-la said irreverently, but, thought Ezra, shrewdly, because dusty New York cabs had overtaken them steadily on the way into Manhattan, some with angry and puzzled hoots.

'I don't know,' said the polite man not so politely. 'You don't get finish like this in any American car,' and he tapped the walnut veneer of what could have been a cocktail cabinet by his knee. 'And anyway, the UK Trade Commissioner has to have a British car.'

'I hope he got a big discount,' replied Hélène, who had an instinct for how such matters are arranged.

The polite man had not yet worked out how to cope with the French lady as Lord Sterling's companion (surely mistress?) on this, he thought – and so did the Foreign Office – fairly urgent, semi-political mission. There had been no mention of her in the dispatch about Lord Sterling.

There was a pleasant fuss in the lobby of the St Regis as the manager, or a manager, welcomed Lord Sterling and his party. Even the Humber, now stationary, looked impressive and appropriate, at ease by the awning. In this safe haven for the rich, Lord Sterling did not disappoint. There were more heavy pigskin cases, each emblazoned with a coronet, than most Americans would take on an aeroplane, and if Madame Hélène's luggage looked rather new, it was of good design.

Particularly telling was the $50 bill Lord Sterling handed to the bell captain when he and his minions had deposited the luggage in the various rooms of their suite. The polite man had been gratified by Ezra's invitation to come and help them settle in and have a drink, and by the explanation of his largesse, that 'the biggest tip should be the first tip'. He was now so soothed that to Madame Hélène's rhetorical question, did he realize how cheap mink coats were in New York, instead of shuddering at the intended breach of Bank of England exchange regulations, he simply said that he didn't know about mink, but there were some marvellous gadgets to be seen at Hammacher Schlemmer where he would be happy to escort her tomorrow, as he understood Lord Sterling was having lunch with the Senator.

'Oh, no,' said Ezra quickly, making a martini, 'she's coming with me; they're old friends. Here, have one of these. I did it the way my wife has them made, stirred not bruised.'

'Thank you, sir.'

'You must ring up Ephie, Ezra,' commanded Madame Hélène. 'He's Lord Sterling's uncle in Miami,' she explained. Really, the man knew nothing.

'Oh my God, he's rung up three times,' bellowed Ezra.

'Who, who?' asked Mme Ooh-la-la from her dressing table, where she was trying to detach an evasive hair from her eyebrow.

'That *schnorrer*, Karnibad.'

'Who, darling?' Less interested. The hair had come out with a tiny *pic* of pain. *Il faut souffrir pour être belle.* Ezra grunted. He was sorting through his messages.

Despite his having arrived at such short notice the response of New York was satisfying. Two predictable official invitations, some generous quarts of liquor from '21', a scattering of welcomes from the wartime American visitors (little Oscar had been busy), a note from the business that $5,000 had been lodged in the hotel safe. But – and here there was no easy explanation – these three telephone messages from little Oscar's own father, the dreaded Karnibad.

'How on earth did he know I was here? He's never done this to me before! Answer me, Hélène!' Ezra stood up and had appeared at the open door of his mistress's bedroom. Following the polite man's departure, slightly slurred after Ezra's martinis, Hélène had taken a swift shower to wash the journey away, as she put it, and was making herself up for the evening's entertainment, which, although it was only to be supper in their suite, still meant putting in some work.

'Before, darling, you were not so famous. Nobody sent *me* any flowers.' She made a little *moue* at the mirror. Ezra looked round the salon. The family was indeed fully represented by flowers, the largest contribution coming from, as the shop girl had put in her anonymous hand, 'Tattie'.

'Very tactful the family is. You're not supposed to be here,' said Ezra.

'Ezra,' said Hélène, interrupting, 'you can massage my neck.'

'And then?'

'And then perhaps I can massage *your* neck.'

Ezra smiled. 'Before dinner?' Hélène's massages tended to develop.

'Why not?' she said. 'It'll give you an appetite.'

Smoking a green, faintly dusty Havana and rocking an impossibly large glass of Armagnac, a present from the delighted management, in his big hands, Ezra felt a little better disposed to the imminent visit of his ex-brother-in-law, Karnibad. For Hélène, sensitive to her lover's unease, had convinced him that their meeting should be sooner than later and had herself telephoned in her mock-secretarial voice to say that Lord Sterling apologized for not having returned Mr Karnibad's calls earlier, that he had only that moment arrived from London and looked forward to seeing him at ten o'clock the following day ('when I shall be out shopping').

'You see, Ezra, flatter him and it'll cost you less.'

'My dear girl, I don't see why he should cost me anything. He's a remittance man paid to stay out of the country – out of England, I mean. When Sophie divorced him he was paid off, finish, *schluss*, sent off to America; the boys were to be called Barnet and he was to be out of sight, out of mind.' Ezra sniffed his Armagnac, and sighed pessimistically. 'So why does he want to see me?'

'Perhaps he wants to pass the time of day?' suggested Hélène.

He smiled at the idea. No one ever came to pass the time of day with him. It was a trifle sad.

'Cheer up, *mon cher*. Tell me about him.'

'Ah.' Ezra drew on his cigar, put down the balloon of Armagnac to give himself a free hand.

Karnibad Sophie met at Deauville, he said, or was it Le Touquet? He was a captain in the Polish Navy, if there was such a thing, and his family owned large tracts of marsh somewhere, and he could throw his monocle in the air at a cocktail party and catch it – in his eye.

'*Tiens*,' said Hélène, although she had heard the story before.

'Furthermore, he had his trousers made in Hamburg and his coats in Paris by Scholte, if I remember correctly. He spoke most languages and knew the *Almanach de Gotha* inside out. He had, I think, some arrangement with the Casino at Deauville, which was how he lived, and I'm told he was very good at the other.'

'The other what?' asked Hélène, who was not familiar with the upper-class pre-war English slang which Ezra, together with his Yiddishisms, occasionally effected.

'You know . . . in bed. Well, anyway, all this was too much for our Sophie, just a poor little rich girl. He got her pregnant and then ... and then' – Ezra started to heave with laughter – 'as a man of honour ... he said he had to marry her! And he did! A man of honour, *oi vey*.' He wheezed and coughed.

'Take a little brandy, Ezra. Then what?'

'Well, luckily there were difficulties about the marriage settlement and we had a better lawyer – that's how she met Freddy. Karnibad got bored when she was having the twins. He took her to Cracow and his family, who were Catholic of course, discovered she was Jewish. And threatened to disinherit him. That shook him, I can tell you; he hadn't thought of that. Then it was easy to buy him off. I thought I'd never see him again.' He sighed. 'My God, my family. It shouldn't happen to a dog. The women are worse than the men. Look at Sarah with that pig man.'

'He is a very funny fellow. I like him. Besides, she's happy. The Doctor's happy with his germs, so ...'

'You know him?' Ezra said accusingly.

'*Bien sûr*, I know him. The family is my business. They tell me everything. Telegram, telephone, tell Hélène,' she added triumphantly.

'And Tattie with that American – not that it matters much,' added Ezra.

'It doesn't matter at all, Ezra, and you should let them marry.'

'Never.' It was almost a yelp.

Three thousand miles from Park Lane Ezra allowed himself some indiscretions, but Hélène, a wise mistress, knew when to stop, and it was clear that she had trod on a corn.

'Anyway, there wouldn't be any children. It's too late and she's too fat. We need children to work in the business. ... My Nicky never cared for it,' and Ezra turned his head into the last of the Armagnac with another heavy sigh.

'Little Oscar, when he settles down, he'll have children,' said Hélène helpfully.

'Little Oscar ... "when he settles down" ... that *schmuck*. That's just what he is. His trouble is he's ruled by his cock and not by his head.'

'And then there's Lucy, and she'll breed.'

'My little Lucy? She's only a child.'

'She is a very lucky child, he is a clever boy and brave. She has a moustache and a fortune, no? An excellent combination.'

Ezra, who had not worked out an attitude to this, considered the conversation had become sterile and replied, 'Hélène, you're too far away. Come and sit on my lap.'

'Ezra, you are incorrigible.' But she obliged and had just managed to take up that absurd position with some elegance when the telephone rang.

'Damn,' said Ezra. 'You answer it, dear, and then you come back.'

Hélène rose and walked to the bureau. How well they furnish a room here, thought Ezra. One could live here quite happily. And how well she moves. Why can't the English learn how to walk?

'It is the desk and they say is it too late to disturb you?'

'Evidently not,' replied Ezra cheerfully.

'It is a message from Commercial Union and they will send it up.'

The two of them prepared for the intrusion and waited in silence. When the door buzzed Ezra intercepted a middle-aged man, too well shaven and pressed to be a bellhop, in the lobby of the suite. He offered a hotel message on a silver plate. Ezra picked it up and read it.

'The desk say the confirmation termorra, sir.'

'Hélène,' called out Ezra, '*viens ici et apportez-moi de l'argent.*'

'*Chéri, j'ai pas de monnaie et j'ai perdu mon sac.*'

'*De l'argent,*' said Ezra insistently.

'Ooh la la.' Hélène scurried up with a $50 bill which she gave to Ezra who handed her the message in exchange.

'Read it slowly, and aloud.'

Hélène read out the message: 'Have seen Nicky's wife stop I think you are going to be a grandfather stop Congratulations and all my love Audrey.'

'Ezra!' exclaimed Hélène joyously.

'*Mazeltov!*' said the messenger, and then, inclining his head, 'my lord.'

Hélène was more or less right. The former brother-in-law arrived at the St Regis the following day nearly a quarter of an hour late, but Ezra's irritation was quickly dispelled by the news that he had come in from Westchester in his wife's car and that the midtown traffic in Manhattan was becoming intolerable. Ezra noticed that his clothes were good but that his fingernails were dirty. Karnibad had, with the years, lost much of the Polish élan which had captivated Sophie in the twenties, but in going to America had clearly landed on his feet, or on someone else's feet in the shape of a brand-new or brand-old wife. He appeared to be active in the new world of television, or at least active in talking about it, because his real concern seemed to be in ferrying his wife to and from her psychiatrist, to whom she was much attached. Ezra assured him that the business was indeed manufacturing cathode-ray tubes which bore a handy similarity to the equipment Sterlings had made for radar during the war. At this moment the conversation faded away and Karnibad asked politely about the twins, his sons.

'I never knew them, as you know, Ezra, but I sometimes think of them.'

'Him,' said Ezra shortly. 'Little Oscar's brother was killed in the war, remember?'

'Oh, yes . . . Such a tragedy.' Karnibad sighed. His manner was so vague that Ezra wondered how many little Karnibads peopled the western world.

Reading his thoughts Mr Karnibad said solemnly, 'My wife and I have no children together . . . but I am stepfather to her children and they have children, too. In fact, Ezra, why don't you come to our place this Sunday for a barbecue? A kind of family affair. And do you know this, we don't heat the frankfurters any more, we attach each end and electrocute them!' This did interest Ezra and he said so, but declined the invitation.

Proof of the conversion to the American way of life of this former Polish gigolo and threat to the family arrived an hour later at the St Regis in the form of a complete outfit of frankfurter-electrocuting equipment – supplied, of course, by Hammacher Schlemmer.

'But how many people in England want to electrocute frankfurters in the open air?'

It had been a good morning. Ezra looked at his mistress over their shared martinis and remembered the advice of an old refugee professor of the History of Ideas or some damn nonsense, who had said to him, 'And never be in New York without a woman – in this city a man needs all the security he can get.'

And then there was something rather special about Hélène. . . . Why did people say chic was indefinable? Hélène was chic in her stockings which were of silk, not nylon, chic in her scent which was always the same, chic in her hat which was almost, but not quite, absurd. And then the veil: how many American women could seriously wear a veil?

The place was not yet full but the few women who had passed their table in the bar had glanced not at him but at her.

'So you see, my dear, not everyone is dangerous, and some people can manage without you.'

Ezra shrugged. 'No, the gallant Karnibad has found another Sophie, certainly rich, probably mad, living in Scarsdale and, I wouldn't be surprised, Jewish.'

'Bravo,' said Hélène. 'And how is your Uncle Ephie? You spoke to him?'

'Not to him, he won't use the telephone, but to a lady who called herself Mrs Steimatsky and sounded like Mrs Steimatsky. But it was only Pat. You know, his nurse . . . Jeremy's nurse, everybody's nurse.'

'*Tiens*, of course! He married her.'

'Why not? This is a woman's country and they run the joint. They kill their husbands, control all the stocks. In America he couldn't *not* marry her. Mind you, she'll never kill Ephie and he's not too good at parting with money. Ephie's fine, she told me, and I'm to go to the people who make UNIVAC. Well, we know what's happening in the computer world, or we should know. But that he should know about Eckhardt Maunchly . . .'

'What is happening at . . . whatever you call them?'

'A little thing called a . . . Oh, but don't bother your pretty little head. Let us talk about more serious things. Your mink coat? You bought one?'

'Bought a mink!' cried Hélène. 'I would never buy a mink coat without showing you, Ezra.'

He smiled. It was a nice way of putting it.

'But I did more or less reserve a coat at Bergdorf Goodman,' she said. 'A blue mink with a little belt and very full sleeves. *Très chic*.'

'Blue?' queried Ezra.

'Well, they call it blue. I show you,' and she stood up. 'Imagine,' she said, stretching with her hands, 'a big collar and a full skirt, very long . . .'

'Am I to understand,' interrupted a voice, 'that you are considering the purchase of a mink coat in this city?' And a gentleman kissed her hand.

'*Bonjour*, madame. Hello, Ez,' and he shook hands.

'Hélène, sit down,' said Ezra.

'Martinis, hm. Ezra, I thought you always drank Scotch.'

'Do you know about mink, Senator?'

'Everything, madame, and you mustn't buy one without me. Some of my best friends are furriers.' He broke off. 'Well, Ez, good to see you in New York again.'

'Yes,' said Ezra. 'You know what happened. Nicky . . .'

'I read about it and I want to offer you my very deepest sympathy. It must be . . .'

'You *read* about it?' interrupted Ezra.

'Yes, this morning or maybe yesterday. A little paragraph on the front page of the *New York Times*. "Son of Viscount Sterling killed in Jerusalem, buried with military honours by the British." That at least must be gratifying to you, Ez.'

'Yes,' said Ezra. The Foreign Office had thought of everything.

'It was an accident, I understand?'

'Yes,' said Ezra, 'an accident.'

'We live in troubled times, we Jews . . .' and he reached for a salted peanut.

'There is some good news too,' said Hélène quietly.

Ezra nodded.

'May I tell him, Ezra?'

Ezra nodded again.

'He is to become a grandfather.'

'Great,' said the Senator. 'In the midst of death, etc. Well, it is true that good sometimes comes from evil. That calls for a traditional celebration. Captain!' he called.

The captain summoned the wine waiter. Ezra awkwardly asked for some New York State champagne which was not on the wine list, and Hélène produced from her handbag – with difficulty, for it was new and she could not manage the clasp – an electric swizzle stick, a present from Ezra.

'Marvellous,' he said, his humour returned. 'I have one of the biggest electrical firms in the world, constantly on the lookout for new products, and I return from the United States with a machine for electrocuting frankfurters and a device for removing the bubbles they put into champagne. In more sophisticated enterprises, the process is known as market research!' Ezra smiled happily.

'Have domestic appliances grown that complicated?'

'No, but they have grown, or will grow. Too many people in the business. We prefer the heavy stuff which is what I'm here for.'

'I would like to hear about that, but shall we order now?' asked the Senator. The captain was hovering.

'Yes, you do that and I'll go to the little girls' room,' said Hélène.

They all stood up. It was one of Hélène's more mysterious qualities that she liked her men to order her food.

The men were each handed an enormous menu adorned with tassels and braid. Ordering a meal at the Brussels was a serious affair for an Englishman in 1948.

'Senator, will you do me a favour?' asked Ezra.

'Anything, you know that.'

'Would the FBI have files on Americans who volunteered to fight for the British in 1940?'

'Probably. They are a very inquisitive lot down there.'

'Can you get a copy if I give you a name?'

The Senator thought.

'I could do that, I dare say, Ez. But a better man for the job would be your friend who was at the Embassy in London.'

'Victor Bridleton?'

'That's right ... he's quite high up in the State Department. He's your man. It would be more acceptable if such an enquiry came from him. Call him up,' he added hurriedly as Hélène returned to the table.

'I haven't had meat like this since before the war. It's enormous.' Hélène gazed at her *entrecôte* now three-quarters demolished. But the men were not to be distracted from their argument. Both Jews, she thought, one an American and the other an Englishman, which seemed to be the Senator's theme.

'You see, Ez, you and I – friends from way back, right? We arrive at this point in history, our Jewish history, from different origins. My father was a janitor; I was born on Rivington Street right here in this city. In this city of two million Jews. A helluva lot of them vote for me. I couldn't just stand by and watch while the British Navy tried to stop our people swimming to the shores of their natural homeland! And we're not going to stand by and watch while those Arabs knock our people back into the sea. So of course with Zionists, all American Jews are Zionists, and so, thank God, are most Americans. You know this country, Ez, you're one of the few Englishmen I know who do, we are a nation of immigrants. Way back all of us who are here came from somewhere else to find a new and better life, or so we thought. And we have prospered and multiplied. There are a lot of us now and we are very strong. There are more Jews in this city than the crazy two million who are now left in Europe!'

'There can't be much room for anybody else. Yet I see some people in New York who don't look Jewish,' said Hélène.

'Yeah,' supplied Ezra in his American voice. 'There are some: the goyim – the audience!'

The Senator smiled but didn't turn his head.

'Exactly. And the only hope, we believe, for the Jews of the world is in the creation of a wholly Jewish state which any Jew can go to whenever he likes, and this has to be established and will be supported by the Jews of America.'

'And in pursuit of this idea, I suppose you approve of stringing up British sergeants, shooting Lord Moyne, a man I know, shooting Count Bernadotte, a man everyone knew, massacring the human contents of an Arab village. That was last month, right? Sending letters which explode in the face of mail clerks, er, er, assassinating people while they listen to Beethoven . . .' The recollection had suddenly made Ezra very angry.

'Of course not, Ez, I deplore those methods. There are extremes in the Zionist movement. The Stern Gang, they did all those things.' With one movement the American picked up the bottle of champagne from the cooler and filled Ezra's glass and then Hélène's.

'Look, Ez,' he said gently, 'I don't know who set up this lunch appointment, and you know I am happy to see you any time, but . . .'

(Damn, thought Ezra, that was a mistake – it made their meeting look official. Why couldn't it have been arranged through the business?)

'You should go home and tell them that you have heard the middle American point of view on the State of Israel. As far as I represent anything, that is what I represent.

'You see, Hélène . . .' Suddenly the Senator was grateful for her presence. Was it a rich man's whim to bring his mistress along to a lunch like this, or was the explanation more complicated? He glanced at Ezra, who was absorbed in testing the electric swizzle stick.

Ezra looked up. 'It has two speeds,' he said, 'fast and slow.'

The Senator turned back to Hélène; her eyes were flattering, encouraging.

'. . . the American people see a little country struggling for independence, a country, moreover, that has opened its gates to the survivors of Hitler's concentration camps. It will be some time before the American people will look kindly upon any European power which has tried to shut those gates.' He looked at Ezra steadily. 'I'm sorry.'

And then, with a change of voice and of attitude, like a victorious boxer who helps his opponent to his feet, he added, 'Look, Ezra, you're a fine man, you've got influence, you're on the Jewish Board of Deputies, and the Anglo-Jewish and – hell, there aren't many Jews in the House of Lords, are there?'

'There are a few of us,' Ezra said mildly. 'And we're not Zionists.'

Although their dialogue was easier, Ezra was still seething in anger and desperation. He remembered one of his father's aphorisms which applied: If you want to lose, see the other man's point of view. The Senator seemed to understand. This thought was transmitted on Ezra's face into a sort of amazed glare.

'We still haven't found Hélène's mink coat, which is what I'm here for, I guess.'

'Well, I saw this one in Bergdorf Goodman . . .'

'Hélène, if I may butt in here, you don't want to buy a mink coat in an uptown store in New York.'

Hélène looked unconvinced.

'Why, you'll just be paying three times what you need pay.'

Hélène looked disappointed. The price was not her problem.

'If you come with me you can see skins which'll give you a coat three times as nice for the same money.'

'Where?' asked Hélène, and she thoughtfully moved one of her crêpes Suzette on to Ezra's plate.

'Downtown, Seventh Avenue, you'll see every kind of fur.'

'I only want mink,' said Hélène a little petulantly.

'Sure, but my dear, around here they cheat you. Look at a mink coat when the lining's off and you'll see the skins have been stretched artificially, a lot of them, to get more coat out of less mink.'

Hélène, who had been impressed by the Senator while he had been making his speech, now looked at him with open eyes.

'*Tiens*,' she said.

'And another thing,' said the Senator, as he handed the hat-check girl a five-dollar bill, 'if you take in skins you don't pay so much duty. And if you talk nicely to Ezra, who I guess has a diplomatic passport, I bet he'll smuggle them in.'

In this mood, warmed by a common ordeal and not unaffected by good food and wine, the three of them tottered into a waiting cab bound for downtown New York in search of mink.

The Senator was convinced his speech had changed his friend's mind; Ezra was determined to forget every word.

5

'The worst thing that happened on the way home was our running out of yellow Benedictine. I kicked up a helluva row and they took it all quite seriously.' Ezra laughed happily.

No one else did. There was nothing funny about being summoned to a board meeting at nine o'clock on a spring Saturday morning.

'You've run out of yellow Benedictine, I said,' repeated Ezra relentlessly. 'Well, that's a fine thing! And the barman called the chief steward and I said to him, ask the captain. And the captain came! And I told him, look here, we are doing three hundred miles per hour a few thousand feet above the Atlantic, it's only three o'clock in the afternoon, and you've got no more yellow Benedictine! Well, thank God the man had a sense of humour and he said, I agree and it's my responsibility. When we land I shall commit hara-kiri. . . .'

'Nothing else went seriously wrong, I hope?' said David.

'No, it was marvellous. You know you can go upstairs to bed on those aeroplanes?'

Little Oscar and David exchanged glances. With whom? they wondered. (There had been rumours.)

'We should go to America every year – for a recharge. You, you and . . .' He hesitated as he glanced at Chaimy who returned his look with a smile.

'You're right there, Uncle, they wouldn't let me in.'

There was a silence. Everybody present knew that Chaimy was a lifelong card-carrying member of the Communist Party.

Sir Arthur cleared his throat.

'Yes, Ezra, how is the political climate?' And instantly regretted his question, for it was a subject which Viscount Sterling notoriously enjoyed and he, Sir Arthur, saw himself being late for lunch before the races at Lingfield.

'Well,' said Ezra briskly, 'what you don't get in the papers here is, of course, the *atmosphere* in America today. IRA demonstrations. Newspaper headlines in New York about White Russian ladies falling mysteriously out of apartment-house windows . . . And all because of the Russians. You know that Truman only signed the European Recovery Act because Acheson convinced him and the rest of America that if he didn't, the whole of Europe would burst into flames?'

'You mean the Marshall Plan?' asked little Oscar.

'Yes,' said Ezra impatiently, 'it's not cakes and ale for old time's sake; it's because they're frightened of revolution. That's why they support German recovery. They think our nationalization here is the first step towards a Communist government. I tell them we do very well out of nationalization, thank you, look at our stock market, look at . . .' he hesitated. 'Look at Sir Arthur here. Does he look as if he's going to end up swinging from a lantern?'

Sir Arthur, pink-cheeked and well-breakfasted, his Lingfield Park member's badge nestling under a large carnation and about him a faint odour of Mitsouko, did indeed look as if he had other plans.

'By the way, David, how *is* the radio business in Germany?'

'Fine, we're everywhere in the British and American Zones – nowhere in the Russian and French, of course – so I'm *all* for German recovery. They're excellent workers, honest, hard-working, if only they had the equipment. . . . That's where I put my money – in Germany!'

This speech from one normally so cool and from a man who had only three years before strangled a Nazi general with his bare hands, or beaten him to death with a club – Mr Wilson forgot how the story ran exactly – prompted him to protest.

'Not everybody is quite so sure about Germany as you are, Mr Blacker,' he said icily. (Mr Wilson had fought in the National Fire Service during the war and was, though an accountant, patriotic.)

'I'm sorry,' said Ezra. 'I seem to have created a distraction.' He cleared his throat.

Distraction? thought the others. What else had this meeting been so far? Had the Chairman gone out of his mind? Little Oscar had his elbows on the boardroom table and was leaning forward in an attitude of eagerness, but his eyes were listless and he looked as if he were nursing a hangover. Mr Wilson had avoided David Blacker's cool stare by studying the blank piece of paper which should have been the minutes. Sir Arthur was toying with a tiny gold object attached to his fob and all radiated unease except for Chaimy, who was absorbed in a private game of making patterns with matches from the box stationed beside his blotter.

'And I forgot to tell you I spoke to Ephie and he's got married,' said Ezra abruptly.

Little Oscar rubbed his eyes. 'The old goat,' he said.

'Not so old,' said Ezra.

'Oh, come on. Uncle Ephie must be at least . . . at least . . . well, he looked a hundred when I drove him up from Margate, and that was in 1940.'

'I'll tell you how old Ephie is,' said Ezra slowly, drawing on his cigar. 'Now if Father were alive he'd be . . .'

My God, thought Mr Wilson, if they're now going to have one of those particularly Jewish conversations about the age of remote relations I shall, for the first time in my life, scream; and he glanced for sympathy in the direction of Sir Arthur, the only other Gentile.

'. . . Seventy-four. That's all Ephie is. And he knows what's going on, too. I *think* he might have known about this.'

Ezra had produced from the jacket pocket of his sports coat an object about eight inches by four, flat and studded with minute batteries in varied colours, sizes and shapes. He turned it over; on the reverse was stencilled a diagram of what looked like the marshalling yards of Hamm after a bad night.

'What's that then?' asked little Oscar.

'I don't know, Oscar. You know I don't understand such things, which is why I asked our technical director to come along this morning and tell us. Here, Chaimy,' said Ezra, raising his voice. 'Ever seen one of these?' And he flung it down the centre of the boardroom table to where Chaimy was playing his game.

The directors of Sterling Industries had little knowledge of electronics, but they were sure items like this should be handled delicately and as one man, they gasped. They also watched for Chaimy's reaction.

('Never could stand the fellow,' Wilson said to Mrs Wilson, 'but there's no doubt he's got brains.') Now he thought, does he have to have such filthy fingernails?

Chaimy stared at the object in front of him, absently stubbed out his Woodbine, nearly missing the ashtray provided, snuffled into a dirty handkerchief, removed his spectacles and started to clean them. Only when this had been accomplished did he lean forward, pick the thing up and scrutinize it.

'No,' he said quietly.

'No, what?' asked Ezra sharply.

'No, I have never seen one of them.'

'Do you know what it is?'

'Yes, Uncle,' still without looking up. 'It is what we call a "p.c."
– a printed circuit board.'

'But if you've . . . if you've never seen one, how do you know
what it is?' asked Sir Arthur practically.

Chaimy looked at him. He didn't dislike Sir Arthur – he was so
obvious. It was that Wilson, with his blue suit and Brylcreemed hair,
who was the real enemy, a typical representative of *la trahison des clercs*.

'But what does it do?' persisted little Oscar.

Chaimy ignored him.

'There have been diagrams of printed circuits for some time in
papers – you know, scientific papers – which I get, mostly from
Cambridge.'

'Cambridge, Massachusetts?' It was David, the sharp one.

'No,' answered Chaimy gently, 'Cambridge, England, and in
answer to your question, Oscar . . .'

He brought out a tiny screwdriver from the pocket of his ancient
brown corduroy jacket and began scratching. 'Hold on.' From the
same pocket he produced another small instrument. 'You see,' he
muttered, 'we are in the era of miniaturization and for that we need
magnifying glasses. Soon oor eyes will be useless. . . . Ah, yes, this
does nothing.' He held it up. 'This is just a model – probably just
for demonstration purposes.'

Ezra looked a little disappointed.

'The lines you see here' – Chaimy tapped them with the screwdriver – 'which look like a railway terminus, don't they, will be
etched out of, I would say, copper and replace wires and then little
things –' he turned the object round – 'germinium diodes, capacitors,
resistors and, finally, transistors, which, gentlemen, will replace
valves. . . .'

At that moment if someone had dropped a paper clip on to the
thick carpet of the board room at Sterling Industries, it would
have been heard.

'You see, electronics has relatively few elements and has relatively few components. It's just a question of the order you put them in and their relationship, input/output biasing and so forth. And, finally, that's based on logic and mathematics,' Chaimy mumbled.

'This here,' he held it up, 'I would say uses diode transistor logic or resistor-transistor logic. So it shouldn't surprise you, David, that a lot of the *ideas* come from Cambridge. Though there's Shannon, of course, MIT in '38, I must admit.'

'It seems to me, speaking as an outsider, that this . . . whatever-you-call-it, could be developed commercially, and that we might have been told about it before?' Speaking as a politician, Sir Arthur had sensed this was the question in everybody's mind.

'Yes,' replied Chaimy with a sigh. 'But would you have listened? You see, you, Sir Arthur, read Greats at Balliol. Uncle went to Harvard.'

(Mr Wilson wished that this electrician would not call the Chairman 'Uncle' at board meetings.)

'Mr Wilson here,' continued Chaimy calmly, 'is an accountant and can presumably add, subtract and multiply to everyone's satisfaction.' (This raised a smile where it was known there were a lot of little Wilsons.) 'But how many of you got beyond School Certificate in physics? That's the trouble with the board rooms of this country, Uncle.'

Ezra was gazing into space.

'But, Chaimy,' put in little Oscar, 'if this thing replaces wires and *valves*, what are we doing gearing up for the television boom everybody's talking about, manufacturing valves? Our business is based on valves.'

'Well, first, commercial manufacture is a long way off, and secondly, transistors don't apply to television receivers whose screen is, after all, a valve.'

'So what do we do?'

'Nothing, just wait and see.'

They all looked at Ezra except for Chaimy who seemed to have assumed the proceedings had closed and was trying to stuff as many boardroom cigarettes into his tiny Woodbine packet as possible.

'And are the others – Pye, Plessey, Thorn – are they all waiting and seeing, Chaimy?' asked Ezra, still staring dreamily at the ceiling.

'I would think so,' replied Chaimy airily. 'They've all got people like me, as you know – only more respectable people, of course –' (a glance at Wilson?) 'telling them the same thing.'

'And these boffins at Cambridge, can they be believed?' Ezra was now staring quite hard at Chaimy who, oblivious, had found another empty packet of cigarettes to fill.

'Nah, I shouldn't think so.' Chaimy, the scientific disquisition over, had reverted to his affected proletarian voice. 'Those fellows don't give a fuck about money. They don't want to make anything. It's the old story – television, penicillin, atomic energy, we think of it, they make it. Buy it from the Yanks, when they've got it right, pay royalties.' And he stuffed the battered cigarettes into his pocket and looked up as if about to depart.

At the mention of royalties there had been a stiffening of interest in the room; it was an axiom in the business that royalties were received, not paid.

'Do you think, Oscar,' said Ezra in a cold voice, without taking his eyes off Chaimy, 'that you could find some cigarettes to give our colleague when he goes home?'

'Chaimy,' he continued evenly, 'Chaimy, you may be right, that we should just wait and see, but I don't like that sort of advice and we will get our people in America to look at this . . . er . . . thing from a contractual point of view. You may also be right when you say it is difficult for you to explain to simple souls like us, to *schmocks*' – Ezra snarled the word – 'like us, these new developments in electronics. But where you are wrong, Chaimy' – and here Ezra picked up a pencil and pointed it at him like a dagger – 'is when you say you read about these things in papers and then don't even try and tell me about them. Tell me, tell me.'

Ezra shouted at him, as if they were alone in the room, while the rest of them sat tight, feeling they were about to be washed overboard. 'Chaimy, have you forgotten how to talk to me?'

Ezra's voice had sunk to a whisper, almost a lover's whisper. 'You remember you managed to explain to me before the war well before the war, about what we now call radar? I listened to you, didn't I? We made the bloody thing. What other country in the world had a nation-wide system for advance warning of enemy aircraft? In 1936?'

Chaimy made no answer.

'No, I think you may be wrong,' continued Ezra, still jabbing at Chaimy with the pencil. 'You may be derelict, but I don't believe it's fair' – he lingered on the word – 'of you to blame the board rooms of England while you sit up in Islington waiting to read about this new stuff in learned papers! God forbid that you should write a learned paper one fine day! You are not a fool, are you?' Ezra screamed.

Chaimy, his cheek gone, on the verge of tears, shook his head helplessly.

'Then you can explain to me what's going on under our noses in England, that I should have to go to New York . . . that . . . that . . . *alterkaker* of an uncle of mine . . .' Ezra appeared to be failing for words, but like a first-class firework, the appearance was deceptive. The big bang was to come.

'And,' he went on, 'less unkind remarks about British board rooms, please. Wasn't it my good friend Simon Marks who put together PLUTO – you know, Pipe Line Under The Ocean – with ping-pong balls or something? He's got a board room, hasn't he?' His eyes flashed round the room and they all flinched as if an express train had passed too close for comfort.

'That's just defeatism – all the Americans have got is a lot of Americans. There's nothing wrong with this country but that people like you make it so. We're the only nation in Europe to have come through the war standing on our own two feet. We still have an Empire, we still have quality, we still have brains, and, Chaimy . . .' – Ezra leaned forward for the final lunge – 'if you don't use yours on our behalf,' but he tapped his own chest, 'I'm going to have to find somebody who does, right?'

Bang on cue, the pencil snapped.

Good, thought David Blacker, that must be the end. He closed his eyes and sighed. Hearing the first Viscount Sterling in full patriotic flow (the Jew for all seasons, the Jew they loved to honour:

if he went on like this they'd have to make him a duke) was no one's idea of how to spend a sunny Saturday morning. An exhausted silence had fallen over the sunlit room.

'Now, Chaimy,' Ezra had begun again, but in the tired voice of a mother pleading with a child to go to bed, 'I've an idea for you. The next time there's a cheap day excursion to Cambridge, take the train – you can put your bicycle in the guard's van.'

Like a little withered old child, Chaimy began to cry. (It is truly said that the kindness and not the harshness in the headmaster's voice pushes boys to tears.)

'. . . And talk to those people. Maybe you'll find a nice young left-wing research graduate you can hire.'

Chaimy snuffled appreciatively.

'We can take them on as consultants,' intervened Mr Wilson pompously. 'That's the best thing taxwise,' he added quickly as Ezra cut him off with a look which said: You may have a point but just now, shut up.

'Spend what you like. Maybe they want a bursary or something? Now, Oscar, you never gave Chaimy his cigarettes. And' – Chaimy had taken the hint and began to assemble his bits – 'don't forget your thermos.' Chaimy did not approve of drink and always brought a thermos of tea to meetings at the office. This time it had stayed untouched. Little Oscar was trying to help Chaimy with his duffle coat in the middle of which Chaimy turned round, sniffed and said in his normal voice:

'Well, Uncle, you made me miss *shul* and if I don't scarper I'll be late for me game of darts in the Mile End Road. Always play darts on Saturday mornings. Got me own set.' He brought out a little box and with clenched fist gave them the Communist salute.

'You'll get there all right,' said little Oscar as he piloted Chaimy to the door, 'it's downhill all the way.'

'Now he's gone,' said Ezra briskly, pressing a button on the machine in front of him, 'we can all have a glass of wine.' And he stood up and stretched his arms. In unconscious imitation little Oscar and David copied him. A waiter entered the room with a tray of drinks. (Ridiculous, thought Mr Wilson, keeping a man on Saturday overtime.)

'Well, Ezra,' said Sir Arthur, 'got any tips for Lingfield?'

(That too was ridiculous, thought Mr Wilson. He must know Lord Sterling took no interest in such matters.)

'No, Arthur, but I can do better than that for you. That was a good question of yours . . . started me off, I'm afraid.' He paused. 'Doesn't a pony mean something in your world?'

'Yes, fifty quid.'

'Right, then, you've got fifty pounds on the winner of the first race.'

'How's that?' Sir Arthur looked puzzled and felt not a little affronted.

Ezra shrugged and gestured in Mr Wilson's direction. 'He'll tell you,' and he ambled towards the sideboard in the direction of his nephew and the champagne. Mr Wilson advanced in the manner of an old-fashioned butler about to explain the breakfast arrangements to a newly arrived guest.

'What Lord Sterling means, Sir Arthur, is just what he says. So that if the winner comes in at, say, two to one, you get a hundred pounds, if it's an outsider at sixteen to one, eight hundred, if it's a real outsider' – Mr Wilson's little eyes twinkled ferociously – 'at, say, thirty-three to one, you get one thousand six hundred and fifty pounds!'

'I see,' said Sir Arthur coldly.

'And furthermore, Sir Arthur,' added Mr Wilson triumphantly, 'you don't need to tell me the amount because I shall know from the Sunday papers and I'll have the cheque sent to you next week.'

'Thank you.'

'That's all right; it's just Lord Sterling's way of showing his appreciation. Only . . .' – he frowned a little – 'he usually does it with younger members of the family.'

'Hmm, yes, typical. Excuse me, I think I need a drink.'

'Do you know, just after the war when I was in Vienna,' said David to little Oscar when Jenkins had tidied Ezra into his car, 'I heard of a Jew – a perfectly ordinary little chap he had been, a chemist or something, who was castrated by the Gestapo. And . . .' – David paused and stared thoughtfully after the departing Rolls – 'he fell in love with the man who did it to him. That's what Ezra's done to Chaimy. He's castrated him.'

6

Jeremy found himself in the grass and wondered if he were alive. He thought he must be because he felt an overwhelming desire to pee. But how? He tried to move his leg but nothing happened. It was as if his limbs were on holiday. He tried again and this time his hand obeyed and touched something feathery. He felt for the first time pain, little half dull throbs sped to his fuddled brain – damn, a nettle: he must be alive. Suppose he just gave up and peed in his pants, imagine the relief, the warm glow spreading through his flannel trousers; he'd done it once at school, there'd been an initial pleasure, but then clamminess and nastiness. Still he had to do something, soon.

The decision was taken for him by the sound of a car drawing up, two doors opening, a military voice, friendly but concerned.

'I say, old boy, are you all right?'

'I don't know.' Jeremy looked up at what from his angle looked like a wool cloth cap and a spotted scarf without a face.

'Well, we'll soon find out.'

'Don't move him, dear, in case he's broken something.'

'I know perfectly well what to do, thank you, Rosemary,' stated the major (as he must have been), who bent down on his knees and began to feel Jeremy's neck, arms and legs. 'Nothing at all as far as I can see. You're a very lucky young man. Here, let me help you stand up, hold on to me.'

'It's awful, sir, but would you mind if I went to the lavatory, spent a penny?'

'No, absolutely right, good chap, shock and all that. Ro, go back to the car, will you?'

But Jeremy couldn't wait and propped up by the understanding major he peed lavishly over the offending nettles, noting out of the corner of his eye his motor bike skew-whiff in the middle of the road, its beautiful yellow and chrome petrol tank picked out by the low October sun, the splendour of the sight marred only by a large L plate.

'Now I suppose we'd better do something about your infernal machine. It's a bit in the way.'

'I can't think what happened,' said Jeremy. 'I was going along, chug, chug, chug, quite happily when suddenly the bike seized up, bang, and the next thing I knew I was in the ditch, and then you came along, thank God. It shouldn't have done that, should it? Oh, by the way, thank you very much.'

'It's all right, old boy.'

The three of them were now contemplating the delinquent and obviously brand-new machine.

'I mean, should it?' persisted Jeremy.

'How long have you had the thing?' asked the major disapprovingly.

'About two hours. I mean, that's just the point; it hasn't had time to go wrong.'

The major stroked his chin. 'Wait a minute, young man, let me tell you. You bought this new machine, the engine's not run in, you're riding it too fast, the engine seizes up, the pistons stop and, as you say, bang! The next time that happens, you want to pull up this little thing here,' and he bent down and touched a small lever on the right hand handlebar. 'The valve exhaust lift,' he said firmly.

'The valve exhaust lift,' repeated Jeremy, impressed both by the major's knowledge and the fact that his machine possessed such an important gadget.

'Didn't they tell you about this sort of thing in the army? You did do your military service, didn't you?' said the major, aghast at the thought that he might be propping up a conscientious objector.

'Oh, yes,' said Jeremy, 'but not for long enough really.'

The major thought this was not perhaps the time to rehearse his views on the younger generation, especially as his wife interrupted, with 'He's bleeding.'

Jeremy's trousers had been gashed to the knees and there was indeed a little blood around.

'Nothing serious, thank you.'

'Just a scratch,' said the major.

'I still think he needs attention,' said Mrs Major.

'Of course. Now, where do you live, young man?'

Jeremy was about to reply that he didn't live anywhere particularly, but instead he said that he was going up to Oxford, but first was supposed to be staying with some people who lived near here.

'Well, I'm sure we can take you there. Where is it?'

'It's a house called Turners,' said Jeremy.

'Turners,' the couple echoed, looking at the young man with new eyes.

'You mean Lord Sterling's place?' said Mrs Major.

Jeremy nodded weakly. 'He's sort of my uncle.'

'Huh, you'll be in good hands over there,' said Mrs Major.

'Oh, yes, and it's all right because I think my sort of father might be there and he's sort of a doctor.'

'Well, if you want to go to Turners, you're going the wrong way,' said the major. 'It's two miles back. It's not out of our way, we'll take you.'

'Oh, no!' said Jeremy, envisaging the clash of two very different styles of life. 'I'm sure she'll start. I can get there all right on my own. I'll just push on, two miles isn't far, if that's what you say it is.'

'You'll do no such thing, young man. I wouldn't be a party to it. You've had a nasty tumble and you're in a state of shock, believe me, I know about this sort of thing.'

Mrs Major nodded at Jeremy, all motherly. 'He does, you know,' she said with her eyes. With some grunting the major heaved the BSA 350 cc on to its feet and stood it by the side of the road.

'I'm afraid it's too big to get into my little bus.' The major glanced at his plucky Morris 8. 'You'll need at least a fifteen hundredweight to pick that up.'

'Do you think I can just leave it there?'

'I don't see why not, you can always tell the police. And better take the keys, you know.'

'And then there's your luggage,' said Mrs Major. 'Don't worry, I'll get it. You get into the car, you get into the front seat. I'll get your bags.'

Ensconced in the Morris 8, a sense of comradeship and adventure glowed among the three of them.

'By the way,' said the major, taking off his driving gloves and shaking Jeremy by the hand, 'I'm John Bentley and this is my wife, Rosemary.' Jeremy turned round and felt a slight pain in his neck as he shook Mrs Bentley's hand in the back seat.

They really were very sweet, the Bentleys with their little old car, so beautifully kept. He hoped the family's motor cars would be tucked out of sight when they arrived at Turners.

The first gate of the private road leading to Turners was open, but after nearly a quarter of a mile they came to another pair of gates which were shut, but at their approach swung, as it were miraculously, open.

'Crikey, Ro, did you see that?' said the major.

'Of course I did, dear. I *have* been here before.' (It still reminded her of the entrance to Windsor Castle.)

'It's on some sort of a switch,' said Jeremy. 'My uncle's in the electrical business and he has all these gadgets. It's silly, really.'

'Nothing silly about it. Sterling, bloody good show. I've got some shares, I'm happy to say. I'd like to meet your uncle and give him my personal congratulations. Bloody good show,' said the major defiantly as the third gate swung open before him. 'Good God, is that a golf course? A private course, of course. Not many left. I thought they were all ploughed up during the war.'

'It was a convalescent home for American Air Force people, I think, so they were allowed to keep it,' said Jeremy.

'Well, here we are, my boy,' said the major as the Morris crunched to a halt in front of a portico, an opulent and inept addition to the plain 1830 house, and he leant over and opened the car door for Jeremy.

'Won't you come in?' asked Jeremy.

'I think we should see him safely inside,' said Mrs Major firmly, 'don't you, dear?' and she moved herself forward from the back seat.

Jeremy pulled the handle of the bell which clanged clearly, but he knew that red lights would be flicking on all over the servants' part of the house. He suddenly felt rather weak, and prayed for Grose, the butler, to hurry before he passed out. Grose had been a dresser to a famous Shaftesbury Avenue actor before the war and before he went into service and he tended in moments of stress to over-react.

'Mr Jeremy,' he almost shrieked, striking his forehead with a clenched fist, 'what have you been doing to yourself?'

'Nothing serious, Grose, nothing serious.'

'He's had an accident and we thought we'd better look after him,' said the major and he took off his cloth cap.

'Gracious me,' said Grose, digesting Jeremy's muddy face and bloody trousers. 'Good gracious.'

At that moment little Oscar lumbered into view like a curious Alsatian. 'What's all this? Good God, Jeremy – is he drunk or something?' Little Oscar turned angrily to the major.

'He's had . . .' began the major.

'I had a slight disagreement with my motor bike,' said Jeremy, trying to appear grown-up, 'and these very sweet people, Mr and Mrs . . . er . . .' He paused.

'Bentley,' said the major, and at that moment Jeremy fainted into his cousin's arms.

'Put his head down, don't you think?' said the major. Little Oscar ignored him.

'Grose,' said little Oscar, 'don't just stand there. Tell the Brigadier to come here and tell Lady Sterling . . .' and he jerked his head towards the visitors.

Jeremy lay on the bed, where little Oscar had dumped him, fully dressed, his tie loose round his neck and with no shoes. He recognized his adopted father, tried to smile and say something, but no words came. Carefully and deftly, the Brigadier moved his limbs and sunk a needle brusquely into his upper arm. The keys Jeremy had been clutching fell on to the floor. Had little Oscar not been standing by the door, the Doctor might have kissed his foster son on the forehead, so touching did he look. He never should have been allowed to buy a motor bike. The Doctor picked up the keys and waddled out.

'Whatever's wrong with him is not fatal,' he announced, interrupting, as was the family habit, the conversation.

'Ah, good,' said Audrey. 'And this' – she turned to the Bentleys – 'is Jeremy's father.'

'We met in the hall,' said the major.

'I am really in your debt. What happened, may I ask?'

For the second time, in more detail, the major told his story, it being one mint julep later.

While apparently listening loyally (so, to her surprise, were the others), Mrs Bentley was absorbing the scene, their clothes and the décor of this strange and exotic establishment. The bar, as Lady Sterling called it, was in fact a sort of orangery, containing even an orange tree, which boasted one small, shrivelled fruit. The floor was tiled in black and pale grey marble and almost tropical plants were dotted around in huge alabaster urns. The heat was definitely becoming too much, but Lady Sterling had explained that it was for the fish who swam in the fountain. (What they must pay in central heating bills!)

They had been introduced by Lady Sterling, but Mrs Bentley had already forgotten who was who. The dark young man was playing some sort of card game with a very fat lady who had been introduced as Henrietta Sterling, but whom everybody else called Tattie. He seemed to be married to a rather sulky-looking girl called Lucy who looked pregnant, had a faint moustache and was a niece of Lord Sterling's. The cool-skinned beautifully dressed girl had just been joined by the big shambly man – another nephew? – who put a hand possessively on her shoulder. When she moved away to light a cigarette Mrs Bentley noticed that she wore no brassière under her jumper. Then there was Sir Arthur Something-or-other – they really must try and remember his name and look him up in *Who's Who*, though their copy was rather an old one. Finally, there was the American, Chuck, who had explained how to make mint juleps and was in charge of the drinks. With the smell of the lilies, the scent of the ladies, the heat and Chuck's cheroot, Mrs Bentley was beginning to feel slightly sick.

'And I must say the boy has guts,' her husband was concluding.

'Guts?' queried the dark young man, not looking up from his cards. 'Down for eight, and that, Tattie, I'm afraid, is a blitz.' He rapidly made some calculation with a large and extremely elaborate tasselled scoring pencil and looked up with a little smile. 'Call it seventeen quid?' (Christ, thought Mrs Bentley.)

'And damn good manners, d'you know,' the major went on. 'He even . . .'

The major was interrupted by a gust of cold air which made them all sit up as if stung. Two more people in golfing shoes stood where a second ago had been a glass wall. One was obviously Lord Sterling, and the other could have been the professional.

'Ezra, come in, shut the door, and take off those awful hobnailed boots.' Audrey gave Mrs Bentley an 'aren't men awful' look. (What a nice woman she is, thought Mrs Bentley.) The younger man pressed a switch and the glass door rolled gently shut.

'I say, automatic,' cried the major before he could stop himself.

'Now the boots,' ordered Audrey.

'I strained my back. Dreadful hook on the third,' complained Lord Sterling. 'Trouble is, I taught him golf and now he beats me.'

'That's all right, I'll take care of it.'

The younger man stopped to undo the Lord's shoes. Ezra advanced across the marble in yellow-stockinged feet and was introduced.

'Mrs Bentley, Major Bentley. The Bentleys have just rescued Jeremy. He fell off his motor bike,' explained Audrey.

'Where did he get a motor bike to fall off of, pray?'

'Don't worry, Ezra, he's all right, and the machine will be removed.' And the Brigadier twirled the keys.

(Poor Jeremy, thought Mrs Bentley. He *will* be disappointed.)

Ezra nodded. 'Quite right. We can't have any more young men taking silly risks.' (Oh dear, of course, remembered Mrs Bentley. Wasn't their only son killed in Palestine by some terrorist?)

'It's very good of you, sir,' said Ezra to the major. 'You must tell us what happened.'

'He has,' muttered the young man, expertly shuffling the cards.

'Over lunch, perhaps,' added Audrey. 'You will stay to lunch?'

Mrs Bentley's heart missed a beat. (Surely Miranda wouldn't mind?) 'It's very kind of you, Lady Sterling, but my sister is expecting us, and as a matter of fact I really should get on the blower and tell her we're going to be late,' said the major. 'I just wanted to have the pleasure of meeting *you*. You see, I've always held Sterlings and I've never sold a share in my life.'

'You'll have done pretty well then, won't you?' said the Lord. 'And I'd advise you to hold on because there'll be another bonus issue – one for two – when I declare the interim next week.'

This, to the major, priceless indiscretion did have an effect, for the two nephews exchanged sharp looks, the dark one paused in mid-deal to say, 'Now he tells us,' while the big one simply opened and shut his mouth.

It was indeed Ezra's policy to make significant statements in casual circumstances; it exercised his upper hand and this Major Bentley did not look the kind of man who would know how to exploit the information. Lord Sterling gave the room his beatific innocent smile.

'Sorry to talk shop. I'd much rather hear about young Jeremy. But perhaps we'd better telephone your sister.' He nodded to little Oscar who pressed a bell.

A second, or was it a third, mint julep commenced to be manufactured.

The family settled in their seats; this time it mattered, Ezra was listening, too.

Grose teetered in and asked the Doctor, 'Oh, sir, is Master Jeremy all right?'

'He'll live, Grose, especially if you get Clark's to pick up his motorcycle.'

'Yes, sir, and . . .?'

'Get rid of it.' Turning to the major, he asked, 'Where exactly is this infernal machine?'

''Bout three miles down the road, right out of the gate.'

'*Right* out of the gate?' queried little Oscar. 'But he was coming from London, wasn't he?'

'Oh, he was lost all right,' said the major, 'blinding on past the house. We all know Turners.'

'You a local man, then?' asked Sir Ezra.

'Very local, church warden and all that.'

'Ah, yes,' sighed Ezra. 'The church . . . Is the spire falling down? They usually are.'

'It hasn't got a spire,' replied the major stoutly. 'It's a round Norman tower, rather unusual in this part of the world. You see plenty of them in Norfolk, but it *has* got the deathwatch beetle.'

'Oh dear,' said Ezra. 'By the way,' he added absently, 'you will leave your name in the visitors' book, won't you? Sorry, I'm interrupting, do go on.'

The major did go on and the story gained in humour with repetition. Mrs Bentley was rather impressed with her husband.

They laughed at Jeremy's bewilderment over the valve exhaust lift, at his delicacy when waiting to pee, and most of all at the description of his uncle – 'rather fond of gadgets'. The story had already passed into the family album.

Ezra turned to the Brigadier. 'What,' he asked suddenly, 'do you plan to give him at Oxford?'

The Brigadier tapped his tummy. 'Well, he has his scholarship.'

'That's all of sixty quid a year,' said David.

The Brigadier had not sensed that there was a distinct pro-Jeremy feeling in the air. 'I think Sarah's arranged five hundred a year.'

'You gave me that before the war,' chimed in little Oscar.

(Phew, thought Mrs Bentley.)

'And some,' muttered Ezra.

Little Oscar blushed.

There was a silence as Ezra was seen to be thinking. 'What would you give him, Major Bentley?'

Mrs Bentley looked at her husband anxiously and in an instant of panic, shivered for her own savings. (What on earth had all this to do with them?)

But if the words were savage the tone of voice was not. Nevertheless it *was* a challenge and the major took a draught of mint julep as if he were going over the top. He did not like the look of Jeremy's father. Brigadier indeed ... probably Ordnance Corps ... Oh no, he'd been an Army quack, hadn't he?

'I would say, Lord Sterling,' and it was nice to feel them hanging on his words, 'that young Jeremy, with a position to keep up, your nephew, after all, would need rather more than that these days.'

Mrs Bentley sighed with relief.

Ezra nodded many times. The man was not such a fool as he looked.

Which is how Jeremy got his thousand a year.

'Steady, dear,' cried Mrs Bentley, as the Morris approached the first set of gates. 'They're not open yet.'

'S'right, Ro. I may be a bit squiffed, but I can still motor, thank you . . . I say, what extraordinary people, terrifying really.'

'I don't know. I thought you put up a very good show.'

'About the boy's allowance? Oh, Lord Sterling was only playing a game. He just likes frightening people. Montgomery was like that. I met him once in the war. He was a bully too, only more conceited.'

'Still, I do wonder why he wanted our address.'

'You'll probably get asked to a hen party, Ro.'

'I don't think so, they don't have much to do with the county.'

Mrs Bentley was right. Three days later, the reasons became plain when a letter arrived for her husband from Lord Sterling's secretary who had been directed to thank Major Bentley for his recent kindness to a member of Lord Sterling's family, and enclosed a covenant in favour of St Mary's Church for £100 for seven years. The Bentleys looked at the document with awe, but later their nephew, an accountant, told them that with his income it would have cost Lord Sterling next to nothing.

A gentle wind was jostling the curtains. It couldn't be his own room at the top of Sarah's house because that had a pitched roof. He remembered holding some keys, the ignition key of his motor bike. Where were they? Jeremy sat up in bed anxiously. Every limb ached and he felt his bandaged knee through a pair of clean pyjamas. He had obviously been cleaned up when he passed out. He tottered out of bed feeling self-indulgently invalid and drew the curtains, realizing too late he should have used the cord intended for that purpose. Below croquet was being played by four men. He recognized David and little Oscar, then Sir Arthur Coleport, Sterlings' goy director, but not the short, slightly hunchbacked tubby man who was smoking a pipe. He opened one of a barrage of fitted cupboards and a light went on to show rows of hangers with clothes draped in cotton sheets like standing ghosts. They were Nicky's clothes. He was in Nicky's room. The clothes set out for him, he presumed by the butler, were labelled wherever possible. The shirt, suit, socks and handkerchiefs bore his initials or name in full and had obviously never been worn by their owner.

They fitted Jeremy so well he felt like an impostor, and as he walked gingerly down the staircase, Audrey, studying a flower arrangement, could not repress a sharp, 'My God,' when she saw him. She met him at the foot of the stairs, kissed him and ruffled his hair.

'Jeremy, I'm sorry. For a second you looked so like Nicky. His clothes really suit you, really you had better save your clothing coupons and take the lot. I can't think why we've kept them all these years. They're all good stuff. Pre-war, you know. Now, don't you think Grose is brilliant at flowers.' Still holding his hand she took him over to the George II console table upon which there was a vast arrangement being pecked at by Grose. 'He's been to a course at Constance Spry.' Grose tittered appreciatively.

'You look much better now, Mr Jeremy, I must say.'

Audrey led him out of the open front door round to the side of the house.

'I say, Audrey, shouldn't I say thank you to those people who picked me up? The Bentleys, weren't they called?'

'My dear boy, that was yesterday. Your father put you right out. He said sleep was what you needed.'

'And,' asked Jeremy anxiously, 'my motor bike?'

Audrey squeezed his hand. 'Be a good boy. Don't mention that now. Not just for the moment.'

But Ezra did, when he saw him. 'Ah,' he said, jumping out of a heavily upholstered hammock, waving the *Financial Times*. 'Look who's here! The family stunt artist.'

At the sound of Ezra's voice the croquet players lowered their mallets and Chuck picked up a champagne cocktail which stood by a hoop and proffered it to him. Tattie gave him a damp cheek and patted his arm with her fat hand, heavy with rings. There was Geoffrey Nickson, whom he had met at Lucy's wedding, and Lucy, of course (oh God, how could David have married her!), and little Oscar and a distant pretty girl introduced by Ezra as his new *shicksa*. The tubby man turned out to be someone in the Government. Everyone was very kind and old Sir Arthur said he could take over his game if he liked. It seemed churlish to worry about the motor bike or how he could get to Oxford.

'I have spoken to the Warden of your college, Jeremy,' said his father, 'a man who claimed to be called Smith, and explained the situation. He told me to tell you that you would need the permission of the Proctors to drive a motor bike.'

'Oh,' said Jeremy. So that was that. Couldn't he have spoken to somebody lower down?

'Never mind, Jeremy,' cried Ezra. 'Drink your cocktail and I'll show you something else. Your father and I have decided on something more appropriate. More in keeping with a young man in your position, as Major Bentley would say.' And he turned his wicked look on to the Doctor.

What now, thought this poor man, have we decided? He didn't approve of the thousand a year and surely they could see that any more largesse would spoil the boy. When he was a medical student ... Ah well, this family never knew when to stop. Their vulgarity, their ... Then he remembered the new grants promised for his Institute. He censored even his own thoughts. Still it would be helpful if Sarah could turn up occasionally. She could deal with Ezra.

'Let's go to the garages and see if we can find something for Jeremy. Who's for a little stroll before luncheon? Is there time for a little stroll before lunch, Audrey?'

'Well, the garages are probably locked, and Jenkins has the keys and Jenkins is having his lunch. But don't you bother, off you go.'

It was more a parade than a stroll, with Ezra pretending he didn't know where the stables were (but Chuck did); two by two, they trotted down the gravel drive. The stables were Edwardian, deep sombre buildings in brick, the colour of dried blood. They were the part of Turners which Jeremy liked best because he remembered as a little boy sliding down a heap of coke used for heating the greenhouses. There was still a faint whiff of hay and horses and a clock which had a beautiful bleak chime which had escaped electrification and still worked from a pair of gigantic weights which were wound up once a week by an ancient groom who bicycled up from the village.

Jenkins, tieless, stumbled into view at a half-trot, panting and wiping his mouth with the back of his hand.

'Mr Grose said you wanted me, my lord.'

'Not really, Jenkins, thank you. Just having a look round. You might open up the doors.'

In the first garage were two black Rolls-Royces, side by side, like Darby and Joan, Ezra's Phantom III and Audrey's more modest 20/25, known as the little Rolls. There was a silence.

'Nothing for you there, Jeremy. They're all ours!'

The tubby politician sucked fiercely at his pipe. 'I think I see now the point of a phrase I heard in Prague last week. "There's nothing like the arrogance of a parked car." '

'Yes, Richard, I suppose some of your lot would like to do away with this sort of thing,' said Ezra.

'Some of our lot are pressing for fairly savage sumptuary laws to deal with this sort of thing.'

'Well, as I said in the House the other day,' said Sir Arthur, 'you can't build an export trade without a healthy home market.'

'Yes, Arthur,' the junior Minister replied, evenly. 'Any moment now you're going to complain about Nye Bevan's silk shirts.'

'Oh, come on,' said Ezra. 'Next one, please, Jenkins.'

The next garage contained an open black and yellow Delahaye and a severe green Humber. Jeremy gaped at the Delahaye.

'We could go for a spin in her after lunch if you like, Jeremy. It's got an electric gear box.'

'Oh, it's yours, is it, Oscar?' said Ezra vaguely. 'Ah, well; on we go.'

Jeremy was relieved that the Bentleys were not around to be included in this expedition. Ezra was behaving like Solomon in all his glory, reviewing his chariots in the underground park at Megiddoh.

Then there was Chuck's overblown Buick with its US licence plates. 'How do you manage for petrol?' asked Ezra crossly. He had an official ration book.

'Surely you've heard of the black market, Ezra? How do you manage for meat?' Chuck drawled.

In the final garage was the house car used for meeting people at the station, and another one covered with a sort of eiderdown.

'I wonder what that can be?' asked Ezra. 'Go and have a look, Jeremy.'

Jenkins coughed. Blushing, Jeremy advanced and, helped by Chuck, uncovered Nicky's brand-new red MG with matching red leather seats. They all walked round it triumphantly.

Jeremy felt suddenly lonely and dizzy but he managed to blurt out, 'It hasn't got any wheels.'

'That's all right, Mr Jeremy. I put it on blocks when . . .'

Ezra interrupted his chauffeur.

'First lesson after lunch in the Delahaye. We'll skip tea,' cried little Oscar.

'Damn the bloody thing! Damn, damn, damn!' In Ezra's eyes were tears of rage, frustration and self-pity as he struggled to construct a bow tie. He kicked the leg of an expensive piece of furniture.

'Don't take it out on my chiffonier, Ezra. There's plenty of time. It looks Empire, doesn't it? But dear Partridge came round the other day and said it was definitely Louis seize.' Audrey's voice floated lightly out of her bedroom. 'Much more interesting, don't you think?'

'Oh, yes, much more interesting,' said Ezra, grinding his teeth.

'Ezra, do be sensible, this happens nearly every night of your life. Why don't you get Grose to do it for you?'

'I don't want that man's hands round my throat,' growled Ezra. 'You come and do it. Why can't you get me one of those clip-on things they have in America?'

'Because they're horrid and it would fall off into your soup at a Pilgrims' dinner. Sit on the stool and wait for me.' Ezra did so, grew impatient, twirled himself around and hummed a silly song.

When Audrey came in she looked beautiful and happy, thought Ezra. She'd been much happier since that policeman had been around. Such a nice man. Why didn't they do something about it? He wouldn't mind. It was such a bore, this permanent brief encounter business, with Nickson not daring to touch and Audrey too correct to encourage. So long as it didn't happen under his own roof; she could go off to Deauville or somewhere, he always enjoyed *himself*.

'Left over right, right over left,' said Audrey, then paused. 'Tell me, Ezra, why did you take Ooh-la-la with you to New York?'

No two people can live together for long without the occasional clear glimpse into each other's minds. Ezra looked up at his wife's reflection in the glass. Thank God she was smiling.

'Who told you?' he asked dully.

'Oh, Ezra, don't be so silly. Everybody knows you have to have somebody . . . to tie your tie and things like that. It's just that she's getting on a bit, and I thought you could have done a bit better, that's all. Look at you,' and she tapped the neatly made bow tie, 'rich, handsome, famous, powerful. Not even very Jewish looking. As my brother David says, really quite *sortable*.'

Ezra said nothing, stood up and opened an almost secret flat drawer under the white marble top of the chiffonier. 'Here, you, read this.'

He handed Audrey a long official envelope from an office in the State Department. It was a tragi-comic little tale. The writer (it was Victor Bridleton) apologized for not being able to send a facsimile of the FBI file on Charles Beauregard Lambkin and also regretted that information on him was not available after 1940 when the subject left the States and volunteered for the British Air Force. (Oh, my God, thought Audrey, it's about Chuck.) Fortunately Hoover owed him a favour and this was a more or less accurate transcription, which was the best he could do.

The subject was born, he said, on the wrong side of the tracks in a one-horse town, St Francisville, Louisiana. 'One horse, one bank, one insurance company, and one crop-spraying company – him.' He had been reported as a matter of routine to the FBI because the second day of his trial (for the rape of a coloured woman) he quit. 'Now, you wouldn't think that was too bad in the South,' wrote Bridleton 'a little raping here and there.' But it seems there had been complications, viz.: (1) The charge was that he had tied the girl to a bed, flogged her and urinated over her. ('Like he brought his crop-spraying into the bedroom,' interjected Ezra's informant, in brackets with a host of exclamation marks.) (2) He owed money all over town. (3) And worst, his own wife 'was a bit of a whore' – not, it was thought, without a little encouragement from the subject himself. 'Do remember, Ez,' he said, 'this all happened during the Depression.'

Audrey had had enough. She put the letter back in the drawer, snapped it shut, and walked into her bedroom.

'Here, where are you going?'

'I'm going to wash my hands. It's ridiculous.'

Ezra walked after her. 'Now what do you think of our Southern gentleman who makes mint juleps the way only grandfather knew how?' He imitated Chuck's drawl, but uneasily.

'You must be very pleased with yourself, Ezra. All that spying . . . Disgusting.'

'Disgusting, you call it?' snorted Ezra. 'I call it disgusting. I call it disgusting that my sister wants me to have as a brother-in-law a pimp, a criminal, as far as we know a bigamist, and a man who's going to tie her to a bed and pee all over her. Apart from stealing all her money – my money!' he shouted.

Lady Sterling dried her hands on a delicate initialled linen towel, there for the purpose but not often used. 'Don't be ridiculous, Ezra, and be quiet. The servants can hear you.'

'I think they'd be very interested to know just what sort of a person they've been valeting and cooking for.' Ezra choked as much with indignation as with the knowledge that he was in a battle which he was about to lose.

'All that was a long time ago, Ezra, when Chuck was a young man, and it's best forgotten, believe me. And don't you forget, Lord Sterling, that if it hadn't been for Chuck and his friends in the American Air Force – he arranged that – your beloved golf course would have been ploughed up and this house would have been requisitioned for an RAF officers' mess or something.'

Ezra groaned. It was true. All those Hershey bars, the nylon stockings, the tinned hamburgers, the little things that had made the war more tolerable – all had stemmed from Chuck, and his American connections, at least in the first place. But that he had to be indebted did not make him regard the man more sweetly. Audrey noticed the thoughtful expression on his face.

'So,' she said, 'I will continue to regard Chuck as an American gentleman from the South who is very kind to my sister-in-law, and I put you on your honour to destroy that letter and never refer to it again, directly or obliquely, in one of your clever little asides. All right? And if you don't give me your promise you're not the man I married and not a man I want to stay married to.'

Ezra looked at her. This was not the reaction he had expected. Audrey had hit him in a place where he was poorly defended – where honour should be.

'But if he married her what about the money, what about all Tattie's shares? He could cause merry hell in the business. You don't know how tightly balanced the whole thing is. I wish my father had had more sense. If Chuck cared to . . .'

'If he cared to, exactly. But he won't . . . nor will Tattie do anything to upset you. She loves you and she's terrified of you. I'm sure she'ld given some of her shares to the children now. Wouldn't that save tax?'

She could give them all, thought Ezra. 'Yes,' he said, 'all right, I promise. You're a good woman, Audrey.'

In reply, Audrey took Ezra's hand and put it to her cheek. 'Thank you,' she said. 'By the way, I've given all of Nicky's clothes to Jeremy. He didn't seem to have any.'

'As long as they fit him.'

'They fit him beautifully. Quite extraordinarily well. I rather like that boy, don't you, Ezra? Sarah does nothing about him, so I suppose we should.'

'He seems a bit soft to me,' said Ezra.

'Oh give him a chance, he's only a baby. Shouldn't I tell Jenkins to take him to Oxford in my little Rolls?'

Ezra thought for a moment.

'No,' he said, 'he can go in mine. And when he gets a license to drive a car, he'll have his own.'

'Ten, eleven, twelve, thirteen,' said Tattie, pointing a beringed finger at the Minister. 'You've made us thirteen!' She looked as if she was about to cry.

'Oh, tush, Tattie,' said Ezra. 'I'm sure you would agree that it is in the national interest that our Right Honourable friend should dine here off black market meat rather than at Chequers?'

'I'm sure nothing we are having tonight is black market,' said The Minister, smoothly, helping himself to more sole Mornay.

'Fish is all right,' said Ezra. 'Partridges anybody can buy.'

'Partridges,' squeaked Tattie. But I'm not allowed game!'

'Don't you worry, honey,' said Chuck, patting her arm. 'I know Audrey will have fixed something special just for you.'

'Roast chicken and lots of lovely bread sauce, and you can have some of our game chips,' butted in Lucy. And as this sally went down rather well, she added spitefully, 'And I'm sure if Aunt Audrey is short of a pig Mother could fix you up, wouldn't you say, Father?'

Lucy, secure with her new husband, her marriage settlement and visibly now pregnant, enjoyed the occasional thrust. The Doctor blinked misunderstandingly at his daughter. He wished she would show more respect. Not for him, he didn't matter – he had more important things to bother about – but for Sarah. That his wife had been having an affair, since he went to the war, with a Danish pig farmer worried him a little, although it was generally known and accepted in the family. Still, it should not be referred to among strangers. There was a silence of the kind that usually follows malicious, unnecessary remarks.

'Did you know,' said little Oscar in his loud voice, 'that there's a Government crisis and Sidney Stanley has sent for the King?'

Everybody laughed except Jeremy who did not read the newspapers. It was a good joke, if a bit late in the day.

'Sidney Stanley,' explained the junior Minister to Jeremy, as the conversation fragmented happily around the table, 'has been convicted of bribing Government officials with modest gifts like a few pounds of sausages. His behaviour at his trial' (he had publicly congratulated his prosecutor, Sir Hartley Shawcross) 'has made him into a national character, if not hero.'

'You can't help admiring the chap. Splendid insolence,' said the policeman.

'Ah, Geoffrey,' said Audrey, 'I think you've got a soft spot for the Jews.'

'Oh, I dunno,' said Geoffrey, smiling secretly into his plate.

7

Of course. It had all gone much too well at Turners, thought

Jeremy, and it was about time something went wrong. Everybody had been very kind – too kind. Little Oscar had actually laughed when Jeremy had driven the Delahaye into an urn, the junior Minister had tried to persuade him to change his school to read PPE, and had showered him with documents and introductions to economics, and everybody had asked him to stay in London. Lucy, Audrey, Tattie and Sir Arthur, especially Sir Arthur, who, squeezing his arm, had pointed out the advantage of Albany – that ladies were not allowed to spend the night. Finally, Sarah, prompted by the Brigadier, had telephoned, only to him, to complain that he had not asked her for money, to make him promise never to ride a motor bike, and to propose herself for a visit, soon, soon, with a friend who would bring a ham.

Until now Jeremy had never really understood what was meant by the prayer they said every night at school, 'Those to whom much is given . . .' His life had been bounded by Kensington, Waterloo Station, whence he went to school, and parental authority in the shape of his nurse Pat. Sarah, once she had acquired him, had given him maintenance, but no care, and the Doctor who had been away in the wars returned with eyes only for his microscope. Occasionally Sarah took him to lunch at the Berkeley with the cheerful red-faced Danish pig farmer, whom he eventually understood to be her boyfriend, whatever that might mean. Once they had all dived under the table at the approach of a doodlebug and a year later at the same hotel, he had been astonished to see how jolly was a group of former Conservative MPs, as they downed martinis at the loss of their seats in the '45 election.

Those had been the highlights with Sarah; more regular and banal were the entertainments in the company of Pat with whom he listened to the wireless and bicycled in the black-out to the cinema for her weekly horror film. He hummed Tchaikovsky's Piano Concerto in B Flat Minor, which was getting very scratchy, dialled TIM, masturbated and daydreamed peaches and Vichy water in the South of France inspired by an article he had read by Cyril Connolly in *Horizon* which described the world of indulgence, warmth and decay which he never thought could be his. At his boarding school – for the fathers of gentlemen – he had read much in no particular order. He enjoyed Chesterton and O. Henry, and when he read Montaigne's mother was Jewish he had bought out of loyalty the Nonesuch edition of his works. On that touchy point, the question of being a Jew, there had really been nothing to report. Although at school the other boys as a matter of principle disliked anything Jewish or foreign, Jeremy's looks and manner were so inoffensive that he was left alone.

But one half-term little Oscar and David, both glitteringly uniformed and armed with a staff car, had come to take him out to lunch. They questioned him about anti-Semitism and he was obliged to answer that he did not know what it meant. When he returned with a 'tenner' – another novelty – in his pocket, Jeremy was astonished to be addressed by a prefect, hitherto friendly, with the words, 'I never knew Jews were allowed to become officers.' With the two beautifully printed £5 notes glowing in his pocket Jeremy just smiled and walked away. (He had, thought the prefect, rather a sweet smile. Pity he was so dull.)

When Jeremy, who had not been any more distinguished in the classroom than on the playing field, won a minor scholarship in Modern Languages to Oxford, there was a flutter of interest among his mentors who had marked him down as an average boy of dubious origin; so his housemaster asked him to dinner. At table, flown, like the devil, with insolence and wine, Jeremy attacked this worthy for an unkind reference to the cowardice of the French in 1940. It was a fashionable theme throughout the war and most schoolboys echoed their parents' prejudices. Also, Jeremy's only friend among the teaching staff was a dry, bony exiled Frenchman who refused to speak English even on their expeditions to local churches which he could date precisely. Further, Jeremy remembered the tears in the eyes of the beautiful Madame Ooh-la-la – the first time he had seen any woman cry – when the BBC played the *Marseillaise*, having announced the liberation of Paris. He alone at Turners had spotted her emotion and he alone had been rewarded with a squeeze from her soft hand and an even softer look from her eyes. 'Oh, *tu es trop sensible, mon petit. Tu vas souffrir.*' So Jeremy was passionately, adolescently, pro-French. That this fool should trample on such an exquisite memory prompted his hysterical and as Mrs Housemaster remarked after he had left, rather 'unEnglish' outburst.

Jeremy refused to apologize, left the table and was sick in his study. It all shows, Mrs Housemaster further remarked, what a good rule it was never to discuss politics over the dinner table. Jeremy went home prematurely, before the end of term, and in a first-class carriage – *de rigueur* in the family, even for small boys – he brooded about his revenge. He decided on a lavish case of wine for the housemaster in return for a book he had been given, on fishing in the Wye valley – the housemaster's rather than Jeremy's main interest in life – and in Bumpus he bought the most expensive book he could find on French architecture, for the bony Frenchman. Sarah was interested to notice these two items on her accounts and told him that it was about time he had some money of his own. Which is how he had got £500 a year.

No, his life up to now had been smooth enough. But now this agony . . .

'Are you sure there isn't another entrance?' asked Jeremy anxiously as the great car edged its way through a crowd of under-graduates. God, what a crazy time to arrive. Twelve o'clock – they must all have been at their lectures. His heart was pounding with fright. While not actually hostile in their glances, they were not friendly, these hairy duffle-coated fellows: the worst were the ones who affected not to notice Jeremy, the chauffeur, the Phantom III and the large tin trunk on the grid stencilled 'The Hon. N. Sterling'.

'It did say New College Lane,' said Jenkins, a little panic entering his voice too. (Chauffeurs are not a brave race.) There was only one place to station the car without blocking the medieval lane and that was in front of the college gate, which meant almost obliterating the *porte-cochère*. Jenkins, in trying to get out, caught his leg on the gear handle and accidentally touched the horn. The Rolls emitted an imperious *peep* – God, groaned Jeremy, now actually trembling – and a figure emerged with a what's-all-this-about look on his face. His expression changed when he saw the car, at which he nodded approvingly, then to Jeremy.

'You must be Mr Kind, sir. My name's Parrot, chief scout. You can tell your man, sir, to pull her up in here, for the moment. I'll get this thing unlocked.'

Mr Parrot prided himself on recognizing a young gentleman when he saw one. There weren't too many around, not like before the war.

'You're late, very late,' said a high-pitched voice behind him.

'I'm sorry, sir, I . . .' Jeremy turned to see a young man dressed, under his scholar's gown, differently from the others, in a suit, waistcoat, pebble spectacles, cigarette holder, and beautifully made neat, small shoes.

'My God, dear boy,' smiting his forehead, 'you must never call *anybody* "sir". It gives them ideas. One calls the Warden, Warden; the Dean, Dean; the Bursar, Bursar; and Bishops, especially Bishops! – they must firmly be called Bishop. You were saying . . .'

The car had moved under the gatehouse and had settled as part of the scenery. The undergraduates were moving around in a more friendly way, Jeremy imagined, while the chief scout and Jenkins manhandled the late lamented Nicky's tin box on to a trolley. Jeremy felt lonely.

'You were saying?' repeated his new friend.

'Ah, yes, the thing is I fell off my bike and had to go to bed and that sort of thing . . .'

'I can't see why you bother with a bicycle when you have that around,' pointing to the Rolls.

'It was a motor bike,' replied Jeremy, 'and that's not mine.'

'I didn't imagine that it was,' said the new friend, 'but your people are rich. I mean, aren't they?' He sounded concerned. 'I mean, where did you go to school?'

Jeremy mentioned the name of the modest establishment which had bored and boarded him for four years.

'Ah, well,' sighed the new friend, 'I dare say it was quite comfortable. D'you get an allowance? You don't look as if you're up here on grant. I have a few hundred from my family, and £100 from the college for my scholarship, but I don't tell anybody about my private income, otherwise they'd cut down on my grant. I was in the Intelligence Corps. I speak Russian, you know. There was a lovely sergeant, he was bliss, we just crooned *Eugene Onegin* together all day long.' He gave a huge theatrical sigh. 'Did you do your military service?'

One confidence deserved another, felt Jeremy. His new friend was, after all, his first friend, and possibly the only person he knew at the university. He was, if absurd, very funny and possibly rather nice.

'Yes, but only for three days.'

'How exciting!' The new friend clapped his hands. 'But you won't get much of a grant after that.'

'No, but my father gives me a . . .' Jeremy broke off to talk to Jenkins who was hovering nearby, but the new friend thought he was going to say 'a thousand a year' and decided that was the figure to be circulated.

'I'll take Mr Kind to his rooms, if you don't mind, sir,' interrupted the chief scout. 'He's in pre-fab B.'

'Oh, Mr Parrot, how could they?' The new friend clapped his hands, this time in grief.

Jeremy glanced from one to the other. Mr Parrot did indeed look uncomfortable.

'Well, it's nothing to do with us, Mr Yoville. You should go and complain to the Bursar's office, but you won't get very far, I assure you. The college is full up and Mr Kind did arrive after the beginning of term.'

'Oh, that naughty Bursar, he should be spanked,' screeched the new friend, and then in a matter-of-fact voice to Jeremy, 'The trouble is I can't be seen dead anywhere near those ghastly constructions, so you can come and have a drink with me before hall, say quarter to one? You'll have to eat in hall your first day, otherwise they'll get upset. It's 4B, front quad, and don't take any notice of the oak being sported, it's just to keep 'em out. My name's Christopher,' and he extended his hand like a cardinal.

Jeremy held it for a moment, then the new friend fluttered off, stopped in his tracks, turned and yelled to Jeremy as if he were a hundred yards away, 'And don't forget to wear a tie.'

'Very popular gentleman with the scouts is Mr Yoville,' said Mr Parrot soothingly, as he piloted Jeremy to his quarters, 'always so polite.'

In 1945 Oxford colleges had decided either to accommodate the grant-aided ex-servicemen returning from the wars, or to ignore them and stick to their old ways, allowing each young gentleman a set of rooms and a servant or scout to each staircase. New College compromised and put up two prefabricated huts – they had to be called A and B. B had a good view of A and vice versa. Jeremy looked through the outside window, and stood desolate at the sight of his room which had the kind of walls you can't pin anything on and the kind of wardrobe cupboard which falls over if you try and open it. Worse, his scout was Queenie, a leathery short-sighted slut, who managed a smile without altering the position of the cigarette on her upper lip, when presented to him by Mr Parrot.

'Oh, what a luverly thing,' said Queenie when she saw the tin trunk. 'What's that "Hon." for?'

Jeremy, slight and mournful in his Harrods suit, had decided that if he had to lie down in this hut at bedtime, his spiritual home would have to be elsewhere, and his expression showed this.

When the trunk was inside and Parrot had withdrawn, Queenie stood appreciatively in the middle of the little room, the ash of her cigarette about to fall off. It did.

'It's not much, is it, but then you could brighten it up. You could have one half pink, and the other half green, say ...'

'Like an ice cream?' asked Jeremy.

'That's right, luv. Something cheerful. Now is the time for follies. Ta ta for now.'

That was rather neat, thought Jeremy, coming from a char; he must tell Christopher whom he could not wait to see again. It was half past twelve; an alarmingly close college clock, detonating other clangings, told him so. Jeremy wondered how early he could decently arrive at 4B, or indeed, whether it would be more correct to arrive late. Christopher was obviously attached to the minutiae of social behaviour. And, my God, what about the tie? He opened his cousin's tin trunk, and there were his cousin's virgin clothes, so immaculately packed that it was a shame to disturb them, but he had to find a tie. There they were: a dozen Harrods ties from the young men's department, the sort a nanny would choose; well, a nanny had probably chosen them, thought Jeremy, lovingly and pointlessly. He decided to walk in the direction of staircase 4B, stopping by at that memorial in the ante-chapel to the German prince who, coming from a foreign country, nevertheless entered into the inheritance of this place, returned, fought against England

and died. It reminded him vaguely of Nicky to whose death, it was now clear, he owed so much.

Jeremy prised open the heavy outer door of 4B, the oak he supposed, and knocked at the inner.

'Don't knock, my dear, just come in. One only knocks at bed-rooms,' piped the new friend.

What Jeremy saw – barely, because the room, with shuttered windows and curtains drawn, was lit only by two enormous church candles and an androgynous lamp – made him think the remark unkind, if not unwise, for Christopher was dancing with another young man, albeit chastely, to the tune of *La Vie en rose*. Jeremy had never seen men dance together and was not sure that they should, did, or even could.

'Give yourself a glass of champagne, my dear, and when the record comes to an end, put it back to the beginning. This is Sergei, by the way.'

The other one waved a pale hand and the foxtrot continued. Jeremy could now see that the ordinary college furniture had been covered with damask and altar cloths, and upon this had been placed innumerable upturned china hands, obelisks and broken classical statues. A marble-topped chess table supported a bottle of cham-pagne and three rather ordinary tumblers, and he was aware of an odd incensey smell, coming from some contraption smoking above the light bulb in the androgynous lamp. Jeremy was about to take a sip from the none-too-clean tumbler when a noise like a pack of hounds descending from the floor above made him hesitate.

'Hide the champagne,' hissed Sergei.

'It's too late. My God, we are undone,' squeaked Christopher. They looked so stricken, Jeremy thought it was the University Police or whatever, after all men weren't allowed to dance together (were they?).

'It's the Fertilizer with his essay, no doubt. Don't stand too close, he'll drown you.'

A turbulent young man with the head and chest of a bull roared into the room.

'Why do you two have to camp around in this Stygian gloom?'

They were all silent. Jeremy noticed that a certain frothiness had accompanied the word 'Stygian'.

'I need your advice about a word, just one word, the last one, actually,' said the Fertilizer.

'Does that mean we have to listen to the whole thing?' asked Christopher.

'Yes,' added Sergei, 'we are both feeling rather frail.' He performed a little *entrechat*, 'and even if you have no consideration for our feelings, you might think of our friend,' and he nodded in Jeremy's direction, 'who has travelled far.'

Jeremy noticed that Sergei's speech was precise, like that of a foreigner who had mastered the language, and that he enunciated every syllable of 'consideration' like a choirboy.

'I had only intended to offer you the coda, as it were, of the last movement.' The young man did not look at Jeremy. 'The whole work is called "When the Cathedrals Were White".' He sniffed.

'But isn't that Le Corbusier?' suggested Jeremy.

'It was Corbusier's, it is now mine. And, incidentally, I find it improper that the first remark you should address to me is in the form of, as it were, a rebuke – even if you did arrive in the largest motor car invented by Mammon.'

Jeremy blushed and buried his face in the tumbler of warm champagne. He prayed he would soon be able to join in their word games, but, in the meantime, what a horrid man!

'Oh, do get on with it, Ferty,' said Christopher.

Silently, Ferty removed the shade and the contraption from the lamp, stopped the record, sat down and put on his spectacles and began to read while both Sergei and Christopher moaned and covered their faces with their hands.

'Extract from "When the Cathedrals Were White" by Prince Furstenburg,' he intoned. 'We have been fed the splendours of the Middle Ages, let us consider finally the miseries. The medieval monarch is on his unsprung throne with pyorrhoea and a raging toothache. When that abates there is the constant throb of pain of a gangrenous wound in the left leg, pain which would vanish in a few days if only he had access to an item standard in every modern household – a bottle of Listerine. The palace is draughty and stinks from the defecation of elderly dogs which nobody knows how to put down. His only consolation in life is an occasional apricot which right now his eldest son, a deformed sadist who would have been institutionalized at birth in any sensible society, is plotting to poison with the connivance of his aunt, a rich lady to whom he is hideously in debt. Contrast this with a typical scene from modern life: the stockbroker in a first-class compartment on the 9.22 from Lewes. He pats his tummy which gives a grateful rumble as indeed it might, for by medieval standards, his breakfast has been a tiny banquet whose elements have been culled from the far corners of the earth. He extracts from his gold cigarette case an Abdulla number 11.

'As if by magic a discreet flame emerges from his gold Dunhill lighter and he inhales luxuriously. He is conscious of the admiring gaze of the bidet-fresh young woman as he unfolds the *Financial Times* and applies himself to the crossword. The Middle Ages had no glories to compare with these. . . .'

Ferty looked up at his audience which was beginning to grow restless. He put up a huge hand, stood up, strode dramatically to the window and flung open the curtains and rattled back the shutters. Christopher and Sergei pressed their hands more firmly to their eyes.

'Did I hear somebody whisper "Cathedrals"?' he boomed. 'Those dirty and expensive monuments to man's vanity and God's greed. Those vulgar cocktail bars which serve indigestible biccys and perfectly filthy wine from Wandsworth. Far better the stern beauty of Battersea power station – if one has to be on the wrong side of the river – "*um Dessen Glut du mich beneidest*" (that'll shake the old fart, he only speaks medieval German), and as for the fabric and the inventory, why we should ship them off to America and spend the money on . . .' He paused, and added in a normal voice, 'C'mon, wake up, it's all over. This is where I need your advice – spend the money on what?'

Sergei and Christopher gingerly uncovered their eyes.

'Steam engines?' said Christopher. 'Did you know that Ronald Firbank adored his grandfather who built those beautiful bridges?'

'Picnics? Spend the money on picnics,' said Sergei.

'No, no, it doesn't go. It has to be a monosyllable. And spend the money on . . .'

'Gin?' suggested Jeremy.

'What did you say?' The Fertilizer looked at Jeremy with new eyes.

'And spend the money on, pause, "gin",' repeated Jeremy.

'Brilliant. My God, you're a genius,' said the Fertilizer, showering Jeremy with spit. 'I'll put you in my column – I do the gossip for the *Cherwell*, you know. But you'll have to do something about his clothes,' he said, turning to Christopher. 'Where, for instance, did he get that?' pointing to Jeremy's suit.

'Harrods, I should think,' obliged Christopher.

'That's absurd,' said Ferty. 'One only goes to Harrods to be buried or for smoked salmon. Anyway, I'm off – vastly obliged to you, sir,' he bowed to Jeremy. 'You'll be all right. You're in bad hands. *Au revoir.*' And he shot out of the door repeating, ' "And spend the money on, pause, gin." '

'Is he really a prince?' asked Jeremy.

'Oh, only an Austrian prince,' said Christopher a little crossly. 'He certainly liked you. He'll probably give you one of his tatty house orders. Thank God he didn't notice the bubbly. We might as well finish it off,' he said gloomily. 'We've missed hall.'

'I wonder,' said Jeremy, 'if you'd allow me to take you out to lunch?'

'Oh, bliss!' Christopher clapped his hands. 'Whites.'

'The Randolph,' countered Sergei.

'No, Whites,' insisted Christopher. 'Then we can peep into the bottom bar at all those delicious American airmen. Come on,' and he threw off his scholar's gown and led Sergei out into the quad.

Jeremy followed in their wake, slightly shocked, terribly excited, and utterly happy at the prospect of the next three years.

PART THREE

1956

'Can't you sit down?' said Ezra.

'I'd rather not if you don't mind, Uncle,' replied little Oscar, 'not just for the moment.'

It had to be something serious with little Oscar standing there like a great sheepdog and calling him 'Uncle'.

'What is it now? Not another bastard?' He spoke as if it happened every day. 'After all, you are engaged and Sandra's only been gone a week or so.'

'Well, quite, Uncle. You see with Sandra away I get bored and depressed and I don't feel like . . .'

There was a buzz.

'No more calls for the moment, please, Mrs Winterbourne,' said Ezra.

'Just as you please, Lord Sterling.' Mrs Winterbourne's tired upper-class voice faded into the thin air.

'And so?' asked Ezra, as he was disconnected with his finger still resting on the button.

'I've been gambling . . .'

'And?'

'About twenty thousand the wrong way.'

'Huh.' Ezra was quite impressed. 'How'd you manage that here, in England. I didn't think it was legal.'

'It isn't, but everybody does it. A different house every night – this was in Ascot – plenty of stuff to eat and drink, champagne and caviar, you know, then chemmy . . . John Aspinall gives the best parties. It's all straight and he sees that everybody pays.'

'How, pray, is he going to arrange that *you* pay?'

Little Oscar managed a sheepish grin and he didn't repeat what 'Aspers' had said to him when totting up his IOUs: 'Give my regards to the Viscount and tell him I'll fix up a game at his place whenever he likes.'

'And what do you mean, "everybody" plays? Does David play for instance? I bet he doesn't.'

'*I* bet he doesn't,' said little Oscar. The thought of David Blacker cosily begetting heirs – there were now two in Tite Street – was a bit much at this moment.

Ezra looked at his nephew. They both had the same thought.

'And how's the girl friend, how's that going? You are engaged, aren't you? It's about time you settled down. You need somewhere to hang your hat!' He thumped the table amiably. 'And for God's sake, sit down, Oscar, you make me nervous. In fact . . .' He paused, frowned thoughtfully, stood up and said, pushing the humidor across the table, 'Here, you have one of these while I go and have a crap.'

There was nothing for it but to wait, and what a place to be alone in! Ezra's board room – for it was very much his: he had an office of his own but he never used it – was cold and charmless. The board room table was big and bare and on it there were no papers, not even a copy of *The Economist* or *Fortune* which sat unread, except at times like this, thought Oscar, on or near many a board room table. The room was dominated, if a small painting could do this, by a portrait of big Oscar in the uniform of a sapper officer, painted in the field when he had been commissioned at Arras in 1917. Of course – the thought suddenly struck him – of course Ezra used this room as his own because it meant that at board meetings they were not directors, they were people coming to see him, Ezra, in his room. Ezra, the chairman, the uncle of them all, and damnit, the great-uncle. Why should he wait in this dreary room while the bloody old tyrant sat with his cigar straining at the loo? It was his money, wasn't it? If he felt like losing £20,000 at cards, why shouldn't he? He could afford it. He only had to sell some shares – *his* shares, nothing to do with Ezra, they had come to him via his mother who had been left them by Grandfather. Little Oscar stood and bowed in Muslim fashion to the menacing little portrait. He then put out his tongue, said 'Yah boo!' and felt much better, like someone who has been longing to kick a dog but has to wait till its owner is out of the room.

He rubbed his chin and thought he had discovered a spot. He had. At his age, how tiresome. Too much of John Aspinall's brandy and not enough of Sandra; why couldn't the silly girl come back? If she didn't want to marry him she didn't have to; he just wanted *her*. Marriage and marriage settlements – that had not been his idea. My God, it was René! From the very first moment it was René. He had introduced them and *he* had started the rumours about engagements. If only Ezra knew that! For his dislike of René Shalom had not melted over the years; he called him now 'that pederast *and* collaborator'. (Which was not quite fair because all René had done in the war was to fudge a Swiss passport and invite the local gauleiter for dinner and chess once a week in his apartment in the Avenue Matignon. It had been enough for the victorious Resistance to have locked him up with a lot of whores for a few terrible weeks.)

Oscar had been spending the weekend at the Lotti with some girl – my God, he couldn't even remember her name – when René telephoned to ask him to a surprise party on Sunday morning.

'What's so surprising about it if you tell me now?' he remembered asking.

'Oh, that's just what everybody calls them now,' said René. 'But the point is, *chéri, j'ai trouvé un bon shiddach pour toi!*'

'A what?' cried Oscar.

René's appalling home-made French, his Yiddish which was probably as bad, Oscar didn't know, *and* the antique telephones retained by the Lotti made communication difficult.

'*Un mariage . . .*' persisted René.

'Why, for God's sake? *Pourquoi?*'

'*Parce que,*' René leant on every syllable, '*elle est très riche. Le père* is not *grand*, but the mother, my God, *elle est excessivement riche!*' He paused and Oscar sensed that there had been made an extravagant gesture at the other end of the line.

'She was born Lehmann or Schiff or something. Anyway, she's the fourteenth richest woman in the world and *très hochgeborene*.

Banks. New York. A sort of Jewish WASP, you know?'

'Is she pretty?'

At this word, the French girl lying beside him opened one eye, winked gently, detached from a certain part of her anatomy which Oscar had been not so absently tickling, his large hand, turned over and sighed like a contented heifer.

'The mother? No, of course you mean the daughter? Yes,' said René in a less certain voice, 'very pretty. She's had her nose done. But one thing, little Oscar, *chéri*, don't go at it too hard; she's very frightened of men, and very suspicious. She's just divorced her first husband – *un maquereau*.'

'A what?'

'A *gonef*, a thief, and apparently it cost her a fortune. He was an Israeli pilot,' added René as if that explained everything.

René's instincts may have been sound, but his judgement was not. He, Oscar, had not 'gone at it' too hard, but Sandra, wow! *There* was a girl used to getting what she wanted and what she had wanted that afternoon was him. Oscar found himself in *her* bed, in *her* suite, in *her* hotel awash with the delicious and, for him, little Oscar, the great spender, totally new sensation of being a kept man.

'Maybe I'll marry you,' Sandra had said when he got out of her bed to go, as she always put it, 'to the bathroom', and as he lumbered naked in that direction she had called out after him, 'The trouble is I'm so stinking rich. Have you got any money at *all?*'

He was still smiling when Ezra entered the board room carrying a heavy leather-bound ledger. Good, thought Oscar, he can't have spent all that time on the loo and he's brought the family Bible.

'Well, you can go on smiling. You know what this is?'

Oscar nodded. It was a list of the stockholders of A (voting) shares in the business. Apart from the 'outside' directors like Sir Arthur and Wilson who had a few for form's sake, the Pension Fund (trustees: Ezra, Wilson and a sly but docile earl), and Chaimy who, as a cousin of Ezra's mother, ranked vaguely as 'family', and anyway gave all the income to the Sterling Charity (another shareholder), all these A (voting) shares were held by Ezra's immediate family – which gave him in practice, though not in theory, absolute control of the business.

It was not a system which endeared Ezra to the City nor, as his friend Poll MP had warned him, to the Labour Party. But they were not in office and since it was agreed in City circles that Ezra ran a 'tight' ship with 'cheap' management – his rich nephews – no one had seriously tried to rock it, especially as there were regular bonus issues, flowing, as Ezra put it, like honey out of the rock.

Little Oscar had seen the Bible only once before, in 1948 when he had been given shares in compensation for David's marriage settlement, and knew its presence now boded well for him. Like the Chinese unicorn, it only appeared when benevolent kings were on the throne.

Ezra sat down with a cheerful sigh and opened the ledger. 'Now, where do we go for honey?' he mumbled and then in a tuneless voice hummed, ' "and with honey out of the rock would I satisfy thee." Always liked that psalm, Wednesday's psalm. No, not Wednesday's – that's a good one, too. Do you know that, little Oscar?'

Oscar shook his head.

' "Ye fools, when will ye be wise," ' intoned Ezra. 'Wait a minute. Ah, yes, "he that planted the ear, shall he not hear? He that formed the eye, shall he not see?" And,' said Ezra, patting Oscar's knee, 'once upon a time I could say that in Hebrew. You didn't know that, did you?'

Little Oscar believed that, in fact, he did; that, taking advantage of the child's tender years and the early death of his firmly irreligious parents – Ezra's mother had been both a suffragette and a follower of Marie Stopes – old Uncle Ephie had slid a rabbi into the household to instruct young Ezra once a week. Now, thinking only what a good mood the old boy was in, Oscar merely shook his head obligingly.

'Trouble is,' said Ezra, staring at the ledger, 'I'm going blind and that fellow Wilson has such mean little writing. Ask Winterbourne for my new reading glasses, will you?' And he jerked his head towards the machine by his usual seat at the top of the table.

Little Oscar did as he was told and the weary voice of Mrs Winterbourne drifted into the board room: 'Tell Lord Sterling to look in the left-hand pocket of his jacket.'

'Ah,' said Ezra, 'now, here we are: Sterling, Henrietta Esther Ruth, Miss.' He looked at his nephew. 'Now, who would you say had the most shares of the family?'

'I s'pose you and Audrey, surely?'

'Surely nothing.'

'But . . .' Oscar made an expansive, querying gesture intended to take in Ezra's *train de vie*, the cars, the servants, the contents of the flat and Turners, and the golf course. Who had a private golf course any more, for heaven's sake?

Ezra took his point. 'One,' he said, stabbing at Oscar with his finger, 'Audrey didn't come to me with nothing, you know. Lots of nice Sephardic City gold your aunt brought me, and without, in the Depression . . .' He pointed to the floor dramatically. 'B,' he continued (it was a trick of his to change classifications in midstream), 'if you think I pay for Turners . . . well, I don't; the Exchequer pays for it! Have you heard of a little company called Sterling Recreations? It's for the benefit of the staff. It has a golf course, which I play on like any other employee, and it's going to have a swimming pool, you know, behind the tennis courts – which it also owns, now I come to think of it. That's how I manage, my boy, by cheating the taxman. All very undignified, but, as you would say, everybody does it – a stratagem now necessary to life, at least to my life.'

'Why don't you have a farm then?' put in little Oscar.

'Why don't *I* have a farm? I should have a farm,' said Ezra in his Yiddish voice.

'Certainly, and for the same reason – tax! I met a man at the Club the other day who told me half the farm vehicles in the home counties are Bentleys. He said anybody with more than twenty thousand pounds a year was crazy not to be a farmer.'

'What club?' interrupted Ezra suspiciously.

Little Oscar had just been elected to the St James's Club and had been searching for a way to introduce that happy event into his conversation. As St James himself, who had engineered the operation, had put it, 'They don't want too many Jews in the Club of course, but even the Committee are beginning to realize that there are Jews and Jews. They'd run a mile from Ezra, for instance

– even though he is quite *sortable*, but you're a different matter. You went to a *reasonable* school' (St James himself had been the second generation of old Etonian Mendozas) 'and you had a good war in a *reasonable* regiment, and' – he shrugged – 'I'll get old Frank Goldsmith – everybody loves him and knows he's a Jew – to propose you and somebody else who isn't, to second.'

Little Oscar gave Ezra an edited version of his election to the Club, concluding with a brief description of the pleasures of its cold table.

'There's only one club worth belonging to in this town, my boy, and that's mine – the House of Lords. And nobody goes there for the food.' Ezra sniffed. 'By the way, they're transferring eighteen thousand to your account now.'

'But . . .' little Oscar started to protest; it was a typical hand-out from the 'dole' – £2,000 less than was needed.

'I know, I know, I know,' said Ezra sharply. 'You just wanted to sell some of your *own* shares, but you can't. You can borrow the rest from the bank.' Ezra smiled to himself. He had spoken to Jolly Jack Webster's successor and told him to be a little awkward over the loan, but that little Oscar must not sell shares on any account.

He put on his spectacles and peered at the entry before him once again. 'Now, as I was saying before you interrupted me with all that farm talk, the largest single shareholding is . . . Wait a minute.' Ezra took off his spectacles and looked at his nephew. 'Geoffrey could always run it. He looks like a farmer, doesn't he? Give him something to do.' Much as he liked the likeable Geoffrey Nickson, who ran the personnel side of the business with extreme fairness and efficiency, he always considered that department was a postwar gimmick designed to reduce his, Ezra's, prerogatives. They needed a weaker man in that job.

'And nice for Audrey, too,' said little Oscar obligingly, who had seen straight through that one.

'Exactly,' murmured Ezra, who had put his spectacles back on again. 'Here we go. Sterling, Henrietta, etc.' His paper slid along the ledger to the final column. 'Two million . . . two million and er . . . thirteen thousand, four hundred and eighty-three!'

Little Oscar, concentrating on the two million, made a very quick calculation indeed.

'Jesus Christ!' he said.

'Exactly,' said Ezra again and quietly, reverently closed the family Bible and began pacing the room, apparently deep in thought.

'Oscar.' He stopped suddenly.

'Yes?'

'Say something!'

'I was only wondering if Aunt Tattie knew –' he hesitated – 'just how much she's got?'

'Of course she knows,' replied Ezra irritably. 'She didn't before the war; well, *well* before the war when she was, er, ill. And that's of course why she *has* got so much. It went on piling up, year after year, and she never had to spend a penny. But she's a good girl, pays a mountain in tax, lives off her bonus shares, as we all do,' (*I* don't, thought little Oscar, bitterly) 'and would never do anything, er, serious, without asking me.'

'Like getting married, for instance?'

Ezra stared dreamily at his nephew. 'Like getting married,' he repeated slowly. 'Tell me,' he said in a different voice, 'this gambling party you went to – did Chuck take you? Was he there?'

'No, Ezra,' replied little Oscar, 'I managed to get there by myself, and though Chuck does gamble, as you know, he's not really up to Aspinall's standards, and anyway, he's on the other side of the shoe, as it were.'

'He runs an illegal gambling establishment, you mean?' asked Ezra quickly.

Little Oscar replied with half a wince, half a shrug, 'Well . . . sort of.'

'Not the kind of chap to whom one could confidently entrust the disposition of two million-odd shares in the business, eh?' Ezra was beginning to shout.

Little Oscar looked round the board room; it contained nothing breakable. He certainly should breed bulls, he thought, as his uncle glared down at him, tapping the ledger to make his point. 'I suppose not,' he said.

'But on the other hand, if your proposed *mishpochim*, those stiff-necked, circumcised, high and mighty . . .' He faltered. 'Miss Sandra Katz!'

'It's nothing to do with Sandra,' cried little Oscar angrily. 'She doesn't give a damn how much money I have; it's her mother. She's terrified of her mother!'

'All right then, I'm sorry,' said Ezra gently, and he put his hands on little Oscar's shoulders. 'If the mother knew her daughter was marrying a Sterling millionaire . . .' He laughed.

'It's not just that.' Little Oscar wriggled irritably. 'She doesn't like the idea of Sandra living in Europe either.'

'Surely she doesn't expect her son-in-law to live in America? When he has such a substantial stake in a substantial business which he must protect for her *grandchildren*? God forbid,' added Ezra. 'Any Jewish grandmother would understand that!'

Little Oscar thought of Sandra's mother doing the Twist at the Copacabana.

'She's not going to *be* any Jewish grandmother,' he said.

There was a silence. Ezra had clearly moved on.

'So,' he said, as if the discussion had ended satisfactorily, 'there is no longer any reason why I should continue to oppose my sister's desire for married bliss, with whoever she likes, provided the right settlements are made.'

The egg which Ezra had brooded over for so long had hatched a chick which already had the characteristics of a bird of prey.

'Wait a minute. We don't have to raid poor old Tattie's larder,' said the younger man, 'do we?'

'Here, thank you, here, thank you and half a mo', Miss Sterling. I'm afraid there's one more – thank you. Now, if you'd just witness Miss Sterling's signature on these documents . . .' The articled clerk had turned to the unarticled clerk. 'And you'll receive the insurance proposal in a day or two, so you can sign that as well.'

'I suppose there'll be enough to make a settlement on my husband?' Tattie had asked her brother, but Ezra indicated with a languid movement of his head that the articled clerk should reply. That worthy man cleared his throat.

'I would say that even after this . . .' He had been about to say 'generous' but something in Lord Sterling's face, which seemed to stop a foot or so short of his own face, made him change his mind.

'After this, er, settlement, Miss Sterling remains a wealthy woman.'

Ezra smiled. The whole operation had taken three minutes.

'And here are your copies, Miss Sterling.' The unarticled clerk, the fourth member of the party, spoke for the first time.

Tattie looked mournfully at the enormous envelope. It would clearly not fit even into *her* handbag.

'I don't think Miss Sterling needs that,' said Ezra easily. 'You can look after them for her, can't you?'

'Yes,' said the young man, somewhat rebuffed, 'and if Miss Sterling does need anything for reference we can always put a copy in the post.'

Ezra was no longer listening, but that is exactly what the young man did.

2

How irregular liaisons begin, with chance encounters at parties (whose, one forgets), is not as curious as how they endure. Chuck and Tattie had been 'friendly' as Sarah put it, for years, since the beginning of the war, and, as everybody in the family constantly agreed, it had worked out very well. Nobody in the family or its circle could think of anything to say against Chuck. He blocked nobody, threatened nobody, he intrigued against nobody and he did not manipulate Tattie or her money. Not even the interior decorators could think of anything too disagreeable to say about Chuck. He met them all – osteopaths, actors (resting and restless), antique dealers, dressmakers and masseurs – with a warm smile, which seemed real, and a drink.

It was not quite clear, apart from off Tattie, *how* he lived. There was a *garçonnière* in Dunraven Street, a modest but handy part of Mayfair behind Park Lane, which no one (in the family) had seen, and there was some sort of faintly shady club in Shepherd Market to which he had been, albeit modestly, staked. But no one could, or did, say that he took Tattie for a ride.

'He costs her less than a butler and a chauffeur, and he's better

at it than ours,' David Blacker once remarked to his wife Lucy,
who replied, untypically:

'Yes, and such a nice man ... I wonder if they ever "do it"
together?'

'God, Lucy, is that all you ever think of? Eva Krapf told me it
was medically impossible,' and he rolled over and went to sleep.

Tattie's maintenance of Chuck was indeed not lavish by family
standards. There was the rent of his little flat – it would not be
proper for them to live under the same roof, his clothes, possibly,
and cufflinks or lighters from Van Cleef & Arpels or Cartier at
Christmas and birthdays, certainly; supper parties at the Savoy and
the box at Ascot and Covent Garden – but then somebody had to
escort her – and, finally, three meals a day.

The first of these meals was breakfast. Since the one thing Tattie
found unbearable in Chuck was his absence, it had been their habit
to enjoy it together. It was the part of the day Tattie liked best
because then she felt like a married woman. They had the same
breakfast: freshly squeezed orange juice, cornflakes and thick
cream, a couple of lightly boiled eggs or an omelette, croissants,
butter, Swiss black cherry jam and coffee from a French per-
colator. Once Chuck had bought her a waffle iron, but this experi-
ment had been abandoned as the cook could not work it.

Chuck was on parade every morning at half-past nine, having
walked round to Tattie's apartment building from his own little
flat. He would take off his alpaca overcoat and his jacket in the
cloakroom and replace them with a heavy deep blue silk dressing
gown from Sulka which Tattie had provided, pick up the mail from
the big Louis XV boule secretaire in the hall – its twin was said to
be in the Louvre – walk down a corridor lined with eighteenth-
century French glass paintings of the four seasons, into Tattie's
bedroom, where she would be lying impatiently in her enormous
bed, peck her plump and scented cheek, give her a magazine to
look at and settle down in a far corner to digest Tattie's mail and
his breakfast.

She always said, although he was always on time, 'Ah, there you
are, dear!' and then, with a kind of cluck of pleasure, 'Go and eat
your breakfast. It's ready for you.' Then, and only then, she would

tuck into her croissants and her magazine. This morning it was the French edition of *Vogue*.

Tattie shared the family aversion for correspondence, incoming or outgoing, and it had become the custom for Chuck to read out any interesting snippet before settling down to the serious business of the day – racing. At ten o'clock Miss Attlee would collect the post, which she could usually dispose of without troubling her employer, and receive from Chuck and Tattie jointly the instructions for the day.

Opening the mail was normally more of a chore than a privilege. From Chuck no secrets were hid but then, normally, there were none to be had. In his mind he made three categories – 'bills', 'appeals' and 'anything interesting'. There was often nothing in the last category and most of the private letters were ecstatic thank you's from the recipients of wedding or birthday presents; for Tattie was a heavy shopper. ('My,' David Blacker had once remarked, 'the crocodiles that have been slaughtered in her name!')

But these were not normal days. The news that they were to be married, with Ezra's official blessing or at least his *nihil obstat*, had been quickly circulated in the family and now, with the announcement in *The Times*, the *Telegraph* and – Miss Attlee's idea – the *Jewish Chronicle*, there had been a volley of telegrams which Chuck put in a separate file for Miss Attlee to answer. It had been agreed that marriage talk would be held over lunch, and so Chuck proceeded with the familiar and soothing routine.

'Are you interested in spastics, honey?' Chuck had opened the first envelope.

'Not really, dear, are you?'

Tattie had put a little too much cream on her cereal and it bothered her momentarily.

'Spina bifida?'

Tattie wrinkled her nose and swallowed. 'Doesn't sound very nice.'

'Oh, heck, you'll have to go to the spastics do. You're a patron. There we are, "Miss H. Sterling" on the masthead with all those lords and ladies is my little girl! And it's a musical, so you'll like it.'

Yes, thought Tattie, she would quite like it and it was comforting to know that the cost of the tickets for her party came, in some funny way, off tax; even more comforting when her name as patron would read: 'Mrs Charles B. Lambkin.'

'All right then, but I don't want to have anything to do with spina whatever it is.' She sounded as if by attending a film première at the Odeon Leicester Square she would be in danger of contracting the disease. 'By the way, dear, you never told me what the "B" stands for.'

'Beauregard, after General Beauregard. He was a general in the Civil War,' muttered Chuck.

'Really,' said Tattie, laying down her knife. 'That's nice. I never knew that. . . . "Mrs Charles Beauregard Lambkin" – my, what a pretty name,' she said in passable mimicry of Vivien Leigh. 'How did you come to get such a nice name, dear?'

But Chuck did not answer. Not even when she wondered aloud whether, since Ezra didn't want a big reception, the Berkeley wouldn't be more suitable than Claridge's. Or, come to that, they could even have it here. 'Couldn't we . . . oh, never mind.'

Chuck was deep in some document or other and merely grunted.

'Chuck dear, what is that you're reading?'

'Hold on, honey, hold on.'

Tattie tutted impatiently and returned to contemplation of a photograph of a young lady, a quarter her size, arched provocatively but disdainfully in front of an impressive gendarme. She didn't suppose she could wear it but the material was nice. She bit into her croissant.

'Tattie? Tattie, will you listen to me?' said Chuck sharply.

Tattie's mouth was full and she mumbled something.

'*Please*, honey!'

Tattie mumbled again on a slightly crosser note.

'Tell me, just how much love and affection,' he leant on the words, 'do you have for your nephew?'

Tattie put down her magazine and blinked at Chuck through her spectacles. 'Oscar? I'm very fond of him, you know that, and so are you, dear, aren't you?'

Chuck was staring at her very hard and Tattie felt frightened. Oh dear, and it was going to be such a nice day.

'You're talking about his marriage settlement, I suppose? It's all right, dear. Ezra said so. And then there will be one for you and . . . And they said I would still be a . . . er . . . wealthy woman. So there's nothing to worry about, is there?' Her voice petered out and she reached for a croissant so snug and reassuring in its napkin.

Chuck was still looking at her oddly. He said slowly, 'Honey, did you read this,' and he held up the document, 'carefully before you signed it?'

Tattie gulped. 'No, they said it was all a lot of legal rigmarole and Ezra said I didn't really even need a copy. He . . .'

'He said that?' snapped Chuck.

They looked at each other – the man now angry and the woman more frightened.

'In consideration of love and affection for your nephew, you have given him about two million pounds, which I would say is about four-fifths of your fortune.'

Tattie paused in mid-croissant. He had her attention now and her head began to throb. Why were people so difficult? Outside, surely the daffodils were blooming. Young people were sauntering in the park, looking at each other. When would he make love to her? Not a fool, she had decided – years ago – to suppress thought, because it was troublesome. Eating, talking, listening to music were easy. Thought and concentration were difficult and reminded her of pain.

'So what can we do?' said Tattie feebly.

'Quite a lot,' said Chuck with more conviction than he felt. 'Send for her,' he added.

Tattie pressed a button. Miss Attlee arrived, somewhat flustered because it was a quarter of an hour before her accustomed time. She bore a notebook.

'Sit down,' said Chuck.

This, equally, was an unusual order from an unusual source. She regarded Chuck gently as an element in her employer's life, not quite an equal. She knew that the rent of his flat was paid and she resented that not at all, and her private reflections on their relationship were that Miss Sterling could have done a lot worse. Miss Attlee sat uneasily on the edge of a large daybed which might have belonged to a mistress of the Prince Regent.

'You don't need your pad, Miss Attlee, just listen,' said Chuck. (Miss Attlee without her pad was like a car without a steering wheel.) 'What I am going to tell you will in any case become evident to you as Miss Sterling's confidential private secretary, loyal to her – uh – interests?'

'Yes, indeed, Mr Lambkin.'

Chuck paused and looked at Tattie, apprehensive and indifferent in her rich sheets. 'Now, in our long association I have never presumed to interfere in Miss Sterling's affairs?'

Miss Attlee nodded approvingly. He had been exemplarily detached, but it was nice that this was about to change.

'But something has happened which, as a friend and, uh . . .' – Chuck found himself blushing – 'future husband of your employer, requires, sorrowfully, my attention. Miss Attlee, I know we can rely on you to help.'

Another nod.

'Miss Attlee, she has signed away her fortune, unwittingly I believe, and this is something I am determined to protest.'

There was a grunt from the bed which sounded like dissent, but neither cared.

'How did it happen, Mr Lambkin? I am amazed. The family are usually so kind to Miss Sterling.'

'I don't know exactly how it happened, but I suppose they figured the best way of protecting her estate from death duties would be to hand most of it over, like to someone younger. Mr Oscar Barnet, in fact.'

'And it's definitely been done?'

'Signed, sealed *and* delivered.' Chuck handed her the document. 'Look it over some time.'

'And this,' he went on, 'is a proposal for an insurance policy which – provided she signs this – Miss Sterling is to pay for, designed to protect the settlement *she* has made against tax in the event of her death within seven years.'

Miss Attlee thought for a moment and then stood up. 'By George,' she said. 'That's not fair!'

'I'm glad you agree, Miss Attlee. Now, the first thing to do is to get Miss Sterling out of the country, away from . . .' He gestured angrily, stood up and began pacing the room.

'Quite,' said Miss Attlee, reaching for her shorthand pad, a gleam in her eye. Had Miss Attlee been a war-horse she would have pawed the Aubusson.

'Paris tonight, and then . . .'

Chuck swung on his heels, clicked his fingers and said, 'I know, a cruise of the Greek islands. Yes, that's it, where no one can find us.'

'It's not right, it's not right,' muttered Tattie. But they ignored her.

'Ring up that man – what's he called? – Nicoloudis. He charters yachts, doesn't he?'

'Where shall I find him, Mr Lambkin?'

'I dunno. Yes, I do. You call Mr Mills's secretary at Les A., Les Ambassadeurs, and she'll know. He'll be staying at Claridge's or some place, and you tell him that I, that is to say we, Miss Sterling and I, want to charter a boat. It doesn't matter how big it is – in fact it shouldn't be too small. . . .' He glanced in Tattie's direction.

She had sat up in bed and was shaking her head from side to side and saying in a sing-song voice, 'Don't do it, dear, don't do it.'

'The best one I heard of,' he went on, 'is the *Radiant*, do you remember, honey? Last year in Cannes we were invited on board for a drink and you said what a nice boat?'

'I haven't got any clothes for a boat,' said Tattie sulkily.

'Well, honey, you go out now and buy some. Go to Hartnell, Molyneux, Creed, or you could walk across the road to Rahvis'; she'll fix you up.'

'I still think it's a bad idea. It's not right to be so . . .,' she couldn't be bothered to find a word, 'with Ezra. Miss Attlee, you tell Mr Lambkin he's not to . . .'

Tattie broke off in alarm as her secretary advanced across the room and now stood a few feet from her pillow with her fists clenched.

'Madam,' she said, 'not only will I not say anything to Mr Lambkin, but if you do not allow us to help you I must insist that you accept my resignation. You have been cheated, madam, in a way any English court would find intolerable.'

Throughout this speech the pain in Tattie's head had begun to blaze, but as she sank back on to her pillow, defeated, she felt some relief.

'All right,' she muttered. 'I'll get dressed.'

'That's my girl,' said Chuck, and he walked over, kissed Tattie's damp cheek, patted her hand and turned to his ally. 'Miss Attlee, that's a point. We need a good lawyer. Do you know of one? It has to be a really first-class firm.' The only solicitor of his acquaintance, a cheerful little Jewish fellow who often drank at the Club, was currently in gaol for investing his client's funds with the book-makers.

'I have a cousin, Mr Lambkin, a second cousin actually, who is a partner in . . .' Miss Attlee mentioned a famous name which was, however, lost on Chuck.

'Are they really the tops?' he asked.

'Well,' said Miss Attlee sweetly, 'they do act for royalty, and, now, if you'll excuse me . . .' She bowed slightly to Tattie. 'I must get on with my work.'

'That's true,' said Chuck. 'So must I.' And he followed her out of the room.

Chuck sat at a mahogany table turning the pages of a back number of *Punch* and failing to receive a frisson of recognition from the jokes. The walls of the little room were almost obscured by stacks of black tin boxes bearing the sonorous names of the British aristocracy, and some, indeed, could have been long-dead descendants of Queen Victoria. Hell, had he come to the right place?

But he trusted Miss Attlee and this morning she had been superb. The Board of Trade had been telephoned about the temporary export of Tattie's jewels, insurance policies against every conceivable misfortune – including, as it is Greece, earthquakes, the broker had insisted – had been taken out. A boat had been hired; not the *Radiant*, or the equally exotic *Camargue*, but a perfectly adequate vessel called the *Atlanta* which happened to be available through a cancellation and was berthed at Piraeus. She had a crew of six – a British captain, a French chef, an engineer, a couple of deck hands, a steward and even, the agent had pointed out with some relish, a cabin boy. And her deep freeze groaned with deep-frozen meat bought in Cannes.

The guests had been no problem since the essential characteristics – usefulness, inoffensiveness and availability – were well represented in the family's circle of friends. Maurice Krapf, the doctor – his presence helped to increase the group's travel allowance; Jeremy – he was after all Greek, wasn't he; Sir Arthur and his friend; Hélène; and Lucy Blacker and her two boys had all agreed to join the party. Eva could look after Maurice's practice, Jeremy said the gallery wouldn't miss him, Sir Arthur no longer had a seat in the House of Commons to detain him, the friend had another friend to look after the shop in the Fulham Road, Lucy, though rich, was too mean to say no and it wouldn't matter if the boys missed a few days at the end of term. Only Hélène had been honest. She had actually exclaimed, 'Ooh-la-la,' and added cheerfully that like all good tarts she would go anywhere and do anything if paid for.

The expedition had been billed as a pre-marital honeymoon and what could be more natural for Tatcie, now allowed to become Mrs Charles Beauregard Lambkin, than to wish to celebrate her happiness with a cruise of the Greek islands with some of her friends. After all, she could afford it. Chuck smiled. The man at Cooks – they had deliberately not used the man at the business who usually took care of the family's travel arrangements – had been ecstatically efficient. Suites of rooms awaited various members of the party at the Meurice in Paris, the Excelsior in Rome and, in case the sheets on the good ship *Atlanta* were damp, at the Grande Bretagne in Athens. Chuck had checked the controls with the precision of a pilot and felt ready for take-off.

But now this. Chuck looked again at the names. The fact that Ezra was a viscount, albeit a Jewish one, lent, he thought, a little dignity to his rather squalid mission.

'Mr Brooker will see you now, sir.' A small boy with a squeaky voice and a plump bottom – now *he* should have been a cabin boy – had entered the room and stood smiling in the doorway. Chuck was led into a corridor, up some stairs, down some more stairs and into the presence of Mr Hubert de Quincey Brooker. He too looked as if he should still be at high school, with his mop of corn-coloured hair, beaky nose, beardless chin and – obviously a prop – a pair of pince-nez below a pair of remarkably cold blue eyes which scrutinized his visitor with almost childish directness as they shook hands.

'Sit down, will you, Mr Lambkin.'

The voice was clipped, petulant, sure of itself. As he did so, Chuck noticed, in the corner of the room by a window which looked straight into an ancient horse-chestnut tree, a figure hunched up at a desk apparently copying into an exercise book.

'My clerk,' remarked the young man brusquely. 'Now, sir, if you begin at the beginning and take your time, I am all yours, as they say. Enlighten me.'

And he leant back in his leather armchair and stared with half-closed eyes at the ceiling for the next twenty minutes. He asked no questions and only interrupted Chuck's narrative twice, the first time when the pendulum clock started to strike twelve, whereupon he leapt to his feet, moved hurriedly to a corner cupboard from which he produced a decanter, poured out two glasses, put one on Chuck's side of the enormous mahogany desk and silently sipped his own, waiting for the clock to subside with a pained expression on his face.

'That Mr Lambkin, that instrument of torture was bequeathed to me by one of our late partners. He knew I loathed the noise it made. He was a very malicious old man.' Chuck thought the shoulders of the silent figure in the corner, still writing, gave a slight twitch. 'And I warn you, Mr Lambkin, in five minutes it will do it all over again!' His voice had risen indignantly. 'So at twelve o'clock I toast the old bugger in his grave – he was a teetotaller, you see – and at five past twelve I have another swig.' His blue eyes glittered and then grew cold again as he said, 'You were telling me that in your opinion the enclosure of a copy of the settlement could have been an error because in Miss Sterling's recollection her brother,' and he emphasized the word, 'had said that they "might as well look after them for her", or words to that effect?'

This was, word for word, what Chuck had just said.

'Well, that's about it, Mr Brooker. Your cousin, that is Miss Attlee, said no English court would tolerate . . .'

'Gwynneth?' asked the solicitor. It had never occurred to Chuck that Miss Attlee bore any other name, and he was about to continue when the clock gave a wheeze and in response to the young man's alarmed shaking of a finger, fell silent and waited while the solicitor, after a further draught of sherry, flicked through the notorious document, muttering occasionally something which sounded like 'M'yaas!'

'Tosh!' he said finally, when the last stroke had died away and he had apparently digested the papers before him.

'What's that?' queried Chuck.

'Gwynneth's view of the matter. Once we're inside a court of law with a thing like this we're sunk.' The young man waved down Chuck's question with a gesture that was both imperious and reassuring. 'There are better ways of recovering Miss Sterling's fortune than by an action in court. British justice is expensive, time-consuming and neurotic. I spend most of my time keeping my clients away from the law. And judges nearly always favour the rich and respectable, whatever they've been up to – and I gather from your own account, Mr Lambkin, that you are neither?'

Chuck coloured a little but nodded. He remembered Miss Attlee had warned him that her cousin was considered by some to be eccentric.

'M'yaas.' The young man stared at the ceiling and the room was silent save for the tick-tock of the odious clock.

'Tell me, Mr Lambkin, is Miss Sterling feeble-minded?'

Chuck started. 'What?'

'You know – soft in the head, mental?'

A rush of affection for Tattie turned inside out and became anger at the sight of this arrogant young man who now seemed more like an enemy. Chuck decided to control himself.

'Certainly not,' he snapped. (Does he think I'm that much of a creep?)

'You must try not to get cross with me, Mr Lambkin, if I am to help you,' was the calm reply. 'So there is no history of mental disorder? You did say that before the war she lived in some sort of home.'

'She lived in a kosher boarding house in north London some place, and you could say it was the party line, the family line . . .'

'To pretend,' interrupted the solicitor, 'that for her protection, etc., etc. Oh yes, we know that one, don't we, Watkins?'

There was, doubtless as intended, no reply from the still-silent scribe.

'M'yaas.' Another silence. 'And, tell me as a matter of interest, how did Miss Sterling escape from such an obviously disagreeable institution?'

'Well, when the business went to the Stock Exchange and the money floated in . . . Well, I guess Tattie just floated out. She can be quite determined sometimes, you know.'

'Yes.'

'Yes, sir. Look, Mr, uh, Brooker, I know this girl pretty well by now. She's not stupid. But she can act stupid to suit herself because she's lazy; she doesn't like trouble for herself or for anyone else. She likes pleasure and presents and trips and clothing and, yes, food. She hates crossing Ezra, but she won't go back on us now. Mr Brooker, she's loyal, I assure you, and . . .'

'You brought the letters?' interrupted the solicitor.

'They're in the other folder.'

The solicitor examined the ten blank sheets of writing paper, each with Tattie's signature at a different place.

'M'yaas.' Another silence. 'And when will Miss Sterling be out of the, shall we say, sphere of influence?'

'They spend tonight and tomorrow in Paris. . . .'

'M'yaas, don't like that . . . too near, Paris. So I'd better wait until Greece.' He was talking to himself now, but about what, wondered Chuck. 'Greece, jolly good place, Greece. Nobody ever rung up Greece and by the time it hits him you'll be swanning around the Cyclades, won't you? I take it the boat's not on the telephone, is it?'

'I should think that this one probably is. But, please, Mr Brooker, what are you thinking about?'

The younger man looked at him blandly. Then, 'Ah,' he said, 'you don't follow my train of thought? Well, when Lord Sterling receives my letter his reaction will be to telephone his sister and tell her not to be such a silly girl. . . .'

'But I told you she – Miss Sterling – is now quite determined. She won't talk to him.'

'My dear sir, I believe you, of course, but how much safer if she *can't*. Blood is thicker than water in these chambers and Jewish blood . . . In fact, it is important that Miss Sterling doesn't speak to Lord Sterling on any matter at all from this moment on. She might just blurt something out.'

Chuck shook his head.

'Come, sir, you must allow me to advise you. She should only speak to you. I insist on this. And you said "they" just now. Who exactly are "they"?'

'You mean the party accompanying my – er – Miss Sterling?'

'Just so.'

'Well, on the first lap it's just Sir Arthur Coleport and his . . .'

'Conservative MP for somewhere in the Midlands, director of Sterlings, and then bang! from behind a bush by an uncooperative policeman, with a Guardsman or something after a beano at the Dorchester. Routine stuff. We know about that too, don't we, Watkins? Yes, I know him. Can he be trusted?'

'Yes, I should say so, but to do what?'

'To make sure Miss Sterling answers no telephone calls. I'm sorry to labour the point, Mr Lambkin.'

'Tattie covenants him seven hundred and fifty pounds a year, I believe, and Lord Sterling was not very helpful over his little trouble. Perhaps it had not been the only time. . . .'

'Good. It's perfectly simple. He tells the hall porter that the doctor has recommended that Miss Sterling's health does not permit her to receive telephone calls directly, a note of reasonable denomination changes hands and bob's your uncle, there's one customer unnobbable till she's safe at sea. M'yaas.' He stared at the ceiling. 'You see, Mr Lambkin, when the document covering the insurance provision is not returned signed, *and* the bird has flown, someone may begin – to use another metaphor – to smell a rat, no?'

'Yeah, I see.'

'So you had better tell our Gwynneth to write a bland letter saying can the document await Miss Sterling's return, or should it be forwarded on to her.'

Chuck nodded.

'And that should be done today, please.'

Chuck nodded.

'M'yaas.' Back to staring at the ceiling.

Silence.

'But,' asked Chuck, 'if the case *did* go to court?'

The younger man shut his eyes as if in pain. 'I've told you once, my good sir, but let me spell it out for you. It goes like this. We field a good chap, okay, possibly a Jew, and if he's also a Zionist *tant mieux*, fire in his belly and a big bleeding heart. I know the very man but this is all hypothetical. We plead undue influence, hint – I'm afraid – at least at gullibility, say no one could love her nephew *that* much, etc., etc. They have a quiet chap who says now, come, come, look here, look at the background to this case. It is true that Miss Sterling's wealth is based on an inheritance from her father, but who made her really rich? Who doubled and redoubled and quadrupled her fortune by his intelligence *and* integrity? Then he digresses to explain to the jury how easy it is for a man in so powerful a position as Lord Sterling to manipulate the financial basis of the company he controls, to favour the directors – who do the work – at the expense of the shareholders who simply draw the dividends, through watering the stock, creating options, high salaries and so forth: all, incidentally, current and legal practice.

'But, m'lud . . .' – Hubert Brooker was still stretched out in his leather armchair, face upwards, and he now stabbed a finger at the chandelier – 'if you consider Lord Sterling's relationship with his family, and particularly with his sisters and particularly with *this* sister, who for many years enjoyed the expenses of a luxurious establishment, remained the biggest single shareholder, he has behaved like the honourable man he is known to be by society, the City of London and . . . his Monarch!' He paused.

'Something like that,' he added in a normal voice and then to Chuck, 'You see, they're not going to weep for a lady down to her last half a million.'

Chuck nodded glumly and was about to ask a question when the younger man resumed his forensic stance, that is almost flat on his back, and started to intone again.

'You see, m'lud, a man in control of a large but essentially family business and, incidentally, one of the chief exporters in the field, can be forgiven if he feels it his proper duty to ensure that the direction of affairs never passes into *im*proper hands. And what more sensible arrangement could be devised than to suggest that his sister hand over, in her lifetime, to his and her nephew who is in any case her heir, a sufficient quantity of shares *he* has made so valuable, to ensure continuity at the helm? Members of the jury, if we are looking for evidence of undue influence we should turn our eyes in a quite different direction. . . .'

The solicitor reached out for one of the documents on the desk. 'Watkins, would you be good enough to take this down to Mr Pendleton in Tax and see if he can find any holes in it?'

Watkins, surprised, with his face full of ham roll took the document and stumbled out of the room.

'. . . In a quite different direction,' repeated the younger man. 'Mr Lambkin, an American by origin, has been the constant companion of Miss Sterling for the past fifteen years and they are now to be married. If you wonder why the courtship has been so prolonged I should explain that Miss Sterling hesitated before an alliance which she knew would distress her brother who was known to disapprove of the gentleman; although I understand he treated him courteously and he was often invited to his Lordship's country home. Mr Lambkin is the part proprietor of a small drinking club in Mayfair. His rent has always been paid by Miss Sterling. He . . .' The solicitor broke off. 'Mr Lambkin, may I ask you, have you ever been the subject of criminal prosecution?'

Chuck had ceased to feel any anger. He just felt numb, pained and puzzled. Whose side did he think he was on? Yet the removal of Watkins from their presence before he went into his heavy piece did indicate that this strange young man possessed, somewhere, a heart and possibly, second sight.

'You are my client and I must know everything.'

'How did you know, I mean, or guess?'

'Dear sir, when a man has absented himself from his own country for a considerable period, the reasons, in my experience, tend to be discreditable. Forgive me, solicitors have such unpleasant minds. You see, they'll drop that in – if they know about it. Do they?'

'Ezra just might. He just might,' replied Chuck.

'. . . Drop it in, be rebuked by the judge, apologize, and sweep on leaving us flat on the floor. The two "killers" being that the settlement does not leave either of you destitute and that Lord Sterling doesn't mind a cuckoo in his sister's nest, providing most of her eggs are stored in a safe place. And there's no question of alienating the rights of any children because I gather your intended is well past child-bearing age.'

'You're right.'

The solicitor paused. 'Lord Sterling must have been waiting a long time for this. That's why he kept her locked up before the war, don't you see, in case she had children.'

Suddenly Chuck did see. 'Tell me, Mr Brooker, you often have cases like this?'

'The whole time. My dear sir, I call this the bad behaviour department. Were it not for the rapacity of the English upper class and the hatred, especially among the nobility, of fathers for their sons, and vice versa, I would be out of business. Here, have some more sherry.'

'You certainly have a gift for words, Mr Brooker.'

'Oh, please call me Hubert.'

'Right, uh, Hubert – and most people call me Chuck. And I would prefer to have you on my side in court, if we may return to the subject in hand.'

'Oh, no, no,' said Hubert. 'No, for many reasons. First, under the crazy antique British system, which God preserve, a solicitor may not plead; secondly, as I hope, and indeed thought, I had demonstrated, we would lose if we went to court; and thirdly, I will certainly not act for *you*.'

'You just said I was your client!'

'In fact, but not in law. But I *will* act for Miss Sterling. Don't you see, my dear sir, Chuck, that in the lists of actions it must appear as *Sterling* versus Sterling. That is our only weapon.'

'Ah! I'm beginning to get the message – scare tactics?'

'Yes. Of course we threaten to take them to court but we never do – we never can, we have no case. But they will settle, in our favour, somewhere between here,' and he slapped the side of the desk, 'and those grimy buildings in the Strand.'

'You sound very certain, Hubert.'

'I am certain, Chuck, if you let me fight this my way – and my ways are not the ways of the law. Why, in a case like this a paragraph in the gossip column of the *Daily Express* is worth more than the good opinion of a chorus of judges.'

'You mean William Hickey?' asked Chuck.

'Well, more or less – there are at least four of them. The point being that when you get to be Viscount Sterling your reputation is worth more than two million pounds. Even if he is not a man of honour – and I have reason to think that he is not – his public behaviour must be impeccable. And what would the world think if it were known that he had pulled a fast one on his sister? What would they say in the City, in the House of Lords, at the next meeting of the Jewish Board of Guardians?'

'But Ezra . . .'

'Oh, yes, Chuck, my dear sir, he has to be made to see this and much more. I see a serious leader in the *Guardian* raising the question of control in these days of voting and non-voting shares in public companies. I see Michael Foot or someone on the left asking the Chancellor when he is going to tax the rich. . . . A *bon mot* from Nye Bevan. . . . Don't worry, your opponent has imagination and he will *deal*. I remember my cousin, Tom, at the Foreign Office told me a story about Lord Sterling's behaviour over the death of his son. . . . M'yaas,' concluded Hubert thoughtfully, and leaning back again in his chair, he added quietly, 'and besides, you realize, Chuck, my dear sir, that Lord Sterling has already reacted in our favour.'

'How come?'

'Let us imagine that an aunt of *yours* – from whom indeed you expect to inherit – *une tante à héritage*, as the French put it – settles a large sum on you, which you know to be an almost sacrificially large sum, wouldn't you, er, give a tinkle and say, "Gee, thanks, Auntie"? Or scribble a note and send her a damp bunch of violets? Or something? But you tell me there has been no communication from the fortunate beneficiary. The silences of Mr Oscar Barnet are to me, fraught with significance. Would'nt you agree?'

'I don't know where you're taking me, Hubert.'

'I gather, too, that there is no hostility between your, er, household and Mr Barnet?'

'Absolutely not. He's a great guy, little Oscar, a bit wild, but a fine guy. We both like him. I knew him when he was a kid.'

'M'yaas.' Pause. 'Then he has not been told of this settlement because Lord Sterling feels guilty. Either way is good for us. Guilt weakens resolve. M'yaas.'

'I don't quite go along with you there, Hubert,' said Chuck slowly.

The younger man shot forward in his chair and looked hard at Chuck. 'In what particular?' he snapped.

'Well, Ezra is a tricky man, secretive and capricious, keeps his cards close to his chest, keeps those boys at each others throats like a man training gladiators. He may have other reasons for not saying anything. He likes drama, too. He'll toss it off to Oscar one day – "Hey, there's a coupla million I got ya!" – like it was a box of matches.'

'M'yaas.' The solicitor's glare had not wavered. 'Right. There is one change of tactic. My letter will be at Lord Sterling's office by the close of business today.'

'What does the letter say?' asked Chuck anxiously. The younger man clapped his hands happily.

'Oh, it'll just tickle the imagination, suggest visions of Sterling v. Sterling, ask where the writ can be accepted. . . .'

'You don't think that a bit, uh, hasty?'

'My dear sir, you must never confuse haste' – he had picked up a paper knife and held the blade to his throat – 'with speed.' And with surprising venom he lunged at Chuck. Then he laughed.

'You see, this is not a campaign where you build up your forces like at Alamein. We are not just willing to wound, we are not afraid to strike. And we must *show* this. . . .' He paused. 'Gwynneth will reply in different terms. She will say that she cannot return the insurance proposal because Miss Sterling instructed her to send it to me. I do have it, do I not. Ah, yes. Secondly, I will need your power of attorney because when we sit round a table, *then* I shall act for you too.'

'So I can go out and join Tattie?'

'No, not yet.'

'Why not, for heaven's sake?'

'I, er, may need your advice,' he said surprisingly. 'You will see Miss Sterling before she goes?'

'Of course. I'll take her to the airport in my old Buick.'

'Oh, how lovely. I adore vulgar American cars! You will tell her that, er, the document unsigned is invalid, that from now on there will be a complicated legal wrangle, that the matter is bound to be settled in her/your favour, and so forth. It is important that she be calm and confident, but equally that she does not speak to anyone.'

The door opened and in came the deplorable Watkins who had acquired another ham roll.

'No holes, Mr Brooker.' He put the document on the desk and shuffled off to his corner.

The solicitor nodded and smiled.

Chuck descended the stone staircase as quickly as he could without slipping, for he had a date to lunch at Claridge's with Tattie and Sir Arthur and he was late. Outside, a group of fledgeling barristers, all with black coats, striped pants, waistcoats and some with umbrellas, were sitting around eating sandwiches out of their briefcases. Further off four lunatics were playing tennis. A couple of them were admiring the Buick. Just as the aged engine spluttered into life, Chuck noticed out of the corner of his eye a man dressed like the rest of them and sporting a gold chain on his waistcoat *and* an Anthony Eden hat, watching the proceedings with amused hauteur. He was black.

Chuck recalled a cartoon in which a black bus conductor is saying, 'I don't know whether to stay on in this job or go back home and be Foreign Minister.' The British were great; pity they had to lose out. He had never believed all that stuff they fed you at school: that Englishmen were ruthless with the natives, hungry for trade and power and hypocritical, too. Look at what happened today! You could hardly call Mr Hubert de Quincey Brooker hypocritical; devious yes, even ruthless – there had been a scary look in those blue eyes when he made with the paper knife. He had been very sure of himself, but then he was young. Just how young, wondered Chuck. He must ask Miss Attlee; though maybe now he should call her Gwynneth.

The porter at Claridge's knew him and the car, and arranged to have it parked in a near-by mews. Yes, it was a great country, England – no better place to live.

3

Like other powerful men, Ezra used both open and secret diplomacy. Sometimes he found it politic to let the world know what he wanted. He would confide, said Audrey, in a taxi driver, if need be. His viscountcy, for instance, had been his idea. Once mooted, it had seemed natural, obvious and inevitable. He didn't always listen – maybe he had already made up his mind – but he did, on occasions, ask. This was such an occasion.

'Mrs Winterbourne.'

She came in. It was a summons.

'Have you seen this?'

'I'm sorry, Lord Sterling, I didn't have time.'

'Read it.' He handed it to her. 'Sit down, woman.' Courtesies were reserved for persons of no account. 'What do you think?'

Mrs Winterbourne sighed. 'It's a try-on. A piece of impertinence.' Mrs Winterbourne was loyal, out of instinct and calculation.

'And?'

'Ignore it. If you will allow me, I will acknowledge the letter and say that no reply will be forthcoming.'

'Good girl. I can't even read who it's from.' He added irritably, 'The initials are H. de Q. B. Ah, yes, it's one of the partners.'

'Forget it, sir. That's my advice,' and Mrs Winterbourne withdrew.

But the letter would not be forgotten. Before Ezra's face and everything he saw that morning, was Chuck drawing on his cheroot. His all too friendly eyes crinkling at the edges were suddenly sinister; his noncommittal remarks, committal; his casual air, contrived. He was the enemy. Ezra read the House of Lords papers – Scottish licensing laws, water troughs for horses in Hyde Park, a new town somewhere – but he saw only the face of Chuck Lambkin, the enemy. *Delenda est Carthago, delenda est* Chuck, he said to himself. Chuck had to be destroyed.

After lunch he asked Geoffrey Nickson to stay on.

'How much does it cost to get someone beaten up?'

'Ezra!'

'Oh, come on. You have friends at Scotland Yard. They're all in the same business. Don't be so coy.'

'You mean you want a job done? I don't know what you'll have to pay, and frankly, Ezra, whatever's on your mind, I'd forget it.'

'That's what everybody says, but I can't and won't.'

'Besides, beating people up is not your style, Ezra, it's not right.'

Ezra stood up.

'Not right!' he shouted. 'Of course it's not right. Do you know who I have to deal with? A man from the underworld. A bum! A gangster! A hoodlum! A drunk!' He banged the board room table with every word. 'Do you know if he went back to his home state he'd be put behind bars? He's a convicted . . .'

'Chuck? No!'

'Yes, that charming, soft-voiced, mint-julep-swilling Southern gentleman friend of yours is nothing more than a cheap blackmailer – not so bloody cheap, as a matter of fact!' He paused and began again in a quieter voice. 'I didn't object to his living off my sister for the last, what is it, sixteen years, as her gigolo, *cicisbeo, maquereau, gonef,* whatever you like to call it. But, by God, he should keep his place!' Another bang for emphasis. 'But now he wants his hands on Tattie's shares in the business – the shares I made her rich with! And for which . . .' – Ezra hesitated – 'I had made more, uh, suitable arrangements. Do you understand?'

Geoffrey nodded.

'Do you think I want a man like that with votes in the board room? Conspiring, why not, with my nephews to throw me out?'

Geoffrey smiled at the idea.

'It's not so crazy! Look what happened to King Lear. I've always felt sorry for that chap.' Ezra sat down again and sighed.

The two men looked at each other with affection.

'Christ!' said Geoffrey.

'It's nothing to do with him,' said Ezra. 'Just you find me someone.'

'You mean a bent copper? I still don't like it, but I'll do it.'

'. . . Find me someone,' muttered Ezra.

'That's an order, sir?'

'That's an order, sir.' He thought it supererogatory to require of Geoffrey his discretion. He was a good man and would not blab to anyone – not even to Audrey.

'I suppose it'll cost about three hundred quid.'

Ezra was no longer interested, but when Geoffrey had gone he asked Mrs Winterbourne to assemble an envelope containing £500. They'd better hire the best.

The copper provided by Geoffrey was properly, almost exquisitely bent. But, in his anxiety to obey Lord Sterling's demand for discretion at all costs, a 'villain' – as he put it – had been selected who may have been discreet but was certainly past his prime. That night, or more accurately, very early the next morning, Chuck was walking back, reasonably steadily, from the club in Shepherd Market to his little flat in Dunraven Street. There was no one about; it was an hour when, in the words of the musical, the streets belong to the cops, but there was no sign of a policeman.

The man got out of a Humber, tightened the belt of his overcoat, sniffed the morning air, and walked briskly towards Chuck who was by now at his own door, one hand in his pocket, the other clenched on what could have been a set of keys. Chuck, suddenly sober, pretended to be drunk, and as he heard the approaching steps, fumbled with his own latch key which he, in fact, turned in the lock. His timing was perfect, for when he was swung at he kicked open the door and the man in the camel-hair rushed noiselessly past, landing with a thud and a crack on the chequered marble floor. The noise woke the night porter who appeared in braces and slippers.

The man on the floor looked up at them.

'Christ, I've broken me bloody head open.' And then, leaning forward on an elbow, he gasped, 'My God, I never knew it was you, guv. They never . . .'

'My friend had a fall,' Chuck interrupted with a warning voice. 'I'll just take him upstairs and wash that cut.'

'Oh, all right, sir,' said the night porter. 'You don't need me for anything?' It was more of a statement than an offer, and he shuffled back to his cubbyhole.

'C'mon, man, c'mon, Monty, on your feet! It is Monty, isn't it?'

'S'right, guv, and I know you well, Mr Lambkin. You're a gentleman,' he said, as Chuck squeezed him into the tiny, ancient elevator.

They did not speak again until Chuck had extricated Monty from his heavy overcoat – it now appeared he might have sprained his wrist, removed his double-breasted jacket, revealing a pair of bright red Turnbull & Asser braces, dabbed his cut with Listerine, applied a piece of Elastoplast and sat Monty down in a chair with a tumbler of Jim Beam. The glass was crystal from Messrs Goodes – a present from Tattie – and the bourbon had originated in the PX.

'Now,' said Chuck grimly, 'give.'

'Well,' said Monty, drawing on his glass, 'I think I'm too old for this sort of job. I must say,' he added, 'you're a gentleman all right.'

'Who hired you?' asked Chuck sharply. Monty stirred uneasily.

'Oh, c'mon, guv. Fair's fair. That wouldn't be professional now, would it? For me to tell you that, I mean.'

'Okay,' he sighed. What was he doing at four o'clock in the morning succouring a valetudinarian thug who had been hired, he was sure, by his future brother-in-law, one of the most respected men in the kingdom, to do him over? Had the world gone mad?

'Did they give you any reason?'

'Yeah, it's some money you owe the bookies, isn't it?'

Chuck just stared at him. 'How much do you get?'

Monty hesitated. 'A hundred and fifty down and a hundred and fifty when I done it,' he blurted.

'Quite a heavy sum for a bookie, wouldn't you say, Monty?'

Monty examined a well-manicured paw in perplexity for some time. 'I dunno,' he concluded. 'They said they wanted a pro-fessional job. . . .'

'Huh,' Chuck permitted himself.

'And above all they said, be discreet, so they only wanted one man and they chose me. . . .' He looked up at Chuck, eyes full of Jim Beam and self-pity. 'Maybe I should give the money back?

Sure, I can't collect the other half, not now.' He looked dispiritedly round the room. 'You wouldn't let me down, would you, guv?'

Chuck didn't answer. He was thinking.

'Listen, Monty. Listen carefully. You go back and you collect the rest of the money, 'cause you tell them you've earned it, see?'

Monty nodded and an expression of semi-intelligent doubt crossed his crumpled face.

'And you show them this . . . if it's who I think it is they'll know you couldn't have gotten it from me too easily.'

He threw an object across the room which Monty failed to catch.

It was an elderly Zippo lighter embossed with the USAF crest, in enamel, which had over the last sixteen years lit many hundreds of Chuck's cheroots.

'And I want it back, okay?'

Monty nodded.

'And, Monty, there's something you can do for me. . . .'

Monty brightened.

'Happy to 'blige you, guv. *C'est la vie,*' he added unexpectedly.

'Supposing you wanted two people – very important, very protected – scared. Who would *you* hire?'

Monty thought.

'Well, guv, I don't know that I can help you. You see it wouldn't be right now, would it, seeing as how I'm working for the other party?' He paused dramatically. 'But you know Eddie Chapman, don't you? He's a mate of yours. He's not in the game any more, but there's nobody Eddie doesn't know.'

When Monty had gone Chuck poured himself a generous measure of the precious Jim Beam, popped a couple of Mogadons into his mouth and went to bed, hoping that when he woke up it would not be too early to call Eddie Chapman.

Drugs need the co-operation of their victims and Chuck's anxiety for the action of the day was such that his own private clock overcame the sleeping tablets and he awoke, though blurrily, at his usual hour in time for breakfast with Tattie. But of course, he realized, with a pang that surprised him, Tattie was by now in Rome. It would be good for both of them if he could speak to her.

He tried to ring the Hassler – the hotels had been changed since it had been remembered that when in Rome the family stayed at the Excelsior – reasoning that because of the difference in time the party, or some of them, might be stirring at this hour. Eventually he was connected by the operator to the switchboard and after much clicking and clacking was told by an American-accented voice that none of the guests he named was available. Chuck smiled at the efficiency of their arrangements and decided to ring his solicitor at his Kensington house. The telephone was answered by a child with its mouth full, who breathed heavily into the mouthpiece. Then a familiar clipped voice was heard in the background which said, 'Caroline, go back and polish off your Rice Crispies, there's a good girl,' and then more loudly, 'Morning, Brooker here.'

'Good morning, Hubert.'

'Ah, yes, Mr Lambkin, Chuck. What can I do for you?'

'I'm sorry to disturb you, Hubert, at this hour, but something has happened which might interest you.'

'Oh yes?' The voice sounded doubtful. But its owner listened carefully to Chuck's recital. Then came the familiar, and now comforting, 'M'yaas.'

A pause. Then:

'You don't think it could possibly have been somebody, er, that you owe money to?'

'I don't owe a red cent.'

'Or the settling of some old underworld score,' suggested his solicitor cheerfully.

'Hubert, *please.*'

'Forgive me, Mr Lambkin, er, Chuck, but do admit that your, er, acquaintance does stretch into some insalubrious areas of er, er . . . Still, it's good news they're obviously rattled and it's not the action of a confident party.'

'No, and I intend to make Ezra feel a lot less confident.'

'How, pray?' The tone was sharper.

Chuck told him.

There was a long pause and then, 'M'yaas. I think, Chuck, that we had better pretend that this part of the conversation has not occurred. I cannot advise a client to break the law; indeed, I must attempt to deter him. ... I take it that you are absolutely determined?'

'Absolutely.' Chuck enunciated every syllable.

'And when do you propose to embark upon this criminal adventure of which I have no knowledge?'

'Today seems like a good day,' replied Chuck easily.

'M'yaas. Very important. Then phase two of the psychological warfare will start tonight.'

'Can you tell me what this is, Hubert?'

'Certainly. You are entitled to know my moves in this affair just as I am entitled not to know of yours. Lord Sterling will be telephoned by a newspaper rather late at night, wherever he may be – and I assure you they can be quite as ruthless as your friends in locating their quarry, and usually more efficient – and asked the whereabouts of his sister, who seems to have disappeared. Just that ...'

'You don't think it's a little dangerous involving a newspaper?'

'It is indeed, but I think you know my strategy, Chuck, and what you have just told me only reinforces my view that it is correct. I bid you good morning, sir, and we will speak to each other tomorrow. There is no point in our communicating before that.'

And the line went dead.

After Waterloo Napoleon rattled back to Paris ahead of his Grand Army, ordered a bath and a prostitute and began to compose a not totally truthful account of the day's events for his faithful subjects. But then he was only forty-six at the time. After *his* defeat Ezra minted an aphorism which filtered through the family and the business though its inspiration was never known: 'Don't fight a losing battle; surrender.'

Ezra and Audrey had been invited to the first night of a radical play at the Royal Court Theatre by its chairman, not so much out of friendship as for fund-raising, and they sat down in the first row of the balcony just as the lights went up on a set of a bed-sitting room where a young woman was ironing some clothes. Ezra did not particularly enjoy or understand the play which involved a group of young persons ranting at each other. Come the interval, he saw

Chuck lounging in what passed for a box at the Royal Court. He was alone. He stood up, flicked his famous Zippo and lit one of his long cheroots, blew the smoke evenly in Ezra's direction, turned around and made an exit. During the second half of the play his seat was empty. Chuck was so cool in his manner that Ezra's spine tingled in fear; after all, according to the book he should have been in hospital. *And the lighter?*

After the performance two Rollses stood obediently right outside the theatre entrance and during the polite haggling between the two owners as to whose chauffeur could be dismissed two men charged out of the pub at the side of the theatre, knocked Ezra down into the gutter and strode on across Sloane Square without looking round. It had happened so quickly that the few who saw the incident were unable to act or even to protest. Ezra was helped to his feet by Jenkins who said, 'Must've been a couple of drunks.' The chairman, envisaging the disappearance of a handsome subsidy, dusted Ezra down and apologized for such uncourtly behaviour. 'Oh, that's all right, Neville. As Jenkins said, just a couple of drunks,' but he noticed that Audrey had gone white.

The telephone call came as the coffee, cigars and brandy were being offered at the chairman's flat. It was a lavish apartment, spattered with Impressionist paintings. 'Monet on the walls,' was Ezra's customary *bon mot*, but he didn't feel in the mood. A butler approached Ezra and said in a self-important voice, 'The *Daily Express* is on the telephone, my lord. They want to know the whereabouts of your sister. Will you speak to them, sir?'

Oh, the naïveté of servants! He always maintained they were in that profession because they would fail in any other. The chairman, noticing Ezra's second of distress, was nimbly on his feet, and interrupted to instruct the servant to reply 'No comment' to the fellow.

'As a matter of fact, sir, I think it's a lady.'

'That it certainly will not be,' replied Ezra, recovering himself.

As soon as was decent Ezra and Audrey took their leave, although Jenkins was not due till midnight. The chairman suggested that they could almost walk home, but they both quickly asked for a taxi, to which the chairman, agreeably, personally escorted them, paying the driver in advance. In the lift, Ezra had promised the

Royal Court rather more in support than he had intended to give.

In the car husband and wife were silent and when it drew up to their apartment building in Park Lane, Ezra tapped on the glass partition which slid reluctantly open.

'Driver, could you be kind enough to help Lady Sterling to the entrance?'

The driver looked from the entrance to his cab, a distance of perhaps fifteen feet, and sniffed. Then he noticed the earnest expression of his fare and the white face of the lady. He grunted out of his seat, farted at the unaccustomed exercise and opened the cab door for them. With one arm Ezra held Audrey and with the other, tightly, the hand of the driver which he did not release until they were safely inside.

Then, 'Audrey, have you a fiver?'

Audrey, without demur, opened her handbag.

'Oh no, Lord Sterling – it is Lord Sterling, isn't it? Yes, I thought I recognized you. Oh no, that I could not possibly manage to accept.' He was chairman of the local Labour Party ward in his native Clapham and was not in favour of lords. 'Consider it as a favour, Lord Sterling. I have already been paid once.'

'I would appreciate it if *you* would consider it as a favour,' said Ezra, handing him the note.

'All right, then,' said the driver briskly, taking the money, 'on the strict understanding that I give it to the wife for the WIZO. She collects for them, you see. We've a boy in Israel and they need all the help they can get. Barry Krost's the name, by the way.'

They all shook hands, embarrassedly watched by the puzzled night porter. Ezra's expression indicated that their acquaintance was unlikely to be renewed, but Audrey managed to say, 'Really, how interesting.'

'Yes,' replied Mr Krost. 'They need all the help they can get, I say, what with that effing Nasser. . . . Ah well, good night, folks!'

Ezra sat on Audrey's bed and removed his shoes. Audrey fetched him a tumbler of whisky and sat by him. Neither had spoken.

'Ezra, I didn't tell you, but I saw those men earlier today. . . .'

'Which men?' whispered Ezra, but he knew perfectly well and she knew he knew.

'When I went to have my hair done, they were there when I went in and then when I came out . . . in a big black American car, the sort you see in films, a gangster's car,' and she shivered. 'And just as Jenkins had started up they roared after us and forced us into the side. There was nearly an accident.' She paused and added in a flat voice. 'Ezra, what's going on?'

Ezra groaned.

'You haven't broken your promise to me, have you, Ezra. . . . It's something to do with Chuck?' she said more sharply.

'No, dear, I haven't broken my promise, and what's been going on will now stop going on.' He stood up, took his whisky, patted her thigh and said, 'Trust me, will you, Audrey?'

In his stockinged feet Ezra walked to his study and dialled the only number he knew by heart. 'Mrs Winterbourne?'

'Lord Sterling.'

'Do you have Mr Lambkin's telephone number?'

'Well, it's in the book, isn't it?' Mrs Winterbourne did not sound as if her mind were on her job. She was probably in the arms of her stockbroker lover and possibly slightly giddy from drink. It was fairly late. But then there was a sharp intake of breath and a change in her voice.

'Mr Lambkin?'

'Yes.'

'He rang up. He wanted to see you tonight. I told him you were going to the theatre. I thought that was a sensible enough thing to say, but then I think I must have told him which theatre. . . .'

'And where I was going afterwards?'

'No, I don't think so. . . . Oh dear, have I done the wrong thing?'

'No, my dear,' said Ezra gently, 'you have done nothing wrong. Just ring him up and tell him . . .' He paused, searching for the right phrase. 'Tell him to send his man to see my man.'

4

The stars were wheeling around in the most dangerous way as if about to fall out of their sockets. The street was no more trustworthy, thought Jeremy, and the whole of the Plakka was attacked by vertigo, lurching from side to side like a drunken ship. Ah, there's the clue. He sat down gingerly on the tipsy pavement vainly willing the sea to subside. God, he was drunk. For the umpteenth time he counted the small notes in his pocket. They never diminished, however many cans of retsina one consumed in however many tavernas. The serious money and his passport were in a plastic Sterlings sales dossier which he had substituted, at the last moment, for the briefcase he did not possess. The stone steps were growing cold. With difficulty Jeremy slipped the folder under his bottom and sat on it, hoping the solidity it represented might permeate his body – like leaving some truffles in a basket of eggs. Osmosis. 'Oshmoshis,' he said aloud. Oh dear, it was no good. The street began again, quite firmly, to rotate. Why had he brought the ridiculous object with him anyway? Why hadn't he left it at the hotel? He had left it behind in at least three tavernas and had it courteously returned to him. He mustn't lose it. It contained his money and his passport and the name of the ship, or did one say boat . . . no. 'Yacht,' said Jeremy aloud.

What a silly word! What a silly word. Jeremy giggled and began to croon, 'Stille Yacht, Heilige Yacht, dum de dum, dum de dum . . .'

Some people passing looked at him curiously.

'It's all right, I'm English,' said Jeremy.

They smiled and one gave him the Churchill V–sign. He tried to reply in kind but his fingers would not perform.

He wondered if he was going to be sick.

He was.

He had made the distance to the gutter – a good eighteen miles – and had vomited quite neatly, but now the problem was to remove himself from the scene of the disgrace. Up the street, or down? Safer up. Towards those shaky stars. *Semper ad astra.* Jeremy crawled one layer up and sited himself on a fresh step, carefully clutching his folder.

He surveyed himself. He was still drunk and now his head ached. He tried to focus on the immediate past. Ferty had said it was only natural for the guard's van, no, the vanguard, to be drunk, as the people employed on such missions tended to be young, dispensable, irresponsible and, arriving in a foreign capital, what on earth could they expect?

Ferty, a fast-talking stringer for an impeccably stolid firm of New York brokers, now called himself Prinz von *und* zu Furstenburg, but was known by his contemporaries in the City simply as 'Bei-bei'. He had terrified Jeremy with prophecies of evaporation of the modest settlement Sarah had handed him if he did not hedge by buying stock in a heavily-tipped-for-takeover Midwest corporation which specialized in sanitary equipment. 'What could be safer?' he had frothed. 'And they are all so constipated in the Midwest. . . . Do admit.' Nevertheless, this so unromantic stock dwindled to nothing in a surprisingly few weeks and Jeremy learnt the meaning of the letters NV on a portfolio – no value. When he protested all Ferty replied was, 'Sorry, dear . . . You remember Eisenhower's last speech. Well,' he coughed, 'so.' On the verge of tears – how could Ferty be so flippant about his money – Jeremy had tried to sound cold and indignant.

'So the market's very sensitive about that sort of thing. Sorry, dear, bye-bye.'

The memory of this unhappy speculation should have sobered Jeremy, but he felt only nausea and resentment. Ferty had swept into the Grande Bretagne with a noisy party of slightly battered debutantes, just as Jeremy was going up to his room, and had insisted he join them for endless gin fizzes in the bar. The expedition, for they belonged to a very large yacht at Turcolimanis which was en route to a very small island owned by a Greek called Sami, seemed to be funded by an American lady with a bright yellow wig and a merry manner. 'She *is* a Gould,' hissed Ferty, 'but from the wrong side of the blanket, my dear, and she likes me because I get her drachmas on the black market.' After many rounds, where Ferty's assistance over her currency problems continued to please the American lady, the party repaired to a restaurant in Kolonaki, the core in a limousine and the court in cabs, where she was vulgar enough to complain, not at the size of the bill presented to her – because the equivalent in real money eluded her – but at the number of people she had entertained. She had singled out him, Jeremy, not because he was the latest addition to her guest list, but

on account of his goddamn plastic bag and she hadn't come to the
eternal city to entertain a load of bum travelling salesmen. Loyally,
Ferty had decided to abandon her, had piloted her back to the ever-
patient limousine, and the rest of them had decided to go slumming
in the Plakka with Jeremy, the instrument of their release from that
dreadful woman, as temporary hero. But not for long. After the
third or fourth taverna, searching for better bouzouki music, more
retsina, Jeremy found himself alone and shivering on this step.

He decided to walk it off. After endlessly stumbling with a
drunkard's confidence in the direction of his hotel, down endless
silent streets, he came across a bench and decided to take a short
rest. He stretched himself out on the hard wood, sweeter to him
than a feather bed, and fell instantly asleep.

He never remembered the headlight on his white face, a car
stopping, being lifted into the back seat, stacked into an elevator,
being undressed and laid out on a divan, like a foolish flower.

The sound of a key being turned twice in a lock made Jeremy
blink open his eyes. There was some more fidgeting, the sound of a
big man moving about, and he promptly shut his eyes again. When
it was safe, Jeremy saw that his host was indeed a big fellow but
was moving dexterously round a tiny kitchen, unpacking groceries
and humming something from *Carmen*. He looked to be about
forty, with thinning hair, compressed lips and eyes, well built,
easy and controlled. He wore a seersucker suit with dark blue and
white stripes, white shirt and a dark tie. Jeremy sat up.

'Hello,' he said.

The man, in the process of lighting the gas cooker, did not
immediately react, but this done, he turned round and walked
towards Jeremy.

'Why, hello, young man, and how do you feel this morning?' He
spoke quietly in a Texan accent, barely moving his lips, and
sounded concerned.

'Oh, all right, thank you. And I must thank you for being kind
enough to look after me. I'm sorry to be such a nuisance.'

'Don't you worry about that, Jeremy. You see, when I first saw
you on that bench in Constitution Square I thought you might be

one of our boys, but then you looked too . . . uh,' he was going to say 'cute', 'but your hair was too long. Look at that note I left for you on the table, and you'll know all.'

Jeremy looked. On the table by the divan stood a glass of drinking water, two fat tablets and a note written in a large shopgirl's hand:

Jeremy [it read], here is some Alka Seltzer. If you take a shower or want to make some coffee, read the instructions first, otherwise you will blow yourself up. Back at one but won't wake you.
Sincerely, JAKE B. GOODY, USN

'But you didn't come back, did you?'

Jake smiled with every bit of his huge face.

'Yes, I came back at around one and you didn't wake up. And last night I came back – quite late – and you didn't wake up. . . .'

'So today is tomorrow, as it were,' said Jeremy. 'Omigod.'

'You weren't drunk, you were very, very drunk – almost doped. So you've lost a day. You're still due plenty more. Where'd ya bin, Jeremy?' He pronounced it Jurmy and looked for a moment severe.

'Well, there was free champagne on the plane. . . .'

'Yes, I forgot you'd only just come into town.'

'How do you know that? And . . . and howd' you know my name, come to think of it?' But he failed to sound indignant, his head ached so.

'Jeremy Kind, you are about twenty-five years old, a naturalized British subject, born in Hamburg, and you probably represent Sterling Industries UK Office Equipment. . . .'

'I certainly do not.'

'And you need something to eat,' Jake said in a changed voice. 'Get up and I'll fix you breakfast.' He turned towards the kitchen, changed his mind and said, 'I had to open your folder to find out who you were and where you came from. I figured your mummy and daddy might be worrying about you.'

Jeremy thought this was not the time to explain that he was without the benefit of those institutions, but he did ask, 'How did you open it? It's supposed to be locked.'

'It was, but there was a lil' key, tied to the handle,' and he turned again.

'Oh, don't go before you tell me who you are, please, er, Jake.' Jeremy tried to sound humble; the man was really rather nice.

The older man turned back. 'All right, then, but it's not very glamorous. My name you know, Jake Goody. I'm a procurement officer for the U.S. Navy and I buy everything from carbon paper to cabbages when the fleet's in. So when I found' – he walked over to a desk – 'this in your briefcase,' and he put a brochure in Jeremy's lap, 'I thought maybe you and I could be in business.'

Jeremy was staring at the brochure which showed on the cover a lady with prominent breasts gazing hungrily into a filing cabinet. Clipped to that was his card, a relic of his six months' stint at the business when he left Oxford, and attached to that was a letter dated what must be today, addressed to Sterlings' Export Division in London, signed by Jacob B. Goody, DSv., USN, asking for a quotation for an inordinate number of the sort of articles with which big businesses decorate their offices.

'What on earth do you want all this stuff for?'

Jake shook his head admiringly. 'Why, Jeremy . . . do you believe in the soft sell? C'mon, let me show you how to work the shower.'

A few minutes later Jeremy let out a piercing shriek; he had found the water too cold, had turned the hot tap too sharply and been rewarded by a dose of scalding hot, bright water. By the time Jake appeared to adjust the machine, Jeremy was shivering with cold again.

He contemplated Jeremy's naked form with disguised interest. 'Yeah,' he said, 'it took me some time to get acquainted with that apparatus. Wait till you see the freezer. She's a brute with a mind of her own.'

Jake, it did not take Jeremy long to discover, was only passionate or solemn about the minutiae of life. He was, as Jeremy's New College friend Yoville would have said, thoroughly anal – tidy, cautious, a saver, perhaps even mean, but considerate and friendly. Their breakfast consisted of fresh orange juice from an appliance the like of which Jeremy had never seen, croissants from Zonar across the street, regular coffee from America, milk and butter via Holland from the PX, and honey from Ymethus. There was the right amount of everything. Jake would not be drawn on any serious topic – the role of the Sixth Fleet, the ambitions of Nasser ('He's in the driver's seat, he's got his foot on the gas pedal. . . . I dunno if he has his hands on the wheel.' Jeremy sensed that this observation was not original with Jake.) All he offered about himself was that he was born on the wrong side of the tracks in Texas some place, that he looked after his parents in a retirement home in Miami, that he would shortly leave the Navy to become the local representative of an American bank. His fortune, he explained, was his face; not because it was so 'purty', but because he looked so honest, which was why he had his present job – the previous guy having been too tender to Athenian contractors.

'Haven't you been,' asked Jeremy, 'a bit tender towards me?'

Jake almost blushed. 'Well, yes, but, you won't believe it but we really do need all this stuff, as you call it, Jeremy, and your prices look all right, and with the cost of freight going up we're allowed to make purchases in Europe. I just thought . . . I just thought it would be nice for you to make a few dollars from Uncle Sam. A gesture – a little uncharacteristic, I guess, but I sorta liked you on sight,' and he almost blushed again.

'Well, I hope it comes off,' said Jeremy airily, but noticing Jake's downward glance of disappointment at the tone of his voice, he added, 'No, really, if it did it would shake them – the family, I mean.'

Jeremy, as he told Jake, had not been much good at the business. After Oxford, where he got a fourth, he had promised Sarah and Ezra to give it six months' trial, and had started off as a trainee. But that didn't work because everybody, including the instructors, thought he was a sort of spy; so they whisked him into the head office and then round the world almost. But that was no good because all the agents did was get him drunk and expect him to make passes at their daughters or their nieces or whatever.

'And did you, could you?' asked Jake.

'Well, there was one time on the beach at Durban with a girl in the moonlight, and that sort of thing, and I believe that's all there is to do in Durban. . . . Nothing much happened.'

'Has it occurred to you, Jeremy . . . No, tell me some more, do go on.'

'Well, that was my world tour and I didn't sell one typewriter ribbon, let alone an intercom set which was the most interesting thing in my division. I wasn't allowed near any of the heavy stuff – radar and electronic gear. . . . And so I gave up and they were quite relieved really.'

At the recollection of his duty to a part of the family and his dereliction, he cried out, 'Oh, God, I shouldn't be here. I'm supposed to be on the boat, already checking the stores, or some such non-sense. I'm supposed to know Greek but I don't know a word. I tried to buy a copy of *Teach Yourself Greek* but they only had old Greek. Oh Christ,' and he jumped up from the table to look for his briefcase. 'No . . .,' he murmured a moment later.

'What now, Jeremy?' queried Jake softly.

'They've taken all my money, or someone has. There was the equivalent of a hundred pounds in drachmas, and it's nearly all gone. I thought they were supposed to be honest. . . .'

'Well, considering they're so poor, they are honest. But late at night on the Plakka and you were very drunk. . . .'

Jeremy considered. The last time he had been handed back his case by a *mikro* it had been with a particularly winning smile, he remembered.

'And they probably left you enough for the cab home?'

'Yes,' said Jeremy, fingering the solitary remaining note. 'They did.'

'Jeremy,' asked Jake, walking into the other room, 'what exactly are you supposed to be doing here?'

Jeremy told him, and concluded: 'And what you didn't know is how neurotic they get when things go wrong. If they're there and I'm not, and I'm supposed to be, they'll ring up the hotel. They'll think I've been kidnapped, they'll get on to the agent if there is one, and make him get on to the Consul. Not that I matter particularly . . . that's just the way they are. Even Aunt Tattie. And also,' added Jeremy with a burst of wisdom, 'it'll be worse because they'll be bored and having nothing else to do.' He looked helplessly at Jake. 'I'd better get changed in the hotel and get a taxi to the Piraeus. But then I haven't got enough money for the bill and all that. . . .'

Jake looked at his unexpected guest affectionately and allowed himself to pat his knee.

'Take it easy, son. I have a plan.'

The Chevrolet, with its US Navy numberplate and glass darkened against the eastern Mediterranean sun, smooched along the quay and came to a quick standstill with the rear doors exactly opposite the gangway of MV *Atlanta*, the only yacht in what was clearly not a yacht basin. Jeremy, slightly hot in one of Nicky's endless Harrods suits, felt ransomed, healed, revived (if not forgiven), both apprehensive and secure by the side of Jake, who wore his uniform with two glaring rows of ribbons. The fair-haired driver, a sailor with a nose so snub and a face so pink that he looked like a freshly scrubbed pig, opened the door and stood to attention as Jake and Jeremy climbed out. Jeremy wished that some of the inhabitants, if that was the right word, of MV *Atlanta* would be around to witness the performance but, alas, the first human being – if you could say that, thought Jeremy – was Jericho, one of Lucy's twins, who was sitting on the taffrail swinging his white little legs.

'Gosh, Uncle Jeremy,' he shrieked, 'are *you* in the doghouse!'

'Charming child,' muttered Jake. 'By the way, Jeremy, what do I call your auntie? Is she Lady something?'

'No,' said Jeremy, childishly awkward at the outsize bouquet they had decided to invest in, 'you call her . . .' and he had a moment of inspiration, 'Mrs Lambkin.'

The atmosphere under the luxurious awning rigged up aft of MV *Atlanta*'s main saloon was endemic to those situations where people are gathered together (and paid to be so) for the purposes of giving pleasure to their hostess. Tense. As Jeremy had predicted, they were already bored and he felt like Daniel entering a den of overfed lions. Chuck had clearly not arrived and Tattie's irritation had infected them all. He, Jeremy, could therefore be blamed for the heat, the oily water, their cabins being on the wrong side of the boat. . . . Plus the fact that, because Chuck was not there, the lions though not hungry, were badly in need of drink. Lucy, with typical family hauteur, ignoring the presence of a stranger, was the first to consolidate the idea.

'Jeremy, where on earth have you been? We looked for you everywhere. You were supposed to be here checking the stores and you weren't. You didn't even spend the night in the hotel. Mr Lemnis was going to get on to the police, weren't you?'

The fat Levantine gentleman in the yellow suit and matching shoes, at whom Lucy briefly looked while pecking angrily at her crochet throughout this outburst, smiled sweatily. There was a silence. If Lucy had not spoken for them all, she had given the official family view. Everyone was looking at him and only Mme Hélène with any kindness; the others, Sir Arthur and his boyfriend, the faceless Dr Krapf, and the two little boys, with eyes cold and curious.

'I do apologize, Mrs Lambkin, for my intrusion on your yacht, but I am totally to blame for your nephew's absence. Permit me to introduce myself, Commander Jake Goody, United States Navy.' His cap tight under his left arm, Jake bent low over Tattie's hand, which he took in perfect Naval Academy fashion, and then stood up straight. 'You shouldn't be too angry with him, ma'am, because we've been doing business together.' His small trustworthy eyes flickered over the rest of them, sure and easy, but his look returned to Tattie. 'You see, young Jeremy here is quite a salesman in his quiet way, and I believe I've bought some of your product. One of my chores is buying for our Sixth Fleet here. . . .' There was a ripple of interest. 'Oh, nothing lethal, you understand, just office equipment, filing, cabinets, intercoms, that sort of stuff.'

'But . . .' Lucy looked up at Jeremy.

'You know, Lucy, when I was on that course at Watford; when I was in the business. I still have the brochure,' he whispered.

'Ah,' said Lucy, satisfied, and returned to her crocheting.

'There are some flowers for you, Tattie,' said Jeremy quickly.

'Silly boy, wasting your money like that,' said Tattie, mock-huffily. Jake and Jeremy managed to exchange glances.

So what if they've been to bed together, thought Sir Arthur's boyfriend, Patrick, there are worse ways of getting an order and he *is* sexy in a sluggish sort of way.

The American's *very* attractive, thought Hélène.

I like him, thought Lucy, peeping up from her crochet. He's a man you can trust.

'Why don't you ask your friend what he would like to drink and introduce him, for heaven's sake,' said Tattie.

'Arthur Coleport,' said Sir Arthur, rising from his wicker chair. 'Get the steward, will you, Paddy. And what can we offer you, sir?'

'This is Sir Arthur Coleport,' said Jeremy hurriedly.

'Well, Sir Arthur, I guess in this sort of weather I find hard liquor difficult to take, so I stick to champagne,' said the boy from the wrong side of the tracks. The introductions proceeded, Jake taking each one seriously, in the American way.

The steward had arrived, a sulky Corsican reminiscent of the late Pierre Laval and equally blue-chinned. '*Una bottiglia di sciampagna, per favore*, Alfonso,' hooted Sir Arthur, and glancing around the company he saw Tattie fussing with her flowers, Lucy placid with her crochet.

'No, better be safe, *due*.'

'And tell the chef there'll be one more for lunch, Alfonso,' piped Tattie.

'Oh, Mrs Lambkin, that's too kind . . . uh, may I tell my driver?'

'That's all right,' said Jeremy, 'I'll tell him. What time?'

'Tell him to go have some lunch and come back at three.'

Jeremy nodded deferentially, junior to senior, salesman to customer, with a mixture of intimacy and respect.

From that moment on it was a bowl of Jello. Jake was a hit all round – Placed at Tattie's right, he listened to her complaints about the quality of fixtures and fittings aboard the *Atlanta*, sympathized with her over the discrepancy in the stores – Chablis half a dozen short, Cointreau two bottles short, no Armagnac at all – and everybody knew that Chuck, her future husband – she wasn't Mrs Lambkin yet, by the way – needed a variety of liquors for his famous cocktails. Jake fended off Mme Hélène with a few inaudible compliments, agreed blandly with Sir Arthur about the villainy of Colonel Nasser. Jeremy, stuck between Solomon Lemnis, the business agent, exiled from Cairo, and Lucy who was fussing over the twins' diet, watched himself move from pride in his new friend's undoubted achievement to jealousy at being excluded from his attention, for not once did Jake look at him.

At one moment the question of bouzouki was mentioned and

addressed as a matter of course to Jake, the authority on matters Athenian. He mumbled that something could surely be arranged but this was too much (or too little) for the neglected Mr Lemnis, who leapt to his feet and began to sing and dance with surprising nimbleness in Greek. His *bonhomie* restored by the applause, Solomon Lemnis began to explain how, when Mr and Mrs Lambkin found it convenient, he would arrange for bouzouki to be played for them on the boat, under the moon, performed by the finest players in all Greece, at the drop of a handkerchief, and at his own personal expense.

There were more hurrahs and Solomon Lemnis beamed. 'And by the way,' he added, holding up his hand with the diamond on it, 'if you would like to join me on Friday night at my cousin's apartment – we say *kiddish* – you are most welcome. It will be a simple family affair. . . .' He faltered as he saw an expression on the faces of his hitherto captive audience, that they did not doubt him for one moment. 'A simple, er, family affair,' he repeated. 'Ah well, another time.'

Jake provided a happy distraction by taking his leave and offering Mr Lemnis a lift back to Athens. At the same time he steered Jeremy ahead of him. Walking down the deck Jake said, 'That Sir Arthur, I didn't know they came like that any more. Well, Jeremy, how'd I do?'

'You did very well, Jake, thank you,' said Jeremy.

'Oh hell, it was great fun. What's worrying you?'

'Nothing. I just hope you're serious about that order. That fat man seemed to think I was trespassing on his territory.'

Jake slowed his step. 'Yeah . . . we'll have to take care of that. Hey, I put my address and telephone numbers in this envelope. No, don't open it now.'

They had reached the car and Solomon Lemnis was hopping after them. The driver showed Jake into the back seat and motioned for the fat man to be installed in the front. Muttering that he thought he had left something in the car, Jeremy opened the other back door and while he briefly searched the floor, took Jake's hand and kissed it. He withdrew but Jake just had time to tickle the hairs on the back of Jeremy's neck.

Jeremy watched until the car turned off the quay. He opened the envelope. Pinned to an elaborate list of where Jake would be when, was a wad of mint drachma notes and a note in Jake's hand: 'In case you need a cab.' He didn't count them.

5

On the plane to Athens, Chuck looked at his watch, the standard Cartier with Roman numerals, but curved to the shape of the wrist. It was 10.30, but Chuck reckoned that as he had got up at 6 he could call it 12.30, and what with one thing and another that entitled him to a drink. He pressed the button in the armrest. The steward was there immediately. Had they bourbon? No, but they did have Canadian Club ... and ginger ale? 'That'll be fine,' said Chuck magnanimously, 'rye 'n' dry.'

He could afford to be generous; the terms were excellent. Hubert and Ezra's lawyer had been unprofessionally expeditious. Hubert, detached in his manner to Chuck as they moved towards victory, had called on Ezra's man in the Temple, his senior after all, and a move, he explained, that would be interpreted as a concession, which it was not. Chuck and Hubert had lunched immediately after at Hubert's club, the Garrick, handy for the Temple, and as they sat down Hubert slipped a note pencilled in his professional hand into Chuck's menu. It said:

Item. Miss T's shareholding in Sterling to be regarded as divisible into 20 parts.

Item. 12/20ths to Miss T. 5/20ths to Mr L. as marriage settlement. 3/20ths to Mr O. Barnet as marriage settlement.

Item. Miss T. to leave Mr O. Barnet her Sterling shares.

Item. An insurance policy to be raised to protect this against death duties. The cost of the premium to be divided between Miss T. and Lord S.

Item. Neither Miss T. nor Mr L. to sell Sterling A shares without first informing Lord S.

Item. Lord S. to pay costs.

'Potted shrimps and cold pressed duck, please,' said Chuck. A waitress had appeared, a motherly lady. She nodded.

'Now, dear, what is it today?' She turned to Hubert.

'Why not?' said Hubert, snapping the menu and giving it to her with one of his friendlier smiles.

'You will have observed ... er, Chuck, that this note is not in legal language, but it's none the worse for that. Remember also that we were only ever concerned with the shares in the business and that your wife's properties and chattels, which I understand are considerable, were never in jeopardy.'

Christ, thought Chuck, have they converted him?

'Secondly, the requirement that you and your wife inform Lord Sterling of your intention to sell shares is really very mild indeed and we concocted it as a sap to his Lordship's principal neurosis, viz., that control of the business could pass out of his control. M'yaas. You see.'

Hubert leant forward intently. 'You must understand the man. He's interested in power not money; as long as he can manipulate the shares he doesn't care who owns them. That was the motive behind, as it were, the raid. And once he was reassured that you had no ... er, political interest ...'

Chuck made a dismissive gesture.

'Exactly, the day was won. He can't do this forever – the thing's getting too big for one man – but by then I think he will hope to be dead. M'yaas.' He paused.

'Further, your wife,' Hubert continued, '– your future wife's undertaking to leave her nephew her shares in the business is in no way legally enforceable, though I'm sure you would not wish to divert her, as a man of honour, from so, er, sensible a course of action. M'yaas.'

Hubert's cold eyes froze on Chuck's face.

'Oh, sure,' said Chuck uneasily. My God, they *had* converted him. He paused. 'Hey, Hubert, what do you think, truly?'

A completely different expression overcame the younger man – one of pure joy.

'Truly,' he laughed in such a way that some members turned to stare. 'Truly, I think it's bloody marvellous.' And they were friends again. 'It was a close run thing,' added Hubert.

On the plane after the first slug of rye 'n' dry had stolen into his stomach, Chuck pulled out Hubert's note, the pencil now faint from much inspection. He also patted his pocket to reassure himself that Ezra's letter to his sister was still there. He had insisted on that. It wished her well.

She's a good girl, a brave girl, my Tattie. He glowed.

After lunch at the Garrick Club, Chuck had walked through Leicester Square round Piccadilly to Wartski's in Grafton Street (where Tattie of course had an account and where he was known) and bought a Fabergé egg inlaid with gold and with an emerald clasp. It was mounted and would serve as a receptacle for Tattie's sleeping pills. It had cost him more than he had in the world, but it was worth it. Chuck felt virtuous until the thought suddenly struck him: Christ, did Jews believe in eggs?

A fit of violent coughing from a seat two rows back on his right followed by a loud 'Bugger!' interrupted his thoughts, and he looked round (the first-class compartment was almost empty) to see a figure – it could not be, it was – a woman choking over a cigar. She wore green leather with heavy gold chains round her neck and a huge cross which clanked as she spluttered.

'Now I've lost the sodding thing.'

'Can I help you . . . er, madam?' The ubiquitous steward with little to do in the first class.

'Indeed you can, young man. I've knocked over the champagne and my contact lens has fallen out.'

'Oh, we'll soon find it, madam.'

'Oh, no, we won't,' she boomed. 'It's the size of a nail clipping and, if you think about it, obviously transparent. I've never found one yet. The trouble is they're so bloody expensive and you can't get them on the National Health.'

She raised her voice further, as if inviting approval and sympathy. Chuck turned away and noticed the well-dressed passenger across the aisle slowly lower his eyes and tighten his grip on his newspaper. Chuck could tolerate any kind of behaviour in private but his Methodist upbringing resisted ladies who swore in public. He resolved to keep his distance. The plane droned on.

And so did Sir Arthur. 'Mind you, he was a big man, was Oscar – I suppose that's why they call little Oscar little Oscar – so that when he took this crowbar he really knocked the stuffing out of those machines.'

'Why would he want to do that?' asked Lucy, frowning at her crochet.

'Because, dear girl, as I told you, he'd sold a lot of calculating machines – you know the kind that go whizz whizz whizz, you still see them in provincial French banks – to this insurance company in Leeds. And I'm talking now about 1910, well before the First War, and the firm had gone broke, as I told, you so big Oscar went in and smashed them.'

'But what did he care if they'd gone bust?' persisted Lucy with a typical mixture of logic and heartlessness.

'Down for three, Doc,' said Tattie.

'Golly, this is going to cost me a fortune,' moaned Dr Krapf.

'Because, dear girl, he'd sold them on hire purchase and he was worried that they'd flog them second-hand and bring down the price of his product by flooding the market!'

'Oh,' said Lucy.

'Now d'you see?' said Sir Arthur triumphantly. 'It was also . . . in those days, the policy of the business to give long credit and charge high prices. That's one of the ways they got started. What none of you realize,' continued Sir Arthur, 'is how long my family's been connected with the family.'

It was growing dark on deck; Tattie had not finished her gin rummy but did not feel like moving inside. The sunset was not disagreeable. Sir Arthur would not see that none of them cared too much about his family. 'Now, this'll interest you, Tattie. . . .'

Tattie made a faint movement with her hand and shut her eyes. There was a soothing breeze and the buildings were now deep pink.

'My father knew your father because he was his MP in Leeds, where the first office was. And he knew the man who was then in charge of excise in that area – quite a big job, you know, sending chaps round breweries and checking upon the schools with alcohol in their laboratories.'

'It doesn't sound like a very big job,' muttered Lucy.

'What's that?' queried Sir Arthur. 'Well, anyway, this feller, he was called Mason actually, let your father into England when he didn't speak a word of English, and gave him money when he hadn't a bob in the world. And d'you know what Oscar did, the moment he'd made a few quid? He . . .'

'And where on earth have you lot been?'

Four figures emerged from the gap in the taffrail; one tall, one slight, and two tiny. They became recognizable as Sir Arthur's friend, Patrick, the French cabin boy, called *mouche* for convenience, and the twins.

'Oh, Lucy, don't take on so. The boys had a wonderful time,' said Patrick, flapping his arms.

'*Je m'excuse, madame*,' said the *mouche* simultaneously.

'Don't just stand there. Can't you see they're shivering with cold? Go and get some bath towels. *Vite!*' commanded Lucy.

Sir Arthur was not too pleased either. That cabin boy was too pretty for his own good. Surely Patrick could have managed the motorboat without him?

'Now, you two,' said Lucy, countermanding her own recent instructions, 'you run downstairs to your bedrooms, or whatever they're called, and have a hot bath.'

'We don't need a bath,' squeaked one twin, 'we've been having a bath all day.' This sally struck the other twin as extraordinarily funny and they both ran below, doubled up with laughter.

'Well den, Sir Arta, de sun sure way down under de hardarm, so don't we get a drink?' said Patrick in his not-so-far-from-base mock-bog-Irish voice, as he walked over to his patron to pat him on the cheek. He stopped as the beam of a car's headlights swivelled across the deck.

'It must be Chuck,' breathed Tattie, suddenly alert.

'Surely he'd have sent a telegram?' suggested Lucy.

'He probably did,' replied Sir Arthur, 'but remember what I always say, Greece is not part of Europe, we're in the Balkans.' Arthur was becoming a bore, thought Tattie, and she must remember not to ask him again; but any unkind thought about anyone or anything fled from her mind because it was, indeed, Chuck.

'You didn't tell us you were coming. . . .' She tried to hide her happiness.

'Honey, I did . . . but never mind. Here I am,' and he spread out his hands, high, wide and handsome. 'Hi, gang!'

Giving his arrival additional *cachet* was the dithering presence of the Captain, who was glad to see the man who had chartered the vessel.

'Hello, Lucy there, where are the boys?'

'In bed, I hope,' said Lucy, pleased.

'And Sir Arthur, and Patrick, how nice, and Doc.' He shook hands with them all and then spun on his heel for there was Hélène, on cue, in the well of the companionway, freshly rested in her 'of Troy' cocktail dress.

'My God, Hélène, you look a little lovelier each day!' He bowed low and kissed her hand. 'For you, I'd have launched two thousand ships.' Miming as if he had forgotten something, and clicking his fingers, he walked over to Tattie's chair and kissed her on the lips.

'And for my own true love.' He pressed into Tattie's hand an envelope and a small package, then turned to the watchful company, radiant with triumph.

'Just a note for Tattie from Ezra,' he said. 'Now, is someone going to fix me a drink?'

It must have gone well. There had been rumours.

Chuck had thought of everything, except an adaptor for his electric razor, and was shaving with Captain Hook's ancient badger-hair brush with its yellowing ivory handle, the ivory-handled cut-throat razor, a cracked wooden bowl containing some cracked shaving soap. There was also a leather strop for honing the blade and a leather box containing colognes in tiny silver-topped decanters and a battery of first aids in case, the Captain explained, Mr Lambkin should happen to cut himself. Happen! said Chuck to himself as he added another little blob of cotton wool to his face, why he was going to look like Father Christmas for the ball. Damn! Some more good American blood had just been spilt.

'What is it, Chuck, are you all right, dear?' said Tattie from her position in front of the dressing table mirror.

'No, I'm not all right, Tattie. Look at me,' and he strode into their stateroom.

'My God,' said Tattie, horrified in front of the glass. 'Your face is covered with blood. I'll send for the Doctor.'

'No, no, honey, it's nothing really,' and he wiped his face with a flannel. Poor thing, he thought, she's probably never seen a man shave. Tattie was trying on pieces of jewellery for the party – trying them on and not taking them off.

'I can't think of anything to wear,' she said weakly.

'Well, honey, you've had a damn good try. If I'm going to look like Santa Claus, you'll be the Christmas tree. The Lord forbids earrings, otherwise you'd have a chandelier hanging on to each lobe. Now, come on, honey, concentrate. . . .'

'It's all very well for you, you men don't have this problem. Oh, I wish you had let me bring Estelle,' she moaned.

Estelle was her maid and one reason for Miss Sterling's *parure* not being too exaggerated was that the jewels were laid out for her. Occasionally Tattie would cheat and pop one more ring on a finger when her maid's back was turned.

'I think the decision must be, with that pink dress, diamonds, only diamonds,' Chuck added sternly.

'But I could still have the two little sapphire brooches.'

'No, Tattie, don't you see, that introduces another colour. I want you to be pink and white, like a marshmallow.'

There was a knock on the door and a voice said:

'It's me, Arthur, can I come in?'

The sight of his host and hostess covered respectively in blood and diamonds unnerved and enthralled Sir Arthur. 'I say, what have you done to yourself, dear boy?'

'It's the Captain's steam razor which I find difficult to control.'

But Sir Arthur's eyes, round with admiration in which there was no room for envy, were on Tattie's dressing table.

'Gosh,' he said. 'Oh, Chuck,' – he recovered himself – 'there's a journalist come aboard, from the *Daily Express*, wants to interview you.'

'Can't you tell him to piss off?' asked Chuck, dabbing his face.

'Chuck!' protested Tattie, as she reluctantly removed a clip.

She had no objection to being in the papers. Why should it always be Audrey who got the publicity in the family?

'I don't believe so, Chuck,' said Sir Arthur slowly. 'She's clad entirely in green suede and looks like an all-in wrestler.'

God, it had to be her, thought Chuck.

'Does she have a great big cross round her neck?'

'I didn't see that, but she does wear boots. Why, do you think you know her?'

Chuck nodded. Maybe the cross was but a device for protection against the hazards of aerial travel.

'Keep her talking, Arthur, can you? Tell her I'll be right up, but tell her nothing and don't let her get inside, right?' It was the new, authoritative Chuck speaking.

'All right, old boy,' said Sir Arthur. 'I think I know how to deal with the fourth estate.'

I wonder if he does, thought Chuck. There had been no coverage in the national press of Sir Arthur's own little troubles, but that might have been due to Ezra's efforts. Hubert had used the Hickey column effectively at a crucial moment and he could hear him explaining that no hound, or to be precise, bitch of the press, once unleashed, would meekly return to kennels while the scent was still fresh. The Hickey lot were not in the marriage bureau business. If anything, the reverse.

Chuck strolled through the saloon where the chairs and tables had been pushed to the sides to give room for a buffet which the chef, in a clean white hat, was titivating.

Alfonso had shaved and looked almost cheerful. The Captain, who had earlier confessed to an artistic nature, was quite unself-consciously arranging some flowers. 'Everything to your liking, sir?' he asked.

'Why yes, Captain. Better than that; you've done a great job.'

'Well, we try to put our best foot forward on these occasions. If it's worth doing, do it properly. That's what I always say. . . . *Non pas là*, là,' he interrupted himself to correct the *mouche* who was trying to balance a wine cooler on the buffet. '*Non, pas là*, là.'

'Yes,' said Chuck, 'she looks like a shipshape ship,' and he walked on deck.

A naval cruiser, probably American, lay at anchor; lit up and dressed fore and aft. She was a fine sight, strung with a necklace of lamps, some of which had gone out. It was faintly hazy and the lights of an aeroplane crawling across the sky were brighter than the stars which tonight the angels had left unpolished. The standard attendants of MV *Atlanta* who, since she was tied up on a quay not normally frequented by yachts, remained loyal to her alone, had been augmented tonight. They had heard about the bouzouki, perhaps, so that in addition to the permanent, hopeful taxi and the bootblack whom no one had yet patronized and the sinister men in suits playing with their beads and the bevy of little boys who just stared, there were groups of young men walking in one direction crossed by groups of girls walking in the other. There was a feeling of friendly expectation in the air, thought Chuck, until he saw the green suede figure temporarily barricaded between Arthur and the gangway on the other side of the boat.

Chuck dabbed at his face with a handkerchief, but couldn't see clearly enough to know whether he had stopped bleeding. He lit a cheroot. At the flash of light the creature in green turned her head and caught his eye. Sir Arthur made a gesture of polite self-dismissal and walked tactfully forward, allowing her to march round the stern of the boat towards Chuck, who stood perfectly still. Since he had seen her on the aeroplane she had abandoned the cross but had acquired an astrakhan hat and an eyeglass. Chuck felt like part of the fold the Assyrian comes down on, a lamb about to be devoured by the wolf.

'Mr Lambkin, I presume.' Her voice was not as disagreeable as her manner. Chuck nodded slightly.

'*Daily Express*, Hickey column,' she announced.

Drawing on his cheroot and exhaling the smoke slightly in her direction, Chuck acknowledged this with a second nod.

'I see we're having a hooley,' she said, pursing her lips and moving her jaw forward.

Chuck raised his eyebrows and inclined his head slightly to the right.

'A party. Well, I dare say you've a lot to celebrate, Mr Lambkin, but we understand Lord Sterling is not exactly, er, overjoyed at the prospect of the, er, proposed, er, nuptials.' She munched on the word and her eyes crinkled into a happy smile.

Chuck tilted his head to the left, no answering smile in his eyes, and blew smoke from his cheroot in such a way to cause her to step back.

'Wait a minute,' she said coolly, 'I must get something to write this down.' She unzipped her suede battledress, revealing a fur lining that must once have constituted the entire wardrobe of some animal and extracted a notebook into which she began scribbling.

What? thought Chuck.

'Tell me, Mr Lambkin,' she cooed, 'this drinking club you're the owner, or part owner of, it's in Bayswater somewhere, or is it in the West End?'

Chuck drew thoughtfully on his cheroot, edged slightly towards her, blew a thick stream of smoke straight into her eyes. Her exclamation of disgust changed into a bellow of rage as she fell backward, through the gap in the taffrail, into the formerly wine-dark but now, alas, oily Aegean sea.

To the Greeks on the quay, for whom no disaster is funny, the incident was proof that the tall man with the cigar was part of the Mafia. He had pushed the lady into the sea and she would surely drown. None looked down more apprehensively into the darkness than the lady's taxi driver whose meter registered the equivalent of one month's rent, and then they all started to shout and raise their hands. Captain Hook was adjusting a carnation when he heard a shout and a splash, which he understood immediately. That bloody little *mouche* had taken out the *Albatross* and not fastened the taffrail.

'*Homme* overboard!' he boomed. 'Alfonso, *dites à Gonzales de sortir le petit bateau et apportez-moi un torch, vite.*' Captain Hook had only one language for all foreigners and it was mostly French. He bounded on deck and saw the charterer calmly smoking a cigar. 'Someone fell overboard, sir?'

'Yes, Captain, but I think she'll survive.'

He was right. The sounds coming from the inky darkness were, after some spluttering, anything but distressed. There was laughter, a shout of 'God, what an arse I am . . . now I've lost the fucking

Hasselblad,' more 'God, what an arse I am,' more laughter, then, '*Donna e mobile*', *fortissimo*, then another snatch of song which Lucy, had she been around, would have recognized as stemming from their old school, Cheltenham Ladies' College. Chuck leaned over the side of the boat and flicked his famous Zippo which fluttered blue and yellow but which did not go out.

'Make for the light, ma'am,' he shouted.

'That's all right, I'll manage.' She hove into view, Alfonso had found a torch and the three of them hauled her aboard. The asktrakhan had gone but not the eyeglass which swung like a pendulum from her sodden torso. Once on deck she stood up briskly and shook herself like a dog. She addressed herself to Chuck.

'Terribly sorry about my behaviour. Ghastly manners that, bursting in on your house party. Filthy trade, journalism.' She panted. 'Learnt my lesson. Do forgive. Name is Jacqueline Graham Taylor. Most people call me Percy. How d'ye do?'

Chuck took her hand. 'Welcome aboard, Percy,' he said, but he meant it. She comes straight out of P. G. Wodehouse, he thought. 'Come, let's get you some dry clothes.'

'I'd be happy if the chef could lend me . . .' she said.

Chuck looked at her bulky form and smiled.

'Yes, maybe you could take over, Captain?'

And odd procession walked for'ard to the fo'c'sle hatch.

How did she know we had a chef, wondered Chuck. She had done her homework.

Like all veteran party-givers, Tattie was a prey to first-night nerves and like many, she tortured herself by arriving too early upon an empty scene. She sat in the only armchair, which had been specially positioned by the door to the after deck, drumming her fingers. She wished she'd not bitten them so savagely when she was a little girl. She felt sad. Why? Well, there is no foundation for the gloom. 'Poor little rich girl,' she hummed. Wasn't there a song about someone who gives a party to which no one comes, or was it a famous short story? She could ask Lucy but the sight of her purling and plaining away at that infernal crochet put her off. Couldn't she, tonight, for once, have left the damn thing in her cabin?

'What's it going to be when it's finished?' she asked.

'Oh, this? I dunno really. I suppose a sort of nursery rug. . . .' replied Lucy without looking up. She had all the stolidity and concentration on the matter in hand of her father and none of Sarah's dash, thought Tattie.

'And where'd you get that pretty frock?' pursued Tattie, but without enthusiasm.

'Oh, d'you like it, Aunt Tattie? You won't believe it; I got it at C&A, just changed the buttons and belt and put on the clip you gave me, and really, you'd never know, would you?'

You would, thought Tattie. It was ridiculous, considering how much money the girl had, that she should look like a typist. Thank God she didn't have to leave her any shares. At least little Oscar knew what money was for.

'Can I get you a drink, Aunt Tattie?' Lucy broke the silence.

'No, don't you worry, dearie. I'll have a little champagne, but not before anyone comes, if anyone comes.'

'Don't be like that, Tattie . . . they'll come.' In Lucy's experience there had never been a shortage of people to consume free food and free drink.

'D'you know who you've invited, apart from the lady who fell into the sea? Funny business, that,' mused Lucy.

'Chuck said she was very nice,' Tattie reproved her. 'Well, there's us, that's, let me see, one, two, three . . . Eleven. That's all I'm sure of. I think Mr Lemnis will come with his family. And there's Jeremy's friend, the American.'

'Oh, yes, I like him.'

'And some friends of Jeremy's from Oxford.'

'They'll be drunk,' said Lucy.

'And there's my masseur, Janni, now I hope he comes. He's the only person *I've* asked. You should have him, Lucy. He did wonderful things to my neck.' Tattie closed her eyes and stretched her arms. She felt happy all of a sudden. Maybe because she heard the sound of the first arrivals on deck.

'How much does he charge?'

'I don't know, girl. Now, you go and get Chuck.'

But Lucy had no need to go on her errand because Chuck's voice

could be heard below. 'C'mon, you, we have company,' as
he rapped on the doors of the cabins in which the guests had
quickly learned to skulk, to postpone the evening's entertainment.
Curious, they emerged, and watched through the port as the crew
deftly handed aboard what could only be segments of Lemnis's
family.

'They remind me,' said Sir Arthur, 'of those pink mice, made of
fudge, they used to give one in Istanbul before the war.' They
filed politely into the saloon, marshalled from the rear by Solomon
Lemnis, like a troupe of theatrical moles, were presented with
pride by their producer and in turn presented, shyly, to Tattie
caskets of sweets, as soft and shiny as themselves. Then they
seemed to melt away, and later no one remembered their going
because suddenly the more regular sort of guests descended upon
MV *Atlanta*.

It was Ferty's group. The expedition had been a disaster, he
explained to Jeremy in a showery whisper. Sami, the Greek, had
taken evasive action. His yacht had been available but the key to
the drink could not be found, and when they arrived at his island
that had been locked up too. Sami himself was nowhere around and
they had crammed themselves into a taxi and driven back to
Athens, parched and indignant and swearing to dish Sami and all
his works the moment they got back to London. Jeremy, knowing
the humour of the metropolis wondered if they would succeed.

'Yes, quite, you're right, it would be fatal,' said Ferty. 'I can't
tell you how grateful I was to get your note. I hope your aunt won't
be cross that we're so many.' Jeremy assured his old friend that the
reverse would be true. 'Oh, good,' said Ferty. 'I must introduce her
to Lord Symington, he's someone we picked up last night, very
rich and not very nice – a cousin of the Marquess of . . . oh God, I
forget. I must be tight.' He signalled out from his group, which had
headed straight for the bar, an elegant grey-haired figure in a
Guards blazer with poached egg eyes.

'Tom, this is my friend Jeremy.'

'How are you?' said Lord Symington, and went on talking to a
large English girl with tombstone teeth. Jeremy enjoyed an instant
vibration of dislike, as if the man had said that he didn't mind

taking their food and drink but that did not mean they could presume. Still, he was a lord and that should have pleased Tattie who would be too excited to notice his disdain. He glanced in her direction. Tattie was talking to a rather pretty, obviously American woman in a long dress and corsage whom Jake, he had noticed with the faintest snatch of his heart, had escorted. He went over.

'Jeremy, this is Laura McGrath,' said Jake. 'Fortunately her husband, who is our attaché at the Embassy, has been called to Paris.'

'Yes,' said Laura, 'something to do with NATO, and aren't I lucky? What a beautiful home you have here, Jeremy, and everything so beautifully done!'

'Well, it's not really anything to do with me. . . .'

'Zonk,' said Jake softly under his breath for Jeremy's benefit as he led his lady away, making sure there was a replacement. It was Percy. Wearing the chef's trousers, Chuck's shirt, a scarlet silk scarf provided by Hélène – they had had fun dressing her up. She swaggered up to Tattie, bowed low like a page, clasped one fat hand in both of hers, knelt and uttered the words:

'My saviour.'

Tattie looked pleased. 'Well, as long as you don't get cold, dear.'

'Don't worry about me, madam, and forgive my sandaled feet. My boots are baking in your oven.'

'Oh, I'm terribly sorry about your accident – oh, do get up – they are so careless on this boat.' The edited version of the incident given to Tattie had confirmed her in her resolve to keep the boat at anchor. If dangerous things like this could happen in a harbour, how much worse would it be at sea!

Solomon Lemnis had been standing by and clearly wanted an audience.

'Ah, yes, Mr Lemnis. Where are the musicians, by the way? I thought you said . . .'

'Yes, indeed, Miss Lambkin, er, Sterling. Oh dear, there are plenty of musicians, plenty of them,' and he made a dolorous gesture in the direction of the quay. 'In fact, we have too many musicians, as a matter of fact.'

'Musicians coming out of our ears?' suggested Jeremy.

'Yes, exactly.' Solomon Lemnis nodded to Jeremy, as if he had made a serious contribution to the problem.

'Why won't they come and play?' asked Tattie.

'The trouble is, madam, there are two bands, the one I ordered and the one I did not,' he said loudly, and glared round the saloon, hoping to spot a guilty person, but people seemed to be otherwise engaged. 'And, of course, they are in disgrace and therefore neither will play.'

He reached up to the sky in despair. 'It's a question of *philotimo*!'

'What's that?' asked Tattie crossly.

'Oh, I can explain. Very tiresome, very Greek. You come across it all the time,' said Percy gruffly, swallowing a hunk of beef sandwich she had somehow contrived from the rather fussy buffet.

'Leave it to Percy. She'll sort 'em out.' And she touched Jeremy on the sleeve, took a bite out of her sandwich, stuck her eyeglass on and marched off, clutching Jeremy by the arm. 'Hold on to me, dear boy, will you? I'm like a hen in the dark; I don't see too well.'

Only in the dark, thought Jeremy, can she be said to be like a hen.

Percy regarded the two groups of musicians, angrily smoking cigarettes, and the attendant crowd of gapers, stood quite still under the quayside light and called out, 'Spiro!'

There was a silence and about seven men turned their heads. One advanced to the pool of light where Percy had theatrically placed herself, the eyeglass glinting, her massive hair thick on her shoulders. She looked like something from outer space.

'He's a good man, this,' muttered Percy to Jeremy. 'He's been driving me around looking for your bloody boat, and he speaks English.' She did not add and perhaps did not realize that her Spiro had been so generously treated that he had decided never to let the Kyrios, or rather, Kyria out of his sight. He glanced doubtfully at Jeremy, standing meekly in the shadow, and standing on tiptoe whispered into her ear.

'Bloody silly,' Jeremy heard her reply. There was some more whispering.

'Pathetic,' said Percy. 'And tell them they're not behaving like Greeks, you tell them, Spiro.' Percy stood in the spotlight, hands on hips, supreme, a *dea ex machina*, provided with thunderbolts and gold; then, when her messenger had reached the warring parties, like a matador who has fixed the bull, she turned to Jeremy. '*Philotimo*, hell, they were just arguing about how to split the fee. You see, two bands arrive for one gig, right? So immediately they think there's one fee, right? So which is the better band? Big argument. Come on, let's join the party.'

'So what happens now?' asked Jeremy.

'Don't look round, but I think we're being followed,' replied Percy. 'I told Spiro to say they'd both get paid. That's all right, isn't it? Your aunt wants music, doesn't she? And she'll have it . . . wherever she goes. By the way, where did you dig up that creep Symington? Fearful fellow, terrible bum, cousin of mine.' They had reached the gangway.

'Oh good,' said Percy, allowing herself a swift backward glance. 'Spiro's coming too.'

'Well done, Percy. You're terrific,' breathed Jeremy.

'Oh, d'you think so? I am glad,' and she patted his retaining arm.

'I can't imagine where they can plug in those amplifiers,' said the Captain.

Chuck was fending off a ravenous deb who was suggesting herself as a guide to the Greek islands and to anything else apparently. 'At least we could go to Hydra for the day? It's a super place, and I know a super rich Greek lady who's crazy about blue. Blue house, blue boat, blue dresses, and she'd love to give us all lunch.'

'You'll have to ask the boss, young lady,' said Chuck, and pointed his hand to the door where Tattie presided, luminous in pink and white. In the doubtful pause which followed Lord Symington managed to insinuate himself.

'You want to be careful with that woman, Lambkin. She's supposed to be some cousin of mine, but she's really a gossip columnist,' he said importantly as if the two roles were incompatible.

'Really?' said Chuck.

'Yes, and she'll print every word one says, and if that doesn't make one a big enough fool, she'll make it up. I don't know how she got on board your boat, but . . .'

'She very nearly didn't,' said Chuck. 'She fell in.'

'Someone push her?' said Symington brightly.

'No,' said Chuck. 'How could you think such a thing, Lord Symington? We have found her a most rewarding guest.'

Symington snorted. 'Look at her now, and for a woman over fifty.' Percy had commandeered the best-looking man in the party, a Greek who had come with Tattie's masseur, and was acquiring a few Greek steps in anticipation of the dancing. The music began. Symington shuddered.

'I think I'll get myself a drink if you don't mind,' he said. Really, these Jews, who were supposed to be so bright, were often incredibly naïve. He must remember to get a copy of the *Daily Express* the day after tomorrow. Then they'd see what he meant.

At the early stages of the party the disparate groups kept an unclear structure, moving according to Heisenberg's uncertainty principle, but not splitting up. Madame Hélène was reassuring Captain Hook about his command of the French accent. '*Mais c'est chic, votre accent, mon capitaine. Oui, c'est méro. . . .*'

'What does that mean, dear lady, merrow?' asked the Captain, enthralled.

'Why, *mérovingien.* It's what the Parisians say when they want to make a compliment.'

'Jolly good show. *Très bien,*' said the Captain, luxuriating in her Chanel No. 5 and wondering whether, perhaps later . . .

Sir Arthur was watching the young Greek cavort with Percy.

'You must admit he's rather a dish, Paddy, but I don't think our journalist friend will get much change out of that one.'

'And nor will you, old man,' retorted his companion, equally fascinated. 'We don't want any nonsense from you on dis trip. You just stick to de dooty-free booze like a good old knightie.'

The bouzouki had an endless quantity which flitted into the night. Songs with bitter words fell on to heedless but increasingly receptive ears, and the dancers gained adherents. The dances were not difficult to perform, badly, provided a literal link for the company, arms round shoulders, and made everybody thirsty, then hungry, then thirsty again. The distance between the crew and the guests remained as the moon rose, but Percy picked out the *mouche* like a jelly baby from a tray of sweets, and performed a *pas de deux* with him from her own repertoire, ending in her loosening her generous hair and, to the applause of all, swinging him round and round her head. Finally she dumped him on Jeremy's lap, gasping into his ear. 'There, that's what you want, isn't it?'

Red-faced, but who could see that in that light, the boy disentangled himself and clambered back into the ranks where he felt safer from assault.

'Gosh, I could do with a shower,' said Percy.

'Let me show you, Percy, and let's see if your clothes are dry,' offered Chuck.

'Oh, I do hope you don't think I overdid it? You're not packing me off, are you? As a matter of fact, I should go anyway.' She looked at her (waterproof) watch. 'Phew!'

'Not at all, not at all,' said Chuck warmly. 'You know you're the life and soul.'

'I want a word with you anyway.'

When they were below Percy explained. 'You see, I'll have to file something on this story, otherwise the office will raise hell. Strictly speaking, I'm back on the foreign desk now, on the way to Cyprus and Cairo, but I did promise the Hickey people some copy. It won't be much good as far as they're concerned, but at least it'll get me off the hook. Now, let me see, I changed in that nice French lady's cabin, so my clothes should be there.'

Chuck tried to open the appropriate door. It was locked. They heard the sound of shuffles and scuffles within and they both rolled their eyes at each other in mock alarm. 'I'm sorry to disturb you, Hélène, but we're looking for Percy's clothes . . . you know, that suede outfit.'

There was a faint gasp and then Hélène's voice, serene and controlled. 'You will find zem just b'ind where you are standing in ze drying closet and 'er boots are zere too.'

Percy gave a naval salute and jabbed her finger at the locked cabin door. Chuck nodded eagerly, but said in a matter-of-fact voice, 'Thank you, Hélène, so long.'

They removed Percy's kit and Chuck whispered to her, 'You'd better come with me to what he calls the owner's stateroom.'

Percy found her notebook and began scribbling. Then she looked up. 'Anglo-American occasion in Athens.' She quoted, 'Almost as boring as small earthquake in Peru, isn't it? Never mind,' she added grimly, 'that's what they're going to get. Mr Charles . . . any other names?'

'Well, you could mention Beauregard, Tattie likes that. . . .'

'So do I, so do I. Right: Mr Charles Beauregard Lambkin, a Southerner who flew for the RAF before America entered the war, right? Dee da dee da . . . wedding at American Embassy, representatives of the American Navy . . .'

'Whazzat?'

'Jake Goody,' snapped Percy, cheerfully pencilling on. 'Dee da dee da . . . Athenian society . . . close to Court circles . . .'

'Whoa there!' said Chuck, laughing.

'What d'you mean?' answered Percy. 'You'll ask that little fellow who looks like Eric von Stroheim, Miss Sterling's masseur? He does the Queen's neck, doesn't he? How much closer can you get? Court circles . . .' she chanted, 'chartered the *Atlanta*, Lord What's-his-name's luxury yacht, but because of the international situation, dee da dee da . . . only as houseboat, party-loving Lord Symington (hee hee) cousin of the Marquess of dum de dum. This'll keep 'em quiet – they like to litter the column with the peerage and isn't there a prince up there?'

'I believe so, a friend of Jeremy's.'

'Fine, I'll check with him. And tell me, er . . . what er, do you and Tattie, Miss Sterling, do together . . . you know, common interests?'

'Well, I do her betting for her and we sometimes go to race meetings.'

'Constant race-goers since the war,' intoned Percy. 'Lord Sterling's only unmarried sister . . . family well known for its interest in Jewish . . . can I say Zionist?'

'No, you cannot.'

'All right then. Jewish and other charities. Okay.' She snapped her notebook shut. 'I just have to get the name of that prince and then we're away. Incidentally, if you want to get rid of any of that lot I can take at least four back to Athens just as soon as I've put on my clothes.'

'Good thinking, Percy, and bye-bye and thank you for everything. You might call us in London, in quieter times.'

'I will.' They shook hands solemnly.

Jeremy, commanded by Chuck to 'clear the decks', found the peer and the prince solicitously feeding each other champagne. 'My father,' said the man with the poached eyes, 'was a proper snob, a pure snob. He only considered Plantagenets. Anybody later than that was a *parvenu*. I say pure because he cared nothing for rank or fortune. I mean,' he said, glaring into the dark and burping on the champagne, 'he wouldn't have been seen *dead* on this boat. Jews, Christ! No, no. He admired one man, chap called Disney – *Mister* Disney – who could trace his descent in a straight line for a thousand years. Lived in Essex. My father used to tank him up with gin at the Club. Told the rest of them at Whites they were all scum compared to this chap. Didn't go down well.' He noticed Jeremy. 'I say, d'you think we could have some more of this stuff?'

'No,' said Jeremy. 'I'm afraid it's bye-bye time.'

'Ah, Jeremy,' said Ferty absently. 'And you mustn't forget the *haute juiverie*.'

'D'you mean this lot?' The peer waved towards the American warship, but he clearly referred to his hostess below.

'Lord, no, they're nothing to do with the *haute juiverie*.'

'The fella is a UK peer,' said the younger son of an earl.

'That's nothing,' replied the dispossessed prince, 'just a military stroke industrial complex preferment. Like that ghastly Montgomery.' They all shuddered. 'No, the whole point about Ezra is that he married a Mendoza and that got him into the *haute juiverie*. The Goldsmids, the Pintos, the Waleys, the Lindos, the Sassoons, the Montefiores.' Ferty rolled out the names with frothy relish. The silence was impressive.

'Those are the people who matter,' Ferty continued. 'Did you know Disraeli's younger brother went to Winchester?' The other did not. 'But that is the connection Ezra needed. Don't you see? Just as William Pitt was nothing until he married into the Glanvilles.'

'The Grenvilles,' said Jeremy, who had picked up a little English history at Oxford.

'So Ezra Sterling was just an Ashkenazi, a German from Leeds until he married Audrey Mendoza. D'you imagine that the flotation would have worked so brilliantly in the thirties without the support of those old Jews in the City?'

Jeremy was doubly amazed. That his friend was taking the affairs of that square mile so seriously, and his concentration on the Jewish sector. Perhaps he was contemplating a similar match?

It had also never occurred to him that Ezra had in any sense emerged. Turners, the cars and their chauffeurs, the business, the family, and the magic carpet of their money, had always seemed part of the firmament.

He yawned. 'Now, will you please go home, otherwise I shall get into trouble.'

The last liberty boat carrying the sailors who had fallen by the wayside and been unable to stand up again, ploughed a white furrow in the moonlit harbour on its way to the big ship and carried a swell to lollop MV *Atlanta* gently from side to side, reminding those aboard her, who were still awake, that they were, technically, afloat. Tattie was applying her night cream when a bottle of eau de Cologne fell over on her dressing table. She tucked it into her velvet embroidered tissue holder – for safety. Chuck was lying on his bed, handsome in his nightshirt, reading a three-day-old copy of the *Herald Tribune* and smoking a final cheroot – a filthy habit in the bedroom, thought Tattie, but manly.

'I thought it went off all right, didn't you?'

'Yeah, honey. Pretty damn well. Now, be a good girl and go to bed.'

The doctor slept as if he knew that nobody cared. Lucy shared a cabin with the twins who had caught a bit of sun, she had thought when she tucked them up. Jeremy had a dream from which one face, sulky, blushing, long-eyelashed would not disappear. Sir Arthur and his friend snored spirituously and separately.

There was a sharp click followed by a dull whirr. It woke the Captain – skippers sleep lightly – and he tried to disengage the arm which held his watch from under her still shoulder and still beautiful neck. She woke and looked into his face.

'*Mon capitaine,*' she said softly.

'Hélène,' he said, and kissed her hair, the haven of that lovely scent. 'That was wonderful. Thank you.'

'*Non, non, mon capitaine, c'est moi qui te dit merci,*' she smiled, remembering that some doctor had told her that high-ranking naval officers were always impotent because, whereas the sailors could go to brothels, the officers had to sit around frustrated, playing bridge and drinking gin. Her *capitaine* seemed to have avoided this malady. *Bon dieu,* twice, within an hour! Maybe he had not been high-ranking enough.

'I think maybe, Hélène, you should think about returning to your cabin' he whispered. 'After all, we don't want . . .'

'No, no,' she agreed, 'you are right. Not that again.' She giggled. 'Being caught in the act. It was like Feydeau.'

That was a French word the Captain did not know, nor right now, want to.

He leapt nimbly out of the bunk and pulled back the curtains. The moonlight was enough for her to see her way out. She noticed how trim he had kept his body. 'Go carefully and take this torch and your dress,' he added hurriedly.

'I see you are a man of experience, *mon capitaine,*' said Hélène lightly.

'Well, then,' he said, opening the door for her quietly, 'er . . . *à demain.*'

'One thing I can't abide,' said Jeremy authoritatively, 'is "brunch". It's a silly word for a silly institution. Now, I don't know what to eat.'

'You can't expect breakfast after midday, even in the best of hotels.' Lucy was always on the side of the commissariat. 'Have a cup of coffee and pretend it's breakfast.'

'*Tiens, mon ange,* let me help you,' said Hélène and she poured him some coffee, broke a croissant and dipped it in the milky mixture and popped it into Jeremy's mouth.

'Ah,' said Jeremy, 'that is nice.'

'You're a spoilt boy, Jeremy. It's about time you did something,' said Sir Arthur in quite a friendly way.

'Oh, if I only had a hundred thousand pounds,' sighed Patrick, not totally irrelevantly.

'Well, I have a hundred thousand pounds, I think, or I had, and it's not that easy,' said Jeremy.

The doctor looked up from his green-covered Penguin and then went on reading. Lucy thought Jeremy's attitude to money showed a lack of respect and, since she had much more, decided the conversation should change direction.

'I've never seen anybody eat and drink the way your Oxford friends did last night,' she said.

'They weren't my Oxford friends, they were Ferty's friends,' protested Jeremy.

'Oh, that Ferdy . . .'

'It's not Ferdy, it's Ferty, short for fertilizer because he sprays everybody when he speaks.'

'. . . is the most awful snob. He kept asking me if I thought the family were part of the *haute juiverie*. What on earth did he mean by that?' asked Lucy.

'He meant, the silly fellow, were the family descended from the Rothschilds or the Montefiores,' supplied Sir Arthur. 'And the proper answer would have been – one of Ezra's favourites, this,' and he winked knowingly, '*moi, je suis ancêtre.*' There was a silence. 'Napoleon said it first. It means,' said Sir Arthur tapping his chest, 'I am the ancestor.'

'Ah, *c'est joli.* I never heard zat before,' chimed Hélène, but the hiatus in the conversation was not filled until the arrival of the Captain.

'Morning, morning, gentlemen, *bonjour*, madame. Good morning, Sir Arthur. Have you heard the news?' The latter was addressed as Senior British Citizen. 'I listen to the eight o'clock shortwave broadcast from Bush House and they said all the foreign pilots are leaving the Canal and the Egyptians are going to run it themselves.'

'Then I give their economy three weeks,' said Sir Arthur.

'That's actually more or less what one of the commentators said, Sir Arthur.'

'Exactly,' said Sir Arthur. 'Disraeli bought the Canal for England and we should protect our interests, along with the French, by force if necessary.'

'Oh, you old imperialist, you,' cried Patrick. 'Why can't you let the little black feller do what he loikes in his own country?'

'Like Hitler, you mean, boy? I don't think you understand what's at stake. . . .'

'Maybe I do and maybe I don't,' said Patrick coolly, and perhaps he spoke for the rest of them, as no one else seemed inclined to comment.

'Percy's gone off her head,' said the Number 3 on the column as he handed the message to the Number 1.

'What's this then? "Bloody Hasselblad"?' He pointed to the left-hand corner of the piece of paper. Number 1 still had a hangover at five o'clock in the afternoon; in his position he was invited to a lot of parties.

'It's a cable,' said the Number 3 patiently – really his boss was losing his grip. 'They often repeat words from the last line. Why a cable? She probably couldn't get through on the phone. Athens,' he added in explanation. He waited. 'Shall I spike it?'

The Number 1 looked at his assistant through bloodshot eyes. He wants my job, he thought, and I dare say he'll get it, but not just yet.

'Do you mind if I read it first?' He did so slowly. 'I don't know how we can get her another camera,' was all he said.

'But the story, we can't run that, can we?'

'It seems innocuous enough to me.'

'Exactly, but who does she think we are? The *Tatler*?'

His superior nodded. 'Look,' said the Number 3. 'Lord Sterling is one of the richest men in England. This American is some bum with a boozing club in Soho or somewhere. . . .'

'Shepherd Market, I believe,' said the other wearily.

'Okay, doesn't matter. He hasn't got a bean, she has many beans, and she's the size of a house. He's after the lolly. His Lordship is none too delighted. A lawsuit in the air. Lovely story and then we get all this . . . all this . . . marshmallow.'

The Number 1 sighed. 'Look son, ever been to Korea? No, sorry, that's unfair. What I mean is Percy has, and she's tough, and she fears no man. If this is her story, this is her story. How d'you know she hasn't done a deal with him? In return for playing patsy now, she gets something later. Something much hotter? Right?'

It was the younger man's turn to nod in agreement.

'So?' he asked.

'So, you lead in with a para about Lord What's-his-name who owns the boat they chartered, he's had a lot of wives and you run the story. And when something better turns up for the later editions, kill it. It makes a change from all this Suez business, you know, the rich at play. . . . And get me a couple of aspirins, will you, there's a dear boy.'

But nothing better did turn up, so that when Audrey had digested all she could manage of *The Times* and had turned to the *Express* (late London edition) for the Osbert Lancaster cartoon and the William Hickey column, there it was. She read it twice, folded the paper, sighed and looked at the ceiling of her bedroom. It needed painting, she noticed. She sighed again and pressed a button on the intercom.

'Ezra, have you seen the *Daily Express*?'

'No, dear, but I can offer you *The Times*, the *Manchester Guardian*, the *Financial Times*, and since it is Friday, the *New Statesman*, the tone of whose editorial suggests that this journal is being wholly subsidized by the Egyptian government. Why should I want to read the *Express*?'

'Come and see me and do up your dressing gown,' commanded Audrey. He had grown negligent in this respect, and Audrey had read an article in a women's magazine nominating this behaviour characteristic of middle age.

Ezra's styles of speech indicated his preoccupations; today's suggested a speech in the House of Lords.

'Can I sit on your bed, dear wife?' he asked.

'No,' said Audrey. 'Go over there. I want you where I can see your face. Damn, now I've lost my specs.'

'Round your neck, my love?'

'Oh, Ezra, quit fooling, as Chuck would say.'

'It's about him? Them?'

Audrey nodded and began reading. 'It's headed "An Odd Couple". Then there's a question mark. "Motor Vessel *Atlanta* is one of the most luxurious yachts in the Mediterranean and comes complete with a crew of six including a French chef, air conditioning in the staterooms and stabilizers. Owned by Lord Carlyon whose recent divorce from the former model . . ." '

'Come to the point, can't you?' interrupted Ezra.

'Wait a minute, I didn't write the article. Now you've made me lose the place. . . . Ah, "former" . . . Yes, "she is now under charter for an undisclosed sum." '

'Of a thousand dollars a week,' muttered Ezra.

'. . . "to Mr Charles Beauregard Lambkin, an American from the South, who has made London his base since the war." New paragraph.'

'Does it say,' asked Ezra ponderously, 'that if Mr Charles Beauregard Lambkin attempted to revisit his native state he would be clapped in jail?'

Audrey slapped the newspaper down on her bed. 'No, Ezra, it does not – it's a very nice piece. And I thought we solemnly agreed never . . .'

'Yes, dear, I'm sorry. You know I don't like being read to.'

'Do you want me to go on, or not?'

'Please.'

' "Last night Mr Lambkin gave a party for his bride-to-be, Miss Henrietta (Tattie) Sterling, a sister of Viscount Sterling, the wealthy electronics tycoon and chairman of Sterling Industries. Among the house party are Sir Arthur Coleport, Miss Sterling's niece Mrs David Blacker and her nephew, gallery owner Jeremy Kind, Mrs Gloria Gould, Prince 'Ferdy' Furstenburg . . ." '

'Who the hell's that?' asked Ezra. He had a residual distaste for Germans.

'Surely a friend of Jeremy's? He brought him over to Turners once or twice. They were at Oxford together.'

'Yes, I know, pimply boy who spits. Go on.'

'. . . "and playboy peer Lord Symington were among those who danced to the two bouzouki (the characteristic Greek music) bands which played until dawn." ' Audrey took a deep breath. 'New paragraph,' she said, looking up at Ezra whose face was expressionless.

' "Intimates of the couple are not surprised at the engagement, for they have been regular racing companions since they met at the American Embassy at the outset of the war, when Mr Lambkin was a Battle of Britain pilot. Appropriately, the wedding will take place at the American Embassy." New paragraph.'

' "Will Lord Sterling be flying over for the ceremony? 'I doubt it,' Mr Lambkin told me. 'He's a very busy man but I dare say there'll be a family reunion at Turners when we all get home.' Turners is Lord Sterling's country home, outside High Wycombe. It has thirty bedrooms and a private golf course." ' Audrey looked up. 'Thirty bedrooms?' she said absently. 'I never counted them. . . .'

Ezra whistled softly. 'The *chutzpah*,' he said slowly. 'Tell me, Audrey, isn't that column supposed to be . . . rather, er, bitchy? Yes, of course, most of the people I know don't like to be mentioned.'

'And don't like not to be mentioned?'

'Quite. Even so, that's pretty soft soap. I wonder how he fixed it.' Despite himself, Ezra smiled. If he were to be beaten, better by a winner. He stood up and pointed to the paper.

'That'd amuse Oscar. You could ring him up.'

'In New York?'

'Why not? I'll book a call for you from the office for twelve o'clock. They get up earlier in New York. I want to know how he's getting on with his new relations.'

6

Trifles only cause bitter rows between people who know and love each other well. (There could be doubt that Sandra and her mother loved each other, but love each other they did.) An argument in a car about the route to a house in the country when one has made the other late (which one?), the placement of guests at a dinner table, the position of a sofa when it is decided late at night to change the layout of the room, the view that anybody with the faintest degree of sensitivity could see that those colours clashed horribly. (Why do we prefer our judgement rather than our taste to be questioned?) It may be the particular in dispute is but a tripwire for the protagonists leading to mines of deeper discontent buried by years of tolerance or tact (or love). At such explosive moments issues are aired with such venom that the flies on the wall wash their hands in grief. Taunts are exchanged by one party over the physical, or mental, or moral, or sexual, or financial, or social condition or prowess or standing of the other. Cocktails of hatred are distilled and exchanged and as with cocktails, the more alcohol they contain the more telling the result. 'And by the way,' they sometimes conclude, '*he* says you have bad breath.'

There was no shortage of drink in any of Sandra's mother's households. Their burning, terrible row was over the venue of the wedding reception. It had been smouldering before Oscar's arrival in New York; he had gathered this from Sandra who had met him at the airport. 'Mother's cancelled the St Regis and you're staying with us but we're not to sleep together because of the maids.' This had been her greeting. Then she had kissed him. 'She's in a state of nerves. She wanders around the apartment plumping up the cushions and every time she sees me she stops singing *It's So Nice to Have a Man About the House*, and gives me a filthy look like I am the nigger in the ointment.'

Oscar laughed and squeezed her hand. 'It's good to see you.'

Sandra ignored this platitude. 'She behaves like *she's* getting married and she wants it at the Plaza.'

The question of whether the ceremony should occur at all seemed suddenly to have been superseded by the question of where. Oscar wondered how and why.

'So she's quite happy about the whole thing?' asked Oscar when they had reached the safety of the limousine.

'Sure, she's happy. She might cross-examine you, but that's her wanting to play games. I tell you, all she's worried about is the Plaza. She wants a big affair at the Plaza.' Sandra nodded her head conclusively.

On native grounds, in New York City, she looked less exotic, less sure of herself, than in Europe. She was prettier, he noticed, quietly dressed and more girlish. Maybe she had put on a little weight.

'I like you when you're sulking,' he said. 'You look pretty.'
Sandra smiled through her concentration.

'And I don't want the Plaza. I've been married before at the
Plaza and I hated it. Can't she imagine the humiliation? Whatever
will my friends say, do you think? Hi, Sandra, haven't we met here
before. I can hear them now,' and Sandra bit her lip in almost
tearful anger, making herself look, thought Oscar, even prettier.

'Darling, can't I talk to her?'

'Ever tried talking to a Panzer division? Look, all I want is for
them to put up the *chuppa* in the hotel downstairs, have a few
people up for some drinks, then get the hell out of it.'

'Where to?' asked Oscar anxiously. He had understood that this
trip was for reconnaissance only and had made his arrangements
accordingly; there was a board meeting in ten days' time which if
he missed David would be sure to . . . He had not planned on
staying away long enough to conclude the campaign.

'I thought of Rio,' said Sandra. 'Mother hasn't got a house in
Rio.'

Oscar felt a flash of excitement rush through his veins, like the
feeling he had enjoyed in Paris, in Sandra's gravely opulent suite.
He must remember he was marrying a rich girl. To hell with David
and the business. Life was bigger than that.

'Yes,' he breathed. 'Rio . . . Sandra, d'you remember the France
et Choiseul?'

'Do I remember the France et Choiseul?' She patted her tummy.
'Rooms 20, 21 and 22,' she echoed happily. 'You know, next time
I think we should be higher up.' She smiled and seemed to have
forgotten about the Plaza for the moment.

Furry-mouthed and head buzzing from the transatlantic journey,
Oscar had showered then fallen asleep. He awoke, washed the
sleep dust from his eyes, dressed and walked down the corridor to
the other half of the apartment. His prospective mother-in-law was
playing patience. 'Damn this thing,' she said, 'it always comes out.'

'Don't you know anything more difficult?' He didn't know what
to call her; surely not Mother.

'Yeah, but then they don't come out and I get really mad. Now
you've woken up, we can have a drink.'

'What time is it?' asked Oscar, an English reflex.

'Time for a drink,' said mother-in-law.

'Well, I suppose in London it'd be . . .'

'Don't you worry about London, young man. You're in Manhattan and you can fix me a martini. You'll find everything over there,' and she waved a glittering hand in the direction of what appeared to be a greenhouse. Picking his way through a forest of palms and rubber plants Oscar found the bar and made a mean martini.

'That's better.' She knocked it back in one. 'Now, how's business, Oscar, and you can still call me Georgy. My first name was Ruth but it didn't suit me.' She exhaled happily.

Ruth – pity, compassion, tenderness. No, it didn't suit her. She was right.

'Where's Sandra, by the way?' He felt bound to ask.

'Shopping. We can relax. Go ahead.' Georgy freshened her glass.

'You mean my financial circumstances?'

'Well, yeah. I checked on your family. They're rich, but what about you?'

Oscar looked a little startled at her directness.

'Well, don't you think a mother is entitled to be concerned over the welfare of her only child, especially after one very uncomfortable experience. Do you know, Oscar, that he had a weak seed.' She leaned forward, her eyes gleaming. 'How's your seed?'

'I've no reason to suppose there's anything wrong in that quarter.'

'Yeah, Oscar, but that's negative. I'd like to be positive; maybe you should have a test.' She ruminated.

Oscar did not feel inclined to disclose proof of his fertility by mentioning his bastard, who being nearly sixteen probably had seed of his own by now.

'I can let you have details of my trust.'

'Trusts don't mean you have any money,' interrupted Georgy. 'Boy, do we have trusts in our family, trusts for domicile, trusts for education, trusts for children who don't exist.'

'True, but part of my trust will be released on my marriage.'

'Oh,' chortled Georgy. 'So you're marrying Sandra for your money?'

'And I will inherit about three-fifths of my aunt's money.'

'What's she worth and why?'

'She is Lord Sterling's sister and has the largest holding in the business, worth about three million. . . .'

'Dollars?'

'Pounds.' It was little Oscar's first hit.

The door opened and Sandra tumbled in, covered in packages which she threw on the sofa and then herself, her long legs outspread. She removed her sunglasses.

'Mother, you've been drinking.' She turned to Oscar. 'How many's she had?'

'I made your mother a martini,' he said loyally.

Sandra sniffed. 'And the sun, as we British say,' she pinched little Oscar's cheek, 'is not yet over the yardarm.'

'Well, we can't expect much at the Wassermans, as they're both being dried out – they have this apartment with the beautiful view of Central Park. They're having some people to meet you, then . . .'

'What have you gone and done, Mother? Oscar may be tired.'

'He's just woken up. He's been asleep all day. He's not tired. Then we'll got to "21" and see if there's anybody there. And if not, there's the roof at the St Regis and I've booked a table at El Morocco. . . .'

'Mother!'

'I thought for his first night he might like a family affair, just the three of us,' she said plaintively.

Oscar would have to get used to their habit of discussing him as if he were not there.

'Has he brought a tuxedo? A dinner jacket?'

Oscar nodded.

'Then get into it,' said Georgy placidly, dealing herself a hand of patience, 'and you get into something too.'

Sandra and Oscar exchanged looks; it seemed sensible to obey.

The question of the Plaza Hotel remained submerged for three hours, through many more martinis, in Georgy's conversation. They had taken in every port of call and it was clear to Oscar that the evening had been planned as a sort of parade, with himself as a newly acquired escort for display to his future mother-in-law's circle or a section of that circle. Those they had met and hailed in restaurants were smoothly tailored, soft-voiced, slightly overfed Jewish people – he knew not to call them Jews – with one glaring common bond: money.

Settled at a favoured table in the sparkling gloom of El Morocco, with Sandra momentarily in the powder room, Georgy patted his arm with her gloved hand. 'Oscar,' she said a little thickly, 'you wowed them, and I'm happy to have you in the family. . . . You know our crowd, our family, are part of this city. We made it what it is. Anyway,' she half giggled but it became a hiccup, 'we made it. And along the line we acquired some traditions, you know what I mean? We acquired traditions. Being British you'd know about that, wouldn't you? Acquired traditions.' She seemed to like the phrase. 'And one of those traditions is . . .' – she rushed out the words to beat an oncoming hiccup – 'we always get married at the Plaza Hotel!'

Suddenly Georgy was drunk, thought Oscar, and now here was Sandra. At her approach, without looking up, Georgy said, 'I'll take eggs Benedict. Oh, it's you, ah Sandra, I was just explaining to Oscar here that our family . . .'

'Had acquired some traditions?' She looked at her mother coldly.

Oscar stood up. 'Like dancing with your fiancée,' he said easily, taking Sandra's wrap from her shoulders and her handbag from her hand. 'Excuse me.' He bowed to the older woman and led Sandra off. They danced well together and they knew it. Sensuous but correct, Sandra held him tightly and Oscar enjoyed the inevitable healthy reaction.

'Let's put her to bed, my darling, and then . . . to hell with the maid.'

Oscar nodded and broke away. 'Yes, but don't we have to eat something?' he asked as he took her back to the table.

'Yes, hell, we do.' Not only the meal but mother too lay between them and fulfilment. But mother would not go home.

It was their third dance together and Oscar was growing impatient as his desire mounted. 'By the way,' he said, 'she's acquired – oh, damn that word – she's got another obsession, apart from the Plaza: my spunk.' And to emphasize the pointlessness of this pursuit he held her a little closer. 'She's talking about a test and I'm afraid the answer's no. Who does she think she is?' he said angrily.

Sandra moved her hand from his shoulder and stroked his cheek. 'Don't worry, sweetheart, I think I can take care of that.' She looked thoughtful. 'Look, you ask her to dance and I'll have the captain bring the check, okay?'

Oscar was aware that the excitement he had felt with Sandra had not subsided when he was holding her mother in his arms on the dance floor. She danced in a more brittle, stylish, dated way, daintily and with obvious delight. She began again. 'You do understand, don't you, Oscar? I was married at the Plaza, my mother was. . . .' And then she broke of. 'It's so nice to have a man about the house,' she hummed.

'That's not what they're playing, Mother. Do you mind if I call you Mother? It comes easier.'

'You call me anything you like, honey chile. Ah'm just putty in your hands. You dance so good,' she drawled, a note of self-mockery in her voice. Maybe she's sobering up, thought Oscar. Was that good or bad?

At the table Sandra was counting out dollar bills. Mother shoved them away. 'Captain,' she said, 'I'll sign the bill and you can bring us three cognacs, right?' The captain bowed. 'On the house,' she added firmly. The captain inclined his head, a little less.

In the cab home, Mother started up yet again, Plaza-wise. Oscar noticed Sandra's face lit up by a street lamp, suddenly taut with misery. He sat between mother and daughter, holding hands. He squeezed Sandra's.

'Put your head on the back of the seat and look up at the buildings,' he ordered. 'Aren't they something?' The vision of the skyscrapers reeling, viscous, and strangely insubstantial through the distorting glass, shut Mother up temporarily.

A wave of tiredness swept through his frame as they waited in the lobby for the elevator. He was holding George's arm, not entirely out of courtesy, but for fear that she would collapse. The golden-haired cherub with the white gloves (and the permanent wave?) who finally handed them into the plush little box had the tact to avoid his eye. It was a stylish place, this.

'Good night, you two,' she said, after their ascent, 'and you two say good night, won't you? Tomorrow is a busy day.' She walked stiffly, not down the corridor to her room but towards the study.

'Mother,' said Sandra warningly. 'There's some cognac in one of the three books,' she whispered to Oscar.

'I'm going to check my diary,' she responded with dignity and then, in a voice which was almost regal, 'Good night, children, go to your rooms.' They did. She waited until they did.

In the bathroom Oscar started opening cupboards as one does when unobserved in strange places. He found a complete new battery of gentlemen's toiletry, Jicky by Guerlain. *Eau de dentifrice* by Docteur Pierre, some sort of ointment (which made him blush) for spots and a brand-new electric razor with a blank guarantee. He smiled. The gesture was a manifestation of the sort of attention which made one forgive whoever had thought of it – and it had to be Georgy – quite a lot. Naked before the mirror he made himself an Alka Seltzer and a toast. He raised his glass. 'God bless René Shalom!' he said aloud.

Oscar examined his body with satisfaction in the mirror. He had most of his own teeth, his hair recessed a little on the forehead giving him (said Sandra) an intelligent look. He put out his tongue – not too good. He felt his balls. More than adequate, as Sandra had often said, which was reassuring as one could not be the judge of that part of one's anatomy. He squeezed the flesh below his rib-cage. There was too much of it; next winter Oscar decided to join a club and play tennis indoors, or squash. David played squash. . . . Then he heard a crash and the sound of splintering glass.

Sandra sat before her mirror removing her makeup and applying a night cream with gentle loving strokes, always upwards she remembered. It was a moment she enjoyed and compensation for not sleeping with Oscar who detested the performance and the subsequent stickiness. She adjusted the flaps of the mirror and leant forward to observe that angle of the face which was elusive any other way. Not bad. She didn't even look Jewish. Everyone said, had said, in and out of earshot, tonight and on other nights, that they made a handsome couple. They were quite right, they did. The pilot had been pretty but not handsome, and then there was the question of his seed. . . . Sandra felt her breasts and considered when they would start to swell, also thinking of Oscar, whether there was any other part of herself it would be nice to feel. She decided no, not tonight, and fortunately too, because she saw in the mirror that her mother had silently entered her bedroom and stood at the door, swaying, an unlit cigarette in her hand, her eyes glittering.

'Oh, you pretty little thing,' she said.

'I thought you'd gone to bed,' said Sandra coldly.

'You're lying. You know I didn't go to bed. I went to check on my diary. Tomorrow is a busy day. I have to call the Plaza.' She paused but Sandra, who had started anointing herself all over again, did not. 'And call Rabbi Goldblum . . .'

'Goldstein,' corrected her daughter.

'Goldberg, Goldblatt, Goldbum, what do you care? And then, sure I had a little nightcap. You wouldn't grudge your mummy a lil' nightcap? It's one of the few pleasures she has left.' She hiccuped. 'I like your man, by the way, and, by the way,' she giggled, 'I think he rather fancies me. . . . You don't want to let him go like the last one.'

'I didn't let him go, Mother, you got rid of him,' said Sandra, finally provoked and then, regretting her reaction, she said in a bored voice, 'Oh, go to bed, can't you?'

'You may be a little whore, but you don't know how to hold on to men.' Her mother flicked the lighter but had difficulty in trying to connect the flame to the tip of her cigarette. She staggered, swayed, and fell down by Sandra's dressing table. Sandra did not move or speak.

'Aren't you going to help me?' She tried to raise herself.

Silence.

Her mother grunted and then snickered. To her horror Sandra saw that she had lit the lighter and was approaching her nightdress with the flame. She struck out at her mother with her foot. Her mother clutched at the drapery over the dressing table for support and brought down the mirror which crashed on the bare painted wood, and a shower of bottles fell on to the carpet. The noise alarmed them both, but Sandra was quick to notice that no harm had been done. Trembling with rage she shouted:

'You're a disgusting old woman. I hate you. And by the way, Mother,' she spat, 'you can quit that stuff about seed because I'm pregnant, preg-nant,' she screamed.

Georgy's eyes, round with fright, suddenly filled with tears. 'Oh, my God, oh, my God, I'm the wickedest woman in the world, in the whole wide world,' she sobbed.

Then Oscar came in.

Sandra decided to attempt no explanation for the moment. 'Can you help me take her to her bed?' and she began picking up the bottles and disentangling the table and the gauze. Oscar picked Georgy up – surprisingly light – and to his astonishment received a wink in acknowledgement.

'The wickedest woman in the world . . .' she repeated. Oscar carried his future mother-in-law down the corridor and laid her down on her bed. 'The wickedest woman in the universe,' she moaned.

'There isn't life on any other planet, Mother, but if there is I hope to God it doesn't look like you.' Sandra turned calmly to Oscar. 'I'll undress her, you go and fix her a sedative. You'll find all sorts of things in there.'

Oscar was confused by the different boxes of pills and their nomenclature. He settled on some aspirin which he crushed into a glass of water with the handle of a toothbrush. After all, she would soon be deep in the embrace of alcohol, the most ancient and salutary drug of them all.

They slept together in his bed, but they did not make love. Sandra talked – about her mother. It was a monologue which grew increasingly affectionate. Oscar fell asleep with his hand on her belly, where gestated his son and heir who, if he remembered his biology lessons, must be at least three inches tall.

It started early enough with the telephone ringing. Little Oscar put out his hand, knocked over a glass of water and picked up the instrument.

'Hello,' he said huskily. Then, clearing his throat, he managed to say with more briskness than he felt, 'Good morning, Oscar Barnet here.' It was a reflex acquired in the business.

'Is it Mr Oscar Bar*nett*?'

'Yes.'

'Hold on, I have a call for you,' said a nasal New York voice.

'We have located Mr Barnett, London, will you put your party on the line.' There ensued the familiar burr of the British telephone, a click, a peep, a squeak, and a roar, followed by silence. After a moment Oscar looked at the instrument dumbly as if it held an answer, and replaced the receiver. Almost immediately it rang again.

'You hung up on me!' said New York crossly.

'I'm sorry,' mumbled Oscar.

'That's all right, we'll try again.' The same procedure repeated, then Oscar heard Audrey's voice alternating between loud and clear and drowned by the Atlantic.

(inaudible) '. . . the St Regis.'

'I've moved.'

'So I gathered . . . that American lady . . . efficient.'

'Yes.'

'Have I woken you up?'

'Not really.'

'Obviously I have,' said Audrey. (That's better.) 'Ezra and I wanted to know how you were getting on. Very well it sounds to me. You've wasted no time.'

'Well, we've decided to get married here.'

There was an electric noise sounding like a wave crashing on a rock.

'What?'

'I only said Ezra will be disappointed . . . and of course Freddy and Joyce.'

'There are good reasons,' said Oscar urgently.

'Anyway, it is the prerogative of the bride's mother.' (She can say that again.) 'Let us know when and where, won't you?'

'Of course.'

'And Oscar . . . Oscar, are you still there?'

'Yes, yes.'

'Get a copy of today's *Daily Express*. I'd read it out to you but the line's too bad.' It suddenly improved. 'There's a piece about Tattie and Chuck.'

'Nothing unkind, I hope?'

'No.' Audrey raised her voice. 'That's the' (words lost) 'thing about it.'

'All right, I'll get it. By the way, how's Ezra . . . er . . . taking it?'

'He seems quite happy now.'

'Oh, good.' That was good news.

'You'll tell us when you're coming back and I can arrange something this end for you both. I'll consult Freddy and Joyce, of course.'

'Of course.' He could not think of anything more to say.

'Here, there'll be quite a small do, in a hotel. . . .'

Another sound of the seashore.

'They always get married in hotels but under a *chuppa*.'

A faint sound, this time human.

'Give my love to the family. Bye-bye. Thanks for calling.' Oscar hung up wondering how much he'd got through. He patted the space where Sandra had lain and decided he might as well get up, the fact, rather than the content, of Audrey's telephone call having charged his brain.

Little Oscar had been moved into a position of impotence by Ezra's attempted raid on his Aunt Tattie's treasure. He had not known every move, but there had been sufficient daylight about the robbery for him to see enough of what was happening. He owed loyalty to Ezra as benefactor and tribal chief, and so could not communicate his distress to the amiable and, he thought, disinterested Chuck at the doubtful methods used for his own advancement. Equally, Ezra would have dismissed any protest from him as spineless humbug. Obviously, at the height of the struggle Chuck dared not risk a dialogue of any kind with Oscar. So that when Chuck, victorious, had rung him up, suggesting a drink ('Like *now*, I'm on my way to the airport'), they nearly collided outside the revolving doors of the Dorchester so anxious was each to put his own so justifiable case. Chuck had no 'territorial claims' on the business; little Oscar none on Tattie's fortune which would, in the fullness of time, pass on to him, he understood. Their good relations, temporarily threatened by the possible success of Ezra's intrigue, had been restored by a martini or two, and indeed the old semi-avuncular feeling was strengthened by the experience of common ordeal, of having been pawns in one of Ezra's gambits. They parted happily, each understanding the other's anxiety to be out of the way while Ezra's sore head recovered, Chuck to Athens and little Oscar to New York.

To hear from Audrey over the transatlantic telephone that Ezra was 'quite happy now' meant that all was well which ended well. Oscar felt if the day yielded nothing more, it was already well spent. He wondered how David would have handled the situation.

Sandra was lying on the sofa, her sunglasses pushed up on her forehead, looking at American *Vogue*. Her mother, in a snood, was dialling a number with a gold pencil, her cigarette holder clenched between her teeth.

'I hope you're not aiming to get married in white.'

'H'm,' said Sandra, flicking the pages of the magazine. 'It seems to be the dominant colour in this feature on brides.'

'Huh, for the second time and in *your* condition?'

'Oh, Mother,' said Sandra lazily. There seemed to be a conspiracy between them to forget the trauma of the previous night.

'Is that Rabbi Goldberg's office?'

'Goldstein,' murmured Sandra. 'Hullo, darling, did you sleep well?'

'Yes, thank you, my love, did you?' said Oscar.

'Yes, I did. Come here and give me a kiss.' Mother threw them a murderous look. She had obviously recovered her bad spirits.

'Oh, Miss Himmelfarb. Yes, you can help me, I guess. I want a day in the near future when the Rabbi can marry my daughter. . . .'

'Yes, obviously . . . perform the marriage ceremony.' She cupped the telephone and hissed. 'I am dealing with a cretin. What do you mean – the days of Omer? Who's counting? Oh, they're over. I *am* glad. And if they get married on the first of the month . . . they won't have to fast? Oh, they'll like that. Of course it's a popular day. And the Rabbi's busy? Will you tell him, Miss Himmelfarb, from me, that I would appreciate his rescheduling his diary for that day. This is an emergency, Miss Himmelfarb.' Again she cupped the receiver and said to her daughter, 'Shall I say I'll renege on the Old People's Home?'

Sandra shrugged. 'Mother, you don't need any lessons from me.'

'And if he can't, Miss Himmelfarb, tell him he can forget about that card room for the Beth Holim.' This last threat provoked a furious buzz from the other end of the line and she held the telephone away from her head for the others to hear it. 'He knows my number, Miss Himmelfarb. Be good enough to have him call me.' And she put down the telephone. 'Was I talking like a robber baron?' she asked.

'Baroness,' said Oscar. 'Mother' was again the phenomenon René Shalom so enjoyed, playing the power game.

'You see,' she said to Oscar, '– oh, have you had breakfast, by the way? Fine. You see, I never realized . . .' She looked meaningly at her daughter. 'So the Plaza is out of the question.' Did she mean that establishment was a temple of chastity, not to be defiled by a pregnant bride? 'But even so, we must have God in the ceremony, don't you agree?' The telephone burred.

'Ah, Rabbi.' She took a deep breath. 'Goldstein. How good of you to call me. Yes, er, no, it isn't sudden. They have been engaged for, er, some time. . . . Well, a mother is the last to know these days. . . . Yes, in Europe. Oh, indeed, a nephew of Viscount Sterling. An emergency? Well, it has been a long engagement . . . and I don't think I need go into details with you, Rabbi. After all, you're a man of the world. . . . You understand, oh good. Yes, I am very happy. Oh no, that was just my little joke. I guess it's gone through any- way. Fine, sure – fine. Oh, that's wonderful. You'll fix it with the hotel? Fine, wonderful, thank you, goodbye.' She turned round. 'We're in business, kids. Next Thursday.'

7

The tangled fuse of the Suez affair spluttered through the summer of '56. Nobody knew if it was connected to an explosion or whether it would fizzle out into loss of a little more face by the British whose mid-twentieth century fate was to decline. Precisely this Prime Minister Anthony Eden, acting high (some said on methadone) and mighty, seemed determined to avoid. The fuse straggled through

England, estranging friends and even families, looping together as allies former enemies, and, as the days lengthened and then shortened again, the debate became more shrill, the talk of plots between British, French and Israeli governments grew wilder.

The split in the family was predictable. Freddy and Joyce had been against Suez from the early days and had joined one of the committees being set up in (mainly) intellectual enclaves throughout the country. (No Member of Parliament is in receipt of so much advice from his constituents as the tribune for Hampstead.) Little Oscar had been emphatically in favour of intervention but *soon*, before world opinion grew familiar with the Egyptians' occupancy of the Canal, and he feared the moment might have passed. Sandra, between reading books about childbirth without fear which gave her nightmares, was too occupied to think about it, what with the architects and interior decorators she had manded and countermanded in her efforts to dismember Sarah's large and obstinate house in Maddison Place. It had been a sensible idea, thought the family, for the newlyweds to have half of Sarah's house, since Lucy and Jeremy had long since left home, Sarah was mostly in the country and stayed at Claridge's when she came to London with her pig farmer, and all the Brigadier needed, as Ezra put it, was a chair, a microscope and somewhere to pee. (The poor fellow had recently had an operation on his prostate gland.)

David did not doubt little Oscar's experience of Egyptians – treacherous, feckless, incompetent, dirty, starving or effete – and had respect for the capacity of Israel, which he had visited, to finish them off, upon a reasonable pretext, and provided the Great Powers would not intervene. Lucy, domestically inclined, was concerned with honouring her mother Sarah's birthday which involved turning the house upside-down and, urged on by the twins, spending a lot of money on fireworks, as the date of the celebration was 5 November – a Sunday. If asked, she would probably have echoed the comment of Anthony Eden's wife to Lady Churchill (or was it the other way round?) while watching a debate in the House of Commons from the Distinguished Visitors' Gallery, that 'the men must have their games'.

Audrey shared Ezra's attitude, modified by speculation often raised in the St James's Club as to 'Anthony's *équilibre*'. Tattie's views had not been canvassed and Chuck, whose would not be either, was out of town 'on business'. The couple, if they were that, had kept to themselves since their return from their Greek cruise which, Ezra, observed, had 'begun, middled and ended moored to a quay'.

At a routine lunch after a routine board meeting, Ezra had asked Poll where he stood.

'I think that is well known, Ezra.' The implication that so, too, now, was he, did nothing to cool the subsequent hostility. 'I've been against it from the first, even when Hugh Gaitskell supported it. It is nothing to do with our tanks in Cyprus being gummed up when they unwrap them.' He glanced at little Oscar whose point this had been. 'I have never pretended to a knowledge of matters military. . . .'

'No, indeed,' muttered Ezra; 'not the combative type.' This was not quite true, he thought. Indeed, he wondered if he had been wise to exchange the Conservative, docile, if disgraced, Sir Arthur for this aggressive and rising socialist MP who did not know how to behave as a protégé.

Poll ignored this. '. . . But surely even the most incompetent expedition launched by us, the French *and*,' he turned in acknowledgement to David, 'the Israelis, indeed could hardly fail against an unsupported Egyptian army.' He had the politician's trick of obliquely associating another's opinion with his own by simply recognizing the other's presence. 'No, the real point is that you cannot lead a country – a modern country – into a war without consensus.' And he gestured towards Freddy who was leaning forward with interest. (It was said in Hampstead, and in other left-wing circles, that Poll MP was a man to watch.) He reached out for a cigar but put it down on the table when Ezra snapped:

'What d'you mean consensus? Can you not feel the mood of the country? The man in the street – the ordinary working man – wants action; the people who normally vote Labour.'

'Yes, if you read the Old Codgers' column in the *Daily Mirror*, they do.'

'You must admit, Ezra,' began Freddy. But Ezra cut him out

with a sharp chop of his hand. This was a duel and he wanted no interruption.

'And what's wrong with that? They're the people who vote you into Parliament. It's your duty to represent their opinion.'

'That, in itself, is a most questionable thesis, if I may say,' replied Poll in his donnish voice. 'I would maintain the opposite view, namely that my duty, as a tribune, is to lead and educate. Some people do not understand the wider issues involved: our responsibility to the developing nations, the reaction of the United Nations, to say nothing of the United States. Besides, to turn Nasser from a hero into a martyr would do no good at all,' he concluded quietly and picked up his cigar.

'But that's my point,' shouted Ezra from the top of the table. 'Our prestige in the world . . . Everybody understands the use of force to apprehend a criminal. Nasser's an old-fashioned threat. He's made more nonsense of our strategy by stealing our property. Don't try and tell me the Americans don't understand respect for property! And as for the United Nations, what use have they ever been to God or Mammon? Ask the Israelis.'

'Ezra,' said Poll calmly, 'I'm a better friend of Israel than you'll ever be and I have always supported the rightful aspirations of the Jewish people, but on this occasion I shared the view of my Jewish colleagues in the House of Commons and voted against this . . . this fiasco.'

'They're traitors too,' said Ezra quickly.

It could be seen that something had snapped in the usually imperturbable Poll. He rose to his feet, his face white.

'I do not think the discussion can be profitably prolonged.'

'Oh, you'll finish your cigar with us, won't you?' said Ezra easily.

Poll looked down at the unlit cigar in his hand, moved forward to the humidor in the centre of the table, replaced the cigar and gently shut it.

'No, thank you, I think not.' He closed his eyes for a moment. 'Good day, gentlemen.'

Ezra exhaled a cloud of cigar smoke, and yawned.

'Audrey told me Clarissa Eden said that at times she felt the Suez Canal was running through her drawing room. Maybe we'd better keep it out of here from now on. Tell me,' he said to no one in particular, 'do we really need, in the business, a Labour politician on the board? I mean, old Arthur had his point, in his day . . . when we knew nobody, but now?' Ezra shrugged.

David Blacker studied Ezra's expression through his slim fingers. His reference to Sir Arthur made him wonder whether the old fox had planned the scene they had just witnessed. After all, Poll had replaced old Coleport and Ezra's question suggested the seat – the only hot one in the board room – was once again vacant.

'While it's sensible to be friendly, for a business like ours, with people who are likely to have power one day, I'm inclined to agree that we don't need anyone from the Labour Party. You see, when the next Labour Government gets in they're bound to cut down on defence expenditure, which is an increasing . . .'

'You said "when", David?' It was Mr Wilson, a pillar of Purley's Conservative Association.

'Certainly, Harry, you know the British system. It works like the pendulum of a cuckoo clock: in . . . out . . . in . . . out . . . tick . . . tock. Of course it's "when", but if we're going to have politicians, we need one from each side, surely? Like the National Union of Teachers, which pays for one MP on each side of the House.'

'Well, not really, David,' said little Oscar amiably – the recent row had purged all animus and left a pall of benevolence over the luncheon table. 'We're not in politics as such. I think we should look at the top people in the civil service . . . like John Henry Woods.'

'Yes, I know him, knew him in the war, Board of Trade, has a limp and a funny eye, good man.'

'Exactly, and Marconi have got him,' said little Oscar.

'Oh, have they? Then why can't we get someone like that?'

'Go to the Ministry of Defence, why muck about?' interpolated Chaimy, stubbing out his Woodbine in a saucer and ignoring the adjacent ashtray.

'That's an odd one coming from you, Chaimy,' said David, voicing the general feeling of surprise.

'I don't see why, comrade. If you lot are all *meshugana* enough to want to blow yourselves up, let's do it on Government money! I'd like to know how they think in Research and Development.

Those are the contracts which are going to matter. My toys are getting more expensive. You tell the men from the boys by the cost of their toys.' He hummed. 'That's our school song.' He grinned, showing a gap in his yellow teeth.

'Who is there then . . . in the Ministry of Defence?' asked Ezra.

'I don't know, Uncle, and if I did it's not my job.' He made a self-deprecating gesture. They all nodded. The possibility of Chaimy entertaining a senior civil servant at the Savoy Grill was, in the phrase of the day, just not on.

'There is a man,' said little Oscar thoughtfully, 'er . . . at the Ministry of Defence, called Matthew Fforde, I believe. I don't know if he's got his "K" yet, like John Henry Woods, but that's not crucial. He was in Lend-Lease in Washington at the beginning of the war and asked me to come and see him when he was in the War Office, after Anzio, liaising on weapons with the General Staff. A bright guy, I thought. He must be in his late fifties, so he'll have a few years to run.'

Ezra's eyes gleamed. 'Get him,' he said.

'Shall I bring him to lunch?'

'No, you and David take him to lunch and if you both like him, hire him. You're going to run the business, you're going to have to live with him, not me.'

They all exchanged looks. Ezra's not so subtle references to his imminent withdrawal from the business were taken as seriously as the late Dame Nellie Melba's farewell concerts.

'He might come expensive – more than Arthur, or, or . . .'

'So what? Give him more than he expects. A car and a driver, all the perks they don't get.'

'And if he's there for a little while yet we could make him a proposition now?' David lisped.

Ezra nodded. 'And talking of directors, I have a feeling that our departed friend has a letter of resignation buzzing in his head. I don't want him to leave us with a bad taste in his mouth.'

'You mean money, Lord Sterling? Well, the best way to do that, if you're concerned with Mr Poll's tax, is to turn the thing round and for you to request his resignation.'

'I see.'

'In that way, the Revenue must regard any payment we make him as compensation for loss of office, which would attract no tax.'

'It makes no difference to us?'

'No, none, Lord Sterling.'

'So that for his sake . . .'

Mr Wilson nodded. 'I'd better get it done right away. . . .'

'If you would be so kind.' In that considerate fashion Ezra fired Poll MP.

The Blackers' house in Tite Street, Chelsea, had been built before the war for a client who must have wished to conceal his wealth. The exterior was Georgian, unadorned and dull. Obligatory in the thirties, there was a tradesmen's entrance and a staircase to the servants' quarters at the top of the house. Each bedroom, except the servants', had a bathroom *en suite*, as the estate agents say, and again as they say, there were toilet facilities on each of the four floors, though in keeping with the modesty of the elevation, from the street it was only possible to see three floors.

Lucy filled her house with her children, her nanny called Tibbit (which was also her name), a rotating *au pair* girl, generally from Scandinavia, who became after a probationary period of three months spent in demure co-operation and crying in her room, delinquent and ungrateful, when she acquired a lover. There were no pets.

The furniture was boring and the furnishings ditto. Lucy did not share the family taste, or at any rate that of her mother, her Aunt Audrey and her Aunt Tattie – especially Aunt Tattie – for spreading money over the walls, as she put it, and no one could detect that here was the house of a millionairess. Although she possessed the symbols, furs and jewellery, all presents from the family or from David, they spent most of their time in cold storage or at the bank and were only worn for family occasions when some degree of opulence was traditionally *de rigueur*. Lucy just liked to watch her money, and her children's money, grow, and never interfered with this process by moving her investments around; unlike David, who, when he was at home, spent hours in conversation with his broker.

Her own contribution was to save money by concentrating on her own and her household's expenditure, to which end she had acquired a water-softening device to prolong the life of the pre-war central heating, banks of washing machines, and, through the good offices of one of the factories, a deep freeze of commercial proportions, full of Brussels sprouts. The main event in Lucy's life since her marriage had been during a power cut – the winter of 1953 – when the contents of the deep freeze, including a salmon Oscar had sent from Scotland, had gone rotten.

As she neither drank nor smoked and positively enjoyed travelling by bus, Lucy was ideally placed to practise her passion in life. To her neighbours, aware of her connection with the Sterling family and at first apprehensive at the news that the house had been bought by rich Jews, who had no business to be in Chelsea, Lucy's style, or lack of it, was reassuring. To them, she appeared a devoted wife and mother, contributing appropriately but no more to the local causes in Chelsea – to the churches, Catholic and Protestant; to the political parties – the Conservative; to the preservation of trees, and to anything else in that cause-minded borough which came knocking on her door or dropping through the letter box. If they were rich, it was agreed, the Blackers didn't show it; and if they were Jewish, they didn't have any funny habits. In fact, they didn't seem to have any habits at all.

Having married David, Lucy never looked at another man; nor indeed did she look too hard, once she had acquired him, at her husband. Perhaps it was a family characteristic, though she was not as indifferent to David as her mother had become to Jeremy. It was simply that she did not protest, even ritually, to her friends, to the family, to herself, at his frequent absences.

When the bleak (and absurd) alternative slogan had been offered to the British public, 'Export or die', Ezra observed that David had clearly decided to live. He was never still. There was not a good restaurant in Düsseldorf, Zurich, Milan, Paris, Brussels or Houston at which David could not, he boasted, sign the bill. Since he had taken over the export side of the business, a shock had run through the overseas agencies as great as when Joe Chamberlain electrified the Colonial Office. Letters to the export department were answered, and in the writers' own language. 'We speak everything here,' he would say, 'except English.' 'Oh, yes, we speak American.' Vintage pre-war agents had been replaced, as it were, overnight, by a new breed of nasal young men who dressed expensively, drove their fast cars fast and had one characteristic in common. 'They're all hungry,' David explained cheerfully.

René Shalom had been detached from the electronics side of the business, which he freely admitted was beyond him, and Solomon Lemnis, now in Beirut, had written letters to Audrey and Tattie threatening to present his case, knee-deep in tears, in person; so he, too, had been similarly compensated. It was a gesture Ezra relished making because while he rejoiced in David's success, he should know that the feelings of the family counted. Little Oscar watched with awe, tinged by dismay, as David built up new centres of profit for the business throughout the world, responsible to himself.

David might be married to the business but he did not neglect his family. True, when he rang up he seemed more anxious to talk to the boys, on whom he doted, than to Lucy. And true, he returned from his trips abroad so exhausted that she had not, for the first few days, the heart to demand from him her due pleasure. But, she *could* always say, 'David rang me up from . . .' wherever it was, and this, coupled with the fact that she would find no evidence, external or otherwise, of any infidelity on his part, satisfied her, and the family. (It often struck Lucy as odd that David, with his wavy black hair only faintly flecked with grey, his beautiful hands and hard blue eyes, did not keep a mistress within a cab ride of every international airport. He never said what he did in the evenings when abroad and she supposed he was too tired. . . .)

They quarrelled rarely, and then over commonplace issues like mother-in-law and money. Eirene Schwarzer described her daughter-in-law with contempt to her bridge-playing cronies in Hampstead as frumpish, *gar nicht elegant* – it had more bite in German – mean, dull and recently, since she had met little Oscar's glittering new wife, no help to her son in his career. Lucy had refused to learn bridge so that dinner parties either way became impossible. (This was, of course, Lucy's intention.) Eirene had antagonized her own grandchildren and laughed when they imitated her accent and treated her generally as a poor and irrelevant relation. Why, in Berlin before the war, *her* family moved among the *hochgeborenen* and entertained the most distinguished people in the land. It was agreed after a few disastrous dinner exchanges that David should take tea with his mother at her home as often as he liked, off her famous china.

The money thing was different, and Lucy flared regularly on this topic. Before the boys could stand up David had brought them from Brussels a delicately constructed carousel which played the tune from *La Ronde*, as daintily carved figures swung higher and higher. David had watched affectionately as Joshua and Jericho crippled this expensive and unsuitable toy in their pudgy but powerful little hands. The nursery cupboards filled with discarded toys and games, for he never returned empty-handed. It was a shame.

Lucy didn't mind the rows of almost identical suits from Huntsman, the piles of monogrammed shirts from Sulka, the shoes from Lobb, all rigid on their trees, for this extravagance could be thought appropriate in a businessman of his standing who was a sort of ambassador, after all. But she did resent his giving money to Jeremy, a spineless romantic, for his crazy adventures. When Jeremy had started his 'Art for the Artless' campaign, hiring out pictures which he put up in school corridors and changed every fortnight, David had put in money. When that had folded and Jeremy had started his gallery David had put in money, and not peanuts either. £10,000 a throw! She had complained.

'Don't you worry, my love. It counts as a business loss. I can deduct it.'

'D'you mean to tell me those things Jeremy gets up to count as businesses? You must give me the name of your accountant.'

'You don't need one, my love. Mind you,' he said thoughtfully, 'you could do worse than have a word with Ferty Furstenburg.'

'Him, why are you suddenly so busy with him?'

'He's not to be underestimated. He's done a few good things for me in the market.' Ferty had become a merchant banker and often rang David late at night, in German.

'You met him through Jeremy, didn't you? I wouldn't give him the time of day.'

'Oh, come on, Lucy. He's no fool. He was quite a success on that yacht, wasn't he? You mustn't despise him because he has to be polite to rich ladies. It's a phase they have to go through, those boys in the City, if they have connections and no money.'

'I don't dislike him for that. It's just that he eats so much and he spits.' Seeing a cloud of irritation pass over her husband's face Lucy relented. 'But he might as well come to the party; he is a prince and I'm sure he'll charm the pants off the Thompsons.'

'Who are they, for instance?'

'Oh, just ordinary people I happen to like and see. Neighbours really. The Allfreys and the Nicholsons and the Thompsons, why not? It fills the place up and it's a change from the family.'

'Goyim,' said David, lightly.

'So what?' asked Lucy. 'They've children the same age as ours, they live like us, and they like *me*. What sort of life do you think I lead . . . when you're away?'

That shut him up.

'Do you think Ezra will come? It is a Sunday night and . . . Chuck and Tattie?' He had started a fairly fat red herring; Chuck and Ezra had not been seen under the same roof recently.

'Mrs Winterbourne telephoned,' replied Lucy, pursing her lips. 'Lord and Lady Sterling would like to drop in after dinner. They are coming up specially from the country. Shall she send a case of Krug? No, I said, don't bother. And as for Chuck and Tattie, Tattie and Chuck, of course, they're coming. It's fireworks night, isn't it, and it's about time Ezra grew up.' Not for the first time David admired his wife's common sense.

'Bravo!' he said.

'You can give me a kiss,' said Lucy.

Lucy was sufficiently family-minded to recognize that when she gave a 'do' for the family it had to be properly done, so she shifted into another gear. The house and garden were filled with flowers, and dotted with little gilt chairs from Searcy's who provided the bulk of the food, the drink, the glasses and the waiters, at an expenditure, in time, of one telephone call. The caterers' fare had been augmented with the sort of costly goodies the family expected at one of their parties. Mounds of potted shrimps, hillocks of *pâté de foie gras*, wild rice from Fortnum's, and a vast tin of silky grey caviare glistened in the candlelight. And the eyes of the twins shone too, but they had been told to touch nothing until the guests arrived.

'I don't understand it – they don't like anything sweet but they do go for the expensive grown-up things,' Lucy complained.

'Ah well, they've got to get used to it sooner or later,' replied David philosophically. 'Did you remember to get some oysters?'

'Yes, I remembered not to get some oysters,' said Lucy. 'They make such a mess.'

'How many people are coming, do you think?'

'I counted forty-three, but there's plenty of everything so it doesn't matter.'

'Oh, by the way, I told Wilson he could come. I mean,' he corrected himself, 'I invited him.'

'And all those children?'

'Yes, of course.'

'Brilliant,' said Lucy.

'Well, the fireworks . . .' He shrugged.

'I must admit it's rather tiresome that it falls on a Sunday this year. If it were Saturday they could have had a nice lie-in.'

'Oh, let them lie in . . .'

'Yes,' echoed the twins, 'let them lie in!'

The bell rang.

'Oh, can we answer the door, can we answer the door, Mummy?' And they ran out of the room. Lucy and David smiled at each other.

It was the Krapf family – the two of them. Ah well, somebody had to come first.

'England has gone mad,' announced Eva, peeling off her white gloves and revealing her celebrated investigative hands. 'As I was saying to Doc the other day, Edda Ciano – we met on Capri in '48 you know – was quite right. If I were a man all I'd want to do would be to make love, make war and gamble.' She looked round the too small audience challengingly. Her remarks were so out of character and context that her hosts were speechless while Doc, who had heard this fusillade before, had noticed the tin of caviare with its blue and gold lettering. It was a big tin, by any standards, and he was very fond of caviare.

'But you're not a man,' said one of the twins, slightly baffled. Then, bored at the discussion, he turned to his mother and asked, 'Mummy, is that lady who *is* a man, is she coming?'

'I hope so, darling.' Percy was now a popular guest of the family and a particular friend of Lucy.

'Lucy, I'm sorry, I never said how wonderful you look. Oh, and this delicious champagne – Krug, isn't it? So few people give one good champagne, but it is so important, don't you agree?'

Really, thought Lucy, the woman is quite odious, and she was a gynaecologist! The idea of being touched by her was nauseating. Would somebody else please come?

Lucy did look quite good, thought Eva. Her hair was swept up to show off a graceful if slightly fussy neck. Her shoulders were flawless and she'd had a shave, or a depilatory, and as for the sapphire and diamond necklace, well, one couldn't complain about that. It just showed that if you had enough money anyone could be a beauty.

Lucy tore herself away to greet her friends the Thompsons and their children, the Nicholsons and their children and the Allfreys and their . . . But no . . . they were too small. 'We're sorry to be so early,' the mamas chorused, 'but the children were terrified they'd miss the fireworks.'

'I'm not starting until everybody's here,' said David, addressing their eager faces, 'but you can go out into the garden and have a look and you can light the sparklers.' A torrent of children rushed out through the French windows forgetting to shut them so that a gust of cold wind blew out some of the candles. 'Oh dear,' said Lucy, 'we'll have to do something about that.'

Then came Sarah and the Brigadier and the pig farmer. She kissed Lucy lightly on the cheek. 'I'm early because it's my party and I don't want to miss a minute of it. I'm sixty or something,' she said, ignoring the Krapf family – Sarah preferred new faces – and she turned to the Thompsons and the Nicholsons and the Allfreys. 'D'yer think I look it?' She charmed them instantly. 'Introduce me to these nice people, Lucy,' she commanded.

There were now just enough people in the room, thought Lucy, for the next arrivals not to feel they had to apologize for being early.

'What d'yer think of the news?' she heard her mother ask her new friends. Her mother listened to the news, on the hour, every hour. Oh lord, thought Lucy, Suez; but then it gave them something to talk about . . . and none more than Freddy Barnet whose bandaged head astonished them all. Further, he had brought with him a beautiful black man in a white cashmere sweater called Chester Cowles, and a girl who looked rich, American and spoilt.

'My, what have you been up to? Freddy, I thought you were a pacifist!' said David delightedly.

'David, that is precisely why you see me in this condition, because I am a pacifist.'

Joyce looked up admiringly at her husband whose headgear had somehow given him extra height.

'Joyce and I went to Trafalgar Square yesterday for the great rally. I tell you it was like Peterloo, but we'd have won if not for the horses! Have you ever been backed down on by a horse, madam?' Freddy turned to one of the smaller wives in the Thompson/ Nicholson/Allfrey set. He was enjoying himself. The lady in question shook her head. In her world horses knew where they stood. 'First of all they're huge – I hardly came up to their *tochuses*. . . .'

The locals could not understand how Lucy Blacker came to know such outlandish people . . . and that indisputably black, black man wasn't wearing a tie.

'It should be said,' hooted Joyce in her reassuringly lady-officer voice, 'that Freddy behaved terribly bravely.'

They all looked at him.

'All I can tell you is that from now on one must revise one's view of British justice and of British policemen. . . .' They waited. 'Some youngster annoyed them for some reason. Well, admittedly he had long hair, but that doesn't have to make him a criminal, does it?' Some of his audience looked doubtful, but Freddy continued. 'They were beating him dreadfully, four of them, and they took him off to a Black Maria – we were on the edge of the crowd, you see.' Joyce nodded deeply several times. 'And I protested and . . . they shoved me in too!' He laughed. 'They drive like maniacs, jamming on the brakes – apparently they do it on purpose – and I knocked my head on the door of the van.'

They all sighed and someone asked, 'And when you got to the police station?'

'When I got to the police station I told them who I was.' The family nodded gravely. 'And I told them I would lodge a complaint.'

'Yes,' interrupted Joyce, 'we've joined Civil Liberties.'

'And all they said was . . .' – Freddy started to laugh – ' "Don't you worry, sir, we don't like to see a respectable gentleman like you mixed up with the likes of them." Of course I'm worried. Believe me, England is a class-conscious xenophobic . . .' Freddy petered out. 'And they're pro-Suez to a man,' he added.

'And then what happened?'

Freddy had recharged himself with indignation. 'Finally I persuaded a cab to take me home, and Joyce tells me about Hungary! Of course, what d'you expect? We've provided them with a heaven-sent opportunity to play their terrible games without an umpire.'

There was no response from his audience so Freddy turned to Chester and said, 'What do we know about this fellow Kádár?'

'I dunno, but have you heard of a guy called Rákosi? He was really nasty.'

A slight unease fell upon the company at the prospect of a political argument on two fronts until Sarah went up to Freddy, drink in one hand and a cigarette in the other, and said, 'I missed some of that – the beginning bit. Come over here and tell me.' When he had obliged her in this way Sarah commented, 'You're too old, Freddy, for that sort of thing. You're going to be a grand-father soon. How is Sandra?' Like all members of the family Sarah considered Freddy to be little Oscar's father, and that he should be so considered. 'And who's your black friend?' Sarah, again like many in the family often did not wait for an answer.

Freddy explained with pride that he was from Columbia, in New York, and was working on his Ph.D. at the London School of Economics. Sarah screwed up her eyes to avoid the smoke she had just breathed out, and pondered, 'People always say what splendid features when they mean what a funny colour, don't they?'

'Sarah, you mustn't talk like that!' said Freddy.

'No? Not even to family?' and she patted his arm. 'And the girlfriend?'

'Oh, I believe she's a Marshall Field or something, very well off. They're getting engaged,' he added defiantly.

Sarah sniffed and marched off in pursuit of more agreeable gossip.

Freddy stood alone, reflecting how shocking it was – and Joyce agreed – that the family who were but second-generation immigrants from some obscure *stetl* somewhere in eastern Europe (where, as a matter of interest? None of them seemed to know), should have so easily slid into the worst kind of Anglo-Saxon attitudes. Joyce maintained it was because they had abandoned religion. But what had they taken up instead – *religio Milneriana*! That public school nonsense about the right and duty of the British to rule a quarter of the world? Ezra's anti-Zionism, and his support for the war, just started in Egypt – in which views, mark you (Freddy was making a speech to himself), that extraordinary man saw no contradiction – were, er, typical. He felt his bandaged head and sighed. At least he had struck a blow for sanity; they must see they couldn't go on with it.

The room was filling up and so were the ashtrays, on which front, so much more important to Lucy than Suez, she was fighting a losing battle. The same arguments ricocheted round the party but the atmosphere of affluence, of a family home, warm with children, good food and drink, with fireworks in the offing, softened the effect of the shots. New places had entered the language – they had been reading their Sunday papers.

'Look,' said one of the Thompsons, 'the Israelis have captured Sharm-el-Shaikh and got to within fifty miles of the Canal in five days. And they've reopened the Gulf of Aqaba for the first time since er . . . er . . . Why don't we let them finish the buggers off?'

'Yes, jolly good show,' said an anti-Semite.

'All this talk of intervention by the Great Powers!' scoffed the Nicholson.

'I wouldn't place too much credence in that if I were you,' suggested Freddy. 'It's a lot of pious twaddle, the French hold up one hand in dismay and with the other they're supplying spare parts to the Israelis for their Mirages. I tell you, it's a conspiracy . . . stands out a mile.'

'Doesn't matter what you boys try and do,' interrupted the black man who had entered the arena, supported by his American girl-friend. 'There's only one man in the world who matters just now, and that's John Foster Dulles.' He emphasized the name with cutting movements of his beautiful ebony arm on which glistened a heavy gold bracelet. 'And John Foster Dulles is a hard man.' He put up his hand and they all noticed the diamond in his ring. 'And John Foster Dulles is going to say stop!' He turned about, a little unsteadily, indicating that that was that.

'I say, Lucy,' hissed René Shalom, '*qui est cet homme noir? Il est magnifique, n'est-ce pas?* You must introduce me, *chérie.*'

'I'm sorry, René, I don't know who he is. Why don't you ask Joyce – she brought him,' said Lucy. 'And anyway, we're going to sit down and eat. I can't wait all night for Ezra,' and Lucy rushed off on some more meaningful mission.

'Ah,' sighed René to his confidante, a French divorcée who had been too much in the sun, '*vous savez*, Odette, *les noirs, c'est moi.*'

That was not quite fair of me, thought Lucy, when she was safely in her kitchen. Joyce had telephoned to ask if she could bring the black man and his girlfriend, but she had gone on about his academic prowess, leading her to expect something more polite, and in a suit.

Family planning at dinner, or as they preferred to call them supper parties, was casual to the uninitiated, but under the apparently free and easy lack of system lay a sense of hierarchy. It was obvious that Tattie had to have a special chair and the senior members of the family be seated properly and first; Ezra, particularly. But it would be a nice point whether Jeremy, for example, as Sarah's sort of son, had precedence over Hélène, as Ezra's ex-mistress, thought Lucy.

Tonight, of course, there was no such problem because Jeremy as part of the immediate family had a duty to sit at Sarah's table and Hélène was escorted by some French admirer with an impenetrable pair of spectacles and the insignia of the Légion d'honneur in the lapel of his dinner jacket. The Thompsons and Nicholsons and Allfreys – her friends after all – she had seated firmly herself at one large table while her mother and father and the pig farmer (as *maître en titre*), Tattie and Chuck, Freddy and Joyce, and David and his mother and herself – although God knew if she were going to be able to sit down – were at the other, with space left for Ezra and Audrey.

It was not a system which the black man could be expected to comprehend. He just saw two empty seats and wondered why he had to stand up. Still, the caviare which the old fruit kept on bringing him was very tasty, especially when one realized that the chopped onion and the chopped egg were not crucial.

Had she known Lucy would not have cared what was happening in the black man's head. All she saw, returning from the kitchen, where trays of coffee were being prepared well ahead of their need, was her drawing room full of a happy, agitated and well-dressed crowd, enjoying themselves at her expense but, to do Lucy justice at that moment, that factor was nowhere in her mind. Eyes shining, she surveyed the room. To top her happiness, when she exchanged looks with her husband, David blew her a rare private kiss, hinting, she thought, at more to come.

All appeared well, *alles in ordnung* as Eirene irritatingly reassured her. She was talking by the French windows – although a place had been set aside for her at the big family table – in German to the new agent for the business in Paris, a Jew from Geneva. Eva Krapf was sitting on the sofa with the American girl who looked bored and anxious about her black swain, who was enjoying obvious success with René, Sir Arthur and Patrick. Jeremy's friend Ferty seemed to be impressing one of the Thompsons who worked at Lazards. Her new friend Percy was alone but happy (she had checked) concentrating on the food. Dimmi who never grew any older was certainly – Ezra not yet arrived – the most distinguished-looking person in the room. Lucy had her back to the American set, as she put it to herself, for Oscar and Sandra and Chuck (that was tactful) and his old buddy Victor Bridleton and another man – was it a friend of his or Sandra's? didn't matter – had settled into the overflow table in the hall. Chaimy and his unkempt girlfriend, his landlady she gathered, were sitting on the stairs behind them, giggling. The only unintegrated element, noticed the thoughtful hostess, was the Wilson family, crushed in a corner, he embarrassed and she red-faced, spectacles steamed up, looking up occasionally from her plate to count her brood, which the others did not appear to reckon worthy of association. Bloody little snobs! She looked, poor lady, like a rolling pin in frills.

Lucy made a decision. After all, next to the family, Mr Wilson was the most important man in the business, and in crucial matters of shares and such like (David had told her), more important. She sailed up in her best Cheltenham manner. 'We can't have this. . . . Please come and sit down.'

Mrs Wilson paused on a forkful of salmon and looked up anxiously, her piggy eyes flickering in dismay, but her husband grasped her firmly by the arm and Lucy said gently, 'It's all right, dear. The children will manage by themselves.' Lucy conveyed them both to the empty seats at the family table. The family were most affable – Sarah greeted Mrs Wilson by her first name, something she would never forget – and David threw Lucy a glance of gratitude nicely overlaid with unrehearsed surprise and admiration.

Ffffppptt pa pa pa phut. There was a white shower of sparks, then a blue, then a sort of yellow dribble. 'What's that?' asked Sarah quickly.

'It was a firework,' replied David.

'Looks pretty *schwach* to me,' said Sarah.

'Just you wait,' said David grimly. He had bought for £5 each some rockets marked 'Admiralty Property'. 'That's just the beginning.'

'Yes,' said Sarah, looking round the room, 'but who began it?'

'I've a chap called Garside who comes in twice a week to do the garden, extraordinary fellow, he was a major in the Indian Army and he will call me "sir".'

'Ah,' said Joyce. 'Lady Chatterley's Lover.'

'What?' said Sarah, interested. 'I thought he was a pig farmer – I mean a gamekeeper. . . .' She giggled and the Brigadier blushed.

'He was a gamekeeper in the book,' insisted Joyce pedantically, 'but he had been in the Indian Army as an officer, which explains a lot, if you think about it. . . .'

But Sarah did not want to think about it.

'How do you get on with my daughter?' she addressed David. 'I always think she's a bit grim,' she added, sucking on her cigarette.

'Sarah!' protested Jeremy.

'Oh, you shut up – you're not so bloody marvellous either,' said

Sarah amiably. 'Me children are a disappointment to me,' she confided to Mrs Wilson who was trying to control a meringue with her fork. This lady was so amazed that she looked up in horror at her husband. Harry Wilson replied with a look saying, 'Don't worry, this is how they always behave.'

Really, thought Jeremy, the purity of Sarah's selfishness rendered it innocent.

'How is the gallery doing, my boy?' asked the Brigadier with a show of interest.

'Well,' said Jeremy, 'I mean, not very well. You see the art world is a sort of barometer of confidence . . . of the business world. . . .' He faltered, not wishing to encourage a let's-do-something-about-Jeremy half-hour, a minor family pastime.

'Listen,' said Sarah, patting him affectionately on the arm, 'my father used to say, "It's cold or it's hot, it's wet or it's fine, it's war or it's peace, but if they want it, they'll buy it." '

'I will giff you ze pigs when I die, Cheremy. If you luff them. You ze,' said the pig farmer turning his head from side to side, 'I haff no children,' and to emphasize his melancholy he drained a glass of kümmel.

Jeremy would like to have pursued this offer but there was a more serious splutter and a giant Catherine wheel began to rotate outside, causing the grown-ups – the children had already vanished – to rise from their seats.

'That's more like it,' said Sarah. 'Wasn't I nice to be born on November the fifth?'

That, and David's meticulous extravagance, combined to make a display of Gaullist proportions during which arrived Ezra and Audrey and their party, which consisted of St James and a fellow club member who was inevitably a back-bench MP. Fortunately the fireworks were too powerful a distraction for an exchange of views on the all-dominating topic of Suez, especially as the late-comers immediately encountered Joyce, Freddy, the black man luminous in white – Chester Knowles, he called himself – and his obvious girlfriend. Joyce introduced everybody and was pleased, and slightly shocked, to hear Chester suddenly begin to address Ezra in the most ingratiating manner:

'This is a very special moment for me, Lord Sterling. I have heard of you and of your public record, of course, but I never thought to have the privilege of meeting you.'

'Any friend of the . . .' But the rest was lost in the roar of a rocket and Ezra simply indicated Joyce with a movement of his head.

The black man nodded understandingly. 'And I believe you could help me if you will.'

In case Ezra should interpret this as an appeal for financial assistance – which he did not – Joyce said hurriedly, 'Chester's doing his doctorate on Power and Minorities at the London School of Economics.'

'That is correct.' Chester nodded sagely.

'I'll be glad to tell you all I know – it won't take long.'

'Well, then . . .' said Chester, making a graceful gesture suggesting they might both withdraw to the comfort of the drawing room.

'Oh, Mr Knowles, don't you think you should both see a couple more of David's rockets? He will be disappointed. . . .' Audrey, who had a more delicate nose, smelt trouble.

'Of course, Lady Sterling,' and Chester bowed and withdrew.

There was in fact a pause in the ignition of more fireworks while Garside, assisted by David and Oscar and the manly among the Thompsons, Nicholsons and Allfreys, shouted at each other, flashed torches, and generally stumped about. One of the twins was apprehended trying to send quite a small rocket up Eva Krapf's flowing embroidered peasant skirt and this delighted Sir Arthur, who said quite loudly to the Brigadier, 'Wasn't it someone in Jane Austen who averred – that's the sort of word she'd have used, isn't it? – that servants, like children and dogs, have a nose for the wrong sort of person?' An argument began between Lucy and David over whether Joshua or Jericho, or both or neither, should be sent up-stairs and locked in their bedroom, but it was mainly for the benefit of the aggrieved Eva and the decision was taken from them by a cascade of gold and silver rain set off by the imperturbable Garside.

Ezra decided to seek out the black man. At least it meant he could sit down.

The living room was now empty and they chose a corner table by the fire where logs were burning. One of Searcy's men produced some Krug for Ezra and, on demand a bottle of brandy and a balloon for Chester, whom he eyed suspiciously but was reassured by a glance from Ezra.

'My thesis, Lord Sterling, is concerned with minorities and political power in England between 1815, the end of the Napoleonic wars, and 1914. . . .'

Ezra was about to say something but Chester put up an imperious hand, whose palm Ezra noticed was a deal paler than the rest of his hand.

'Yes, I know Jews did not exercise much power – politically – before that date. At least no organized power . . . because you cannot consider the peerages Edward VII gave to his Jewish friends as anything more than tokens for favours received. The "troika" at Hyde Park Corner, for instance . . . you know?' Ezra did not.

'Oh well,' said Chester easily, taking a big sip from the balloon of brandy, 'that expensive bit of sculpture with three horses pulling a chariot was put on the top of the arch there by the first Lord Chobham, if I have it right, who was born Stern, a money-lender who had helped the King when he was a young boy.'

'Really, I didn't know that. How interesting.'

'Yes, there are a lot of things you don't know.' And the black man smiled up at Lucy charmingly as she passed. She was bustling past on a domestic mission and was surprised and pleased to see two such different people getting on so well. If Ezra could be so busy with the black man – the one danger spot, she had thought – the party must be a success.

'Tell me, please . . .' said Ezra, noticing that there was no one else in sight and that the crowd was in the garden watching the fireworks which occasionally lit up the darkened room. Ezra experienced a flicker which he dismissed angrily from his mind and determined henceforth to fight this fellow with his tongue, and he was clearly in for a fight. Most of his life he had been protected from this sort of assault. He resolved to pursue the encounter detachedly and with courage.

'Tell me more about your thesis, Mr, er, Knowles.'

'Oh, please call me Chester.'

'Yes, of course. . . . But how does the money-lender, Mr Stern's, purchase of a peerage relate to anything I might . . .'

'Oh, everything, Lord Sterling. You see, my supervisor agreed that in the case of the Jews, as a minority in England, I might slip over the watershed a little into the twenties and even thirties, which is where you come in. . . .'

Ezra, his heart beating a little faster than usual, nodded calmly. 'So?' He drew on his cigar and was careful to turn his head away when he blew out the smoke.

'So, an ethnic minority group like yours has to buy its way into power and pay over the odds, right? So how much did you pay, Lord Sterling, and to whom?'

Ezra blinked and sent a prayer. It was answered.

'The family, and indeed the business, has never been political, like the Samuels or the Markses, who, I'm told, support Nye Bevan. . . .'

'Being apolitical in this country means you support the Conservatives.'

'Yes, you're right, Chester, usually it does. But not in our case. We give each of the political parties the same every year. It's a modest sum – you can see it in the accounts. Except, of course, the Communist Party . . .' – he paused – 'to which we give a lot of money. But,' he paused again, 'you will not see that in the accounts.' There was a big bang outside and the windows rattled.

'Whazzat?' said Chester.

'I think it was just one of David's special rockets.'

'No, no, about giving money to the Communist Party,' and Chester drew the brandy bottle towards him and poured himself a serious dollop. He's on the run, thought Ezra.

'Oh, I should explain,' he answered, 'that while the girls on the floor are young, don't stay with us very long, and are happy to accept a paternal sort of management, the men are, some of them, highly unionized, especially in the laboratories, and their union is the ETU, which is organized, most efficiently, by the Communist Party. I therefore find it wise to propitiate them – with money. We have, as a result, a great deal less trouble than our competitors,' Ezra concluded mildly.

Chester Knowles just stared at him.

'My cousin Chaimy Hassan is himself . . .'

The black man cut him short. 'Do many people know about this?' he asked dully.

'No,' said Ezra, 'only you and me. But if you tried to make something of it, you wouldn't be believed.' Ezra's eyes glittered in the candlelight.

'Could that be perhaps on account of my black skin, Mr Steimatsky?' spat Chester, leaning forward.

Chuck, passing through the drawing room to look for his cheroots which he might have left on the table in the hall, heard part of this last sentence. He stopped and read in his brother-in-law's eyes the simple message – 'Help.'

Chuck walked on towards the hall then, as if catching sight of the black man for the first time, spun round and said, 'Hi! You must be the guy they're all talking about out there. You're on a Fulbright, aren't you? I met the Senator just after the war. Mind if I sit down?' Chuck spoke to Chester as if Ezra were not there.

'Where you from?' asked Chester. 'You American? You talk American,' said Chester.

'Sure,' said Chuck with his friendly smile. 'I'm proud to be American, St Francisville, Louisiana.' And he held out his hand which Chester limply accepted.

'Listen, friend, are there any johns around here?'

'Sure are,' said Chuck and as the black man seemed to have difficulty in standing up, he said, 'Let me show you.'

'Excuse us, sir,' Chuck said to Ezra.

'Do you know that guy?' Chester asked Chuck as he was led out of the room. 'Pretty mean, isn't he?'

'Yeah,' said Chuck.

The downstairs loo was occupied and showed no signs of being vacated. The equivalent on the half landing was lit up, and the door was open so that when Chester insisted he had to get to a john 'like soon', Chuck suggested they attempt the stairs together. Chester agreed with this strategy. They inched their way up and when they reached the top Chuck gently removed his arm from the black man's shoulder and hit him, as hard as he could, on the chin.

There was no one about and the inspiration had come from the garden where David's second naval rocket – one of his *pièces de résist-ance* – had just tottered into the Chelsea sky. To the jubilant shout of one-two-three-four, rising in volume and excitement, it had exploded once, twice, thrice and then at a beat before the fourth crack, Chuck had struck. How premeditated the blow had been Chuck could not have said, but as he watched the black man first rise slightly, then tumble like an uncontrolled boulder down Lucy's solid Queen Anne staircase, he felt no regret, only fear.

Why had he done it? Not out of hatred for the black man but out of love for Ezra.

The body, for that was all it now was, had gone bumpity, bump, ending in a curve from which it almost gracefully unfolded to lie flat, unmoving, on the floor.

Chuck noticed that his hands were shaking. Surely the man was not dead? Quickly, but not too quickly, he descended the stairs, glanced quickly at the body sprawled in the hall, and walked into the drawing room where, seeing that Ezra was still alone at the table by the fire, he joined him. Still everyone was in the garden. Thank God.

'I heard a crash,' said Ezra quietly. He had long since trained himself not to look round. 'What happened?'

'The Fulbright scholar fell down the stairs,' said Chuck, caressing a clenched fist with his hand.

Ezra slightly inclined his head.

'Did I ever tell you,' said Chuck, 'about when I was spraying crops? It's easy now – you get a plane for four hundred bucks or a thousand at the most. But then, before the war, a plane cost more, and I couldn't beat those niggers at sixty cents a day with their sulphur pumps. But I tried. I borrowed money all over town and I bought me a plane which flew like a scaffold. Pretty tricky. You have to follow the contours of the land from a few feet up. And the farmers were poor. So when I got a contract it didn't add up to much, okay?'

Ezra nodded.

'But the niggers were scared. They thought I was unfair competition. Okay? So one day they put some soda pop in my tank. Right? In those days soda cost more than gas. So I crashed, but I

didn't even sprain my ankle. They were good planes, those . . . But
I had to quit.' He concluded, 'So now I don't like niggers any more.
He was harassing you, wasn't he?'

'Yes,' said Ezra, 'he was, but perhaps we had better forget it.'

'You don't think I should . . .'

'No,' said Ezra, 'stay where you are. Somebody will . . .'

And he was right because an Italian, one of the caterers or one of
Lucy's, rushed through the door crying, '*E morte il nero . . . il nero
e morte!*'

'Stay where you are!' ordered Ezra sharply.

'Damn!' said David. The incident could not have come at a more
tiresome moment. The big bombs had been a great success and the
crowd, notably the twins who had advance information and had
been boasting to the other children, were clamouring for the final
shell. It exploded five times, each in a different colour.

'*Signore, signore.*' The Italian was clutching one sleeve of his
duffle coat while the boys were tugging the other.

'Lucy,' he shouted. 'Get the family doctors . . . the doctors in
the family . . . There's been an accident.' Everybody assumed
somebody had been hurt by a firework and torches were flashed
officiously. 'Oh, hell, I'd better take care of it.'

He marched off, just remembering to say to the twins fiercely,
'Now don't you touch anything!'

Eva Krapf came up to him. 'Can I help at all?'

'No, dear, you're a gynaecologist. Just hold on to that American
girl and keep her in the garden. Her boyfriend's broken his neck or
something. But don't let her near him, right?'

He hurried on to the house and walking through the drawing
room just noticed Ezra deep in conversation with Chuck of all
people, and apparently oblivious to the pandemonium in the hall.
The Brigadier was already there bending over the body of Chester
Knowles, as were the servants, and now there was Joyce.

'Is he all right?' they asked, almost together.

The Brigadier, kneeling down, was gently moving Chester's
limbs one by one and merely grunted. Then he felt round his head.
There was no mark on his face. He straightened up.

'Of course he's all right,' he said contemptuously. 'If you think

. . .' He was addressing the lot of them. 'If you think a drunken man can do himself much injury falling down a flight of stairs you haven't seen as many drunks as I have.'

A look of relief, to be replaced by an expression akin to disappointment, appeared on the servants' faces and one of them stopped crossing herself. Now a dark stain appeared between the legs of the black man's beautifully cut trousers.

'Oh, shoo off, the lot of you,' he snapped. 'And somebody get a blanket,' said the Brigadier. 'Mind you,' he said, 'he's unconscious, so he must have hit his head somewhere down the line.' And he looked at the staircase.

'Well, what do we do?' asked Joyce.

'Take him home and let him sleep it off,' answered the Brigadier.

'Shouldn't he go to casualty at St George's, just in case?' Joyce believed in involving the National Health Service in people's lives as often as possible.

'On fireworks night? You must be joking,' said David.

'In case of what?' asked the Brigadier, glaring at Joyce and on seeing Doc, joining the group, said, 'Have a look at him, will you, Dr Krapf? There seems to be a demand for a second opinion. I'm going to get myself a glass of your excellent champagne, David,' and he walked away.

David suddenly understood why his father-in-law had become a Brigadier. He stayed long enough to hear Dr Krapf say, 'Yes, there is a contusion on the jaw,' then he walked back into the garden. Presumably Joyce could arrange the transport. It was, after all, her friend.

'Can I get you a drink, Ezra?' asked the Brigadier.

'No, thank you. Chuck's looking after me very well.' The Brigadier was the only member of the family who would not have been seized by the import of that casual remark; but then he was not interested in their politics. 'Our coloured friend, will he survive?' Ezra called out.

The Brigadier returned with his glass full, and with a fart, sat down. 'Sorry,' he said. 'Yes,' he said, taking a gulp, 'for many years. I've told them to send him home.' He sipped his champagne and did not notice the look exchanged by the two other men.

'How?' asked Ezra.

'How what, Ezra?' replied the Brigadier.

'Will they get him home?'

'Oh, there are enough cars outside.'

'Yes, but if he's unconscious . . . carrying him . . . He's a big guy, you know,' said Chuck.

'Yes, you're right. Jenkins can take him in my car,' said Ezra. That would be a considerate gesture, he thought. 'Any friend of the family is a friend of mine. Could you arrange that, do you think, for me, Chuck. There's a good chap.'

It was decided that Freddy and Eva Krapf, now firmly holding on to the American girl, should take Chester home in Ezra's car, with orders to return to Tite Street after safe delivery. But when Jenkins heard of the plan and the condition of its principal he was shocked.

'I'm not having that, sir,' he said to Chuck. 'I know what'll happen, he'll be sick all over the upholstery, and it's not leather, you know, like you can wash it off with soap and water, it's cloth and you can't get it out. It'll stink forever!' With advancing years Jenkins had lost his timidity.

'I tell you what, Jenkins, if anything does happen we'll get a new car, how's that?' Jenkins gazed at Chuck in wonder and disbelief.

'That'd be bloody marvellous. I dunno why his lordship makes us keep the old tub on the road. The springing! Why there isn't any! Oh, my aching back!'

'A promise,' repeated Chuck.

There was no one present at this exchange to speculate how he could keep it.

David and Lucy were so adroit at avoiding comment on the incident that many people did not hear of it until days later. In the meantime, more hot punch was served outside and more champagne in the drawing room for the senior citizens who were beginning to feel the chill. (Sarah had a comment when told by her husband what had happened and how he had handled the incident: 'Well, I like an accident. It makes yer feel pleased it wasn't you.')

There were more fireworks too and when David asked Garside the stock position, he replied, 'Plenty more, sir. Don't worry, plenty more of everything.'

Jenkins's prophecy was fulfilled – in Prince's Gate. The black man in the back of the car suddenly opened his eyes, rubbed his jaw, and announced, 'Gee, I think I'm going to throw up.' There was not quite time to stop the car, wind down the window and hold out his head, to stop some of it dribbling down the inside of the door.

The smell did persist, and prompted Ezra to order a new Rolls, and since the two seemed to go together, a new chauffeur.

PART FOUR

1966, 1967

1966

oⒺo

'Remember the old Rolls, Oscar?' Ezra fastened his seat belt. 'Goodness me, these things are badly designed.'

'Do I not. How often have I told the story of getting it up to a hundred on the Ashford by-pass at the beginning of the war?'

'How foolish of you. You never told me. Well, at the time of Suez I had to sell it because it was such a greedy car, and of course, we got nothing for it. Now, I am told, people are collecting them, and it would be worth a fortune. Did I tell you Jenkins won the Greyhound Derby? Only an old man crippled with arthritis would breed greyhounds, don't you agree?'

'Do you know how many cars you've had in the last ten years, Ezra?'

'Couldn't count them, or the chauffeurs for that matter. Something snapped at Suez, you know, Oscar. I know it's an unfashionable point of view but I agreed with Winston – "I'm not sure I would have started it but I would have finished it!" Something like that. And I'll tell you another thing, Oscar.' Ezra leant over to tap little Oscar's knee but was restrained by the seat belt. 'Damn this thing,' he muttered and undid it. 'A fellow in the House told me the other day that his brother was at the FO and saw one of their chaps, an American in hospital, just after we climbed down – a high-up fellow in the State Department, and when the Englishman complained at Dulles's behaviour, he sat up in bed and said, "Why did you take any notice?" '

'Extraordinary,' said Oscar.

'Not at all, not at all. Ever hear of Admiral Parker?'

'No.'

'Of course not, nobody has. He was the man who ordered Nelson to withdraw at the Battle of Copenhagen, and when he saw the signal he moved the telescope to his blind eye. Right!' Ezra beamed.

'Point taken.'

'England's falling apart. The women play Bingo in the afternoons, watch television in the evenings, and on Sundays the men wash their Japanese cars.' Ezra looked out of the window of the Rolls at the semi-detached houses with disgust. 'That lot! We've never had it so good, hah!'

'Well, Ezra, it's true, isn't it? Have we ever had it so good? I mean, since Suez the business has ... what, tripled? And as I always tell Sandra when she complains about the traffic – don't be cross, they're all customers. That lot,' he too pointed, 'keep us going.'

'Hey there, what's happened to little Oscar in his old age? Since when have you become such a supporter of the mobility – as it was called in the eighteenth century?' Oscar was silent. 'Has Freddy converted you to Hampstead socialism?' Ezra went on teasingly.

'Quite honestly, Ezra, now that I come to think of it, I must be reacting to Sandra. Her views on politics come undiluted from her mother and I understand what René meant when he called them Jewish WASPs, except that lot, or that crowd, are genuinely not aware of being Jewish. They take less interest in Israel, for instance, than you do.'

It was Ezra's turn to be silent.

'How is little Mariamne?' he asked.

'Just like any other ten-year-old. Only we think she's prettier and cleverer. She's brilliant at the piano apparently, but all she talks to me about is ponies. She wants a palomino.'

'What's that?'

'It's a kind of horse, sort of goldeny, and naturally very expensive.'

'Then she shall have one,' said Ezra.

'Oh, please not,' said Oscar. 'I've told her it'll have to wait until we ...' He bit his lip like a schoolboy.

'Don't tell me you're going to desert me, and get a house in the country or Gstaad or somewhere.' David had bought a chalet in Switzerland to rhyme with his bank account in Zurich and earned from Ezra a black mark for each.

'We did think,' – Oscar swallowed – 'that when Mariamne gets a little older – and she really is crazy about horses – of getting . . .'

'Oh, I know what you mean,' interrupted Ezra crossly. 'A Queen Anne rectory with seven acres and a paddock an hour and a half from London on the motorway. What's the point when there's all that and more at Turners? Why do you think I bought the place? It's for my children and my children's children.'

Oscar smiled. Ezra had described exactly the house Sandra was looking for, but all he said was, 'There isn't a paddock at Turners.'

'There will be, *and* a bloody Pallor-whatever-you-call-it. Then perhaps my great-niece might honour me with a visit, eh?' Ezra jabbed little Oscar with his finger.

Oscar blushed. His daughter was rather a haughty little girl (from her mother of course) and had once referred to herself as an 'establishment child' in conversation with Ezra.

'It would certainly be a lure, I must admit. I'll talk to Sandra about it.'

'Huh.' Sandra's inability to be in awe of Ezra put him slightly in awe of her. He preferred the family to marry into a certain amount of dependence. And that little Mariamne was – as are all only children – spoilt.

'Isn't it about time, Oscar, that you and Sandra . . .'

'Had another child?'

'Exactly.'

'The time has passed. I've told you often enough she couldn't bear being pregnant, and that business about women being naturally programmed to forget the pangs of birth somehow does not apply to my wife.'

'My family are lazy progenitors. I shall die without seed as in the old Hebrew curse,' said Ezra dramatically.

'What about your own grandson, for Christ's sake?' said little Oscar, annoyed by the old man's use of self-pity to trespass on a delicate zone. 'He must be coming along.'

'Eighteen on June the third,' replied Ezra quickly. (A little too quickly?) 'But, as you know, Oscar, he's lost to me. He must be one of the few kibbutzniks who still believe in the system. I understand a lot of them want "out", isn't that what they say nowadays?

Some Israelis have even gone back to Germany, they tell me, and they all want to go and live in America. But not the next Viscount Sterling. Oh, no. His granny has been sending money to that kibbutz for years. She thought I didn't realize that, his grandpa – that's me, you know – starts sending him money for his birthday and what does he do with it? He trots round to the secretary of the kibbutz with the money and says, here you are, and a few months later I get a letter from the treasurer saying the committee have decided to use the money we sent for a swimming pool, for a cotton-baling machine or some damn nonsense.'

'Probably more use,' suggested little Oscar.

'Yes, it probably is, but not more use to me. Now he'll have his own money, and then later he'll have a lot, and there's nothing I can do about it. Those bloody tax consultants, why did I listen to them? All his shares could be sold on one day by some ignorant Israelis. Can you imagine? After all the trouble we went to with Chuck and your Aunt Tattie – remember? – I should be gazumped by my own grandson. Huh!'

'Well, it hasn't happened yet, and David . . .'

'David got nowhere. I sent David to see him.' (This was not wholly true, thought little Oscar, as David had slunk off to Israel on his own bat.) 'And the boy is totally intransigent. England and things English he has rejected, totally. That includes the business and the family. Apparently he has some obsession that we killed his father. David told me his Hebrew was better than his English and he's even changed his name.'

'Yes,' said Oscar. 'Niki something.'

'Yes,' repeated Ezra. 'Avi-something. Don't even remember my own grandson's name. Ah well. *O tempera O mores.*'

Little Oscar looked at his uncle's gloomy face with a smile. Ezra quickly acquired the idiom of others, and it was not always easy to say from where, as in the cases of 'out' or 'gazumped', but the Latin tag could only be from the House of Lords.

Ezra glowered balefully at the traffic as the Rolls crawled forward. 'I thought the whole point of going to the country on Friday morning was to avoid the traffic on Friday afternoons. Did you remember your clubs, Oscar?'

'They're always kept at Turners.' Ezra knew that perfectly well.

'How's business, by the way? Your side, I mean? I never really understand what you do any more, you boys.' This admission was the standard prelude to some sharp questioning, so little Oscar wriggled in his seat. Ezra had taken to appearing at the business sporadically and preferred intimate to public sessions. His memory for figures and details had not diminished with age, but, reflected little Oscar with secret satisfaction, he could not be expected to remember figures he had not seen.

'Oh, the Defence stuff, you mean. That's going very well, almost embarrassingly so. You must get Chaimy to tell you his top-secret adventure.'

'You tell me.'

'I don't know anything about it. As I say, it's top-secret and he wouldn't tell me anything. . . . But I dare say he'll tell you. It was all laid on by Matthew Fforde.'

'So Sir Matthew is beginning to earn his corn.'

'And how. Can you imagine getting Chaimy, who's a card-carrying Communist, clearance to see one of our most secret weapons?'

'Well, I can, in fact,' said Ezra. 'Chaimy's so . . . obvious.'

The car was speeding now.

'Ah,' said Ezra, 'the English countryside, unbeatable . . . Do you know why? Because it's looked after by people, like me, who water it with money. There's not a stitch of England that hasn't been treasured for centuries. Something Americans fail to understand, you know, Oscar.'

Little Oscar smiled. Making Ezra add a farm to Turners had been a good move.

'Why are the gates open?' asked Ezra of the chauffeur as the Rolls turned into the private road.

'I believe the house is open to the public today, my lord, in aid of the nurses.' On such occasions it had become the custom to leave the electrically operated gates permanently open. There had been too many accidents.

'Oh, God. So it is. Damn. That means Audrey won't come

down till later. I hope they don't crawl all over the golf course. Do nurses play golf?'

They usually took about an hour and a half to play nine holes, Ezra, Geoffrey Nickson and little Oscar, which brought them to 12.30 of a Friday afternoon, and a glass of carefully iced Krug before lunch, normally presided over by Audrey. Ezra played steadily scoring more on the green than on the fairway. Geoffrey was by now a good player, with a handicap of 4, little Oscar played dramatically and erratically, losing his temper (and quite a few balls) and taking Geoffrey's quiet advice with ill grace.

'Never mind, Oscar.' Ezra would tell him after a particularly vicious hook. 'It's not really a game for Jews.'

Little Oscar, if he saw Ezra's ball lying in the rough, would kick it on to the fairway, a practice Geoffrey had not learnt to condone.

At the eighth hole, thinking that Ezra looked tired, little Oscar was about to tee up Ezra's ball when Ezra said crossly, 'I can manage that for myself, thank you.' And he did. He hated to be regarded as an old man and had never used the electric golf buggy which the employees at the business had given him for his last birthday. However, he did allow Geoffrey to carry his clubs.

On the ninth hole Ezra missed an easy putt. He looked up at little Oscar. 'What did you mean,' he said slowly, 'in the car, when you said "embarrassingly so"?'

'Oh, the missile business. Well, the Ministry got their sums wrong, so we make a couple of million more than we thought, before we even write a programme.'

'What does Chaimy say about that, I wonder?'

'Oh, he doesn't know,' replied Oscar easily. 'If he did he'd probably want us to give it back,' and he laughed.

Ezra stared at his nephew, his grey eyes blazing with rage. 'That's exactly . . .' he began and then he noticed Geoffrey's anxious face, and collapsed.

Time stood still.

The golf buggy was, miraculously, on charge in the hut a few yards away. They lifted Ezra into the seat. Geoffrey stood by the controls and little Oscar put Ezra's panama hat low on his forehead and held his head up by his hair as the vehicle trundled forward. He waved at the few curious people who noticed them on their way to the house. People who visit gardens on open days have to be curious.

'Can we get him as far as the lift in this thing?'

'Through the house, you mean?' asked Geoffrey.

'Why not?'

'Oh, I suppose so . . . they're all double doors.'

He wondered why little Oscar was holding on to poor Ezra's hair. They stopped the buggy in front of the electrically operated glass doors of the orangery. There was just enough of an opening for Geoffrey to slip through and press the switch. The doors slid open and they had to lift the front wheels of the machine on to the chequered marble floor. Pettit, who like his predecessor Grose, enjoyed this particular function, was arranging the weekend flowers on the great console in the hall. His mouth fell open in astonishment when he saw the strange procession.

'Get Dr Raven and tell him Lord Sterling's had a stroke . . . or a heart attack. Anyway, tell him to come at once,' snapped little Oscar.

'Sir, it's not Dr Raven any more. He's retired. It's a . . .' He hesitated. 'It's an Indian gentleman.' He paused. 'The staff like him very much.'

'Well, get him, Pettit, quick, whoever it is.'

There was only room in the lift for two. Little Oscar hugged Ezra like a lover as the little box, so horribly like a coffin, whined slowly upwards. Some colour seemed to have returned to Ezra's face – it was difficult to tell in the pale yellow light – as he opened his eyes which were full of pain and said, 'Heart.'

Geoffrey was waiting by the lift to help Oscar carry him to his bed, where they undid his belt and took off his shoes.

'I hope to God it's not a stroke,' said Geoffrey.

Little Oscar shook his head. He was thinking hard.

'Hadn't we better tell Audrey?'

'Certainly not, on no account,' said Oscar. 'I'll go downstairs and wait for the doctor,' he added.

'All right then, I'll stay with him. Maybe he'd like a glass of water.'

Little Oscar nodded. (What's on his mind? thought Geoffrey. He's behaving like a conspirator.)

Ignoring the unstopped bottle of champagne, a melancholy reminder of what should have been, Oscar walked behind the bar and poured himself a quarter of a tumbler of Hine, which he drank in two gulps. He saw his hands were shaking. Half ambling and half trotting across the hall to Ezra's study, he was stopped by Pettit.

'I got through to Dr Xavier himself, Mr Oscar; he was just sitting down to lunch, but he said he'd come now.'

'Which means?'

'Just a few minutes, sir, he only lives in the village, in Dr Raven's old house.'

'So you'll show him up straightaway.'

'Yes, sir, of course.'

'And I'll be in the study. I have some telephone calls to make. By the way, do you know how the direct line works?'

'I think his lordship just used to pick it up and the connection is automatic. She will be there – Mrs Winterbourne. Lord Sterling always telephoned her before luncheon.'

'Oh, did he?' (It was eerie how they had both slipped into the past tense.)

Pettit followed him into the room. Oscar picked up the unmarked black telephone, oddly the only old-fashioned looking instrument in a house full of gadgets, and immediately heard Mrs Winterbourne's cool voice.

'Good afternoon, Lord Sterling.'

Little Oscar gulped and nodded at Pettit to go away. 'We . . . Mrs Winterbourne . . . it's Oscar Barnet.'

'Oh . . . is there anything wrong?'

'Yes, Lord Sterling has had an attack.'

'Oh my God.' Mrs Winterbourne was no longer cool. 'Is it serious?'

'I don't know. The doctor's on his way. But in the meantime, there are two things I would like you to do for me, please.'

'Yes, Mr Barnet.'

'Will you get hold of Brigadier Kind, wherever he is, and ask him to telephone Lord Sterling urgently. Just that, do you understand?'

Mrs Winterbourne did not, but she replied, 'He's probably on his way to his club, Mr Oscar.'

'Fine. He'll know of a heart specialist. The local man here is an Indian apparently,' said Oscar.

'Oh dear,' said Mrs Winterbourne.

'Secondly, er . . . where in the world is Mr David?'

'Hold on I'll tell you.' There was a rustling of papers. 'Today is Friday the . . . yes . . . he's in Honolulu.'

Oscar remembered. The business shared with an American company an assembly plant for transistors in Hawaii. It was very simple, David explained. You flew in with $5,000 worth of little bits and then weeks later you flew out with $500,000 worth of equipment, thanks to hundreds of pairs of tiny Chinese hands.

'Right,' he said. 'Then Mr David should have a copy of the following statement. I'll give you a personal note later. Ready?'

'Yes, Mr Oscar.'

'Take this down, please. "At a board meeting of Sterling Industries Ltd. held this morning, Viscount Sterling announced his intention of retiring from the chairmanship of the company, er . . . in order to attend", no, no, "in view of his increasing private and charitable interests." Got that?'

'I'll read it back when you've finished, Mr Oscar.'

'Good. "The Board appointed Mr Frederick Barnet MA as Chairman and as Joint Managing Directors, Mr David Blacker, er, DSO, BA, and Mr Oscar Barnet . . ." '

'DSO, BA?' supplied Mrs Winterbourne.

'Yes.' Of course, I never thought of that, we both have the same things. '. . . Right. To continue, "Lord Sterling agreed to accept the office of President of the Board of Sterling Industries, in which capacity he will be available for consultation at . . . er . . . ah . . . all times." Would you like to read that back?'

Oscar had seen a battered Volkswagen draw up to the house. Pettit ran out to meet it and was extricating from the driver's seat an almost square, very dark man in a blue suit, who carried an ancient Gladstone bag. He looked like the newly accredited representative of a small Asian country which had waited a long time for independence.

'Fine,' said little Oscar when Mrs Winterbourne had finished. 'Send that out as a press statement on Monday. Right? And . . . er . . . let me think – the Stock Exchange closes at three. . . .'

Ah, thought Mrs Winterbourne, now I see what he's up to. The last time Lord Sterling had to cancel some engagement through illness the shares had dropped sharply. Clever little Oscar.

'Are you there?'

'Yes, sir.' It seemed appropriate.

'So ring up the City Editor of *The Times* at, say, four, and tell him that only he has this information in advance. All right? And copy it in a cable to Mr David, with this to precede it: "Ezra had heart attack this morning and in your absence we issued the following statement. Please communicate. Yours Oscar." And, Mrs Winterbourne . . .'

'Yes, Mr Oscar?'

'I will try and telephone Mr David.'

'Yes, of course.'

'But I don't want anyone else to know what has happened until they read about it in the papers. Otherwise there'll be the most God-awful panic. Not even Lady Sterling.'

'I understand, Mr Oscar. Will you let me know what the doctor says?'

'I will indeed, Mrs Winterbourne.'

'And I'll get the number of Mr David's hotel in Honolulu for you.'

'Thank you. Goodbye.'

Little Oscar put down the receiver with a sigh of relief. He had taken the only possible action, and Ezra would have approved, he was sure.

How sure was he?

He had invented a board meeting and made changes in the most senior offices of the company, an action against the Companies' Act and possibly a crime, if it was not condoned and regularized, which could be easy, or not. Who would kick up a fuss? Surely not David, unless he expected to be Chairman. Hell, of course he did. But promoting the two of them to the vague position of Joint Managing

Director and so fossilizing their rivalry was both logical and in accord with Ezra's style. Most reassuring had been Winterbourne's apparent, no real, and immediate acceptance. She was the bell-wether and thermometer of the business, the confidante of Ezra, and was shrewd and courageous enough to spot anything objection-able in what he had said and to protest. ... Or to sabotage his intentions? No, come, come, he reassured himself, she had called him 'sir' at one point in their conversation. That was significant.

The real hazard was Wilson. He was, after all, the company secretary and he, Oscar, had trespassed on his territory. Wilson must be telephoned tonight. No, better, early in the morning after *The Times* had gone to bed. He would explain that his action had been motivated – good Wilsonian word that – by a concern for the business. The Stock Exchange was ignorant enough to regard Ezra as the mastermind and genius of the business, and hysterical enough to act on that belief. If the rumour of a heart attack reached the City unexplained the shares would have a heart attack too. Ezra's condition could be serious; he would certainly never be the same again. A mild heart attack was, he believed, like painful in-digestion, but Ezra had fallen like one of the princes and, indeed, for a moment he and Geoffrey had thought he would not rise again.

There was no point in ringing up Sandra. Anyway, she was with Audrey. Sandra, unlike Lucy, who was content to take the money and chew the cud, would be – in this situation – like any other all-American wife: pushy. 'Why didn't you make yourself Chairman, you dope, and wait for the flak?' Sandra grew more like her mother every day. What makes people more like their mothers every day?

Geoffrey was standing outside Ezra's closed bedroom door. In answer to Oscar's questioning look, he shrugged. 'Doesn't want me in there. Not too much excitement from now on.'

'Quite so.'

They stood uncertainly in the broad corridor, two big men, like schoolboys.

'Er ... Geoffrey.'

'Yes, Oscar?'

'I'm sorry I snapped at you just now. About telling Audrey. You

see I have a duty to see that news of . . .' – he gestured to the closed
door – 'should come out in our way, in our time. . . .'

'Because of the shares, you mean?' Geoffrey had been in the
family long enough to know their obsession with the fall of the
shares. It was mentioned morning, noon and night. Friday's closing
prices at the weekend at Turners was a highlight. Woe betide any
guest who did not bring down a late edition of the *Evening Standard*.
For people who had been so rich so long, he had thought it odd,
until it occurred to him that a fluctuation of a few pence multiplied
by a few million, added up. 'All right then, I'll wait until the
doctor's finished, then I'll go home if you don't mind. On Fridays I
usually give George Perry lunch at the pub. There's no need to
change the routine, is there?'

Oscar nodded appreciatively. Perry was the farmer at Turners.
'By the way, Geoffrey, is there anywhere here where we could put a
paddock?'

But he was interrupted by the door opening and the appearance
of the very dark gentleman, who turned round to shut the door
carefully and then announced.

'He will sleep.'

'And?' asked Oscar.

'Then,' said the very dark gentleman, 'he will wake up.'

The Indian's accent, as if he were imitating Peter Sellers, caused
little Oscar to wonder how a Welsh regiment could have so inflicted
and infected an entire subcontinent.

'I gave him a very mild sedative. I understand Lord Sterling is
not in the habit of taking drugs of any kind?' He had turned to
Geoffrey Nickson, who made a gesture indicating that now that Mr
Barnet had arrived, his own opinion would be irrelevant.

'Yes, he hated drugs. I don't think he ever even took an aspirin.'
Again he bit his lip; that past tense. The doctor moved unself-
consciously ahead of them down the corridor and was waddling
swiftly.

'I think we should have a little talk, Mr, er . . .'

'Barnet. I'm Lord Sterling's nephew. Isn't there anything . . .?'

'And you were playing golf at the time?'

'Well, actually we had finished playing golf and we were just walking back to the house chatting . . . when suddenly . . .'

'Chatting?' repeated the Indian. He walked on down the staircase still ahead of both of them, then stopped and turned round to look at him. 'What about?' he asked.

The insolence in the question was dimmed by a smile of such beauty on the face of the Indian that Oscar stood still and silent. The Indian walked on down the stairs.

'Oh, just business,' he muttered. He wanted to ask about an ambulance, a nurse, another opinion (the man had told him nothing), but he felt foolish at the thought of addressing that uncompromisingly square back.

At some stage, the doctor having been asked to stay to lunch, Geoffrey made his excuses and left.

'So what do we do now, Dr, er . . .'

The two men stood facing each other in the hall.

'Xavier,' said the Indian, extending his hand. 'I have another name but it is somewhat burdensome to pronounce, so I am known as Dr Xavier. My family comes from Goa, and most Goans are called Xavier. In answer to your question, Mr Barnet,' and he raised the hand holding the Gladstone bag to tickle a substantial nostril, 'we can do nothing' – he paused – 'but wait.'

'Until?'

'Until the patient is rested enough to regain his strength, then we can take him to hospital for a cardiograph. Only that will reveal the extent of the damage. At the moment one can only guess . . .'

'And what is your guess, Dr Xavier? Oh, sorry, may I offer you a drink?'

'What a very sensible notion.'

Oscar chose the study as the more suitable setting for such as this. The doctor sat down and eased apart his legs.

'Whisky?'

'Please.'

'Ice?'

'Oh, no thank you. I do not think one should distort whisky of that quality with ice.'

'Ah, I see you are a connoisseur, Dr Xavier.'

'I recognize the bottle. Chivas Regal, I believe?'

'Right.' Ezra's bar in his study at Turners was a replica of the one in London and only the costlier brands were carried.

'One is only a connoisseur of what one cannot afford, would you not agree, Mr Barnet?' said the Indian, rolling his first mouthful round his mouth. 'Imagine the tedium of a claret of the first growth with every meal. One's palate would soon leave one.'

'Is that so?' asked Oscar, puzzled.

'I doubt it. It just appealed to me, as a paradox.'

Oscar stared at him. 'How do you happen to fetch up here?'

'I'll tell you about that over luncheon if I may, but now we should be talking medicine, don't you agree? Your uncle has experienced a fairly serious heart attack, I would guess. Is it his first?'

'As far as I know, and I don't understand it. He wasn't suddenly exerting himself. He wasn't even carrying anything.'

'Ah, my dear boy, that is the popular myth you are expressing. One can have a heart attack in one's sleep, while relaxing over a pint of beer in the pub, or in the middle of a telephone conversation. But often, of course, under moments of hidden stress, like at the wheel of a motor car, or at moments of frustration. Tell me, is Lord Sterling a man of even temperament?'

'Good God, no. He says what's in his mind, why shouldn't he?'

'Yes, of course, that was a foolish question. What a juggins I am. Obviously he is a powerful man, uninhibited by normal constraint and, therefore, not subject to the frustrations or stress felt by so many of Her Majesty's, er, subjects.' He smiled – his Number 2 smile. 'And then of course he is Jewish. That one must not forget.'

'What's that? What's that to do with it?' asked Oscar, not amused.

'Everything. You see, my dear sir, we do not know much about the heart, but there are at least four diseases endemic to Jews and two are related to the heart. Do you think I might have a little more of this absolutely delicious . . .?'

Oscar took the outstretched tumbler and poured a handsome measure. He wondered how far this strange man would wander before coming to the point. 'Tell me, Dr Xavier, what exactly is a cardiogram?'

The doctor inhaled on his Gauloise. 'It was invented here in

England, in Colchester, I believe, and perfected in America –
obviously – and it tells us what is happening and has happened, in
the case of a seizure, to the heart. There are two types: one operating
on Einthoven's galvanometer and the other on a cathode ray.'

'Ah,' said Oscar. 'We probably make them, or the bits at any
rate. How big is it?'

The doctor looked round the study for guidance but found nothing to help him. 'About the size of a tea trolley,' he said.

'Right,' said Oscar, and pressed a lever on Ezra's telephone. He
felt an absurd need to impress this fellow. 'Pettit!' There was no
answer. 'Oh, damn the man,' said Oscar, and then: 'Oh, there you
are.' Pettit had just opened the door.

'Luncheon is served, Mr Oscar.'

'Good.'

'And Brigadier Kind telephoned, sir.'

'What! Why didn't you tell me?'

'It was a reversed-charge call, sir, from the Reform Club. The
Brigadier wanted to speak to Lord Sterling, and I thought it best,
sir, to tell the operator that his lordship was not available.'

'Oh God!' He was cross with *himself*, but the man could not
know that. And need not. 'Well, will you be kind enough to ring
him back, straightaway?'

'Of the Kind Institute?' asked the Indian when Pettit had
withdrawn.

Oscar, now pacing up and down, nodded abstractedly.

'Not, if I might venture a comment, in the right field.'

'No, indeed, but he happens to be my uncle – he's Lord Sterling's
brother-in-law – and he must know someone.'

'Yes, of course, how very interesting.' Dr Xavier seemed about to
say something else but instead, as Oscar stared out of the study window, he stood up, ambled to the bar, poured himself a third Chivas
Regal, sat down again in the green leather armchair, and sighed.

Oscar watched this performance without comment. The man's
mad, he thought.

'You are a member of a rich and powerful family, Mr Barnet,'
began Dr Xavier, without a trace of uncertainty in his speech, 'able
to command the services of the most distinguished physician in the

land, but I beseech you to listen to a word of advice from a humble village GP.' The sight of Dr Xavier caressing his whisky, his firm belly buttoned up in a single-breasted waistcoat, his incredibly dark face, flashing white teeth, and a yellow silk handkerchief strolling casually across a well-cut blue suit, was not typical of a humble English general practitioner.

'Yes,' Oscar managed.

'Ask your uncle for a young man, one who wants to prove his mettle, and cut a dash. I would not send my worst enemy one of the Queen's physicians. They are a vain, bad-tempered lot, old and overworked, and frequently not in the best of health.'

Oscar pondered this. 'Dr Xavier, I think you are a very clever man,' he said finally.

'I know,' said the Indian, and then came the beautiful smile. 'I know.'

2

'I tell you, it's just another goddamn sparrow,' said Mariamne, squinting through the binoculars.

'Are you sure?'

'Ab-so-lute-ly goddamn sure,' said Mariamne, enunciating every syllable.

'Where did you get that awful expression from, my girl?' asked Audrey from the other end of the breakfast table.

'From Mother,' replied Mariamne, her eyes still screwed into the binoculars. 'Isn't it funny, I don't miss her a bit,' she added thoughtfully.

'That is the sort of sentiment one feels, but does not air,' said Ezra.

'Whazzat?' She put down the binoculars.

'He means you can think it but not say it,' explained Audrey.

'Oh,' said Mariamne, bored.

'Now here is something, just look at this fellow, Mariamne. Why can't you ever spot one of these?' And Ezra jabbed at a page in his bird book. '*Oriolus oriolus*, why you can roll it around forever on your tongue, the golden oriole!'

'You're in the wrong country, silly. We're not in the eastern Mediterranean.'

Audrey looked up from an envelope she had just slit open. 'Mariamne, shouldn't you be doing your scales?'

'Oh, can't I go and see Shushi?'

'Yes, after you've done your exercises – half an hour.'

'Oh, goddamn scales,' said Mariamne, but she flounced obediently out of the room in her jodhpurs, brown velvet cap and yellow Aertex shirt, the standard equipment for little girls in love with their ponies.

'I like that little creature,' said Ezra as the sound of her practising trickled into the morning room. 'She'd make an excellent duchess. What did she mean when she said she didn't miss her mother?'

'She meant nothing; they adore each other,' said Audrey, absently staring at the envelope.

'Or maybe she'll run off with a black railway porter,' mumbled Ezra, readjusting the focus on the binoculars. 'She's right, it is a goddamn sparrow.'

Audrey studied her new model husband. A wave of affection swept through her. She wanted to cry. At all costs he must be protected. Some of the doctors predicted another ten or twenty years of trouble-free existence, but Xavier had told her that heart attacks are usually followed by heart attacks, and this – she looked angrily at the cutting – was just the sort of thing to set one off. He had been so good, giving up cigars, drinking one glass of whisky at night (for his arteries), measuring the rainfall, observing the birds, as excited over a new calf as he had been over a new issue. And now this – if it were true. It was all the fault of that bloody little Oscar, she suddenly saw.

'Ezra?'

'Yes, my love?'

'You remember when you had your . . .' She stumbled.

'Heart attack?' Ezra helped her.

'Yes. You were with Oscar.'

'And Geoffrey.'

'But you were talking to Oscar, and you were cross with him' something to do with a defence contract, you told me, some swindle. Audrey checked herself.

'A miscalculation, we decided to call it. It can happen in the best of families. You're quite right, I was angry with him but I no longer am.'

'And it's all been sorted out?'

'I believe so. They were kind enough to spare me the details, but the terms have been changed. Why do you ask?'

'Oh, I was just wondering why he never rang me up when it happened.' Audrey changed to a different, but allied subject.

'He didn't want to, er, alarm you. He didn't want anybody to know. An excess of zeal or caution, I suppose you could say.'

'But he rang up the Brigadier?'

'A medical man,' replied Ezra evenly. 'Anyway, there's nothing you could have done, was there?'

'Except be *told*,' said Audrey firmly. 'People like to be told things. That wasn't very kind. Oh, that reminds me, you've got Harley Williams coming to lunch and Xavier said he'd try and come in.'

'Old Chest and Harley Williams, that'll be expensive.'

Audrey clicked her tongue. She supposed that the Chest and Heart Association was a good cause.

'Yes, I'd much rather you gave Xavier a new car. He'll kill himself in that thing one day.'

'Alas, dear Xavier is not a registered charity, and things being how they are . . .' Ezra shrugged.

Audrey assembled the post, putting the unstamped envelope and the cutting it contained into her handbag. Why were the senders of anonymous letters also so mean? She looked at her husband and gave him a smile she did not feel, but which he returned warmly. She was proud of him now; there had been moments when his intelligence had been too cutting, his ambition and his way of playing with people too cruel for her daily taste, but the heart attack and the *coup de vieillesse* which followed had uncovered in him springs of wisdom which she had not known. It had come as a sweet surprise to them both to realize that if Ezra was feared and admired it did not prevent his being loved, and not just by the family and the business, but by people in the village. They had sent flowers and sent up prayers in their round-towered and, thanks to him deathwatch beetle-less little church.

'God has been good to me,' he'd said. 'They needn't have bothered Him.'

And now this, which could destroy everything Ezra had stood for – or claimed to have stood for, if one were honest – throughout his life. Recalling a childhood habit, she decided to study the cutting more closely, on the loo.

A sharp crack, as of a piano lid being impatiently shut, a squeaky curse in which the word 'goddamn' was discernible and Mariamne rushed into the room, thwacking her diminutive thigh, crying, 'Come on, grumps, inspection time.'

'Don't you ever feel the inclination to play with people of your own age, Mariamne?'

The little girl considered. 'Not really. I am a spoilt and only child, and they don't usually like other children.'

'Ah well, then you can go and get my hat and stick and I'll accompany you with pleasure.'

'Don't let her ride unless there's someone else around,' said Audrey.

'Why not? Do you think I'd have a fall?' cried Mariamne, suddenly childlike and pink with anger.

'Hush, little one,' said Ezra, rising to his feet.

STERLING BUSINESS ALL RIGHT was the headline.

Ever heedful of the groans of the British taxpayer, the *Eye* has to report that the giant electronics firm, Sterling Industries, is not finding it so simple to return the £2M they overcharged the Government on a defence contract. This 'miscalculation' (see *Eye* No.   ) was first detected three months ago, and shortly afterwards the Chairman and founder of the company, the first Viscount Sterling, resigned from the helm. (There can be no connection between the two events.) The current Chairman is his lordship's brother-in-law, Mr Freddy Barnet, by all accounts an amiable and addlepated figurehead. But the power is held by Lord Sterling's nephew, 'little' Oscar Barnet, and by one David Blacker, a nephew by marriage, who are the Joint Managing Directors. (The relationships in this Jewish family themselves need a slide-rule to disentangle, and their interlocking shareholdings have often caused distress to their friends in the City.) A question has been tabled in the House and one man who is unlikely to reach forward and take the family off the hook is the estimable Poll. Now one of the HMG's Ministers, he was fired by Lord Sterling after a choleric board room scene back in 1956.

It is hoped that news of this distasteful peccadillo does not reach the ears of Viscount Sterling, a Jewish millionaire and famous for his patriotism. Now retired to his Oxfordshire estate and apparently not in the best of health, Lord Sterling is now 106.

Audrey rose from her position, added the cutting to the paper already in the bowl and flushed the lavatory.

3

The colonel was damned if he was going to take his man to some seedy kosher restaurant in the East End; that was one bit of the file he would forget. Equally, the Club was out. His man would be far too conspicuous, if only because he never wore, and apparently did not own, a tie. Further, one of the less dim members might notice that a member known to be working at the War Office was lunching a man who might just be spotted as the technical director of a company which had taken the Government for £2 million. True, his man's life work had been at Sterlings – an unusual span of loyalty for a technical man – but then wasn't he related somehow to the boss? However, he was, from the records, too unworldly to be involved in any fraud, and this expedition was nothing to do with that complication.

His man, the boys had explained to him, when they required his presence, was working on a graphic device, incorporating a TV-like cathode-tube display screen which used an electronic light pen to edit data appearing on the screen. The data concerned would be transmitted from a guided weapon, which in flight would come through too fast to be read by the human eye. It was not

enough to slow down the transmission; the boys wanted it fragmented intelligibly but simultaneously on to different screens. So
they wanted to talk to the boffin – or maybe they were just bored?
thought the colonel.

In any case, the two of them should not be seen at the Junior
Naval and Military. No, it had to be downstairs at the Ritz or
better, upstairs, which was nearly always empty and where they
understood eccentric behaviour. To be on the safe side, the colonel
put into his briefcase a brand-new Old Wykehamist tie. That would
shake him. A nice touch, and his own idea. Card-carrying Communist indeed! Once one realized the man was not only a nut but
also a fraud, the whole thing fell into place and getting security
clearance had been no problem. His common accent, his shiny suit,
his seedy rooms in Islington, his pub life, very inventions which
could have been put to some use, one would have thought. But, no,
his man was a sphinx without a secret. There was nothing there
except a brain, and now that had been hooked for life. The colonel
was sorry for the people who would have to follow Chaimy from
now on. Chaimy: how do you pronounce it? 'Ch' or simply an
aspirated 'H'? He would address him as 'comrade', it would be
more fun. Come to think about it, he was rather looking forward to
the expedition. Made a change from the intense young men and
harassed generals one normally had to deal with in this business.

The colonel put on his bowler hat, his muffler, for it could be
chilly in . . . (what was he saying, even *thinking*?), his British warm,
and strode out into the corridor, an archetypal red-faced Whitehall
warrior, a link in a chain of command which could blow up the
world.

The car was a ten-year-old Mulliner-bodied Bentley, grey and
none too clean, a typical landowner's car. It also had a stylish but
quite pointless chrome loop where otherwise the rear passenger's
side windows would be, obscuring, but casually, the occupant from
the public gaze. He drove himself, and in the pre-lunch traffic jam
up St James's, glanced for the umpteenth time at Chaimy's file. He
knew it by heart.

It was intriguing that his man, obviously 'very able' in the jargon
of the forties, had started the war as an aircraftsman, second class,

and ended the war as an aircraftsman second class. Yes, there it was, 'refused a commission 1942'. Probably some poppycock about not wanting to leave the ranks. What nonsense! Chaimy's war had been spent in the company of other boffins, staff officers, WAAFs making tea and mostly underground. His one brush with authority cannot have endeared him to the officer class, perhaps was not intended to? Returning from examining the wreck of a Boulton Paul aircraft at Llandow airport, he was arrested on Bristol Station by some military police for not wearing a forage cap. He was nearly shoved into a 'glasshouse' because this offence was compounded by some insolent language and the threat of legal action – the man has to be mad, thought the colonel. 'The Department intervened,' the report had said laconically.

He parked the car in the basement of Arlington House, gave the man ten shillings and made a note of the sum in his diary.

Chaimy was there, in the foyer of the Ritz, forlorn and unmistakeable among the golden palms, clutching an enormous black cardboard portfolio.

'Comrade,' enthused the colonel. 'I hope I haven't kept you waiting?'

'No,' said Chaimy sulkily. 'I was early. What shall I do with this? It's very secret.'

'Give it to me. I'll hand it in to the cloaks. What will you have to drink?'

'I don't suppose they have any draught beer?'

A waiter, bent with fatigue, had appeared. He shook his head sadly. 'No, sir, only lager I'm afraid.' He looked at the colonel for encouragement.

'Fine, and bring me a large pink gin, will you?'

The waiter seemed happy at the recognition of a proper customer. 'That's all right, sir,' he said, taking the portfolio. 'I'll look after it for you.'

'When does all the cloak-and-dagger stuff start?' asked Chaimy, watching as his precious computer programmes were shuffled off into the recesses of the Ritz.

'We'll have lunch on HMG – the food's all right provided you don't go for anything ambitious, and then we can chat in the car.'

'I'm kosher, you know,' said Chaimy as the waiter reappeared with the drinks, and another hovered with two menus.

'Yes, I know, so you can have a smoked salmon salad and I'll start with potted shrimps.'

It wasn't until the plate was before him that Chaimy wondered if his host knew that whatever his fellow directors guzzled at board room lunches, a smoked salmon salad was always prepared for him.

'I suppose,' he said grudgingly, allowing a second glass of Meursault to be poured out for him, 'you think you know everything about me. Otherwise we wouldn't be going on this jaunt.'

'Yes,' said the colonel with a sigh (it had been drudgery), 'everything.'

'Tell me.'

'I don't see why not,' replied the colonel quickly. 'I suppose we are all interesting to ourselves.' He glanced at Chaimy as if he should be an exception. 'Mind if I skip the war? There's only one bit I don't quite understand. Those MPs on Bristol Station ... They seem to have overreacted?'

'Ah,' said Chaimy. 'But I was very provocative, comrade. I sang the Internationale, all verses, in Russian, and they didn't like it. Is that all you don't know?'

'Probably. Shall I go on? You'll have to forgive the officialese, it's easier for me to remember. "Subject has lived since demobilization at 117 Noel Road, Islington, N1. Pay telephone in hall. Number CANonbury 4809, in lodging house belonging to Miss Stella Shuttleworth. . . ."'

'Wrong!' claimed Chaimy. 'Stell married some chap along the line, some Czech, I believe.'

'Yes, indeed, a Czech refugee called Gregory Mlinaric, but the marriage was annulled – he was a Catholic – and she reverted to her maiden name, Shuttleworth. Second daughter of Lieutenant General Sir . . .'

'Ooh,' said Chaimy. 'The cunning old thing. She only ever refers to her father as being "one of the impoverished officer class".'

'Subject's daily routine is as follows,' intoned the colonel, pausing as he tried to arrange the largest number of shrimps on the smallest piece of toast, 'and varies only on (1) Wednesday evenings;

(2) Saturday mornings; (3) Saturday evenings. One, visit to a local cinema in the company of Miss Shuttleworth, followed by supper at Robert Carrier's restaurant in Camden Passage . . . I say,' said the colonel, who had been reading the text as if it were suspended from the chandeliers, like the song which descends at thee nd of a pantomime, and looking at Chaimy severely, 'that's whooping it up a bit, isn't it, comrade?'

'I dunno, got to give the old cow something to eat occasionally; she likes her nosh.'

'Right. Two, between 8.15 and 8.25 a.m. walks from 117 Noel Road to Bevis Marks Synagogue, Jewish place of worship, bracket, Orthodox, bracket.' The colonel broke off. 'That rather excited them at first. I suppose if you were up to any villainy it would be a good contact place, a synagogue. All those foreign languages and shawls and things. Wonder why they haven't used it in films, I mean?'

'You go to those sort of films?'

It was his host's turn to look shamefaced. "Fraid so, rather partial, old boy. Shall I go on?' He gazed up at the gilded roof of the restaurant. 'Er. Personal possessions, apart from clothing, box two, collection of old 78 r.p.m. records, no interest, box three, collection of classical music on tape and records, no interest . . .'

'What was in box one, then?'

'Your clothes.'

There was a pause while the colonel poured them both some more wine, anticipating an elderly commis who had moved slowly towards them.

'Wait a minute, how did you have time to do all this? To put all my stuff into boxes. I never saw any boxes! And neither of us has left the house for more than a few hours for as long as I can re-member. We both loathe holidays, and except for last year when some bloody crooked developer started knocking the house down just behind us . . . Well, we were driven out by the noise and the dust – and I believe it was illegal or should be anyway, as those terraced houses are sort of protected. . . .' Chaimy rattled on in-dignantly. 'There was a frightful row about it but nothing happened of course. We all signed a petition. I imagine the man bribed the Council.'

'Tut, tut,' said the colonel as he smeared the pâté over the over-cooked tournedos. 'So you and Stella decided to take yourselves and Mr and Mrs Tench, the newsagents, on a ten-day coach trip to Holland, hoping that by your return the dust, as it were, would have settled. Otherwise, I don't know what we'd have had to do.' He smiled. 'Go on, comrade, eat up, we haven't got all day.'

Chaimy was looking at him open-mouthed. 'You bastards,' he said. 'You bastards,' he repeated slowly. 'And what, may I ask, happened to the poor beggar woman who had been living in the basement? Of that nice little house you destroyed?'

'You must mean Mrs, er, Callais, I think. With the co-operation of Her Majesty's caterers, Messrs Joe Lyons & Co., we secured a room for her in a home for their retired employees, salubriously situated on the edge of Wimbledon Common. Pudding or cheese?'

'This is where the cloak-and-dagger stuff starts,' said the colonel, once they were in the garage under Arlington House. The car was blocked by even grander vehicles including a costly parody of a London cab – Gulbenkian's – and while these were being shunted, Chaimy was told the procedure.

The rear section of the car, besides its chrome dado, had tinted windows preventing vision either way. There was a tape recorder, and a walnut cabinet with a set of silver mugs in a leather case and three diminutive cut-glass decanters labelled in antique porcelain letters, WHISKY, BRANDY and SHERRY. The colonel showed them off proudly.

'No ice?' queried Chaimy.

The colonel ignored this comment. 'My advice is to turn the light out and have some sleep; it was quite a good lunch – in that way.'

He should talk, thought Chaimy, remembering his host's indulgence with the Armagnac.

'It used to be much worse,' said the colonel, misinterpreting Chaimy's expression. 'I had to kit people out with darkened fractured contact lenses, an idea we got from a chap who was experimenting with homing pigeons, worked very well, but hellish uncomfortable, I believe. Ah well, in you go, comrade I'll wake you up in about three and a half hours.'

'Supposing I want a slash, comrade?' protested Chaimy. He used the expression favoured by aircraftsmen second class.

'Ah.' The colonel smiled, dived into the back of the car and produced a china flask of unmistakeable design emblazoned by the coat of arms of the Palace of Westminster. 'As used by their lordships for the Coronation, okay?'

'You think of everything,' said Chaimy.

But they had not taken into consideration the size of his feet. The Bentley had turned off the main road on to a track and woke Chaimy up as it groaned, lurched and squelched, in contrast to the hypnotic ripple of the big tires on the macadamized surface of the last God-knows-how-many hours. It was nearly dark, becoming chilly. They were in the middle of nowhere and Chaimy had a hangover, whose depressing effect continued with each pair of wellington boots he failed to get on. The colonel for the first time lost his composure.

'Damn and blast. Look, d'you mind getting your feet wet? I promise you we can kit you up properly when we get there,' he said humbly.

Chaimy nodded. ''S all right, comrade, got me bicycle clips. Don't you worry.'

The car had stopped by a five-bar gate where the track obviously petered out. The colonel, carrying Chaimy's portfolio, unpadlocked the gate and courteously ushered him through. They trudged up the grassy knoll together. A few sheep looked up from their cropping in mild interest. Then, there was a shout and a figure appeared to their left. It carried a gun under its arm and, worse, was accompanied by a wolf which bounded towards them.

'Oh, my God,' said Chaimy, thinking of his exposed ankles. Chaimy was not a country boy.

'Don't worry, comrade, I'll protect you.' The animal had come to a shivering halt and looked less sure of itself. 'Here, Betsy, there's a good dog,' said the colonel, whereupon the wolf put back its ears, slunk towards the colonel, licked his outstretched hand and was transformed into someone's domestic pet.

'I'm sorry, sir, I didn't recognize you.' Its owner's voice had a distinct lilt. Surely they weren't in Wales?

'That's all right, David. Betsy did.'

'Shall you be coming to the house later then? The missus will be very disappointed if you don't.'

'It depends on how long . . .'

The farmer looked at Chaimy without apparent interest. The colonel brought down some nutty-looking people, but this one was most peculiar.

'You'll let us know, sir, won't you?'

'Yes, of course.' The farmer waved and returned whence he came, leaving the colonel and Chaimy to walk on in the direction of a broken-down corrugated barn about fifty yards up the side of the hill.

It was full of disused machinery, collapsed and rusty. 'This is a bit tricky, comrade, you'll have to hold my arm.'

In the fading light the colonel, who had obviously performed this trick many times, led Chaimy to the end of the barn where there was an ancient safe. He fiddled with something, still in the semi-darkness. There was a faint hum which grew louder with the sound of Chaimy's heart. He was not reassured by the feeling that the colonel was smiling at him. There was a clunk, then silence.

'Hold my hand and lower your head,' ordered the colonel as he opened the safe. Chaimy obeyed. 'Go in, I'm with you.' It was terribly dark and smelt of nothing. The door of the safe shut and the lift began to descend. After ten feet or so, the darkness changed into brilliant splitting light. 'Turn around,' said the colonel. 'You've got your back to her.' Chaimy did so.

'Wowie gumdrops!' he said. 'Isn't she beautiful!'

'Of course, you've never seen one, have you, being in software?'

It was like a conference room in any well-heeled American corporation or university except that there were no windows; the air was being circulated soundlessly but not as soundlessly as if it were not being circulated, thought Chaimy.

They couldn't have been kinder. He had washed his feet; they had given him at least three cups of tea and there were cigarettes in a box just like at the business. And, when it had come to the problem, instead of implying that his, Chaimy's, programme was

inadequate, they had contrived to suggest that though the answers
were there, their own comprehension was lacking. He was sorry
when the colonel came into the room with another man.

'Okay, boys,' he said. 'Everything wrapped up?' He had a
Kissingerish voice.

'I think so, sir, we understand each other. Mr Smith has been
very patient.'

Chaimy blushed. It had been explained to him that all their
visitors were Mr Smiths.

'Very good then. Have we time for an evening show?' A ripple of
anticipation showed on the faces. 'Full moon. Well, two days off.
Twenty-three minutes, dark and cloudy,' said someone.

'Okay, then, let's get the show on the road.' The boys moved
quickly out of the room and the Kissinger figure approached
Chaimy, put his hand on his arm and said, 'We are very grateful for
the trouble you have taken, sir. Please come with me.'

He led him down a corridor, back to the hangar and sat him down
in a surprisingly comfortable chair. A sign went on saying SILENCE,
which was instantly obeyed by men and by machines, and then,
just like the Odeon in Camden Town, the lights dimmed. When all
was black, Chaimy heard a noise like a lift door sliding back and
suddenly, ahead and above, was the sky. He felt the fresh air on his
face. 'It's beautiful – the sky, I mean,' he whispered.

'Yes, and if you haven't seen it for three months . . .' replied the
Director.

'Well done, comrade, you went down very well. I'm proud of you,'
said the colonel as they plodded back to the Bentley

'Down I certainly went; how well I don't know.'

'The Director was very impressed. They don't often roll back the
hill.'

'I imagine they have to wait for a dark night, in case of reflections?'
'Certainly, but even so . . .'

'And the Director wasn't even there, when I was with the boys
. . . he wasn't watching.'

'Maybe he was listening?'

Chaimy digested this; yes, it was a different world down there.

'What did he mean by not seeing the sky for three months?'

'Ah, part of the exercise lies in simulating conditions of nuclear warfare so there is a tour of duty involving three months underground, and there's even a chap there to see how they get on. Remember the black fellow who made the tea and found you those boots? He's the psychiatrist. ... Here, hold the torch will you, comrade, while I unlock this thing.'

They had reached the gate. The colonel motioned Chaimy to the front seat and a few moments later the headlights lit up a farmhouse whose front door was instantly opened to them by the farmer. He helped them off with their boots. The colonel was obviously an honoured guest and treated like a landlord. They were led into the kitchen, the farmer explaining that the colonel preferred to eat there as it was more cosy. The sight of a side of ham hanging from a beam and the open coal fire where the dog sat thudding its tail made Chaimy literally rub his eyes. He thought of the elegant machinery up the road, shuddered and converted this reaction into a contented yawn.

'Oh, good, that's a sure sign you're hungry. You'll feel better when you've had something to eat, Professor,' said the farmer's wife. 'There's proper food here, the Colonel will tell you that. Proper bacon, which I cure myself, not like these lazy English farmer's wives whose hubbies complain at meetings about the import of Danish bacon. And what d'you suppose they have for supper, may I ask you? Why, Danish bacon, of course.' She slung another thick slice of gammon into a heavy iron pan.

Oh dear, thought Chaimy, and the colonel met his glance.

'And free range eggs, naturally.'

'Do you think I could just have a couple of boiled eggs, Mrs, er ...?' asked Chaimy politely.

The farmer's wife smote her brow with a theatrical gesture. 'Ooooh,' she gave out a true Welsh wail, and turned round to study Chaimy with interest. 'You're one of them, are you? And there I was prattling on about bacon. What a bloody fool I am, so tactless.'

'You wouldn't think she used to be the best fence in Chester,' said the colonel when they left the farmhouse.

'Fence?'

'Receiver of stolen goods.'

'I see. Another one of your babies, comrade?'

'Yes, an ideal couple. He was just a labourer and rather dim – there are some jobs which require stupidity, and walking round and round a hill all day is one of them. And she's scared stiff of the law and no fool. Perfect tenants for me.'

Chaimy supposed the area must belong to the Ministry of Defence and that the colonel was the titular landlord, but he didn't like to ask. He was dreading the journey back. 'Back in the black box?'

''Fraid so, comrade,' said the colonel, opening the door.

'Suppose you wouldn't stop for me to buy some cigarettes?'

'No need, old boy, you'll find plenty in this box,' and he flipped open a lid. There were enough Woodbines to last a journey to the moon. Poor Stella, thought Chaimy as he pressed the cigar lighter. She'll probably have run out of cigarettes too, and be too plastered to get any more. She wasn't used to being left alone.

Chaimy felt cobbles rumbling under the tires and thought, how odd, after only an hour and a half. The colonel unlocked him and helped him out of the car. They were in the close of a cathedral, which, if he concentrated on the clouds hurrying past the moon, could be made to sail.

'*Vaut le détour*, wouldn't you say, comrade?'

Chaimy just moved his head. He felt dizzy from the beauty of it, and the strangeness. The colonel took his arm. 'Let's see if we can get in, it's not that late.'

Not only was a door open, but a light was on in the organ loft and after a little audible rustling and a cough, the pipes trembled, into life and a reedlike sound sneaked into the cold air. They both sat in a pew and after a moment the colonel knelt in prayer.

Oh dear, thought Chaimy, now I'm going to cry. And he did a bit and was still snuffling when they went outside.

'Very affecting, that *vox humana*,' commented the colonel.

'I think it's so bloody unfair. Why can't we have something like that; we Jews, I mean?'

'Well, you did have the Temple; rather splendid, I once saw a model. . . .'

'Yes, but we never had the Gothic. .... I dare say it wouldn't have worked, but I love it. I spent most of my time at school in the cathedral, playing chess.' The colonel gripped his arm in astonishment. 'Only with myself, and in my head. And bridge,' he added. 'I was rather good at bridge.'

'I think we both need a drink,' said the colonel firmly, when they reached the car. He poured out some whisky into the silver mugs and they leant back against the car, looking at the view.

'Tastes rather good, never knew whisky taste so well,' said Chaimy.

'Hmm, yes. Can't think why they need the floodlighting with a full moon, spoils the effect, don't you think?'

'Easily rearranged. You could link the brightness of the moon to the brightness of the artificial light.'

'Really?' said the colonel, pouring himself another tot.

'Comrade, the people who built Stonehenge could do more than that.'

'Right,' said the colonel, gulping it down. 'We're off, ready?' He opened the front door for Chaimy, reassembled the drinking equipment and started the engine.

This is a treat, thought Chaimy as the car slid along the quiet streets. Does he imagine I didn't recognize Ely Cathedral or have I passed some sort of test? Or he's bored and wants a *schmooze*, or what, or what?

'Tell me, comrade, as a matter of interest to myself rather than to the department, how d'you square this work with your, er, principles?' the colonel asked him.

'Ah' said Chaimy, and belched. 'The answer,' he said, 'is very simple.'

'How do I reconcile my principles as a Marxist and a pacifist with helping to design those expensive toys of yours?' Chaimy paused. 'No, I'm talking nonsense. The answer is very complicated.'

It's funny how when he doesn't watch himself, thought the colonel, he talks like a gentleman.

'Any man of science who is not a pure scientist likes to see his theories tested, right? In the commercial world there are limits to the amount of money which can be spent not only on research and development, but on manufacture too. In the military world there are no limits. That beautiful thing we just saw, for instance – what company could afford that?'

'Agreed, but that doesn't bother you? If it were ever used?'

'It never will be. I am convinced of that. The people involved will never work them, you see.'

For no reason the colonel put his foot on the brake. 'The people involved are dedicated, efficient, in terms of security they're cleared for everything.'

'Everything, I'm sure. Except perhaps humanity. But I'm not talking about sabotage, or anything so dramatic.'

'Yes?' The colonel sounded unimpressed.

'Simply that the business in these weapons has grown so big, and so lucrative, that the west won't want to destroy the world because too many influential gentlemen have a vested interest in its survival!'

The colonel thought for a moment. 'It's an interesting theory.'

'Show me a way to disprove it. No, I'm much more worried about computers telling each other how much money you owe, or trying to cheer you up by activating electrodes plugged into your brain, or telling the police when a pub is serving drinks after hours, and who's there doing it.'

'Oh, come, come, comrade, now you are going over the top.'

'The computer has made possible the cashless society. Well, isn't that but a step behind the moneyless society? How about that, Colonel?'

There was no answer from the driver's seat.

'The computer can design the most efficient electric lamp,' pursued Chaimy, 'or motor car or new port in the Persian Gulf. It can demonstrate in terms of public benefit the best return for public effort and public resources. It doesn't understand *private* competition and private capital. Not for that matter, privacy. They adore talking to each other, computers. You can't direct them to be concerned about free enterprise, property or the rights of the individual. You can only switch them off.'

About two miles went past in about ninety seconds before the colonel spoke. 'Tell me about the family and the business.'

'From the beginning? It's a long story.'

'It's still quite a long journey.'

The Bentley was slicing through Walthamstow when Chaimy had finished. The colonel had chosen the old Cambridge road to London because it was no fun, he explained, on the motorway, as one couldn't change gear, and that was the whole point of Bentleys.

'How remarkably well informed you are, dear boy.'

'Why remarkably? Oh, I know everybody in the business thinks I'm a loony living in a world of my own. . . .'

The colonel smiled because that was exactly the description on the file.

'But it suits me. That way I'm left alone. I don't have to go to *all* their parties. I'm not involved in their politics, they never ask me for money – you wouldn't think I had any, would you?' added Chaimy slyly.

'I wouldn't think so, comrade,' said the colonel as he double declutched, 'but I know that you have.'

One of the first steps in any security clearance was to look at a subject's bank account for the large movements in and out. This had been simple in Chaimy's case because he had no bank account. A registered packet was sent weekly to his landlady containing cash, and bills were met directly by the business. The balance was used to buy Sterling shares for a trust in his name under the personal control of Lord Sterling. The colonel had been given to understand by the company secretary that over the years that trust had grown to a substantial amount.

'Apropos of which . . .' started the colonel.

'What?'

'Of money. I imagine that Lord Sterling would be very distressed if there was a scandal about the . . . er, miscalculation of the R and D business.'

'Yes, but I think he thinks it's settled.'

'But it isn't. You read the *Private Eye* piece?'

'Stella showed it to me. She thinks they're a pack of fascist schoolboys, but she gobbles it up every week.'

'Fortnight.'

'So . . .'

'So,' replied the colonel, 'I believe the Minister should be made aware of the satisfactory co-operation the British Government has received from a relatively small – in the field you are relatively small, is it fair to say? – British-owned company with a long tradition of service in sensitive areas. In the area of security alone the Ministry should appreciate that cancelled contracts cannot be speedily transferred without . . .'

'Excuse me . . .'

'Yes?' The colonel glanced at Chaimy through the driving mirror as if he had forgotten his presence. Chaimy realized he had interrupted the rehearsal, out loud, of a memorandum.

'Which Minister?'

'Well, it could end up not a million miles, as they say in *Private Eye,* from the desk of Mr Poll.'

'Whom Ezra fired in '56, silly old thing.'

'As they said, but from the little I know of Mr Poll, the reference could be counter-productive, whereas an offer by the company of some sort of *amende honorable* might be received with, er . . . sympathy.'

'Finsbury Circus, you turn right here,' said Chaimy.

'I'd better see you home.'

'Yes, please. She might have passed out completely and I haven't got a key.'

'What sort of a lock is it?'

'Yale, I think.'

'Ah, no problem,' said the colonel.

But it was a problem because Stella had locked the door with a chain and bolt so that when the Colonel mastered the Yale lock, with the aid of an American Express credit card, Chaimy noticed, the door opened only a few inches. So they banged and banged. They then threw coins at an upper window and sang 'Land of Hope and Glory' – Stell's least favourite tune, explained Chaimy. Finally a light went on and voice said, 'Where you bin, mate?'

'I told you I'd be late, mate.'

'Hold on, I'll open up.'

The colonel shook Chaimy solemnly by the hand. 'Thank you, comrade. I'm sure we'll win through.' He stepped back, saluted, and Stella was just in time to see him climbing into the Bentley.

'What have you been doing, love?' asked Chaimy gently.

'Getting pissed, of course. What else was there to do? Who's yer posh friend? Business?'

'I think you could say he's a friend of the family. C'mon, ducky, make me a cup of tea.'

4

The Blacker boys had grown up but, as their father David said, that was not all they had done. They had submitted peaceably enough to the ceremony of Bar–Mitzvah and had accepted with good grace the mound of presents which accrued on that occasion, though they clearly regarded them as juvenilia. They were already marked by their height, bearing and sophistication as young men rather than teenagers, and after a year at a 'progressive' school, which stank of cannabis, they were sent to a more expensive establishment in Switzerland popularized entirely by the children of the very rich.

This was no doubt, in retrospect, the fatal move, since the few drops of filial piety, patriotism, honour, truthfulness, obedience and so forth which they had not rejected in their early years, quickly evaporated in that cheerful, ruthlessly hedonistic international atmosphere. But as David said (again), it did get them out of the country. At the age of sixteen Joshua and Jericho, after a furious exchange, had split the costs of aborting a fellow pupil at Le Rosey. In the same year they had been picked out of casinos in Deauville, Aix (en Provence), Cannes and Venice, and the next year had returned with beards and passports immaculately adjusted by a forger in Zurich, to win, slowly, quite a lot of money on a variant of the Labouchère system. That they stuck to this most boring way of playing roulette should have warned their educators that they were not just naughty but, worse, persistent.

At Le Rosey they had been dubbed 'the tigers in the tank'. Their friends and admirers were legion and tolerant, nay expectant, of their bad behaviour and possibly their only opponent was their father, once so doting, whom they referred to variously as 'Daddyo' or 'old penis envy'. Everyone else in the family, except of course Freddy and Joyce who snorted disapproval at a distance, competed to please and indulge the terrible twins, perhaps unconsciously, as emblems of their own glorious, now apparently internationally accepted, status. Chuck taught them how to shuffle a pack and gave them money, Tattie bought them shirts from Mr Fish and gave them money, Sandra sent them to stay with her mother in the Virgin Islands one Christmas and their grandmother had to pay for the Albatross they smashed and for repairs to their faces. It was then that they grew beards.

To Ezra they behaved decorously and with cunning, showing a hypocritical interest in the workings of the business, and a less hypocritical interest in the price of the shares, of which, thanks to the good housekeeping of their mother, to the early settlements of their grandmother, and to the immunity of their trusts from the incidence of capital taxation in the years of their childhood, they possessed – or would possess – a great number. A portion of these were due for 'liberation', as they put it, on their eighteenth birthday, just a few weeks away, which was the reason for this lunch. Jeremy had been asked to arrange it, not because he was their 'sort of uncle', as they called him, but because he was a friend of Ferty, 'Bye-bye', a man their acquaintances in the world of pop music recommended for his expertise in 'offshore' funds.

'They've had mistresses, motor cars, every kind of psychedelic experience, and now they want a merchant bank,' explained Jeremy.

'Good,' Ferty had answered. 'I'll pay for lunch and if anything happens I'll see you all right, as we say in the Golden Square Mile. The Connaught, one o'clock, Thursday?'

It was already 1.37 and the twins had not arrived. Ferty had heard, and admired, the tales of their bad behaviour, but this was a bit much.

'If they don't come soon I'll be drunk,' he complained.

'Eat some more peanuts,' said Jeremy helpfully.

'I can't, they're fattening.'

'Too late to bother about that.' His friend had grown almost oval in the past ten years.

'Oh, that must be them,' said Ferty as the revolving door into the

Connaught was revolved with unaccustomed zest.

'My God, they're going round twice.'

One twin stumbled into the foyer. 'Cool it, man, will you, you bloody nearly broke my arm.' A distinguished youngish man with grey hair advanced on them delicately. 'Ah, morning, Auguste. Sorry – this idiot here . . .'

'Oh, shut up.'

'Joshy, Jericho!' cried Jeremy, trying to inject into his voice an authority he was far from feeling, for the twins considered no place too seemly for a brawl.

'Oh, hello, Uncle,' they chorused mildly, and when introduced to Ferty they clicked their heels, bowed, muttered something in German as they had been taught at Le Rosey to do when meeting a *hochgeborene*.

For lunch Joshua ordered a steak tartare with all the trimmings ('You know, buckets of tomato sauce') and Jericho chicken curry ('But take out the bones, will you'). They both drank fresh orange juice, Ferty disguising his horror with aristocratic finesse as they silently shovelled the food into their mouths.

'Now,' said Joshua, wiping his face with the back of his hand, 'tell us about this Cayman Islands bit.'

'Ah,' sighed Ferty reverentially, 'you mean Milton Grundy's scheme?'

'Who's he? Born on Sunday, Milton Grundy,' said Joshua.

'A genius,' replied Ferty simply.

Jericho looked up from his task of converting the interior of an innocent white bun into leaden grey pellets with interest. 'Maybe we should go and see him?'

'He is somebody I could possibly consult on your behalf,' said Ferty easily. 'But if we could first discuss your portfolios?'

'Yes, of course,' said Jericho, returning to setting his pellets in V formation.

'Which are, understandably, unbalanced, if not,' Ferty giggled, 'actually hysterical.'

The boys looked at him blankly.

'Well, I've got the figures in my case, but I think 88.4 per cent of what you both have is in Sterling Industries.'

'And the other 11.6?' Jericho again.

'Oh, very conservative. Respectable little packages of blue-chips: Rio Tinto, Burmah, Rolls-Royce. Haven't been changed for years.'

'Yes,' said Jericho darkly. 'Mum doesn't believe in mucking things about.'

'I think you'd agree that the Sterling holding should be diminished unless there are private reasons . . .'

He looked at Jeremy for help. What an impossible pair! He needn't have bothered.

'Ab-so-lu-tely. I couldn't agree more, could you, Jerry? I mean, we want out of Sterling and out of sterling. I'll say . . .'

'You don't worry about upsetting the family?' suggested Jeremy.

'Oh, the old Lord'll probably turn in his grave.'

'He's not dead yet, silly.'

'Oh, I don't know about that,' said Joshua gravely, laying down his fork – on the tablecloth, Jeremy noticed. 'I went there the other day – you were in America – and my view is that he *is* dead. He's walking about an' all that, and talking, about birds and bees and things, but essentially, he's dead.'

'Perhaps he thought it was time you knew about sex?'

Both howled with happy laughter.

Ferty looked uneasy; after all, they were supposed to be talking about money. 'What do you think will happen to the business?' he asked.

'If he falls off the perch?' said one.

'Yeah, hands in his clogs?' said the other.

'Well,' said Joshua, spooning into his mouth a forkful of steak tartare, 'there'll be a great power struggle, won't there, like on TV.' He gulped. 'On my left, little Oscar, bravest of the brave, prince of the blood royal, supported by, er, let me see, Chuck and Tattie certainly, Audrey probably, coached by Sandra, and boy, do those American ladies love power, and Freddy, of course, who is, after all, his stepfather – not that he matters, because he hasn't got any shares worth mentioning and anyway, he'd lean over backwards to be fair.' He almost sneered. 'But don't forget,' he added, 'there's this scandal which might break over little Oscar's head – the slip-up over the two million they keep trying to give back. If there is a fuss . . .' He shrugged.

'Yes, I read about that in *Private Eye*,' said Ferty. 'Do you think it's serious?'

Joshua ignored the question. 'And on my right is Dad, a cunning fighter, supported by Grandma, Mum and . . .'

'The two of you, perhaps?' suggested Jeremy, trying to sound icy. 'By the way, I don't see it as a boxing match, Joshua. Surely little Oscar is the gladiator with the broadsword and your papa has the net?' (He was quoting Ezra.)

Joshua looked at him thoughtfully. 'Yes, I suppose so, if we're still around,' he said, taking only Jeremy's first point. There was a silence.

'I don't know enough about company law,' said Ferty, 'but you two may have to wait a few years before you can participate in this particular drama. You're suggesting a full shareholders' meeting, and I don't suppose the institutional investors . . .'

'You're forgetting one crucial element, brother,' said Jericho, ignoring the interruption and waving his fork. 'Our long-lost cousin Niki. He may emerge from his wholesome kibbutz with a wad of shares stuffed into his plucky El-Al handbag.'

'Nonsense, the next Viscount doesn't give a damn. All he does is pot the odd Arab and carry on hoeing or whatever they do. Besides, any moment now the whole lot of them will be pushed into the sea.'

'Every farmer needs a hoe,' said Jericho in an imitation Trinidad voice. This prompted more laughter. 'That's what Dad said and he's been to see him.'

'In Israel?' asked Jeremy. 'I didn't know that.'

'Kfar something-or-other. Dedicated kibbutznik, he said. So much a week pocket money. Got his own hi-fi set in his cabin, likes the Beatles, happy as a lark. Makes you want to cry, doesn't it? All that money going to waste. Do you think I could possibly ask for another fresh orange juice, by the way?'

'Yes, of course. Jeremy, why don't you and I try another bottle of this Volnay. I think we're going to need it.'

From the nature of the suggestion and the tone of his voice, Jeremy understood that for Ferty the generation gap between us and them had developed in the past few minutes into a chasm. He shared Ferty's distaste for the boys' manner, but was impressed by their coldness, cruelty and precision. They might ass about but they had minds like rattlesnakes.

'So who's the winner if it comes to a showdown?' he asked.

'Seven to four on Dad,' said one.

'Done,' said the other. 'Ponies?'

'I'm not betting with you, mate. You never pay!'

'Now wait a minute!'

'Boys, boys,' protested Ferty. They looked at him, prepared to wait, briefly, for something interesting to happen. 'We can conclude that you do not see yourselves in the family business at any point in the future.'

'You must be joking,' said one.

'We see ourselves in Monaco at any point in the future.'

'Switzerland.'

'And pay that negative interest? *You* must be joking.'

'In other words, you want your capital, or as much of it as you can get hold of, out of the country,' Ferty ploughed on.

'That's it. And trusts can be broken, can't they? A friend of mine has a chap called Arnold Goodman who does all that.'

Ferty quivered at this frivolous reference to that august person.

'Got to get it all out. England's finished. Sick man of Europe. Why go down with the ship and so on. Talking of which, come and see my new car, Jeremy, *mon oncle*. C'mon, mate, we're late.'

The car, a red Mustang convertible with white wall tires of course, was parked on the taxi rank by the island opposite the Connaught. It was very big. A few people stood round it in ill-concealed admiration and dislike.

'I thought you couldn't have a driving licence until you ...' Jeremy began.

'Oh, they're not so fussy in Maine,' said Joshua. 'Look at this licence plate. Isn't that too much?'

'It's his ego trip,' said Jericho. The number read: TWI N.

'Yes,' said Ferty gravely. 'I agree with you, it is too much.'

Two taxi drivers approached. 'We bloody nearly called the police to tow you away. You're bloody lucky ...'

'Yes, indeed, but you did not, and I'm most grateful to you, sirs,' said Jericho in a funny sort of accent and handed each of them a pound note with a little bow.

After some pitiless manipulation of the power steering the Mustang was extracted. The boys waved cheerily and as the car turned into Mount Street Jeremy saw one of them lean forward, remove a parking ticket from under a windscreen wiper, and flick it out of the window.

Ferty put his arm round his friend's shoulder. 'Let me tell you something, Jeremy, my dear. I'm a bit of a fraud and a bit of a con; I've been polite to people I shouldn't have been polite to; yes, you could say that I even married for money – they do say that, you know, in the City – but,' and he raised his voice, 'not for all the tea in China, the coffee in Peru, the tin in the Patinos, the boots on Charlie Clore, not for all the p-p-porphyry on the Coromandel C-c-coast . . .' he spluttered.

'Yes,' agreed Jeremy, 'but do admit, as our friend at New College used to say, they have a certain style.'

'Yes,' sighed Ferty, drying the corners of his mouth with a coroneted handkerchief, 'they have. Now let us finish our luncheon in peace.'

5

Ezra had discovered television. It had previously been banned at Turners because he found the aerials offensive – the servants huddled over a portable set in their part of the house – but now he had erected one tall mast in a pine spinney behind the stables, whence the transmission was expensively piped to all the sets on the estate. The County Planning Authority had requested its removal, but Ezra had countered by offering to demonstrate the efficacy and sound aesthetic of the new device and to give one to the village. The parish council, whose members were all patients of Dr Xavier and friends of Geoffrey Nickson, had accepted to a man, and to a woman. The local newspaper had taken up the cause, casting Ezra in the unusual role of David, with the County Council as Goliath. A man from the Society for the Preservation of Rural England had come to look at it, and stayed to lunch. Ezra's friend, the sly earl, was to raise the matter in the House of Lords if the Council pursued its threat to send a crew to dismantle the offending erection. Ezra was delighted: insulated, as a man of power, from regulations throughout his life, he had found a new enemy – bureaucracy. 'Over my dead body,' had been his reply to the Council's latest move.

(Exactly, thought Audrey. 'No excitements, no frustrations, no aeroplanes and above all, dear lady, I beseech you do not let him play chess. Very bad for the heart. Luckily my wife is too stupid to learn so I am exempt from that fatality.' So Xavier had spoken. It would be tragic if after all Ezra's careful and co-operative resignation, he were to be killed by a row about a television mast.)

'Down for four,' said Audrey. 'And that's – what do you call it – a blitz?' They played gin rummy instead. It amused Ezra to play for enormous stakes – and to lose.

'But you've only taken two cards!' complained Ezra.

'That's the way it goes. Now come on, Chuck, you take over while I go and change. We're dining early tonight because of this documentary film we all have to see.'

'Oh lord, it's like taking candy off a child,' said Chuck, stretching his legs and yawning. 'Time was when I had to do this for a living, remember, Ez?'

'I remember well. My poor sister. Now, will you cut?'

Chuck laughed, as a man who could afford to be ashamed of his past.

'Did Mrs Winterbourne tell the family to listen in tonight, or more precisely, to view, Audrey?'

'I'm sure she did, dear.'

'Good, then they'll have something to talk about tomorrow at the board meeting.'

Halfway across the room Audrey turned round. 'How do you know about that?'

'A few items of interest from the business filter through to the presidential ear. Ah good, a spade double score.'

Audrey frowned. The meeting had been summoned to discuss the possible Government inquiry. She did not fear, or any longer care so much, for little Oscar's future as for the effect on Ezra, whom she prayed they would not involve.

'Do we really have to play gin rummy, Ezra?' asked Chuck when Audrey had left the room. 'I hate taking your money. . . .'

'Oh,' said Ezra with a little smile, 'since when?'

'C'mon, Ezra, you know you've something on your mind and you'd rather talk about it.' He laid the cards on the table. 'Tell me. I've no axe to grind.'

'Yes, I know that,' He was fiddling with the empty box of cards. 'Do you suppose anybody actually washes these washable cards?'

'Ezra, is it something to do with Oscar and this Defence business? Audrey . . .'

'Look, Audrey has had Oscar in the doghouse since she found out he deliberately didn't tell her about my heart attack, which she blames on him anyway. He didn't tell anyone because he didn't want the Stock Exchange to find out. Very flattering, somewhat exaggerated, but perfectly prudent.'

'And the two million quid?'

'Not so prudent.'

'Apart from getting caught, God, two million pounds: that's peanuts. Someone should tell them about the Teapot Dome scandal. It happens in California every ten minutes. And haven't they given it back, for Christsake?'

'Yes, but that's not the point. This is England and the biggest scandal after the war was about two pounds of sausages, remember? And the business is a Jewish business, right? And I may be half dead but I'm something of a totem, right? And it could just be that some of our competitors are concealing their sympathy quite well. There's no business like defence business. *On peut toujours souffrir les maux d'autruy.* We can always endure the misfortunes of others.' Ezra paused and picked up a pencil. 'I'm sure we'd come through a Board of Trade enquiry, or whatever they call that department, with clean hands, and there may never even be an enquiry, but talk of it is bad, bad, bad, bad.' He snapped the pencil between his fingers.

'That's all right,' he said calmly in answer to Chuck's anxious glance. 'Dr Xavier, whom God preserve, said I could break as many pencils as I liked. Now, I've just got to make a telephone call. No, no, I can manage . . . if you will be good enough to keep Audrey out of the way. Ah, all's well. . . .'

The noise of a car on the gravel outside. 'That must be Geoffrey.' He looked out of the window. 'You must remind me to get him a new dinner jacket.'

'The old boy's in pretty good form, then,' said Geoffrey, when he heard what was in store for him.

'Yeah,' said Chuck. 'He smells battle.'

That night every member of the family, as Ezra had suggested, watched the same television programme. For Sarah it was no strain for she and her pig farmer rarely did anything else in the evenings; for the Brigadier it was a nuisance because he had to cut short an Association dinner and hurry back to his flat in Dorset House. (He had finally been ousted by Sandra from the old home in Maddison Place.) Tattie could not very well watch it because she was taking a cure on Ischia, accompanied by the faithful Dr Krapf. (She was not on the rota of those required to attend Ezra at Turners, a source, to her, of some unspoken discontent.)

Freddy and Joyce would have watched the programme anyway, as selective tuners-in to current affairs. Chaimy and Stella, possessing, on principle (which one? they sometimes forgot) no television set, went to the pub where, as customers of twenty years' standing, their request for a change of channel was agreed to despite the disapproval of some of the younger regulars. David, who had to be in London for the next day's board meeting, had asked Jeremy, who had not been on Mrs Winterbourne's list, to join them. The twins had sniffed that something interesting was afoot and insisted on watching with their parents. They had heard of Ezra's directive issued via Mrs Winterbourne, and like everybody else, were intrigued by his choice – a documentary about life in a kibbutz.

On the little screen a small aeroplane swooped low over a recently ploughed field scattering what looked like brightly coloured pieces of paper. 'Tomorrow the kibbutz celebrates its fiftieth anniversary,' purred the honeyed voice-over, 'and now a light aeroplane from Israel's Air Force is playing Santa Claus by dropping presents for the children – modest gifts, packets of sweets, T-shirts and the like – and they are watched from behind the barbed-wire fence by what must be almost the entire population, wouldn't you say, er . . . Dov?'

'Most of the members are here, yes,' replied another voice in a mild Lithuanian accent.

'Of course nobody knows who they belong to,' said Jericho. 'The kids are brought up communally and never see their daddies and mummies, so how could they know?'

'Nonsense, you ignoramus,' said his father. 'They see their parents every day after work and all day on Saturdays. That's enough, isn't it?'

'Do you think we'll see Cousin Niki?' asked Jericho, ignoring the question.

'No, because now he's in Nahal . . . on a military installation.'

'Of course, you've seen him, haven't you, David? You've been to his kibbutz,' said Jeremy. 'I only heard that the other day – you are secretive,' he added.

'Yes, Daddyo, you . . .'

'Now, look here, can't you tell them to go and play ping pong?' David appealed to Lucy.

'Yes, boys, you do that.'

'Oh, Mum,' they chorused.

'Otherwise I'll cut you out of my will,' said Lucy placidly.

'But we want to watch televsion. Didn't Uncle Ezra say . . .'

'There's a television in the day nursery, and don't upset Concepçion by making a lot of noise.' Having paid her fare from the Philippines, Lucy prized her greatly.

'Mithconception,' said Jericho quietly.

They all laughed, but the boys did go.

'I'm not going to let them make tomorrow's meeting into a bear-baiting session with little Oscar playing the bear,' said Freddy.

The man was interviewing an elderly lady cobbler, originally a Miss Bernstein from Ilford, Essex.

'I'd have thought that was a man's work, repairing boots . . . but you must put your foot down, Freddy.' Joyce took his position as chairman of the business very seriously.

'Yes, dear,' said Freddy as the camera traversed a line of men in loin cloths, hauling at a net. 'But where? Look, that's where *gefilte* fish comes from. I never realized . . .'

The Brigadier reflected that if everybody led such conspicuously clean lives there would be no venereal disease and he would be out of business. Still, one could always rely on the Arabs.

'What the hell is sisal?' asked Sandra. 'Do you agree it's typical of the goddamn British Broadcasting Corporation to assume that everybody knows what sisal is?'

'I don't think it is the BBC,' said Oscar, and indeed the picture had changed to a girl in a see-through nightdress, smiling on a swing in the middle of a forest, surely nothing to do with life on a kibbutz. 'Sisal you make rope out of,' he said wearily.

'Honey, you're tired, you're not yourself because you're so worried about that goddamn board meeting tomorrow, isn't that so?'

Oscar nodded dumbly as he watched a woman demonstrate the inside of her oven with idiotic pride.

'Why don't I open a bottle of champagne?' asked Sandra, glaring at the dimpled housewife on the little screen.

'You have seen them in the fields, in their fish ponds, at the work bench.' The man with the mellifluous voice was back. 'Now, let's look at them relaxing in their homes.' There was a shot of a flower-brocaded bungalow at night and small interiors lined with books and the sound of Beethoven flooding from every casement.

'If these are peasants, they must be the most literate peasants in the world.' The voice faded as Sandra turned the knob and, smiling, handed Oscar a glass of champagne. 'Now, big boy, you listen to little me.'

'But, honey, I . . .'

'No, you can look, but listen to me. Do you realize we haven't had a proper holiday for years, not since our honeymoon? What ort of a life do you lead, *little* Oscar?' She sneered at him now. 'All ou and David do is work your arses off just to amuse that wicked ld man and wait for him to have another heart attack.'

'Sandra!'

'Don't Sandra me ... and watching some dopey television programme when the Lord says to. Where does he think he comes from? Sinai?'

'Please,' said Oscar, but it was no good. Sandra was growing more like her mother, as he had said, every day.

'Do you think it's an accident that his own son quit? And his son, the grandson, does he come home ever? Does he hell! He knows he's safer raising carp and being shelled by Syrians.' She pointed to the television where, in complete silence, a tractor was being driven into the sunset with the driver's machine-gun over his shoulder in clear silhouette.

'And now he's trying to steal my own daughter from me, with that fucking horse. Oh, Oscar, can't you see?' And Sandra, bursting into tears, fell at his feet and buried her head in his lap.

'Darling, darling,' said Oscar, stroking her hair. 'I never knew you hated him so much.'

Sandra straightened her head, took his handkerchief from his jacket pocket, and blew her nose. 'Oh, I don't really. He's quite a guy, I s'pose – very brave and all that. I don't think he knows the damage he does. Look,' she said in a different tone of voice, 'didn't you say someone wanted to buy the business?'

Oscar shrugged. 'Every week they come shopping – the Americans, Armand Erpf, IBM, Honeywell, you name it.'

'Why, if that's not a purty name! Honey-well,' said Sandra. 'So why not sell it? It's a big, wide, wonderful world and we've seen too little of it. We're still quite young and we're still quite rich. Remember Buenos Aires? Oscar smiled at her.

'C'mon, baby, let's finish the champagne and go to bed.'

With one hand she squeezed Oscar in a sensitive place and with the other she switched off the television.

But elsewhere the show went on, albeit on a black and white screen which Lucy considered good enough for the children and their maid in the upper room in Tite Street.

'And although kibbutz members achieve positions of power in what one might call the outside world,' (still of man at desk, in position of power) 'they remit their salaries to the kibbutz treasury. Absolute equality is the keynote of the kibbutz syndrome. This man is the manager of a kibbutz guest house, the equivalent of a four-star hotel, and a flourishing enterprise by any standards. He receives the same personal allowance – a few hundred dollars a year – as this lady.' Picture of woman slowly swabbing floor with a squeezer.

'Holy Mother of God,' said Joshua. 'I don't think we're cut out for a kibbutz, brother.'

'You can say that again.'

'Holy Mother of God,' obliged Joshua.

Concepçion, sitting uneasily between the twins on a sofa, the only piece of adult furniture in the room, marvelled that such pieties could fall from such heathen lips, and wondered if, later, she would be raped.

'Although older members of this kibbutz remember the sound of gunfire and shells falling in their orchards' (shot of gaily decorated bunker) 'the scene has been relatively calm in the last few years and a few of the youngsters opt for a Nahal where they receive para-military training' (shot of blond Israeli loaded with equipment struggling through a series of motor-car tires).

'God, they're a bloodthirsty lot,' said Stella, scowling through her brandy and ginger. 'Remind me of the Hitler Youth, and don't try and tell me it's anything to do with socialism, mate, 'cos it's just propaganda! Why are the Jews so good at that, I wonder?' she added in what was intended to be a meaningful voice.

'Ezra was asked that once at the time of Suez, and he said, "Yes, ever since Saul of Tarsus." Rather neat, don't you think?'

'I can't work it out, mate, too subtle for me. But I do know that at some stage in the argument you always quote the first bloody Viscount bloody Sterling. That bloody racketeer. You're in love with him, that's what. You're a crypto poove and a crypto Trot . . . and I want another B&B.'

(Fasten your seat belt, Chaimy, this is going to be a bumpy night.) 'There isn't going to be an argument, is there?'

'That's another thing about you, mate, you don't like an argu-ment,' said Stella irritably. 'It must be the thunder in the air. It makes people quarrelsome and depressed.'

He glanced up at the mirror above the bar. 'Fred, that chap who's just come in . . . seen him before?'

'Fellow with the *Evening Standard*, you mean? Hah.'

'Ask him if he'd like a drink, will you, Fred?' The landlord looked at him. Well, he was a good customer.

'Righto, squire!'

'What are you doing splashing yer money around, mate?' asked Stella.

'I just felt sorry for him – looks as if he leads a lonely life,' replied Chaimy thoughtfully.

The *Evening Standard* was a posh sheet, not often read around the Angel, Islington. The *Evening News* would have been a better buy for someone trying to be inconspicuous. Chaimy's outing with the colonel had made him observant of that sort of detail.

'. . . often welcomed in élite units of the army, like the para-troopers, where their toughness and courage is proverbial. But is patriotism enough?' We were back in the studio now and the man on the screen was suddenly well-shaven and wore a suit and tie. His voice, too, had changed to an indoor silky voice. 'Israel is surrounded, it is a platitude to say, by enemies. Sworn enemies . . .' (Shot of map of the Middle East – 'Whatever happened to the Near East?' asked Freddy – with Israel looking very small in a sea of hostile black, save for Iran which was a delicate grey; shot of Nasser swearing on television, shot of Ibn Saud looking crafty . . .)

'Just like Mimi Hayim, don't you think? Ezra? If you changed his headdress and gave him a big flowery hat?' suggested Audrey. But there was no sound from Ezra.

'. . . And if her enemies should unite in a Jihad or holy war – and there are increasing signs that, led by President Nasser, they might – Israel will need more than prayer for her to survive. But then her history so far . . .' The camera moved in to show that the man's eyes had crinkled with knowledgeable concern, '. . . has shown that she *can* depend on miracles. Good night.'

The credits came up over the same shot of the man on the tractor with the sun fading on the hills of Upper Galilee to the sound of the *Hatikvah*.

'It just shows,' said Ezra, 'that those fellows, trying to plug video cassettes and EVR, haven't a chance commercially. I'm glad I told our boys not to touch it. You see, television is a shared experience. Who would reach for their own tape of *My Fair Lady* or 'How to Repair Your Motor Car', when you can watch that? That programme will have enormous emotional and, therefore, political effect. Millions of people will want to talk about it tomorrow, in bus queues, supermarkets. . . .' He blew his nose. It was no good. When the lights went on everyone could see he had been crying.

'And in board rooms?' suggested Chuck considerately.

The larger part of the British nation had, of course, watched television the night before, but less exacting programmes had been preferred. The directors of Sterling Industries had all seen the documentary on the kibbutz and did indeed, as Ezra had prophesied, have something to say about it before their board meeting.

Mr Wilson, the company secretary, was impressed that Israel appeared to be so progressive and announced that his boys were going to work on a kibbutz – like Giles, the son of the other Wilson, he explained with a snicker. After they had solicitously served one another with strong black coffee, with the exception of Chaimy, who brought his own thermos of tea, Freddy indicated that they might sit down. Little Oscar moved to a position at the end of the table, the furthest removed from the Chairman, and David moved to the seat next to him which could have been interpreted as a gesture of family solidarity or a device whereby he could avoid looking his rival in the eye, should anything untoward occur. Chaimy sat opposite them, with his mug and packet of Woodbines, and the two 'white knights' as the family called them, Sir Matthew Fforde (formerly of Defence), and Sir Albert (the 'man from the Pru' but not actually from that particular insurance company) sat side by side.

The Chairman cleared his throat, then changed his mind and, as if a sudden and more important thought had struck him, said, 'I still don't understand why they don't have camels.'

'They do, surely, Chairman, further south, in the desert,' said

Sir Matthew. (It was clear that the meeting had not started after all. Was Freddy parodying Ezra, or just playing at being a 'card'?)

'Very efficient beasts, camels,' said Freddy.

'Yes, a horse designed by a committee,' said Wilson fatuously.

'No, no.' Freddy looked at him sternly. 'The bedouin looks to his camel for food, drink and clothing, not just transport. More use to the bedouin than a Bentley or a Mercedes is to me or you.'

Wilson blushed. The business had just bought him a Mercedes – quite a large one, the biggest in Purley anyway.

'No agenda?'

'No agenda, Mr Chairman,' said Wilson. 'As you know, this is an irregular meeting, called at the suggestion of Sir Albert.' He nodded at that gentleman, whose face betrayed the acknowledgement by a slight ptosis of the left eye. 'And with your agreement, of course, and there is only one subject for discussion.' He sighed and folded his neat hands on his lap.

'Before we proceed, gentlemen, could we hear from our technical director who recently returned from a visit which might not be totally irrelevant to, er . . .' They all looked at Chaimy whose nose was almost inside his mug of tea and who answered with a startled expression of Who, me?

'We don't expect any details, you understand,' said the Defence knight sagely.

'Well, it went off all right, didn't it?' said Chaimy in his Cockney voice.

There was a silence while Chaimy took another gulp of tea. This was a little cryptic even for a mission known to involve security at a high level.

'Er . . .' This time the Chairman meant it.

'They were friendly down there, up there,' said Chaimy, whose spectacles were now steamed over. He removed them and began to wipe them with a handkerchief, an action which experienced members of the board dreaded and which drew Sir Albert's basilisk stare. 'They seemed to want to give us more work, not less; there was that little problem we sorted out over a programme, and er, they seem quite happy with the bits we flog 'em.' Chaimy picked up his mug.

'He means the components you see,' whispered one knight to the other. Sir Albert's right eyelid dropped in sympathy with his left, for them to see that he saw nothing.

'That sounds quite satisfactory, thank you,' said Freddy. 'Now, the main burden of our discussion . . .'

'Mr Chairman, forgive my interrupting you, but I think I can make it much easier for you . . .'

Freddy nodded. It was Oscar.

'. . . by insisting that the responsibility is mine and no one else's. I don't know one end of a missile from the other, but Defence is in my control financially, and I can spot a couple of million quid moving in the right direction, and at first I did nothing to stop it. Quite honestly, gentlemen, I reckoned that we should hold on to it because, though the Government wouldn't notice . . .' The Defence knight shut his eyes in pain. '. . . *we* would . . . and imagine if it had been against us? Running to them for another two million? "Sorry, sir, we were a little out in our sums"!' Oscar snorted.

He's going at it like a bull, thought David.

'So, if they want my head they can have it. The Chairman has my resignation in his pocket.' Oscar's gesture was decent and British, but even Sir Albert moved his hand a few inches across the board room table in protest at so dramatic a solution.

'And all because of *Private Eye*,' muttered somebody. At this everyone spoke at once, except Sir Albert who moved his head from side to side like a vulture on top of the tower of Babel:

That magazine should be suppressed, it was irresponsible . . .

No, it sometimes had good sources of information. Look at the Profumo affair . . .

Its only sources of information were from drunks at El Vino . . .

It had no money . . .

It had plenty of money – from the Arabs . . .

It was right wing . . .

It was left wing . . .

It was a wing of its own . . . (Chaimy) . . . and so on.

Finally Freddy Barnet, as chairman, tapped on the table with his pencil, turned apologetically to Sir Alfred whose action had indirectly generated the discussion, and said, 'You see, Sir Alfred,

this is a small and . . . er . . . somewhat informal board. I'm . . .
when you agreed to represent the institutional investors here, you
had an idea of the kind of company you would be, er . . . keeping?'
Freddy smiled. It was his sort of joke.

Sir Albert considered this, and finally spoke; looking at little
Oscar he said, 'Yes.'

What is this supposed to mean, wondered Oscar. Approval or
condemnation? He might as well have said 'No.' The man should
bring an interpreter along with him.

The silence was broken by a trickle from the other end of the
table. Chaimy was pouring himself another mug of tea, but thoughtfully, as if he were minded to make a contribution. Chaimy was
hungry; the rest of them had been driven to the meeting but he had
bicycled. In his canvas bag, now a very pale blue and once the
property of the Royal Air Force, were two rounds of sandwiches –
cheese and pickle, and salmon and cucumber. He didn't know with
which to start.

'Mind you,' he said, 'we don't actually know that a question will
be asked in the House of Commons, we don't actually know that an
enquiry will be set up, and we have not heard from the Ministry of
Defence that they propose to pursue the matter?'

He addressed the question to Sir Alfred who, if he was surprised – more than anything by the unexpected inflections in
Chaimy's voice – registered, implacably, nothing. Freddy nodded
encouragingly and Chaimy went on.

'After all, we have been working with them for a number of years,
and there is reason to believe that if we approached them on their
attitude to this, er . . . affair, we might find them more amiable than,
er . . . some of us imagine.' He blinked innocently in the direction
of Sir Alfred.

'What makes you say that?' asked Freddy.

'It's not a saying, Mr Chairman, it's a quotation.' Chaimy sighed
and reached for his canvas bag. He had made his decision – half a
round of cheese and pickle, then half a round of salmon and
cucumber, and after that, with any luck, he might be able to finish
the rest off in the pub with the crossword.

The Defence knight stared at Chaimy. 'Mr Chairman, I would

like to support that suggestion, and if, er . . . someone' (clearly not Chaimy, whose face was full of sandwich) 'would care to propose a motion, I would second it.'

'The trouble is, Mr Chairman,' said David with his slight lisp, 'that whoever goes to the Ministry might end up talking to our former colleague.'

'Ah, Poll,' said Freddy.

'Exactly, who resigned in something of a huff at the time of Suez.'

It was known that Poll's successful rise had been marred only by one commercial failure and that with the business; also that he did not forgive or forget disappointments.

Wilson stirred in his seat. 'Er, through the Chair,' he began, 'I beg to contradict you, Mr Blacker. Mr Poll did not resign of his own accord, Lord Sterling requested his resignation. He was, in fact, fired!' Wilson paused, enjoying the effect he had created. 'The procedure insisted upon by Lord Sterling enabled him to receive, under the regulations then obtaining, a comparatively large sum of money in compensation, tax-free.'

David turned to little Oscar and both shrugged their shoulders. Cunning old Ezra, he had never explained that.

Sir Albert looked a little less bleak. He was an accountant originally, and the discussion was moving nearer to his territory, and, he noticed, had become more decorous. It was thereupon decided that the Ministry, nay Poll himself, should be approached for 'clarification'.

But by whom?

'Ezra,' said Chaimy, picking at a piece of cucumber stuck in his teeth.

If he would agree.

'It'll probably kill him,' whispered little Oscar.

'Good way to go,' replied David, with equal irreverence.

'And the question of Mr Barnet's resignation, Mr Chairman?' asked Sir Albert, moving his pencil from a lateral to a vertical position on the blotter.

'Yes, I was coming to that, Sir Albert,' said Freddy firmly. The ground upon which he was to put his foot suddenly felt more solid. 'I think we would all wish not to accept Mr Barnet's offer of resignation. . . .' Most eyes lowered in assent. 'But since the business is in the public eye at the present time,' Freddy had unconsciously lapsed into parliamentese, 'it may be appropriate to make some sort of gesture. . . .'

Here we go, thought Oscar.

'Mr Barnet has been honest and open enough to admit . . .' Freddy faltered. 'I have a motion from the chair which will be seconded by the Secretary that Mr David Blacker be appointed Deputy Chairman of the company with overall responsibility for Defence contracts,' he concluded hurriedly.

There was quiet in the room while all looked at little Oscar's burning face.

'I may say,' added Freddy conversationally, 'that this arose from a conversation I had last night with Ezra . . . er, with our President. Is it agreed?'

They all nodded their heads.

'That is perfectly acceptable to me,' croaked little Oscar.

'I hope you don't think this was my idea, Oscar,' said David, when it was all over. 'I never even knew . . .'

'Don't worry, dear boy, I believe you. And, by the way, congratulations.' Little Oscar put his big hand on his rival's shoulders. 'Do you think after all these years I can't recognize the handwriting?'

They went off in different directions, and factions, to lunch. Since Lord Sterling had no longer been present the directors' expense accounts had zoomed: a small point, thought Wilson, but significant.

6

The officer nudged Niki in the ribs, pointed, and handed him the night glasses. Niki looked hard but saw nothing. He shook his head, straining his eyes into the darkness and wondering if it would help to alter the focus of the lens. The officer looked up to where seconds ago there had been a split of moon.

'Wait,' he whispered.

They were about fifty yards outside the barbed wire fence of the

Nahal, where a few wan lamps creaked in the wind. The only other sound was the hum of electricity and the rasp of cicadas. A harsh, black, almost burnt piece of cloud slid away from the moon, illuminating for a moment the basalt-strewn landscape, and was quickly replaced by a heavy dull cloud.

'There,' said the officer. Niki thought he might have seen something which was not a rock, not a tree and not a patch of squill.

'*Mechablim!*' whispered the officer. 'Two, maybe three.'

Niki believed him. What did terrorists look like by night anyway? The officer sniffed the air, then, without turning, handed the glasses to the third member of their party.

'Motta, keep these until we get back. We'll go downwind of them. Stay where you are and cover us, but don't fire first. When you see the light, fire into the air – into the air, okay?' He used the English word.

Motta, a Canadian, many years older than Niki, resented this secondary role, but Niki was training to be a commander.

'Niki, follow me. When I stand up, you stand up. If they fire back, you lie down. Okay? Let's go!'

Half crawling and half crouching and crooking his Uzzi in his left arm so that it wouldn't touch a rock, the officer crept off. Niki followed. Time froze, but always the officer moved on, pausing only when the sky momentarily lightened, when he lay motionless like a lizard on the ground. Niki tried to breathe through his nose. Surely the terrorists could hear them panting?

Minutes, or was it half an hour, had passed. The big rocks were smooth, but a sharp stone had torn his shirt. From the watchtower where Niki had often been on duty the landscape looked flat enough, but now he saw how uneven it was. They had crawled to a point where their enemy should be between them and the barbed-wire fence. The officer sat on his haunches. Niki did the same and felt the breeze in his face. The sweat was getting in his eyes so he pushed back his steel helmet and wiped his forehead with his right arm. He had time to reflect that he felt no fear, only excitement.

The officer changed direction and moved quickly, almost casually, to a boulder big enough for them to stand up and lean against. Niki followed his every move. They remained in that position until

Niki felt his breathing grow normal. The officer touched his thigh and then his own lips, making a gesture over his shoulder. Niki heard the sound of voices, he could have sworn in disagreement. The officer, still standing, moved to the exposed side of the boulder holding his Very pistol in his right hand. Niki moved to his side. If the moon had come out they would both have been in silhouette. But the officer did not give it time. He fired the pistol into the air and as the light burst so did Motta's machine-gun. Niki looked wildly around. He could see nobody. But there they were, to the left, almost at his feet. He noticed the whites of their eyes, winking in the blackness of their faces like the tropical fish he had seen in the Dead Sea. He squeezed the trigger. Nothing. Misery stabbed his body. The safety catch! A stream of bullets chattered out of the muzzle of the gun, destroying the many orifices and vessels in the delicate machinery which time had laboured so long to perfect, of the two human beings below him. The screams told Niki he was on target, and only when the officer shouted at him to stop did he realize that the screams had stopped too.

They both climbed down and looked at the bodies. The face of one appeared to be a man of twenty-five or so, bearded with slightly pockmarked skin. The other had no face left, but Niki saw a youngish hand with a gold ring on the middle finger. The officer knelt down, turned the one with no face over on his front and removed the grenades from their belts, tucking three in his own and handing the others to Niki. Both the dead men had light machine-guns but one was, even in the dim light, so shattered that the officer left it. How funny, thought Niki, for guns to kill guns. The other he picked up gently.

'*Karashnikov*,' he said, 'now let's go. Well done, you were very quick.'

Niki wanted to ask a lot of questions. What would happen to the bodies? Weren't there any other *mechablim* around? Finally he chose the silliest.

'Shouldn't we see if they have any identification?'

'What do you mean?' said the officer. 'Like a driving licence?'

It was all very well for the officer – he must have killed lots of people,

in Sinai, or on raids like tonight. They never told you in basic training what it felt like to kill someone. They told you to squeeze the
trigger, not to snatch at it, that to fire from the shoulder was more
accurate than from the hip. He didn't remember anything about
being downwind of a quarry, but the lieutenant had explained over
a cup of Nescafé in the canteen that humans could smell, just like
animals. They never told you about standing above somebody,
because it was more difficult to fire up than down. Simple stuff,
really – after it had happened. Niki smiled in the darkness of his
little room. It was a nice smile, he knew. Lea had told him so.
Maybe if he imagined her with him it would help him to get to
sleep. Why not? He was a hero, wasn't he?

Oh dear, Niki remembered the slogan, there are no heroes in the
Israeli Army, only casualties. And if, the instructor had said on the
command course, again and again, you become an officer you are
more likely to be killed. 'There is no word "forward", only "follow
me".' He didn't feel like a hero now, more like a casualty.

Poor Motta. All that zeal for Eretz Israel and all he had been
allowed to do was to shoot into the air, as a distraction. Clever
fellow, that officer, and nice too; much more worried about his
torn shirt and the scratch on his tummy than about the two dead
men. When Niki had confessed that, far from being very quick to
fire he had forgotten the safety catch, the officer had said, 'Then
you were quicker, weren't you? You see, as my professor used to
say, quoting Cicero, "Anybody can make a mistake – only a fool
persists in it." ' Who was Cicero? He must ask somebody – not the
lieutenant.

He wondered if he should model himself on the officer – a dry
man, a paratrooper, a scholar. Wasn't he a lecturer in the Humanities
at the University in Jerusalem? And, unlike his father, there:
before his eyes, alive and capable of being copied. He, Niki, was,
said his mother's old friends from the other kibbutz, just like his
father, only taller and fairer. But what was his father like?

'Well,' his mother always said, and in his childhood it had
become a sort of chant, 'he was not like Abrasher.' Abrasher was
his stepfather and the father of his half-brother and half-sisters. 'If
Abrasher is hairy like Esau, he was smooth like Jacob; if Abrasher

is tough like a goat, your father, Niki, was delicate, like a kid; if Abrasher glows like a warm fire, your father burned like a furnace; if Abrasher is gentle and patient like a shepherd, your father was gentle too, but it hurt him because he had to contain the fury inside him.'

'What fury?' Niki always asked.

'He loved his mother but he hated his father, and he spoke only of his father.'

Niki turned in his bed and wondered if God would mind if he thought again about Lea, but sleep fell upon him before anything was decided.

7

Once a fortnight, usually on a Wednesday, Ezra enjoyed what had become known as his 'day off'. This institution, endorsed by Dr Xavier and condoned by Audrey, who usually let Geoffrey drive her up to London, was a sort of Mardi Gras in Ezra's usually Lenten routine. In Audrey's absence for the day and sometimes for the night, Turners became the scene of activities and indulgences normally forbidden.

For a start, the current Ashby, Ashfold, Ashworth, or whatever the chauffeur was called, was sent in Ezra's Rolls to procure Mme Hélène. Fatter and myopic, she was still gay, not only presentable but, with the assistance of cosmetic surgery, positively desirable, at least to Ezra who had studied his own condition and consulted Dr Xavier on this very point; for Hélène's right hand had not lost its cunning.

'My dear Lord,' he had said, 'there is a famous doctor in London, who shall be nameless, called Goldblatt or Gold-something, with a considerable following among wealthy noblemen like yourself. In return for lavish fees, he inflicts upon them a regime of terror. Anything pleasurable is forbidden – tobacco, fine foods, wine and love, and they lap it up like nobody's business. Now, I tell you, as I tell all my patients, on the National Health, would our creator have arranged that we enjoy the pleasures of the palate and the pleasures of the bed – the palate and the pallet as you might say, hee hee – until our dying day if, er . . . if . . .' – Dr Xavier had rather lost his track – 'if he had not known what he was doing?' He then poured himself some more whisky. 'My own father produced a son at the age of eighty-seven.'

'I thought he was a Roman Catholic,' said Ezra.

'He was. I have to confess' (beautiful smile) 'that the child was the fruit of an illegitimate union.'

This had been good enough for Ezra. Hélène's visits were hardly a secret from Audrey since their cars regularly crossed around eleven o'clock somewhere about High Wycombe, Hélène in the Rolls bearing fresh *foie gras* and Audrey in Geoffrey's Rover. She did not know that on this particular Wednesday, Ezra had arranged another forbidden delight for himself. The dispute with the Planning Authority was to be advanced, Ezra was sure in his favour, by a visit from Chuck's solicitor.

Hubert had been pleased after all these years to hear from Chuck Lambkin, his former client, intrigued at the thought of meeting his former adversary, but appalled at the subject to be discussed. However, when he had mentioned it to his wife, she had decided that it would be jolly for them all to spend a day in the country and perhaps Caroline could sell Lord Sterling some of her hydroponic plants.

'Super,' Caroline had said routinely. So with a map specially prepared for visitors to Turners by the Automobile Association, and sent to them by Mrs Winterbourne, the 'family' as they referred to themselves had set off.

'I told you, Dad, it was full of gadgets,' said Caroline as the first gate swung open. Hubert wished his daughter would not call him 'dad', but then perhaps she was too big to say 'papa'. He glanced at her via the driving mirror. Her mouth permanently open, a freckled face, tousled hair, her mother's small eyes, and then those two – of course there were two – enormous breasts. 'Hoydenish', people were sometimes kind to say of Caroline. Her current job – even the lowest form of higher education had been beyond her – was in a shop which supplied plants for the West End offices of airlines and the like. Hubert hoped she would not in fact try to sell any to Lord

Sterling, who, to his surprise, opened the door to them himself.

'How very good of you all to come.'

(What an absolutely charming old man, how typical of Hubert not to have mentioned his courtesy.)

'Mrs Brooker, and Caroline, how nice!' Ezra beamed. He even knows my name, thought Caroline, and crossed her huge thighs in her embarrassment.

'You're the gardener of the family, they tell me. Well, there's a lot to see here at this time of the year. May I offer you champagne or coffee? It's a bit early for drinks, I suppose?' He led them across the hall towards the orangery.

'Gosh,' said Caroline, dazzled, 'just like our shop!'

'May I present you to Madame Hélène Delaunay.'

Hubert bowed over the French lady's extended hand which he kissed, and muttered. '*Très heureux*, madame.' He knew that '*enchanté*' was common. He prayed that Caroline would not fall over anything, or attempt a curtsy.

It was decided that in the interval before lunch Hélène would conduct the ladies round the house and gardens while Ezra showed Hubert his television mast, which he seemed very keen to do.

'You must admit the reception is brilliant.'

'Yes, Lord Sterling.' Some cartoons had indeed been visible with extraordinary, and to Hubert, unnecessary clarity. 'But that's not really the point. You see, disputes in the area of planning are about people being refused permission, and contesting that refusal, through appeals ending up with the Minister. Or the other way round. A local authority may give you planning consent which offends local interests, who protest, and that too can end up with the Minister who can overrule the consent. But your situation falls into neither category. You broke the law; you went ahead and did it.'

'Exactly,' said Ezra happily as they passed the stables. 'Bloody silly law, don't you think? One beautiful spire instead of all those tangled wires.'

'Many of our laws are bloody silly,' said Hubert, 'as our judges often imply when sentencing those who break them. M'yaas.'

They plodded on in silence.

'Think of it,' said Ezra, when they came to it, 'as a metal pine tree.'

'All right,' said Hubert loyally. He noticed a formidable section of barbed-wire fence, about twelve feet high.

'That's to stop the boys from the village climbing up the mast and hurting themselves.'

'And anybody else?'

'Yes, maybe I should have it mined.'

Is he mad, wondered Hubert.

'So you cannot take my case?'

'Lord Sterling, you have no case. I can advise you to prevaricate, to delay answering letters, even to send them to the wrong address. To be ill, to be out of the country, and so on. But your only hope is for a change in the law. You see, the trouble is even if they wanted to concede, technically and psychologically, they cannot. Your enemies lack what General Suvorov called "the golden bridge" – a way of retreat. They are bound to administer the law.'

He looked up. Lord Sterling was leaning against a tree breathing deeply, more deeply than was natural. He waited and watched; there was nothing else he could do.

'My friend Professor Yudkin says that if you feel a heart attack coming on, you should take in deep breaths. Long and slow, to increase the supply of blood and oxygen, which, as you can see, is what I have been doing. But I'm not sure,' he smiled, 'whether I did feel a heart attack coming on.'

Neither am I, thought Hubert; it may just have been a way of shutting me up.

'That's all a heart attack is, you know; coronary thrombosis is the grand name and what happens is that a clot cuts off the blood supply and damages the muscles of the heart. Rather like in the old days when the pipes in the central heating furred up. But the body, even one as old as mine, is quite resourceful and grows new routes when the main road is blocked off. If you want a more up-to-date analogy, that is. Tell me, dear boy, how is your client Mr Lambkin?'

'Oh, Lord Sterling, you see more of him . . .'

'Of course I do. Stupid question. Forgive me. And, d'you know, I never met a kinder man, nothing is too much trouble for him. Yes, indeed, I see as much of him as he can bear!' This of a man whom ten years ago he tried to destroy by intimidation, denunciation and assassination, 'a whim of iron', Hubert remembered. 'Give me your arm, will you, I'm like a horse, I hate going downhill.'

'Tell me, you're a successful fellow . . .' – Ezra patted the sustaining arm with his free hand – 'but you don't look happy.'

'Call no man happy, Lord Sterling,' said Hubert not raising his eyes from the slippery pine needles.

'Nonsense. I've heard that and I haven't had a classical education. Look at me. . . .' Ezra disengaged himself, held out his arms, gazed at Hubert out of his deep grey eyes so that he flinched. 'I'm happy,' and he smiled. 'I'm not yet dead.'

Hubert removed his spectacles and then put them back. 'Yes,' he said, and smiling too, offered his arm.

'Of course,' said Ezra as they set off again, 'I have my problems.'

'The mast? I've been thinking . . . if we offered to lower it. You see, it's the skyline that bothers them. They're very skyline-conscious. One of our clients got a few thousand the other day from the Electricity Board because of a couple of pylons which spoilt his view.'

'But if we lower it, it won't be efficient.'

'I said, "if we offer to lower it", Lord Sterling!'

'Ah ha.' Hubert's arm was patted again.

'That would take them a couple of months to work out.'

'Now, since you're so clever, Mr Brooker . . .'

'I beg you to call me Hubert.'

'Yes, and you can call me Ezra.'

'That I cannot do, Lord Sterling.'

'Ah well, since you're so clever, Hubert, here's another problem for you – on a professional basis, of course. My heir – my grandson – is a soldier in the Israeli Army.' He paused and seemed deep in thought.

'A very efficient force, I understand. I met a man in the club the other day who said he invented it. Liddell Hart,' added Hubert.

'He was born after his father was killed. Hubert, you look to be a man of discretion. . . .' Ezra had halted and once more let Hubert's arm go.

'Only if necessary.'

'My son was killed by the Arab Legion, a shell . . .' He faltered.

'Yes, I know,' said Hubert quickly. 'My cousin Tom Brooker, who told you, told me.'

Any other emotion Ezra might have felt was swamped by astonishment.

'Brooker . . . let me see – drunk, hiccups, fairhaired?'

'Cousin Tom is a deal soberer than most judges I know, but he has fair hair . . . or had.'

'Stoops, rather an old-fashioned young man he was.'

'That's him.'

'Right. And the man who killed my son was a British officer in the Arab Legion and knew him as a boy.'

'I believe that was part of the story I was told. Tom said . . .' He was interrupted by a clock which chimed rapidly four times.

'That's lunch. S'all right, we have ten minutes – and they can bloody well wait. But what you don't know, Hubert – hey, you'd better hold on to me – is that this fellow deserted the Legion, and joined the Haganah.'

'I read somewhere that a few did that.'

'And was killed.' Hubert felt the grip on his arm tightening. 'But after Nicky's death he wrote me a letter to . . . to . . . apol . . .' Ezra stopped. 'I'm sorry – to apologise.' He gulped.

Hubert felt a need to change the conversation. 'What no doubt bothers you is something to do with inheritance. Tell me, Lord Sterling, is the child legitimate? I mean, were his parents married?' Hubert spoke as coldly as he could.

'Certainly his parents were married. You can ask my wife.'

'Then he will inherit your title,' said Hubert briskly. 'Here, you need this,' and he tugged his handkerchief out of his top pocket.

'That's not the problem. You see, he is a member of a kibbutz and anything we send him they take. We know that. There are trusts of which he is the sole beneficiary . . .'

'Discretionary trusts?'

'Yes, but two come to him absolutely, one at eighteen like now, and a larger one at twenty-five. It was something all the family did years ago – before some of them were born.'

'Quite.'

'And the kibbutz takes all ... at present. Mind you, I believe when they're twenty or so, they're eligible for a year off, and if he came down here, for a weekend, say ...'

'Quite.'

The house had just come into view. Turners was not one of the most beautiful country houses in England, nor was it the smallest.

'... he might change his mind. And I was wondering if I could leave him this, conditional on his living here ... or at least in England?'

'It would be difficult to prescribe his living here in this house, even if you tie it in with money for maintenance, but you could make British residence a condition, and in any case I would advise you to settle the house on him now, with your wife as life tenant. And we can worry about the land later.'

'Why?'

'Because it pays much less duty. M'yaas.' It was wonderful how talk about money concentrated the mind and dried up the emotions.

At lunch Ezra behaved, as the family would say, like a gentleman. Correctly he sat Mrs Brooker on his right, grew to dislike her mouth, a mean red slit, like the jam in a doughnut, and with increasing cruelty and courtesy plied her with drink. One moment of savagery escaped him, marked only by Mme Hélène who knew and by Hubert who thought he knew, and that was when Caroline declared how much she had enjoyed her swim. 'Ah good,' said Ezra. 'So they found you a bathing suit; one of Miss Tattie's, er, Mrs Lambkin's, perhaps?'

The time came, eventually, for their departure and Ezra insisted on escorting the family to their car, a snazzy BMW.

'I thought *I* would drive back,' said Mrs Brooker to her husband, coy, bossy and drunk.

'Did you?' said Hubert. He had decided to divorce her, both of them. The BMW's back wheels splayed the gravel and they were gone.

'Poor man,' said Hélène. 'They are both so ugly and each in a different way. And now, *mon amour*, I'm taking you to bed, to rest.

'What an absurd luncheon party,' said Ezra. 'I am sorry – was I all right?'

'There was one little moment . . . when I thought you were going to fall asleep. Otherwise you were marvellous.'

'The man is worthwhile though, clever.'

'I'm sure he is, my dear.' She knew that her man, her unofficial man, never totally wasted his time.

Hélène was reading a novel by Simenon. She was diligent in her devotion and nearly kept up with his output. She lay on the bed in Ezra's dressing room and could hear his rhythmic snores. The telephone buzzed. It was Pettit.

'Mr Barnet, Mr Frederick Barnet, is on the telephone, madame, would you care to take the call downstairs? He says he will wait.'

Ezra always maintained that only little people had secrets, so it was known at the business that Hélène might be found on every other Wednesday at Turners. This was useful, because it provided an alternate route to Ezra, who was possibly overprotected by Audrey from matters which would cause him embarrassment or concern.

'Hello, Hélène, how, er, are you?' Freddy sounded nervous.

'Fine.'

'Good, and, er . . . how's the family?' Nervous and not too clear-headed.

'My family? They are mostly dead. *Dans la Résistance!*' she shrilled. It was not true, but Hélène saw no reason why she shouldn't enjoy herself.

'Oh dear, I'm sorry to hear that, I . . .'

'It was some time ago,' Hélène interrupted sweetly.

'How is Ezra?'

'Very tired, very, very tired.'

'Oh.' Freddy could not hide his unnaturally deep disappointment.

'Very tired,' repeated Hélène. 'Why do you ask?' She was not one of those who believed the moon was made of green cheese.

'Because . . . Look here, Hélène, Chaimy's with me and he'd like a word with you.' Freddy felt it was time to change the bowler. He himself had no appetite for intrigue.

Chaimy's French was excellent, if pedantic, and, like a clever sixth-former, he enjoyed exercising it. He had been gentleman

enough to flirt with her the few times they had met, which could
be counted on two or three of those dirty fingers. She teased him
about his subjunctives; she also knew of Ezra's secret regard and
respect for his talents. Chaimy was well fielded on this occasion.

Hélène listened carefully, one hand on her other ear trying to
dampen the sound of an officious electrical noise, which had started
up somewhere in the depths of the house. She understood immediately. The expression '*chacun à son ministre*' is peculiarly French, but,
but . . . '*Mais, ce n'était pas lui qui a volé l'argent!*'

Chaimy explained that it was Ezra's innocence which gave his
mission such dramatic appeal; the patriarch begging forgiveness
for the sins of the third generation (here Chaimy's Biblical references
grew confused). The shepherd ransoming the black sheep, was that
better? (Did the expression '*mouton noir*' mean anything in French?
It sounded odd.)

Hélène said that in her view it would be difficult to deter Ezra
from such an attractive expedition, but that Audrey must be
consulted first. This bewildered Chaimy.

'Because,' said Hélène, 'husbands may deceive wives, but
mistresses, never.' (She was pleased with this remark. It did not
make sense, but it had the quality of an epigram, and suited the
tone of their *marivaudage*.)

8

'Damn,' said Ezra. 'Something extremely embarrassing has
happened. I've been incontinent. Sorry.'

'Whaddya say, Ez?' Chuck leant across and took Ezra's hand.

'As Sandra Barnet would say, I've gone to the bathroom in my
pants.'

'That's all right, we'll soon get your cleaned up, it happens to
everybody.' He pressed the button which lowered the partition.
'Stop at the next men's clothing shop, will you, Ashworth?'

Ashworth nodded. There was now detectible evidence that the
Lord had forgotten himself. Poor old sod!

'Yes,' said Ezra bitterly, 'but it's happened to me! Xavier gave me some little pills, but I never thought of taking one. Damn, damn damn!'

'I'll get you some new underwear, and to be safe, some more pants. There must be a hotel or a pub where we can wash up and change. What's your waist size, Ez?'

'That is the sort of statistic I have, hitherto, never had to bear in mind. Nor I suppose did Job. I never thought I'd envy Job,' said Ezra sadly.

From an astonished young man with long hair, himself ill at ease in a suit, waistcoat and tie, Chuck bought underwear and three pairs of trousers in different sizes, as near in texture and colour to Ezra's jacket as he could remember.

The public house, a vast glazed red-brick Edwardian edifice, designed to regale the good (and numerous) folk of Holloway, north London, with liquor at ground level; with cold, bare linoleum rooms for their 'functions' on the first floor, had been emphatically shut, nay padlocked. But Chuck found an Irish girl scrubbing a step, with a transistor blaring, and with five pounds' worth of Southern charm an upstairs room had been procured for an unspecified period of time. She even put a shilling in the meter to light the gas fire.

The decoration and amenities were strictly coeval with the building.

'Extraordinary,' said Ezra. 'If not for that,' he pointed to his discarded clothes, 'I would never have seen this.' His gesture took in the narrow bed, the spitting gas fire, the threadbare carpet. 'It's like the evacuees. . . . We never knew how sick most of England's children were, until the war. And, d'you know, Chuck, for the first time in the history of England her people were properly fed. Milk, carrot juice, butter, no sweets . . . Marvellous fellow, Woolton!'

Chuck, cleaning Ezra's behind with the patience and dexterity of a nurse, marvelled at the old boy's spirit.

'And now they all eat too much, and they feed too many budgerigars. Do you know that the amount of food consumed by the pets of Britain would sustain the entire population of Calcutta?'

Chuck considered that this revelation had been provoked by the imminence of a visit to the House of Lords. It had been arranged that Ezra would meet Poll in his room in the House of Commons at 11.30 that morning, a discreet venue and a short walk at a time when the Palace of Westminster should be deserted.

'I say, these trousers fit perfectly. Do you think you could get me some more? Do you remember the name of the shop, dear boy? I think I shall abandon Kilgour & French to their American clientele. I gave up Lobb at the beginning of the war, you know, in favour of ready-made shoes, and have been satisfactorily shod ever since. Now, thanks to this deplorable incident, I shall be well trousered. You see how the Greeks say, in every evil there is some good! Now, let's see if the fellow has any champagne.'

Ashworth had moved the car to the side entrance of the public house and was in conversation with the admiring landlord. It was a part of London where Rolls-Royces are not usually stationary. He would look in the cellar if the gentlemen would care to sit in the private bar, as they were standing on the trap door.

'Ah,' said Ezra, 'how nice. I like cellars,' and he moved aside, but not far.

The landlord pattered down the steps and re-emerged with a bottle wrapped in cellophane with a flashy gold label which he proffered to Ezra.

'H'mmm. Very shiny. What else have you got down there? Might I have a look?'

'If you like, my lord, only be careful.'

Assisted by Chuck and watched by two pairs of anxious eyes, Ezra descended the steps.

Once in the cellar Ezra sniffed appreciatively.

'Good place for growing mushrooms. But I understand, like us, they are plague to all manner of diseases.'

'I'd say you'd recovered, Ezra, you're ...'

'H'sst! Chuck, come here!' Ezra interrupted. He had pulled out a dusty bottle and had wiped the dust from the label.

'Oh, that's just a lot of old stock I more or less inherited you might say ...'

It was the voice of the landlord from above.

'The Lord bless us and keep us,' whispered Ezra. 'Moet et Chandon '53 – and *pink*!'

'Left over from a wedding, I'd say,' said the landlord. 'Probably flat now.'

'How much for the lot?' asked Ezra.

'Dunno, sir, it's not even on my list!'

'Say, two quid a bottle, landlord, that all right?' There was a pause in which Chuck could feel Ezra's grip tighten on his arm.

'That's er, two dozen bottles, forty-eight quid,' suggested Ezra.

'All right, my lord, I'll help you shift them.' Ezra took one bottle up the stone steps and watched as the bottles were loaded into the car. Ashworth dropped one on the pavement. The champagne frothed prettily.

'*Oi vey*,' said Ezra. 'We are undone.'

'S'all right, my lord, shan't charge you for that,' said the landlord.

There was a slight hitch. Neither Chuck nor Ezra had enough money.

'Lend me forty-eight quid, will you, Ashworth?' said Ezra cheerfully.

His chauffeur looked at him bleakly.

'Not to worry, Lord Sterling,' said the landlord on a man-to-man basis. 'You can have your secretary post me a cheque or send your man round with it.'

'Nectar!' said Ezra as he dusted the bottle with his spare hand-kerchief in the back of the Rolls. '1953 was a wonderful year.'

'You don't think it was too long ago?'

'Nonsense, my boy. You saw the bottle that *schlemiel schlumped* . . . fizzed like an angel. My friend, the sly earl, whom you are about to meet, and who is well versed in such matters, informed me that good champagne lasts as long as a camel.'

There wasya pause while Chuck thought.

'Fourteen ears,' said Ezra happily. 'So it's just coming up to its prime. You'd pay a tenner for this in Claridge's, if they had it!'

As Ezra was led down the corridors of the Palace of Westminster – fraying carpets and obscure portraits – he congratulated himself on his prescience in compensating Poll so handsomely in 1956. God, as he often said, had been behind him then. How much would it cost now? He kept an account, in another name, in a local bank in

High Wycombe, against such emergencies. He had that cheque book with him.

Yes, with the Minister was a man who had the marks of an official from Labour Party headquarters at Transport House. From the treasurer's department perhaps?

'This is Mr Clark who looks after our publicity at Transport House. What do you think of this,' and he held up a paperback, 'instead of a pamphlet?'

'Anything's better than a pamphlet. Nobody reads pamphlets,' said Ezra, feeling relieved.

'Precisely,' said the Minister. 'Thank you, Andy.'

Andy withdrew.

'Cigar?' asked the politician who habitually, in public, smoked a pipe.

'No, thank you, alas, I . . .'

'Quite, quite. You introduced me to cigars, you know, Ezra?'

'I'm glad to see you both got on so well.'

It was spirited, but the sight of Ezra unnerved Poll. He looked like a dismantled man o' war, pooped, with cannons spiked.

'I remember when you took me to the station one night, after a party given by Freddy and Joyce. You were very kind to me. That was some time ago,' he added thoughtfully.

'A generation ago,' said Ezra. 'I always knew you'd be a success.'

'Then why . . .' began the Minister.

'Why did I fire you?' supplied Ezra. 'Ah, that was in '56 and in '56 I was not so sure.' He smiled tentatively. Poll laughed, with relief.

'But you were sure about Suez, weren't you? Do you still feel the same way, Ezra? May I ask . . .'

'Certainly you may and certainly I do. It was the end of the England I knew.'

There was a pause and the Minister exhaled. 'You were good to me, too, when I left, very good.'

'One tries to behave as well as one can. . . .'

'Yes, you do, but some of your lads . . .' And he rapped the file in front of him.

'Which is why I am here. It is good of you to see me.'

'Oh, we can sort this out, easy enough. Tell me, how is the family?'

'Fine. There have been a few additions since you last saw us; the most delightful is a little girl called Marianne, my great-niece, little Oscar's daughter. She is kind enough to come to Turners now and again.'

'And Jeremy?'

'Jeremy?'

'Yes, Sarah's ... er ... boy. I thought he was bright, had a future, you know?'

'Ah, maybe he still has a future, but it has yet to appear.'

'And your grandson in Israel, he must be ...'

'Eighteen,' said Ezra quickly, and looked up at his former employee to indicate that that was as far as he would like to go in that direction.

The Minister opened a file on his desk. Pinned to the top was a photostat of a tearsheet from *Private Eye*. He looked at it and sniffed.

'I hope you won't misinterpret me, Ezra, if I say that no political option is totally closed to one, until it has been predicted by this journal.' And he waved the offending sheet in the air.

Ezra looked puzzled.

Fine, thought the Minister, if he doesn't know, so much the better. They *do* protect him.

He cleared his throat. 'Listen, this is how it might go. About seven months ago, just six weeks, in fact, before your retirement as chairman of the business, you sent me a confidential letter as an old, er ... friend, former colleague, and Minister responsible, saying that there had been brought to your attention a serious error in the accounts of your business, relating to an R and D defence project. Right? It was an error in your favour, of about two million pounds – and though the sum was relatively small compared to the final amount involved, if the project were accepted by the Ministry, you wanted me to know that you were deeply concerned as to the principle involved, and that if the mistake *were* intentional, the offenders would be punished, and in any event the excess profit would be refunded.' The Minister turned to the next piece of paper. 'Which indeed happened on the thirteenth of October of last year. I replied appropriately to the effect that the matter was not yet my concern, but that I appreciated your characteristic openness and patriotism, etc., etc.' He looked at Ezra to see if he had understood.

'Now, all we have to do is sign the letters.' He stood up and walked over to Ezra's chair, knelt down by his side and held out the letters for him to read.

Ezra digested the two documents, without recourse to spectacles; it was an odd sensation reading a letter from yourself which you had never written, thought Ezra, on your own business letterhead. The very stuff of politics!

'Do you think I've captured your style?' Poll looked pleased.

'And my notepaper,' said Ezra. 'But I can't sign this.'

'Why not?'

'Because the paper you have captured, or retained, is incorrect. When I wrote this letter you were not a member of the board.' Ezra smiled. Poll blushed.

'Yes, of course, just a draft then . . . But you approve?'

'Absolutely, you are very kind. I'll send it round to you in the proper form.' He fingered the letter thoughtfully. 'But how will you deal with the private question in the House?'

'Ah, very simple.' Poll was back on native ground. Sticking his thumbs in his waistcoat pockets, in a parody of a parliamentary performance, he addressed a bust of Chatham on the mantelpiece as if it were the offending back bencher.

'The Honourable Member for, er . . . Piddlehampton is justly famous for his zeal in protecting the public purse, especially in the area of defence. He would be listened to with more respect, however, if he were to choose his objectives with more care, and appear less obviously motivated by pique rather than patriotism. . . .'

Poll broke off and turned to Ezra. 'At this moment, Hansard reports noises from the left, like "Shame!" and "Withdraw!" And then when that's over I carry on and say: "In the case of Sterling Industries I'm proud to confess to an interest."' He turned again to Ezra. 'The House likes a confession. "For some years," I continue, "I was a director of that company, advising them on exports and, due perhaps to that happy and fruitful association, Lord

Sterling wrote to me about the miscalculation referred to, the moment it came to his attention, which was many weeks before it came to that of the Honourable Member. That letter can be made public. It is therefore not a question of crying over spilt milk but of rejoicing at the honour of a British company which so swiftly offered to replace the milk, which was in fact done on, er," I check my notes, "the thirteenth of October of last year!" '

Ezra clapped his hands.

'Half a mo', Ezra, not finished yet. "There is another document in this affair, which I hope the House will now consider closed, prepared by the Ministry of Defence, which I may not on grounds of security make public, and it offers excellent reasons why their long association with Sterling Industries should continue and, indeed, expand. Since the Honourable Member is so greatly concerned in this matter, I will be happy to show the document to him, privately." ' He turned, finally, to Ezra. 'That much, incidentally, is true.'

'Bravo!' said Ezra. 'Now may I applaud?'

'Yes, but the speech may never be made. They might be satisfied with your demotion of the culprit. That was how you intended it to be read, I suppose?'

'We didn't demote little Oscar, we promoted David Blacker.'

Poll smiled. 'I'm very glad to recognize your thinking, and to see it unimpaired. And, apropos of continuity, although it's none of my business . . .'

'You have just demonstrated that anything to do with me is your business,' said Ezra solemnly.

'As you know, I've been a Zionist all my life and now, we friends of Israel are very much concerned for her safety, indeed for her survival. Any moment now there has to be another war. And she'll lose it – on paper at least.'

'Paper?'

'Well, just on relative military strength. But wise or foolish, Israel seems to want a war. I was informed by our Middle East desk that the settlements in Upper Galilee can no longer endure the shelling from Syria and have gone to Eshkol to say they will abandon the kibbutzes unless there is some action. Isn't that where your grandson could be found?'

'Could be found is right,' said Ezra, starting to rise from his chair.

'Can't you bring him to this country? Here, let me help you.' Poll stepped across the room.

Ezra shook his head uncertainly as he stood up; half-denying, half-admitting his need for help of any kind.

'I fear for the continuity of your line, Lord Sterling,' said the Minister as they shook hands.

'Thank you . . . The letter will be retyped and sent over this afternoon.'

In Ezra's world duty had no limits. Anyone hired by the business could expect to be bidden at any hour to perform some not obviously significant task which, in a normal organization, might be delegated to somebody else, or not performed at all. So the sly earl had been 'fagged', as he put it, to look after Chuck in the House of Lords, while Ezra was visiting Poll in the House of Commons.

Apparently the duty had not been too onerous. Ezra found Chuck explaining, with practical examples, the unique quality of Jack Daniel as an ingredient in old-fashioneds.

'There he is, firm of step, bright of eye, with the looks of a con- queror. Don't tell me, Ez, I know. You pulled it off!'

For the first time in many years Ezra blushed. 'You're both drunk,' he said.

'Can't think what indooshed you to give it back,' said the sly earl. 'Government money, fair game. We never did. Hey, bring Lord Sterling a half-bottle of the best French champagne, there's a dear chap!' He signalled a waiter.

Ezra was often amused at the streaks of vulgarity displayed by noblemen.

'That's handsome of you. I've just got to write a note, then I'll be back.'

"Straordinary fellow that, you know. And you, his brother-in- law – you don't look like a member of the chosen race.'

'I'm not.'

'Nor does he, come to think of it. I thought they always married each other. Jews, I mean.'

'They do usually, but not so much in the States, as a matter of fact. I married my wife because she was very rich and very fond of me!'

'Did you, by God, so did I. 'Cept my wife loathed me. Forced into it. Ambitious mother. Shipbuilding. Newcastle. Like the Lycett-Greenes, only less common. Or maybe they were more common, I don't remember . . .' He shook his head. 'Let's have the other half, shall we?' The waiter, who had brought the champagne, inclined his head respectfully.

'I say, I haven't had so much fun since dear Aunt Maisie caught her left tit in the mangle . . . D'you know that song? Oh . . .' he said.

Ezra had reappeared, holding a long envelope.

'Sorry to break it up, lads.'

'I was going to ask you to lunch, as my guests.'

'Really . . .' Ezra looked at the sly peer, famous for his inhospitality, with interest. 'I hope you remember to charge it to the business.' He was not kind, but Ezra reckoned the earl was too drunk to notice. He was right.

'Oh, can I . . . ?'

'Of course, we'll set it against the two million quid. If Chuck would be good enough to tell Ashworth to take this to Mrs Winterbourne . . . We would be delighted to accept, would we not?' Chuck nodded and took the envelope.

'Smoked salmon, Irish stew, potatoes in their jackets, on a separate plate, not mash, and tell the cook to keep a portion of baked jam roll. Cream, not custard. What are you having, Sterling?'

'The same,' said Ezra.

'And our American friend?'

'I'll go along with that.'

'Good, tell the wine waiter what we're having to eat and ask him to bring some wine.'

The young waitress looked at him as if he were a practical joker. They were a queer lot, these peers.

'I always do that; puts them on their mettle, flatters them, and they never sell you a pup. Best club in London, wouldn't you say, Sterling?'

'I say that, I think we all do. It's built on coal, beer and graft, I hope you've explained to our friend, and it's an excellent institution.'

'Not graft,' protested the sly earl, 'theft. Theft on a grand scale. I have an ancestor called Petty, y'know, by name but not by nature, yer might say.' He nodded. 'Sergeant Petty was in Cromwell's army in Ireland and when the time came for the carve-up of the land, my ancestor was one of the few chaps who could work a what-d'yer-call-it – a theodolite. And he thieved quite a lot that way. That's what my nanny told me. Of course, it's quite untrue,' he added.

'Why? It sounds a likely tale.'

'The truth is, it was a chap called Sir William Petty, who surveyed the place, and bought out the soldiery. A respectable fraud, he was.' The sly earl sighed. 'My dear Sterling, haven't you learned not to believe anything one's nanny tells one?'

'I never had a nanny. I suppose my sister Sarah performed that function. You see, Chuck and I are self-made men. Did you have a nanny, Chuck?' asked Ezra with a little smile.

'Not that I recall,' replied Chuck with the same sort of little smile.

The sly earl peppered his smoked salmon thoughtfully. 'Yes, and I suppose your lot don't have ancestors,' said he challengingly

'My friend,' said Ezra, putting his glass of champagne on the table, 'at a time when your ancestors were half-naked savages living in unsanitary caves and worshipping animals, mine had built a city of a quarter of a million people. There was a water system which worked until 1917 when Allenby entered Jerusalem, not as a conqueror but as a pilgrim. Good man, Allenby. They had refined a religion a perversion of which now dominates the western world, whose songs you still sing in your churches. The sophistication and beauty of their palaces made strangers rub their eyes in amazement.' Here Ezra rubbed his eyes in amazement. 'The chariots of Solomon, thundering out from the hollows of the fortresses of Megiddoh and Hatzor, were not equalled in their terrible efficiency until the invention of the Panzer division; their ships scoured the seas for treasures to bring back to the temple which was the equivalent of St Peter's, the Louvre and, er, the British Museum, rolled into one. That was fifty generations ago. Maybe you could raise ten?'

'Bravo, Ez,' said Chuck.

'Gosh!' exclaimed the sly earl. 'What went wrong?'

It seemed a good moment to summon the Moet et Chandon '53 which had, by arrangement, been cooling its heels in a House of Lords refrigerator.

'My!' said the sly earl as he sipped the pinkish-amber liquid. 'We've nothing like this in our cellars. I must admit your lot knows how to live. Where did you get it?'

'It's important to have a *provincial* wine merchant. I often use Avery's of Bristol.'

Chuck did not bat an eyelid.

In the vestibule of the House of Lords, through which peers commonly made their entrance to the chamber, pausing to dismantle themselves of hats and coats – a hook for each peer – a ʝsately person handed Ezra a package which he clearly expected.

'Thank you. Why isn't there a hook marked Lord Sterling?'

'Because you never asked for one, my lord, and you never wear that.'

'Ah, they're for hats, are they?'

'Principally for hats, my lord.'

'You know, Chuck, this is a special place,' said Ezra, sorting out ahe package. 'After thirty years of married life, Audrey still offers the sugar in my coffee. I have never had sugar in my coffee. But mere they notice that I don't wear a hat. Can you lend me a fiver?' This induced the stately person to incline his head slightly.

The package contained a note from Mrs Winterbourne explaining the contents of the package: two identical letters to Mr Poll, one signed in Ezra's name by Mrs Winterbourne (she had become skilful at this minor art over the years) with his own distinctive pen, and the other blank; a packet of Lomotil tablets, which were not exactly as prescribed by Dr Xavier, but which the pharmacist had assured her should have a similar effect. Ezra swallowed two tablets immediately.

'I'm sure it's not protocol to crap in another fellow's embassy, eh, Chuck?'

The package also contained a note to the effect that the Israeli

Ambassador could not see him at such short notice, but he was expected by the First Secretary at a quarter to three.

'My God, we're late. Can you send this next door, or whatever we call it?' He handed the stately person the letter for Poll.

'Ez, are you sure you should be doing all this? Can't we come another time?'

'Don't desert me now, dear boy.'

'You know I won't, but . . .'

'I'll sleep in the car on the way back.'

'Promise?' said Chuck when they were seated.

'Scout's honour. What d'you make of my noble colleague, by the way?'

'The sly earl, you call him. He's a great guy. Adores you.'

'Oh, he's a Jew-lover and a Zionist too. Always has been, him and the Duke of Devonshire. They don't understand the difference, bless 'em. Did he say anything about my aerial? I forgot to ask.'

'Ez, I should ease up about that aerial. You see . . .'

'Ease up!' Ezra turned on his companion. 'Why?'

Trying to calm Ezra, thought Chuck, was like suggesting to a man who was drunk that he was drunk; he just came on stronger.

'Well, apparently your friend has discovered that in the case of a new construction, an apartment building or a hotel, there is less of a problem, but . . .'

'Oh, I know that. Of course it costs money, but money's nothing compared to the cost of ugliness. Have you thought of what we are leaving for our great-grandchildren to contemplate? Haven't you heard of the word "ecology"? A few years ago you had to look it up in a dictionary, now any secondary-modern schoolchild can give you a lecture on it. All those greedy pylons carrying cheap current to all those greedy washing machines will be chopped down and put underground, you'll see, and the people who put 'em up will be disinterred and shot!'

Ezra smiled happily and slapped Chuck's thigh.

'Is that your next speech?'

'No, oh dear . . . My next speech will be made quietly. "C" in "h", as my father used to say – cap in hand. I want them to send my grandson on compassionate leave to England, Chuck.'

'Well, a man in your position . . .'

'. . . Who hasn't exactly been a friend to the infant state . . .'

'You could always *become* a friend.'

'That is what I shall propose, if we ever get there,' he added staring at the unblinking red light at the junction of Prince's Gate and Knightsbridge.

Ezra's irritation at being late for an appointment was mollified by the rare and, for once, justifiable use of the car telephone – a present from Pye Communications – and, later by seeing what could only be a bodyguard outside the high iron fence of the Embassy garden in Palace Green, Kensington.

After some dialogue in, to Chuck, a very foreign language, the front door of the Embassy opened, revealing another, more formidable steel door. When this swung to, Chuck saw a pretty girl behind a bullet-proof glass wall opposite, and noticed a couple of hoods, one of whom toted a light machine-gun. All were smoking cigarettes.

A man in a less dark suit came out of an open door to their right.

'Ah, Lord Sterling I presume and, er . . .' He looked at Chuck politely. 'I'm sorry about the theatricals. They are, unfortunately, necessary, but they always remind me of being in a B movie.'

'I guess I'll wait in the car,' said Chuck.

Twenty minutes later Chuck saw another car draw up. It was a Jaguar with a Daimler-style bonnet. Chuck, an automobile buff, lamented the passing of distinct and elderly makes of car. This one bore a CD plate, but no other indication of ownership, though he was sure from the certain manner of its occupant that it was the Israeli Ambassador returning after a long lunch. Chuck could just see by straining forward and looking through the dense iron railings that the man and Ezra had met in the Embassy garden.

He helped Ezra, who looked exhausted, into the back seat and tucked him up in Audrey's old fur travelling rug.

'No deal, they wouldn't deal,' and he muttered something in Yiddish.

'Now be a good boy and go to sleep. Don't worry, you can't win 'em all.'

'Why not?' said Ezra. 'The fellow came from Leeds and his father knew my father. But it didn't help,' he added, shutting his eyes.

'What did the old man want?' asked the Ambassador as they watched the Rolls depart.

'He telephoned from his car to say that he would be seven minutes late, and he *was* seven minutes late.'

'Seven English minutes,' said the Ambassador.

'He wanted us to sell him his grandson. He offered two million. . . .'

'So? English pounds?'

'Sterling, naturally.' The First Secretary smiled. 'I tried to explain. . . . The boy's doing his military service. I didn't actually say we weren't in the kidnapping business, but . . .'

'For two million pounds?' The Ambassador threw up his hands. 'Look,' he said, 'write me an *aide-mémoire*, it sounds interesting. I'll send it to Abba Eban, rather his cup of tea, don't you think?'

His inferior had nodded; he supposed that, *sui generis*, ambassadors were more worldly than first secretaries. The assignment was not to his taste, and he stared at the blank sheet of paper. He could not even think of a heading.

He reached for his diary (courtesy of the Israel Citrus Board) and wrote in English, 'Tishri, eve of Fast of Gedaliah' – that excellent leader of men, murdered in error by some exuberant Jews a long time ago, his memory honoured by a fast which few must keep. Was there a parable? Would he be responsible for breaking Lord Sterling's heart, which had recently been attacked from some other quarter, and sending him – an excellent leader of men – to an earlier grave? Unlikely, but now he had the last sentence of the report: 'Finally, if this unusual proposition be considered' (he was sure the Foreign Minister would notice the subjective) 'worthy of advancement, the next step should be taken with all due dispatch since, in my view, Lord Sterling – may he live for a hundred and twenty years! – will not.' The First Secretary laid down his pencil with satisfaction; if his career had, earlier, taken a different twist (a better degree, perhaps) he could have been writing this memorandum in the British Foreign Office.

Under the heading 'Appreciation' the First Secretary inscribed,

Ezra, 1st Viscount Sterling, rich, pillar Anglo-Jewish Socy, historically anti-Zionist (perhaps really just indifferent but

N.B. hung-up over death of son in Israel just before war independence). Another N.B. obviously, hints of a father–son relationship of Dostoyevskian intensity. Still in control (he maintains, no doubt correctly) of Sterling Industries, which supplies software and components, and he is certainly in control, through trusts, of a considerable block of Sterling shares. Quote from Lord Sterling, 'Though the supply of arms to foreign countries is carefully monitored by the Ministry of Defence here, it cannot be to the disadvantage of the State of Israel if shares in a small but vital enterprise like Sterlings were held by someone friendly to her needs, my grandson for instance.' Unquote. Yes, but query reaction Defence, Ministry of, British, to dealing with a company with such connections. The grandson is entitled to British nationality which he takes up, along with his inheritance. . . .

Tickety boo. It was all too damn neat.

And then Lord Sterling had started talking about his 'line'. Hell, there were six million corpses out there, across the Channel, without 'lines'. Angrily, the First Secretary stabbed at the paper with his pencil and broke the lead. Temper, temper – time for his second after-lunch cigarette, the eighteenth of the day.

'To sum up,' the Israeli Government undertakes to supply, deliver but not to return one citizen – yes, the boy was eighteen – Niki Steimatsky, of Kibbutz Kfar Hanassi but currently undergoing military service on a Nahal. (Where?) In this event Lord Sterling would transfer two million pounds of Sterling stock to an agency appointed by the Israeli Government. Lord Sterling had accepted the dismissal of his first suggestion – that the money should be given to the boy's kibbutz – as creating an impossible and unacceptable distortion of what the First Secretary chose to call their *train de vie*. The First Secretary had suggested the Technion in Haifa as an appropriate beneficiary. He had also hinted that the boy, who was obviously a dedicated kibbutznik – a volunteer and all that – might not approve the transaction, even if he had been adequately provided for elsewhere. 'There are still some idealists left, Lord Sterling.' This had so distressed the old gentleman that he had fumbled in the pocket of his curiously unmatching trousers and produced a pill. To often his remark the First Secretary had explained that often in their twentieth year, on completion of their military service, the kibbutz wou d send their prize kids round the world. He was sure Niki would qualify and come to England in a couple of years' time . . . or why didn't Lord Sterling visit Israel? Arrangements would be made . . . compassionate leave . . . to anywhere inside the country. Unless there's a . . .

'Exactly, unless,' he had been interrupted. 'I haven't two years to wait, and nor I fear, has Israel.' Those had been Lord Sterling's final words which had given him *his* final words for the report.

The proposition was unthinkable; the problem was to avoid presenting it as an ugly fairy tale.

1967

◦●◦

Jumping was beautiful. First, when the plane had gone there was that silence which was beautiful, and then, as the body fell, the spirit soared and knew that the earth was beautiful and worth inheriting. It must be wonderful to be an astronaut and see the world looking like a globe in a classroom, with Israel marked in green, tiny and touching. 'We must defend this land,' he hummed.

Today should have been his eighth jump, but instead of flying down over the Mediterranean, they were stuck in this citrus grove on the edge of an aerodrome, where all morning planes had been taking off without them. The scene was like a nightmare picnic. The paratroopers had been there long enough for the makeshift latrines to smell, and for their mums and girlfriends to have turned up, despite official secrecy as to their location, outside the barbed wire with chocolate and biscuits and cigarettes, whose empty packets now added to the human detritus.

Niki had spent the morning trying to persuade his section to bury some rotten meat. The ground had been hard and the meat stank; so did the paratroopers. His major had rigged up a shower for himself. That man would commit murder to get a shower.

Day after day, since mobilization, there had been rumours of war, and now that it had begun they had been left behind. To do what? To protect Jerusalem? It was ridiculous; paratroopers were not designed for civil defence, or for burying rotten meat. Besides, Hussein would never dare attack; everyone knew there'd been a deal.

At 14.30 hours, when told their orders, Motta took off his para-trooper's belt and threw it angrily on the ground. 'When are they going to stop *daffka*ing us?'

He kicked his defenceless water bottle, and looked at Niki. In the last year of their companionship at arms, Motta had allowed his envy to move from secret to open admiration.

'What's wrong with Jerusalem? At least the nights are cool, so they say,' replied Niki.

The warm crackling voice of Jack de Manio, like a log fire in the bedroom, woke up Ezra every morning at seven o'clock, the radio being set to switch on at that hour. He felt like millions of other listeners, that de Manio's blend of hopeful weariness, the implication of *surtout, pas de zèle*, the idiosyncratic emphasis on sub-headline items of news, was designed to tickle his consciousness into pleasurable anticipation of another day.

Ezra muttered his waking prayer – 'Blessed art thou who hast restored my soul to me' – which had acquired more force since Xavier had told him that an agreeable way for people in his condition to move on to the next world was by night, in their sleep. ('How do you know?' he had replied.)

'Blessed art thou, O Lord, who hast restored my soul to me, great is thy faithfulness,' repeated Ezra. Jack de Manio cleared his throat reassuringly, and announced that Israel was at war.

Ezra put his hand on his heart. Moving slowly, he got out of his bed – he now slept in his dressing room – and put on his dressing gown and slippers, taking care to move his body methodically in contrast to the erratic whirling of his mind. He opened the door into Audrey's room where the light was stronger. She was still asleep, a slight frown on her face, but otherwise serene and breathing easily. He noticed every detail of the bedroom, for the first time, like a stranger. It was, most people said, the most successful room in the house. Audrey had commissioned an eccentric and far from deferential young decorator, Christopher Gibbs, and had 'let him rip'. The colours had been taken from the Sterlings' Watteau, a severe and luminous *fête-champêtre* which was thought to have belonged to the Kaiser, and they were stronger than the muted beiges and mushroom pinks which featured in the boudoirs of the fashionably rich. Scarlet and green and gold, in damask and velvet and silk, almost scandalized the eye. As a gesture of 'spectacular restraint' in Gibbs's words, the Watteau itself was not illuminated, except by the painter. The Louis XV furniture had been freshly gilded and caught the coruscating sunlight, which as Ezra stood in silent admiration, had begun to spin off the chandelier, specially designed for the room, in Murano, Venice.

Ezra had impressed on the dogmatic young decorator that the Venetians had been taught their craft by Jewish glassblowers, refugees from Tyre in the first century.

And now the Jews were to be expelled again, from their native land, so painfully restored to them.

Ezra walked to Audrey's bedside and pressed a button. A curtain slid back with a whirr; it was not the one he intended to open but it woke her up.

'What are you doing? Are you all right? What time is it?'

'It's seven o'clock, my love, and all's not well with the world. There's a war in Israel.'

'Oh dear, well, what can we do?'

'In the face of eternity . . . we should all do something.'

'Look, Ezra,' said Audrey, suddenly awake, 'it's seven o'clock and far too early to be thinking about eternity. The servants won't even be up. Why don't you go back to bed and see what Jack de Manio has to say at eight o'clock – maybe you got it wrong?'

Ezra considered this. 'Where's David?'

'The Blackers all went back last night; today's Monday, remember? So go back to bed. There's nothing you can do for an hour.' She patted his hand. 'There's a good boy.' She turned over and firmly shut her eyes, leaving Ezra no choice but to obey.

However, when the bedroom door had clicked timidly to, Audrey sat bolt upright, her eyes wide open, if only to blot out a vision of appalling and appealing intensity. The girl, heavily pregnant, who had just swept her ring into the steaming washtub and was thumping savagely with a wooden paddle, had lost her defiant sulky silence, and crept towards the door to watch Audrey leave the kibbutz with her British military escort. And when she thought the car was out of sight she had brought out a handkerchief and waved.

No situation, however dramatic or painful, required of Audrey that she should look her worst; so she went into her bathroom, cleansed her face, Chaneled her bosom and neck, let down and brushed her hair, and chose her most elaborate peignoir in order to visit her husband.

Ezra, she could just see, was fiddling with his wireless. She sat on his bed, held one of his hands in one of hers, and with the other turned off the radio and pressed the button which controlled, here too, the opening of the curtains.

'What a vision!' said Ezra. 'And what a lovely perfume, sorry, scent.'

'Ezra, I've been thinking, about what you said . . . about eternity.'

'I thought we had to wait till eight o'clock.'

'And I've decided you're right. We have to do something – all of us. But there's one thing I want to tell you. I'm not a politician and I don't know about tanks and bombers, but I do know about people. Call it a woman's instinct but there was something about that girl.'

'What girl?'

'Nicky's wife, your daughter-in-law.'

'Funny, I don't see myself with a daughter-in-law.'

'Exactly, but I've seen her and I tell you she's a survivor in a way Nicky never was.'

'Nicky?'

'Oh, Ezra, don't you see? Nicky was too beautiful, too strange, too mad to live long. He was doomed,' she said angrily. 'But that girl . . .'

'That girl what?' said Ezra, and he reached for the radio.

'No, Ezra.' Audrey removed his hand. 'Listen to me. Just this once, listen to me. Get the family down here, the whole bloody tribe, and tell them to bring their cheque books.' Audrey stood up and faced him, her eyes blazing, her hands on her hips, like a fishwife.

'Woman, spoken like a man!'

(Wherefore this sudden rage? A gush of maternal instinct, suddenly unplugged? Love turning inside out, into a Sephardic grudge against his family?)

'No,' said Audrey quietly, 'let's say spoken like Ezra Sterling.' She sat down again on the bed and kissed him; she was herself again,

'You don't think they'll say we've become Zionists, do you?'

'*They* need never know. I'm not going to those ghastly dinners at the Dorchester.'

'So no one will know and no one will love us, not even that girl?'

'Ezra, I don't think you understand. To the second and third generation of the Sterling family in Israel, you and I are the enemy. We're British to them. We let them down over Suez. We ruined the cotton crop, we paid for the Jordanian army – as a woman I can understand.'

'I hope my grandson will have a more enlightened . . .'

'I doubt if our grandson is any different from any other young Israeli. But that doesn't stop us doing our duty, Ezra. Shall you ring up Mrs Winterbourne, or shall I?' She stood up.

'I will. They can come here tomorrow. You'd better arrange lunch,' said Ezra. 'They must be fed.'

'My God. And I don't have any food.' She smote her forehead. 'Ashworth can go to Mount Street and get a joint, and little Oscar can carve. How many of us are there?'

'What, in the family? Thirteen, and the two of us, fifteen, that is counting Chaimy, and not counting Jeremy.'

'How's that?'

'I can remember the trusts. Which reminds me, we'll have to get Wilson, he's on all of them. So that'll be sixteen. Goodness me, you've quite cheered me up. And don't forget, Chaimy's kosher. . . .'

Audrey groaned. 'Oh, can't I?'

'No, you can give him a smoked salmon salad,' said Ezra, switching on the wireless.

All this catering, as her niece Lucy called it, would be worth the trouble if Ezra were really jolted out of his recent melancholy. His interest in the phenomena of nature, thought Audrey, was slight compared to his real passion, the manipulation of man. His sucesss with Poll had never been properly acknowledged since the scandal had fizzled out, as if, said Ezra, the prosecution had withdrawn the case against Dreyfus for lack of evidence. His failure with the Israeli Embassy was private and bitter. It had been a shock to him to discover that while money talked, not everybody listened. The same might apply to that damned television mast he was so proud of.

Ezra heard nothing new until one o'clock when the young Winston Churchill, recalling an interview with Ben Gurion the day the Egyptians closed the straits of Tiran, quoted the old man: 'For us military defeat means probably death for every single one of us!'

He then telephoned Mrs Winterbourne for the second time that day.

'Call Michael Sacher at Marks & Spencer and tell him to expect a hundred thousand pounds.'

'I have already done that, Lord Sterling.'

'I know. This is another hundred thousand pounds.'

'Ah . . . er, Lord Sterling?'

'Yes?'

'Mr Sacher thought you would like to know that he has received a similar telephone call from Lord Bearsted.'

'How delightful to keep such respectable company!'

'And I have contacted most of the family. The Blacker twins are flying in tonight from Geneva.'

'You're a good woman, Mrs Winterbourne.'

'Thank you, Lord Sterling.'

Niki lay flat on his stomach, his steel helmet grazing the crepe soles of the platoon commander's boots.

There had been only one casualty in their section. The Arab Legion's twenty-five pounders, which had opened fire against all expectation, had done little harm to Jerusalem's stone walls, but a piece of shrapnel had hit Reuben in the stomach as they slunk through the dusk down Zaharia Street.

He had screamed, 'Medic, medic, I'm hit. Help me, help me.' It was horrible. Nobody can be brave when they're hit there. The medic had given him a morphine shot and bandaged him up, but they'd had to leave him behind in the doorway of a travel agency. Another man had been ripped to pieces by the spinning wheel of his overturned and out of control jeep, but it wasn't anyone Niki knew. He hoped nothing like that would happen to him – an arm or a leg, maybe, but nothing like that.

Fighting was different at night. You soon heard the difference between the sound of mortars, bazookas, grenades, light and heavy machine-guns, and the curious rumble of the bangladore, the pipelike contraption they needed so badly, which the sappers used to blow up barbed wire. That was the hitch now, apparently. They couldn't get the fuse to take. A brilliant explosion silhouetted the police station, the new flats opposite with so many window frames intact, and the waste land where the Arab Legion had so far not spotted them. It also lit up the sappers, calmly snipping the barbed wire as if cutting out decorations for a party. Then the bangladore detonated and after a second or two the platoon commander flashed the green light of his torch to either side of the scorched path to show up the white lines.

He stood up, grotesque with his blackened face and camouflage. 'Follow me!' he shouted.

The paratroopers obeyed their officer. Niki and Motta and Itchko and Dov and Ami and Yigal and Shimshi and Zvi and the rest of them, all country boys, followed the young farmer towards the storm of noise and danger of the vincible police station, firing wildly and blindly into the shattered darkness.

Ezra's change, or rather acceleration, of plan had been announced over the lunch table to Audrey and Geoffrey.

'I think the old ones should come down tonight, before the others, for a spot of brainwashing.'

'Meaning?'

'So that the young – and I mean, I suppose, the Blacker twins – are presented with a *fait accompli*. It's going to be quite a heavy *finta*, as you Sephardim say, my love. D'you think Dr Xavier would allow me a tiny glass of Armagnac? If one calls it a *digestif* or a *pousse-café*, alcohol sounds innocent. The French have a way of domesticating their indulgences, wouldn't you agree, Geoffrey?'

Sometimes it's like listening to Hitler's table talk, thought Geoffrey, but he managed to say, 'And don't they all have liver trouble?'

'I might let you have a tiny glass of something if you explained what you mean,' said Audrey.

'Well,' said Ezra dreamily, 'there's you and me, Sarah and the Doctor, Sophie and Freddy . . .'

'Sophie! She's been dead for years!' Audrey exclaimed before she could stop herself.

'Oh, then that other woman . . .' He shut his eyes in concentration. 'Bossy, hairy legs, hard voice,' he mumbled. 'Joyce!' He snapped his fingers.

'How very unkind,' said Audrey mildly. 'Now look here, Lord Sterling. You're half asleep already and you're going to have your rest and you're certainly not having a *pousse-café*, whatever you call it. Geoffrey will take you upstairs and then he can go and get those two old biddies from the village to help in the house.'

'Mrs Hope and Mrs Groan, we call them, Ezra.'

'Do you? That's nice. And my emergency dinner party?'

'If the family will come at a few hours' notice – of course I'll arrange it,' said Audrey.

'They'll all come. They'll want to be in on the death,' said Ezra.

Since Chuck was around Turners and Ezra's person so much these days, the fact, once obscure, that she, Tattie, bored him, Ezra, was spelt out. Gaining one's heart's desire did not guarantee happiness. She saw less of her husband than of the man she used to keep; nevertheless, the honorific of Mrs Lambkin, even on the lips of servants, supplied her constant patty-cakes of pleasure. And now Ezra had promised to play cards with her, alone. If it took a war in Israel to achieve that, it was worthwhile. Oh dear, they were off again. Freddy was pontificating.

'I don't know how much Joyce and I can do, Ezra, but I would . . .'

'Don't worry,' muttered Ezra, loud enough to be heard, '*I* do.'

'. . . but I would think the United Nations signifies for Israel more even than this family.'

'Yes,' began Joyce eagerly and in support. 'General Odd Bull . . .' and she was stupefied when everybody, including Pettit and the lumpy Irish boy who was going round with the vegetables, tumbled into laughter.

How childish they are, thought Freddy, and ignorant. It wasn't funny at all.

Tattie had just dealt when someone turned on the ten o'clock news. Ezra didn't even pick up his cards.

'Less than fifteen hours after fighting began, Israel has already won the war,' said a very neutral voice.

'What's that?' snapped Ezra, swivelling in his chair.

'Ezra! Shhh!' said Audrey.

'. . . no more a fighting factor. It's the most instant victory the modern world has ever seen.' There was a pause. 'This report from Michael Elkins, our correspondent in Jerusalem, remains un-confirmed.'

'I'm not surprised, are you, Chuck?' asked Ezra. A large tear rolled down Tattie's cheek and fell on to the empty Asprey's scorer.

'Like I told you, Ezra, that went out *live* to the States, hours ago.'

'You told me?'

'Yes, Michael Elkins, live on CBS! I called Victor in Washington and he'd heard it. Look, Ezra, you've got to do something about the Beeb. It's crazy to have news in the hands of a Government monopoly.'

Ezra sniffed. In his world, the BBC was in a category of in-stitutions which it was sensible *not* to attack, like the Pope and the trade unions – besides the BBC was a good and prestigious customer of the business. But any discussion was stopped by the sound of Tattie crying.

'Oh, honey . . .' Chuck rose to comfort her. 'Don't worry, it'll be all right. C'mon, let me take you to bed. You're tired.'

When Chuck had led her out of the room, Freddy spoke up: 'Poor thing, I never knew she cared so much.' He cast his eye round the room. 'Look, Mr President, sir, I have a motion . . .'

'Seconded, Mr Chairman,' said Ezra, smiling as he rose to his feet. 'What is it?'

'That in view of the absence of information, especially in the area of world opinion, for however much you laugh at the United Nations, it surely is the forum of public opinion that . . .'

'For the love of God, Freddy, is this sentence ever going to end?' demanded Audrey.

'. . . we get David to telex the agencies. Didn't we know about Suez before the Foreign Office?'

'Good idea,' said Ezra. 'Do it.'

'Do you have a night operator?' asked Geoffrey, the policeman.

'I don't know, Geoffrey, but that, as Ezra would say, is David's problem.'

The grenade, exploding in the courtyard, had cut a swathe through the flowers, about the height of his waist. Niki was momentarily aghast at the damage he had done to such a rare and pretty place until he saw the Jordanian soldier fall on his face from behind a pillar. He finished him off with a burst from his Uzzi. There was no feeling, no repugnance left. He had killed too many in the night, some so near that he could have punched them in the head. Once you realized it was them or you, it came easy. There was a silence in the garden of what must be a hotel, so the soldier must have been alone. Typical. The paratroopers would never do that, leave a man by himself.

Niki beckoned to Motta and Zvi to come forward. 'Dump that fellow somewhere out of sight, will you. I'll cover for you but I don't think there's anyone at home.'

They looked at him in wonder and mute protest. He was their commander, but what the hell was the point in . . . ?

'Look,' said Niki, 'it's a nice hotel and it's ours now, isn't it? We're going to come here for a weekend leave. Now you wouldn't want to come down to breakfast and trip over a dead Jordanian, would you?'

They both smiled. Laughing used up energy. But he was right, it was a beautiful place. The man-made fog revealed by the dawn, an hour or so ago, that pall of dust and grit, the product of too many explosions, had not climbed up to the American Colony Hotel.

The paratroopers stiffened as they heard a new sound.

'Mirages,' said Zvi knowledgeably.

'Mystères,' said Motta, not to be outdone.

'Both,' said Niki. 'And if you listen, not much flak. Now come on, let's get going.'

The platoon's task was to clear and search every building on either side of the Nablus road, moving towards the south wall of the Old City. It was a polishing-up operation. There would not be much opposition in the area of the American Colony itself any more.

Diagonally across from the American Colony Hotel (for such it was – they had not noticed the sign), the next building to be searched and cleared was long and low, obviously the house of some rich Arab. There was a gate into a narrow garden, drooping with vines and unripe grapes, leading to a heavily barred front door. Niki didn't see the point of laying a fuse and blowing open the door, so he told the others to enter by the back door. Soon, amongst the crush and roar of more sophisticated breakages, Niki detected the crash and tinkle of a kitchen door being broken in, as if the house-holder had forgotten his key. Then the front door was unbolted from the inside and Motta said in parody of a parlourmaid as seen on British television, 'Coffee or tea, sir?'

'You nut,' said Niki. 'Don't you know there's a war on?'

'Oh, come on, always time for a nice cup of tea, we British say. Itchko's found a stove which works '

'Right, but quick.'

Motta trotted down the corridor and left Niki in the gloomy hall which he could now see was lined with encyclopaedias and tables with silver framed photographs. He picked one up, of a boy about Bar Mitzvah age, looking rather Jewish.

The war seemed momentarily shut away and the only sound in the house was the drip of water from the leaking cistern. It was all that could be heard between the gunfire; there can't have been a cistern intact in Jerusalem. A shaft of light picked up something glittering in a display cabinet. Niki knelt down to look at it and, as he moved, knocked over a little table with his haversack. Oddly, the key was in the lock and opened easily. Inside was a set of six silver and enamel coffee spoons. Niki had never seen anything so pretty. A thread of translucent enamel of a different brilliant colour ran down each shaft and spilled into each tiny bowl. Printed in gold inside the lid of the leather case, in English, was, 'Mappin & Webb, Regent Street, London'. With trembling fingers Niki picked the precious things from the velvet grooves and put them in his pocket. He returned the case to the cabinet, locked it carefully and stood up.

Just in time. A jeep screamed to a halt outside the house and a bulky figure waving a pistol jumped out.

'Itchko, Motta, quick! It's the sergeant-major!'

The sergeant-major, a professional soldier, had an instinct for sniffing out dereliction. He glanced at their guilty faces.

'Right, you lot, where you been? You're behind the rest of the platoon. Come with me. And now you'll be ahead of them if we get through.'

They piled into the back of the jeep where a wireless set crackled. The jeep shot forward a few yards, then stopped at a fork in the road.

'No, not Nablus, we'll take Salah-ed-Din. The tanks have been this way and it'll take us to the Rock.'

'What rock, Sergeant-major?' asked Motta boldly.

'The Rockefeller Museum, my lad, new Brigade headquarters, didn't you know?'

'Dere at last, a proper motor car – a Merc!'

'Don't you approve of the Rolls-Royces, McWhirter?' asked Pettit.

'I won't say dat, Mr Pettit, but too many of 'em does sort of stuff you up, if you know what I mean.'

'The family have always favoured Rolls-Royces, even before the war, I believe. His Lordship used to have three. Now, there's his,' he counted on his fingers, 'Miss Tattie, that's Mrs Lambkin, doesn't have her own, not that she couldn't if she wanted, Mr Oscar, two, and Mrs Sarah, three, and Mr David, four . . .'

The red light winked in the pantry indicating that the man in the Mercedes had rung the front doorbell.

'Go on then, lad, let him in. Don't stand there gossiping. I wonder who he is. He's never been down here before, that's for sure. Could be a bank manager or an undertaker. . . .'

Pettit tittered happily. What a morning it was going to be!

'Mr Wilson, milady,' announced McWhirter.

Mr Wilson bowed stiffly to Audrey, to Sarah and to Tattie, who had already sat down at the head of the table, not because she felt entitled to that position, but because the chair was large enough to accommodate her.

'Morning, gentlemen. I must say, though this is a melancholy occasion, seeing the family gathered here together is rather, er, splendid. Are your boys coming, Mr Blacker?'

David shrugged and looked at Lucy; so did the rest of the family.

'I went to wake them this morning myself, quite early; they'd slept in their beds, but they'd vanished!'

'Well, well, well. In any case, I have their documents if they should turn up. Valuations as at four o'clock Monday afternoon.' Briskly, he opened his briefcase and handed to each a heavy envelope. There was a silence as they received them. They looked at them as if they were unexploded bombs.

'Rather like school reports, wouldn't you say?' ventured Mr Wilson

The family, cheerful until this moment at the blood-letting planned for them, looked with displeasure at their leech.

'Say, Joyce, your friend is an unlucky son of a bitch.' Chuck, seemingly indifferent, was embedded in a newspaper.

'Who's that, Chuck?'

'It says here, in this paper,' Chuck turned to the front page, 'the *Daily Mail*, that among the aircraft destroyed by Israeli fighter-bombers at Amman yesterday was the private plane of General Odd Bull.'

The laughter was shared by those who had been in on the joke of the night before.

'He's a loser,' said Chuck, 'like poor Alger Hiss. A friend of mine had him to lunch and the dog ate his hat. . . .'

All this was most confusing and frivolous, thought Mr Wilson. Where was Ezra?

'Lord Sterling?' he asked Audrey.

'. . . Will be down in a moment,' she replied.

'Shall I go and check?' said the Brigadier.

'No, dear, he hasn't got the pox. You stay with yer wife and tell me how much all this is going to cost,' said Sarah.

A dining room is awkward for lounging, thought Audrey, but Ezra had wanted the seance to be formal, so she was grateful when Sarah sat down at the table as the eldest member of the family, and the others followed her example.

'I think Ezra wanted you to know,' began Audrey, a little shyly because she found pronouncements unbecoming, especially if they concerned money, 'that yesterday he sent two hundred thousand of his own, as it were, and that he's promised two million from his trust to the Embassy here. . . . But that, of course, will take time,' she concluded apologetically. 'Now, I really must go and get him,' and she hurried out of the room.

She almost collided with Chaimy.

'My God!' she said. 'Won't you take off your mackintosh . . . and your bicycle clips?' Audrey glanced crossly at the young Irishman who must have let him in. 'You don't mean you came all the way here like that? Chaimy, you're mad!'

'No, no, milady, took the 7.02 to High Wycombe, then a funny little track someone forgot to axe . . .'

'But the bicycle?'

'In the guard's van, why not?' Chaimy smiled. He did not explain, though it would be agreeable to confide in somebody, that for the first time he had lost his 'tail', it being difficult to follow someone on a bicycle, except on a bicycle.

'Come and let's get Ezra. He'll be delighted to see you,' and she took his arm.

Pettit was tying up Ezra's shoes. 'They don't fit, Pettit.'

'You said that didn't matter, my lord, today.'

'Ah, look who's here!'

'Hello, Uncle. You've got to do something about the gates. They don't work for bicycles. I had to cut . . .'

'They aren't designed for bicycles. You're the only person I know who rides a bicycle. And sometimes I'm not sure if I *do* know you.'

Chaimy blushed unhappily at this incomprehensible but clearly wounding remark.

'Still, you got here; that's the main thing,' Ezra said gently, as Chaimy and Audrey piloted him down the stairs. 'It doesn't matter how. . . .'

The noise of a light aircraft had suddenly grown to the unmistakeable clatter of a helicopter, now deafening, like a battalion of Hell's Angels. Ezra stopped halfway down the stairs and pulled a small black object out of his pocket.

'Hm, ten fifty-seven. Whoever that is, is on time.'

'Is it one of ours?' shouted little Oscar. The family had moved excitedly out of the dining room into the hall, curiosity having overcome discipline.

'Is that a digital timepiece, Uncle?'

'Yes, quite a useless breakthrough. Someone sent it from America. You need two hands to work it, and in the daylight you can't see the figures. Here, you keep it, but don't show it to little Oscar, he might go mad for it. Do you think that machine has anything to do with us? Let's all go and see . . . David?'

David Blacker nodded. It had to be the boys. Noisy, expensive and dramatic.

'Look, Ezra, everybody. I think it would be far more grown-up if we went back into the dining room and started our business,' said David firmly.

'As you wish,' said Ezra. It was a family tenet that in matters of *gravitas* the father's will was paramount. It was naughty of the twins to try and steal the show. The family scurried conspiratorially back to their places in the dining room where they found Tattie still presiding over the empty space.

'I hope they don't land on one of Ezra's greens,' hissed Lucy to her husband. 'Where do you suppose they got that thing?'

'Oh, you can hire them. . . .'

'Eighty-five quid an hour, I believe,' supplied the Brigadier. 'Quite a lot of the profession use them, invaluable in emergencies. Jolly good show,' he added defiantly, for the benefit of Joyce who had started up about 'conspicuous consumption' and matters relating.

'Right,' said Ezra. He tapped the table with his pencil, and the buzz of conversation petered out.

'Mr Wilson has given you your documents and I'd like him to explain the system we have operated, for your approval, and your action this day.'

'Thank you, Lord Sterling. Er . . .'

His speech dried on his hurriedly moistened lips, for the door opened and Pettit ushered in the twins and announced, somewhat unnecessarily, 'Mr Joshua and Mr Jericho, milady.'

At that moment only a firm jaw – like Sir Albert's, thought David – would not have dropped open in amazement. The twins were dressed as for a pre-1914 boar hunt. They wore calf-high boots, knickerbockers, Tyrolean jackets buttoned at the neck with leather frogging at the sleeves. Each slim waist was emphasized by a broad black leather belt, supporting a holster from which peeped the butt of a pistol. The effect was splendid, or ridiculous, depending on one's point of view.

Joshua and Jericho acknowledged the company with a slight movement of the head and then, as if rehearsed, marched to Audrey, kissed her on the cheek, and then paid their compliments, solemn, unsmiling and efficient to their great-uncle, to their grandmother, to their grandfather, their great-aunt, their mother, their father, their cousins, kissing each in turn. Very Jewish, thought Mr Wilson, whose share of the courtesies had been limited to a stiff little Germanic bow.

The performance over, the twins sat down demurely, like brides-maids, hands folded and eyes lowered, but as the last chime of eleven died away, they sneaked a look at each other and smiled.

'That clock's slow,' said Ezra.

'Where did you get those guns?' demanded Lucy, not looking up from her ubiquitous crochet.

'We nicked them from Le Rosey. Colt thirty-eights. With all that money you pay for our education, we thought it would be nice to have something to show for it,' said Jericho.

'And what are you doing with that helicopter?'

'Well, it was the only way we could fit everything in, wasn't it, Joshy? We've got this plane to catch at Blackbushe, which we're taking to Israel, it's Lyki's – he lent it to us.'

'Really? What's your route?' asked the Brigadier, leaning forward with interest and ignoring the hard looks he received from this intervention.

'Le Bourget, Nice, Bologna, Lecce, Corfu, Athens ... Lod, Grandpa,' said Joshua obediently.

'Ah,' said the Brigadier, satisfied. He enjoyed logistics.

'And if we could possibly ... er, do the necessary – that thing's ticking up outside. Then we'll be out of your way,' said Joshua apologetically.

Mr Wilson glanced at Ezra. Ezra nodded. Wilson walked round the table to where the boys were sitting and smoothed out the papers. There was a cheque pinned to the top of them.

'If you would, gentlemen, here, here and here.' Of course the twins had no pens. When these were produced, Joshua looked across the table at David Blacker, whose eyes were shut, as if nursing a toothache.

'S'all right, is it, Father?'

David opened his eyes and contemplated his son.

'Yes, Joshy, it's all right.' He shut his eyes again.

The boys signed three times. They stood up and made as if to leave when Oscar cried out:

'You've just time to hear this, boys. This'll take the sting away for you. It's a cable addressed to "the family", just that, and they gave it to me this morning at the business as I was leaving. It's from your great-great-uncle in Miami. Can I read it?' The laughter had already begun.

'It reads: "Deeply concerned Israel stop have personally donated JPA dollar sign figures one hundred stop suggest family does similar stop signed Ephraim J. Steimatsky." How about that?' asked Oscar amid the general applause.

'Come here, Joshua. Come here, Jericho. Let me bless you, then you can be on your way.'

For a moment Audrey thought Ezra was about to dredge up some half-remembered Hebrew prayer, but all he did was pat them cheerfully on the head and say, 'Bless you, boys, and now be off!'

On the way out, Joshua paused for a second behind his father's chair to lay his hand on his father's shoulder and kiss him briefly on the cheek. David stretched out his open hand and closed it slowly; the boys had gone. Nobody noticed that their grandfather was in tears.

'Israel is in safe hands, apparently,' said Ezra.

'As long as they don't get there,' said David, 'the silly sods.' He blew his nose and rearranged the papers in front of him.

'So, Mr Deputy Chairman, have you some reports?' said Ezra, breaking the silence.

'Yes, Mr President, I have,' said David. 'When the Chairman telephoned me I sent requests for information to the agencies. Incidentally,' said David, looking at Freddy, 'you don't need me to do that; the telex is now manned, or to be precise, womanned twenty-four hours a day, because we can't expect the world to keep our time.' He smiled to himself; it was one of his slogans. 'Well, thousands of dollars later, we get all this.' He waved a wad of print-outs in the air. 'The fellows really went to town. The longest is from São Paulo, but I'm afraid I can't understand it because it's in Portuguese, and we couldn't get a translation.'

'Where's São . . .' began Sarah, but the helicopter had started its engine.

'Where's São Paulo?' asked Sarah again, moments later when the ash from her cigarette had fallen on to the dining room table and the noise from the helicopter had subsided.

'It's in Brazil, Sarah. There are fifty-five thousand Jews in São Paulo and, you may be interested to know, three hundred and sixty thousand in Rio – nearly as many as in the whole of England. And every one of them rooting for Israel, apparently. That's the message. I won't bore you by reading them individually because they all say the same, that is: Don't take any notice of Government statements – and that goes especially for the United States, wouldn't you say, Chuck?'

'Yeah, yeah,' Chuck agreed vigorously.

'But the people of the western world, and that's all that matters . . .' – he glanced challengingly at Joyce, the family's representative for underdeveloped nations – 'want Israel to win, and believe she *will* win. So this time we're on the right side. I'm very happy about your decision, Ezra, I really am. There must be something in the air if those . . .' He gestured with his head in the direction of the departed helicopter. 'If those idiots . . .' he faltered.

'Thank you, David, you did well.'

'There's one more thing, Ezra,' said David, blowing his nose again on a handkerchief. 'The best reaction of all was from René, René Shalom, who called me this morning from Paris.'

'Good old René,' said Sarah.

'You know he lives near the Champs-Elysées? Well, he rang up and held the telephone outside on his balcony. . . . Of course I couldn't hear a thing, but apparently what's happening in Paris is that even the right wing, which was always what René calls "anti-*cinématique*", has gone wildly pro-Israel. The people who used to shout "*Algérie française*", and honk their horns are shouting," *Israel vaincra*" to the same tune.'

'What tune?' asked Sarah.

'Oh, you know, Sarah. *Al-gé-rie fran-çaise! Is-ra-el vain-cra.*' David picked up his wad of papers to beat the tune.

'*Is-ra-el vain-cra!*' shouted little Oscar.

'*Is-ra-el vain-cra!*' murmured Tattie doubtfully.

'*Is-ra-el vain-cra!*' said an American voice firmly.

'*Is-ra-el vain-cra!*' said Ezra. 'All together now. IS-RA-EL VAIN-CRA!'

They all came together now, even Joyce and Mr Wilson joined the chorus, which grew louder and louder.

(McWhirter, whom Pettit had allowed to witness the departure of the helicopter, hurried past the dining room window and was amazed to see his employer conducting a sort of devil's mass. 'What the hell's goin' on in dere, Mr Pettit, d'yer think?' 'It's a sort of Hebrew war chant, my boy, Israel – er, something or other.)

Still they went on. Ezra stood up, turning round and holding on to the back of his chair to support himself. He looked out of the diningroom window towards the stables, and beyond to the spinney of fir trees on the rise behind them. He held up both his hands high above his head, whether in despair, joy, or as a blessing, no one immediately knew, because when he turned to face the family for the last time, his heart had stopped.

2

'Start with this – it must be from the wires.' Except in times of war, the intelligence major worked on the foreign news desk of the evening paper, *Ma'ariv*.

The intelligence captain, an Arabist who normally employed his time on his thesis on the Palestinian cotton trade in the eighteenth century, stopped reading a report on captured Syrian tanks at the interesting point where, whatever else they carried, chocolate and Eau de Cologne appeared to be standard equipment.

'Stop News,' he read. 'Died suddenly at his Oxfordshire home first Viscount Sterling, founder and president of Sterling Industries, British electronic giant. Stop. Heir is grandson, presently studying in Israel.' Underneath the message, which was a photostat with a hole torn in the middle where it had been stapled to another piece of paper, was written, 'Get him,' and besides that a tick, and a squiggled initial.

'So?'

'Now this,' said the major. 'Read it.'

The second piece of paper, similarly holed in its centre, was an original Israeli Foreign Office memorandum.

'The Minister stresses,' he read, 'that the grandson is of military age. It is essential for the security of the State that if he is in a combat unit he should be removed to a place of safety.'

'A place of safety? In *this* country?'

'Go on,' said the major.

'Attached is an *aide-memoire* from the London Embassy, for background information. Obviously no action was taken at the time, but the Minister feels that the death of Lord Sterling puts the position of their heir into sharper perspective.' Blah, blah, blah, thought the captain. He read on. 'Unfortunately, there is no reference to his second name or his kibbutz. All we know is that his first name is Nicholas or Niki, that his father, killed in the War of Independence, was called Steimatsky, and that the kibbutz is in Upper Galilee. Intelligence might help?' He finished reading.

'Intelligence might help . . . why can't they do their own dirty work?

'Any problem they can't solve they hand over to Intelligence, and any problem I can't solve . . .'

'. . . You give to me.'

'You could begin by asking the Federation for a list of kibbutzim in Upper Galilee with English connections, founded before '48. That'll narrow it down.'

'I know nothing about kibbutzim,' said the captain, 'but already I can think of three which qualify - Kfar Blum, Ayelet Hashachar, Kfar Hanassi.'

'Bravo,' said the major. 'You're halfway there. Get them on the telephone. You know the telephones only work in this country during a war.' He walked away.

The captain followed him. 'In the middle of the night? And, supposing I need transport?'

'You can have my car.'

Hell, thought the captain, he must think it's important.

More Americans had been killed by falling drunk out of their jeeps than by enemy action throughout the whole of the Second World War. Niki wondered who had told him that. It sounded like one of Motta's statements. Certainly, though Israeli soldiers were rarely drunk, there were accidents. Poor fearless hand-to-hand Itchko, E. One tank had taken the wrong road and was stuck rigid in a street not designed for the circulation of tanks. Another had overturned, and in trying to rescue the crew now Itchko, the bravest of the brave, who had been seen bashing a Legionnaire in the face with the butt of his machine-gun when his ammunition had run out, had been taken away by the medics, with a sprained ankle. He had cried louder than the paratroopers with no legs - out of shame. They had been forced back by ferocious enemy fire to leave the crew under their tank, just a few hundred metres from the Old City walls, and there it had spent the night, with the crew, no doubt, under the tank.

Search, identify and destroy - that's what they'd been told in Basic, but it hadn't been like that at all. This battle had been confused, messy and maladroit on both sides, stopping and starting for no reason. Last night at eleven o'clock they had been able to sleep, to the rumour of the sighting of forty Patton tanks brought up by the Jordanian army. Now, in the morning, there was another rumour: the fighting had stopped and the tanks had vanished, but there was another rumour: that the paratroopers would not be allowed to take the Old City. Politics.

'I tell you, it's the United Nations. They're going to cheat us again. They did it to us in '56 and they're going to do it to us again.' Motta, who had spent most of his life in a comfortable suburb of Montreal, identified himself closely with the State of Israel. 'It's the old story. Bloody anti-Semites. You don't know what it's like to be the only Cohen in a school of five hundred kids.'

'Quite an honour, I should think,' said Niki, watching the dawn over the Old City. The sun was coming up like a rocket and he felt empty-headed and gay.

'Oh, you sabras have no understanding of anti-Semitism.'

'Only what I've read,' said Niki. He wondered if he should tell Motta about the spoons he had stolen. If he was going to die he wanted to appear before God with clean hands. After all, his father was buried here, on the Mount of Olives.

'Motta . . .'

'Hey, look. The Samal's telling them to take off their packs . . . we must be going in!'

There was a crackle over the tannoy and the clearing of an emotional throat.

'So now they make speeches?' said Motta.

The captain believed in the argument that there must be one intelligent being in every organization, and that until he (or she) is found it is vain to wrestle against the stupidity of the rest.

The duty night clerk in Records in the Israeli Defence Force building in Tel Aviv was their intelligent person. (He wondered how they managed by day). As the night wore on a warm relationship grew between them, over the telephone, so much that the captain hoped he would not be asked to spend a Friday night with the family. (Friendships which blossom in low gear should never be changed up.)

There were no likely Sterlings, or Stirlings, N., from kibbutzim in Upper Galilee serving on reserve, the night duty clerk informed him, but that wouldn't apply, would it, as the boy was in the middle of his military service. There were seventeen Steimatskys, five of them Naphtalis, but that was the closest he could get. On the next telephone call, he produced two theories, the first complicated and negative, the second which had – the captain kicked himself – been the major's in the first place.

Didn't the captain say that the boy's father had been killed in the War of Independence? Well, the widow, an attractive young woman . . . So, the boy might have his stepfather's name? (Huh.) On the other hand, the first name 'Niki' was not an Israeli first name, and surely sufficiently unusual for it to be worthwhile asking a few kibbutzim if they knew any eighteen-year-old Nikis. . . . And, by the way, how was the rest of the war going? History is being made on other fronts, did the captain know in which direction?

The captain did, but wanted the intelligent person off the line. The intelligent person reflected that the more you knew, the less you said.

'*Shalom*, is that the *mazkir*?'

'No, he's away. Didn't you know there's a war on?' Cross at being woken up, elderly.

'I'm trying to trace one of your members, Niki . . .' The captain hesitated, hoping the blank would be miraculously supplied, but there was only silence, followed by a wheeze.

'Who are you? I'm just here to take messages. I can't give out information in the middle of the night. I . . .' Another wheeze, and a muttered dialogue.

'This is Military Intelligence in Tel Aviv. Working on orders from the Prime Minister's office. I need to find . . .'

'Oh yes, and I'm Moshe Dayan,' interrupted the old man.

'He's called Niki and he's eighteen,' he shouted.

Urgent dialogue at the other end of the line in which the captain could discern a young girlish voice, followed by a scuffling noise.

'Wait a minute, my granddaughter . . .'

'Is he rather handsome with one eye darker than the other?' The telephone had obviously been snatched away from the old man by a very young girl who had been overhearing the conversation.

'Yes,' said the captain wildly.

'Well, he's not here. He's Nahal. He comes here on leave, sometimes. He's a paratrooper,' she added proudly, 'he and Itchko and Motta. . . .'

'What's his second name, my dear?' The captain prayed.

Silence. Then, 'Caspi. Niki Caspi.' Caspi, silvery, sterling, sterling silver! Yes! A nice, unobtrusive, not uncommon name to choose.

'Thank you, my dear. Do you remember their unit?' It would save time if she did; *she* was the intelligent one.

'Is there a sixty-sixth Battalion?'

'Yes, thank you. *Shalom* and bless you.'

He put down the telephone. The 66th was part of a brigade whose the casualties had been the heaviest of the – spectacularly bloodless, he understood – war, so far. He went happily into the next office.

'Right,' said the major. 'I'll send the brigade commander a signal asking for the boy to be withdrawn from the battle. He'll ignore it, having better things to do. You may not even get an answer. In the meantime, you stay here,' he pointed to the camp bed, 'and take over. I've got to organize tomorrow's press conference – or maybe,' he looked out of the window, 'it's today's.'

'What are you going to tell them?'

'Nothing; just to keep the smile off their faces.'

Niki kept his eyes on the sergeant's back as he followed him up the shuttered souk; with affection and respect because only a few hours ago he had lain down for the paratroopers as a bridge over some barbed wire.

One company had lost its major in the olive groves of what was once King David's city, but the fighting had been mild compared to the night before. The Legion had lost heart or maybe it had left the Old City; certainly the inaccuracy of the snipers (thank God) as they climbed up the bizarre, narrow passage, past the padlocked booths, smacked of the amateurish venom of a remnant. They had surrendered, hadn't they? On the Mount itself, that Gold Mosque was beautiful, but the Wailing Wall was a mess. It looked like a dried-out cesspit and he had been astonished at the behaviour of the paratroopers, *dovenning* and crying and kissing the dirty old blocks of worn stone, and each other. He never realized they were so religious and wondered if there was something missing in him. He rubbed his face where a blubbery and unshaven Motta had embraced him.

And the two rabbis squabbling over the microphone! And the R.S.M. arriving on the holiest spot in the holiest city in his jeep, and being shouted at by everybody!

The Jerusalem Brigade had captured Abu Tor, and the no-man's-land including the valley of Gehenna which lay between the Jaffa Gate and the King David Hotel. They greeted the paratroopers in the most flattering way, and since praise from other soldiers is rare, Niki began to feel like a hero. One of them was taking messages from the paratroopers which he promised to telephone that evening. He refused money.

'This is not a day for money,' he kept on crying.

But Niki had a cable he wanted to send to England. His stepfather had given him a l.100 Israeli bank note the day he left for the Army – an enormous sum for a kibbutz where money is not current – with the injunction not to spend it all at once, and not to ask where it came from. 'Please have it,' Niki said to the soldier. 'There's no day when you can't take a Herzl!' Parting with the money somehow eased the pain of the stolen silver spoons.

The man gazed solemnly at the note. 'All right,' he said. 'I'll give what's over to the mentally handicapped.' Everybody had thought that very funny.

The section had reached a square marked by handsome old buildings on two sides, and the walls of David's citadel which Niki had often seen in photographs. It looked smaller and crumblier than it should. White sheets hung on broomsticks from all the balconies as if for a ghost's holiday. It must be the Jaffa Gate, the west wall of the Old City. There were no signs of fighting; no signs of anybody. The sergeant looked doubtfully at the iron-clad door of what claimed to be a hotel. There was no point in blowing up what might become company headquarters.

He knocked politely on the door, which opened immediately. They saw an Arab in a well-cut English suit holding a boy of about six by the hand. The boy looked scared. He must have been fed stories about how Israeli soldiers killed their prisoners, thought Niki.

'Good morning, gentlemen,' said the man in the well-cut suit, in English. 'Can I help you?'

'Is there anybody else here, apart from you?' the sergeant asked in Hebrew.

The proprietor looked baffled. 'I'm afraid I can't speak Evrit.'

He's going to have to learn, thought the sergeant. He turned to Niki. 'Two of you search the building, send the runner to tell the major we have a billet, and get Motta to explain to this, er, gentleman,' he leant sarcastically on the word *'adonai'*, 'that if he can't fix up a shower for my commander his life won't be worth two *agarot*, Israeli.'

The little boy now looked very frightened and about to cry. Niki smiled at him.

'Chocolate?' he suggested to the little boy, whose lips were trembling.

The provision of a bath for the major became the main factor in the détente between the civilian and military population of the Petra Hotel. The proprietor quickly recovered his *esprit d'hôtelier* after the occupation of his establishment and reassured the sergeant that a shower could be provided from water he had been prudent enough to buy before hostilities at a cost of thirty pounds sterling. It was kept in a cistern built into the wall of the kitchen and access was through a small metal gate which was, of course padlocked. But he was sure he could find the key. Would Motta, his Canadian friend assigned him as interpreter, please explain to the sergeant that if the paratroopers slept in the hall outside the bedrooms in any quantity, the floor would subside under their weight. He did not wish to be shot as a saboteur. The building was a hundred years old and had been constructed round a courtyard, later roofed in, but not in a manner far-sighted enough to provide a safe dormitory for so many soldiers. So those paratroopers who were not packed four to a room were ordered to bed down in the corridors between the kitchen and dining room of the ground floor.

The intelligence captain, unused to disorder, either in war or peace, when he found company headquarters was dismayed at the scene.

'Have you a Niki C.?' he asked.

'Maybe,' said Motta, 'but he's asleep.' (What a little shrimp.)

'I have to see your commander,' said the intelligence officer firmly, and he hoped militarily, to the *tarash*.

'Then you'd better wait till he's had his shower. He'll be in a good mood then. What do you want with Niki? He's a buddy,' said Motta.

The captain nodded, slumped on to a stool, wiped his spectacles with his handkerchief solicitously and then his brow. But he said nothing. Motta was not surprised at the appearance of an intelligence officer in search of Niki; there had always been about his friend an air of suppressed significance, which he appeared to ignore and never exploited.

'Have you come from far, my friend?' asked the proprietor, leaning across the desk with a glass of arak.

'From Tel Aviv,' said the captain.

'And how is the war? The radio tells us nothing.'

'It depends whose side you are on, sir,' said the captain in English with a little smile.

Motta looked at him sharply. He looked very young to be a captain.

'Look, Captain, why don't you go and see the major? He's probably had his shower. I have to stay here.'

'Up the stairs and right at the end of the hall. He's in the corner room, with its own shower,' said the proprietor.

Two paratroopers guarded the major's quarters and the captain gave his note to the *rabat* who indicated that he should wait.

The major burst out of his room, naked and energetically towelling his head, and glared at the *Shabaknik*.

'What do you want him for? He's one of my best boys.'

'It's not my idea, Major, you'd better ask Abba Eban.'

'Hah,' sniffed the major. 'Politics.'

He examined the document, then the bearer. He was very young to be a captain. He sniffed again. Intelligence. Still, he might know something. 'Come and talk to me. There's no one to talk to around here. They're great lads but not a brain among them.' He tweaked one of his paratroopers by the ear. 'That so, Ami?' The major ushered the captain into the bedroom.

'Tell me, you come from the big wide world – you can sit on that bed – are the Great Powers going to intervene? There was a bad moment you know, last night, when we thought they wouldn't let us take the Old City. Mind you, I don't think anybody could have stopped us. Motta would have gone in by himself. And if he hadn't we'd have gone in without him!' He looked belligerently at the intelligence officer, querying his approval.

'Well, we did our best to delay the effect of world opinion, as it's called,' said the captain. 'We cut off General Odd Bull's telephone.'

'Yes? Bravo! I think I heard that . . .'

'Did you hear that he asked the Arabs to be moved to a place of safety –like the Old City?'

The major slapped his hairy thigh. 'That's good. Oh, I like that, that's good! Look,' he said, 'place of safety: that lad, you can take him if he'll go with you. Trouble is, they're rearing to get at the Syrians. They're a bloodthirsty lot, my boys.'

'Trouble is, Major, if I don't take him, my commander's bloodthirsty too. . . .'

'Right! Ami!' roared the major. 'Tell Niki C. I want him here, quick. You know the tall one with fair hair, he's a *rabat*.'

As he came into the room Niki saw the officer with the unfamiliar tab on his shirt. His hand went to his left pocket where he had the stolen silver spoons. Not possible, surely. How could they have found out?

'I want you to go with this officer to Tel Aviv.'

'But, Commander . . .'

'What?'

'My pack . . .'

'You won't need it. For reasons I do not understand, you're to be removed to a place of safety.'

'Why, Commander?' Niki looked doubtfully at the intelligence officer. He looked too young to be important, although his expression was solemn enough.

'Because . . . because . . . I don't know. He may tell you.'

The major put down his towel and studied the young man. He was, thank God, intact. But not all of them were. A place of safety indeed. He turned to the intelligence Captain.

'I say, you left it a bit late, didn't you?'

Niki was more bewildered than impressed by the *Shabaknik*, but his car was another matter. Except when hitching a lift he usually rode in trucks, tractors or buses. This was roomy and had a driver.

'Don't worry,' said the intelligence officer. 'It's not mine.' He was going on to say that he was not the VIP, but looking at the earnest face of the paratrooper decided on discretion.

The car honked through the smoke and the destruction and the two were silent until the plain which began at the monastery of Latrun.

'My father was killed somewhere around here.'

'Just before the War of Independence started?'

'Yes, how did you know?'

'Ah,' said the intelligence officer.

'I stole some spoons from an Arab house in the American Colony,' said Niki in a matter-of-fact voice, and felt much better. 'Do you think it matters?'

'Nothing matters very much, and most things don't matter at all,' said the captain.

Niki did not recognize the quotation.

'Would you like to look at them?'

'Of course.'

'Do you think they're very old . . . valuable?'

'They're very pretty,' said the captain, 'and it says on them,' he removed his spectacles, 'sterling silver. How apt.' He smiled.

'What's that?'

The captain had been to a summer school in Oxford. How little the paratrooper resembled an English lord.

'Never mind. Look, Niki, you'd better not ask me questions. I don't think I'm supposed to say anything, but I have to look after you, right?'

'Right,' said Niki.

'Tomorrow I have to interrogate prisoners of war. There are thousands of them. Do you know any Arabic?'

'A few swear words.'

'Fine, that'll do.'

3

'Lend me half a crown, will you, in case there's a chap in the pissoir. I've got no English money.'

'I dare say the Caprice has seen a dollar before now,' said David. 'But as you were my best man . . . here. Shall I get us a martini?'

'Oh yes, lovely big mean martinis,' said Jeremy.

'Where on earth were you?' asked, David when they had settled into his usual table in the far corner of the restaurant.

'I was doing a deal with a gallery in LA. Then I hired a car and drove along the coast to San Francisco where I got your cable. In fact, I very nearly didn't get your cable because they nearly didn't accept it, I was told. You're not allowed to send rude messages.'

'It wasn't very rude.'

' "Come back at once you idiot" – I call that fairly rude.'

'Sarah said, "Where's that bloody idiot Jeremy? He's always in the wrong place at the wrong time." And you were. Your office said you were in Corfu. . . .'

'I *was* in Corfu. Then I went to Rome, then direct to America.'

'The boys ended up in Corfu. I'm glad you missed them. You might have tried to get them out of jail.' David downed his martini.

'Jail? How come? Doesn't sound their style at all.'

'Look, Jeremy: a private plane lands on a Greek island just after a revolution. In it there are three young men, and a crate of Dom Perignon. Two of them – Joshua and Jericho – carry bloody great pistols, which they don't even bother to hide, and the third is a waiter from Annabel's.' David shrugged gleefully. 'Mark Birley rang me and said would I try to get my sons to return his waiter – as if they'd stolen a mustard pot.'

'Christ!' said Jeremy.

'Well, you do see that it's not the sort of carry-on likely to appeal to the colonels.'

'Yes, I do see. Where are they now, the boys?'

'In jail,' said David smugly. 'Shall we have another one of these?'

'Hell . . .' began Jeremy.

'It's not hell, Jeremy, and it's not heaven either. It's a jail for foreigners and it's full of American hippies who've been caught smuggling pot from Turkey. Apparently there's a very simple rule in Greece: one kilo – one year. Let's order shall we? I'm longing for *pommes croquettes.*'

'*Pommes croquettes* with everything,' muttered Jeremy.

'But, David,' he said, when the waiters eventually left ('We might as well have a long lunch and get drunk,' David had said, 'and you can pay for it. I'll tell you why later'), 'if you don't even try to get them out, the boys will never . . .'

'Of course I'm trying, you idiot, but it might take some time – during which, Jeremy,' he continued, 'your nephews might even learn the limits to the power of money. They really believe that you can buy anything and anybody. And they behave accordingly.'

'Yes,' said Jeremy. 'Poor Ferty.'

'You fell for that one, didn't you?'

Jeremy's mouth was full of smoked salmon, but he looked hurt and puzzled.

'Did you really think they'd use someone I talk to every night of my life – when I'm here, that is? Who'd tell me what they were up to? No, they just wanted to "suss out Daddy's money man", as they would say.'

'Oh,' said Jeremy, swallowing. 'Tell me why I've got to pay for the lunch. You know I haven't any money.'

'Later. By the way, you'd have a lot less if you hadn't missed the levy.'

'Levy?'

'Of course. That was the whole point, wasn't it? After the Lord's sudden miraculous conversion to Eretz Israel . . .' David broke off. 'Mind you,' he said, wagging his fork, 'not that I believe conversions happen like that. I bet that miserable fellow Saul had nagging little doubts long before the Damascus trip. You remember the decree about that TV documentary we all had to watch? Ezra had been changing his mind about Israel, helped by the fear of death, the continuity of his line, as he called it, and the fact that quite simply, after his heart attack, he had time to think.' He paused and looked thoughtful. 'I must say, with *entrecôte marchand de vin*, these spuds really come into their own.'

'Go on,' said Jeremy. 'You've got to remember all this is news to me; I've just come off the plane.'

'Right. So the war begins on Monday morning. Ezra decides to convene the elders of the tribe at Turners for dinner that night. The rest of us turn up the next morning. There was the whole shooting match, complete with Wilson and all the papers.'

'Papers?'

'Yes, you know, trusts, statements, even cheques. All we had to do was sign. There was no way of getting out of it. . . . Reach for the wine, will you, Jeremy? You can die of thirst in this place.'

'Then?'

David was silent.

'Then?' repeated Jeremy quietly.

David sighed. 'Then, for some reason, we started singing, chanting "*Is-ra-el vain-cra*" – louder and louder. It was a bit mad, and it was getting madder when Ezra stood up with both his hands raised, looked out of the diningroom window, and what he saw, or rather' – David leaned forward across the table, fixing Jeremy with his blue eyes – 'what he *didn't* see, killed him.' He looked at his plate.

'I knew he was going to collapse so I tried to stop him falling. . . . But he pushed me away, fiercely . . . and fell into Oscar's arms. And, Jeremy,' he glanced up again, 'I could see the bugger smiling through his tears.' David sat back in his chair, expectantly.

'Meaning, with that gesture . . . Very theatrical.'

'Exactly.' David drew his fingers across his throat. 'For me, the chop; for Oscar, the accolade, the blessing, the succession, the lot. His dying move – and it's even in the will.'

'I still don't understand what killed him.'

'Ah . . . nor did we. At the time. Then the Land Rover roars up to the house, out stumps Geoffrey Nickson in a terrible temper. He bursts into the room shouting that the aerial had been taken down by the County Council. He sees Ezra lying on the floor, with the Brigadier massaging his heart, and the poor fellow bursts into tears. It was all too much for him.' David neatly sliced a piece of steak, anointed it with sauce and potato and popped it in his mouth. 'Funnily enough, the goyim were much more affected than the family. Pettit – you know, the butler – blubbered around till Audrey sent him off to bed. Wilson shot off to London in his Mercedes, forgetting all his papers. Chaimy said the *Kaddish* in Hebrew and tore his only clean shirt, very properly. Audrey, dignified and queenly . . . as if she knew it was going to happen. Tattie . . .'

'And you?'

'Well, it wasn't my day, was it? Besides, you know the family – no shortage of officer-like qualities. The Brigadier got hold of an ambulance to take Ezra's body up to the flat. Oscar sent for that Indian doctor in case Audrey needed looking after – not that she did. He booked a rabbi for prayers that evening, and was even busy with the press. There was nothing left for me to do, Jeremy. Do you want anything more to eat? Or shall we just have coffee and too much of that Marc de Bourgogne'

'I haven't been so drunk,' said David slowly, 'since that lunch with Ezra and little Oscar at the black market restaurant in Half Moon Street. I remember thinking that it cost more than I earned in a month. I also remember thinking that I would never be poor again, and I thought I had won a passport to happiness. Now look where it's got me!'

'The rabbis say that if you marry a rich wife, you pay a high price,' said Jeremy sententiously.

'I suppose you think Lucy's cold and mean. . . .'

'Lucy *is* cold and mean,' said Jeremy indignantly.

'She's a good wife and a good housekeeper. She has tried with the twins and she lets me do what I want.'

Jeremy wondered what such an exemplary business executive did want which could be denied him by such an exemplary wife and, as if he had understood the question, David continued:

'Jointly, I suppose, we're a boring couple. Certainly Ezra thought so. He never really liked either of us. You see, he enjoyed bad behaviour, eccentricity of any kind, getting people out of scrapes. . . . He liked Oscar for getting into debt; Chaimy because of his bicycle, and bringing his own thermos of tea into the board room . . . that sort of thing. He even liked you. . . .'

'Perhaps he left me something?' suggested Jeremy frivolously.

'Oh, don't be an idiot. He said in his will that having done enough for the family in his lifetime he was sure no one of them would wish to benefit by his death. He left you nothing. He left none of us anything. Why should he? It had all been taken care of. Audrey all right. Turners goes to Niki and an enormous insurance policy pays most of the duty. And, here's a clever one . . . You know who I mean by the sly earl? Well, he gets five grand the day he presents the second Viscount Sterling in the House of Lords. How about that?'

'It'll never work. Bribes beyond the grave.'

Jeremy was ashamed that he felt so hurt at being left nothing.

'He left something to Arthur – old Sir Arthur Coleport; again, you see, a bit of guilt, plus pleasure in remembrances of things nasty . . .'

'Yes, but what's all this about my . . .'

'I'm coming to that. Every time I suggested we pay you out of your commission he just said, "Art for the Artless" and roared with laughter.'

Jeremy blushed. 'What commission?'

David put up a hand. 'And then he said, "Wait till he's down to his last hundred thousand."'

'I'm way below that, don't worry,' said Jeremy impatiently.

David hiccuped and started to clean his immaculate nails with a toothpick.

'Do you ever hear from an American called Jacob Goodchild or something?' he asked finally.

'Jake Goody, yes, every Christmas. Why?'

'I was looking in your file and he seemed to be the one who started it all. . . .'

'Started what?' asked Jeremy, his heart beginning to pound.

'Started this,' said David, handing him a cheque to which was pinned a compliments slip which he steadied himself to read first. 'Commission to June 1966,' it said, 'Mr J. Kind, Esq.' (Some illiterate girl clerk, but never mind.) Jeremy stood up and walked round to David's seat and kissed him.

'I like the thirteen shillings and fourpence,' he said, sitting down.

'And the thirty-eight thousand whatever?'

'I like that too . . . how did you pull it off?'

'It's yours, you idiot, you earned it. In fact, you could have sued us for it. That was Oscar's point. He's delighted. He sends you love, by the way. Everyone's pleased for you, Jeremy. Freddy was shocked that you hadn't had the commission, regularly like the other agents. Now that Ezra's gone, the business can't play games any more.'

'All from a few filing cabinets . . .'

'It began like that, and then your connection in the U.S. Navy moved on to higher things and now it's depth-finders – all based on radar, you see. You may not know it, but we make the best depth-finders, for light marine craft, in the world.'

'Do we?' said Jeremy, grinning.

'Much appreciated by the U.S. Navy. You're listed as the agent. You get the commission, till the cows come home – business policy, family business.' David twiddled the tulip glass with the amber liquid and raised it in a toast. 'Fear not, the struggle naught availeth,' he lisped. 'What are you going to do with it? Spend it on something silly?'

Jeremy had a vision.

'I shall make peace between the Arabs and the Jews,' he said unsteadily.

'That ith thilly.'

'What'll you do?'

'My struggle continues. That's all I can do, all I know and all I care for. Little Oscar thinks he's won, but he hasn't. I have the biggest shareholding now, in my pocket. Look at this.' He handed over a piece of paper. The cable was addressed to 'Blacker Sterling London' and the message read: '*Lachadnu Yerushalaim Shalom Niki.*'

'*Lachadnu* means "we have captured"; the rest you may be able to understand.'

'So? The second Viscount Sterling has captured Jerusalem. . . .'

'Yes,' said David, taking the cable from Jeremy and folding it carefully, 'but why does he tell *me*?'

Jeremy was about to suggest that the evidence might be precious but was little enough basis for a life's campaign, when he saw that David had signalled for the bill.

'I thought I was going to take you to lunch now,' said Jeremy angrily.

'What's the point? With you it comes out of net income, with me it goes straight to the Chancellor of the Exchequer. You're a legitimate expense, my boy, bringing in dollars to beleaguered Blighty. The fact that you didn't know what you were doing is neither here nor there.'

David signed the bill with the slimmest of slim gold pens, added a generous percentage, than an extra fiver from his wallet.

They were the last in the restaurant.

'Oh, and let's have one more for the road.'

He produced another fiver and waved towards the trolley of succulent bottles.

'In fact, you're obviously so good at it, I don't know why you shouldn't work with me.' He looked at Jeremy seriously. 'We'd have fun. Start a marine division. Have an experimental yacht – in the South of France? Oscar's benign these days, Jeremy. A benevolent king on the throne.'

'Now you're being silly, David. My American contact, as you called him, was just that – a little touch, an absurd piece of luck. . . .'

'We don't discount luck in business. . . .' murmured David.

'And I don't want to join your fraudulent system. You give me a marvellous lunch, and it costs you nothing. You make a lot of money from weapons of death . . .'

'We only make the little bits,' said David mildly.

'The whole so-called greatness of Ezra was based on death. . . .'

'Come on, Jeremy, you're talking like a lunatic. Just because you're a misfit, out of tune . . .'

'I don't want to know your tune. I don't want to sing your bloody song!' he shouted. 'And I don't want to go along with this family business business. Sarah bought me in 1940!'

'Shush, man, so I sold myself in 1948. So what?'

But Jeremy would not be shushed.

'Frankly, David,' he said in a quieter voice, 'I'd rather be my sort of failure than your sort of success. I know I'm no good, but at least I try. I consider my actions in the face of eternity.'

'And with a very red face, too, by the look of you, Jeremy. What rubbish you're talking. You can't ride the system and buck it at the same time. Give me back that thirty-eight thousand then.'

'No,' said Jeremy belligerently. 'Why shouldn't I try and make peace between the Jews and the Arabs? Israel is another nonsense. Do the people who produced Spinoza and Einstein and Freud and . . .'

'Karl Marx.'

'And Karl Marx, if you like, have to end up as another little nation, with its own army, and air force, and navy? Couldn't we have done something more original than that?'

David took a deep breath.

'Look, Jeremy, you're a dear, sweet, silly boy and we love you. But you don't understand the ways of the world. It's not consistent, it's not in black and white, and it sort of works. Take Chaimy, for instance. He says he's a pacifist, he says he's a Communist.'

'And?'

'And he's quite happy doing his sums, being followed by security men wherever he goes, and awaiting daily the coming of the Messiah.'

David pushed back his chair. 'In the meantime, I'm taking you home. You can sleep it off. I'll see you at the memorial service. In the circumstances, I think you should attend.'

Epilogue: 1967

°☺°

'Paddy, did I ever tell you about big Oscar and the immigration man?'croaked Sir Arthur.

'You did, and I wish you'd stop sniffling. We'll be at the Church or whatever soon enough.'

'Well, what did happene then?' asked Sir Arthur crossly.

'With the very first money that big Oscar earned when he came to this country,' intoned Patrick, 'he sent a five-pound note in a registered envelope to the immigration officer at Hull. Right?'

'Quite a lot of money in those days, m'boy.'

'Yes, and you always say that too.'

'I hope it teaches you the meaning of honour, Paddy. Both big Oscar and Ezra were honourable men. . . .'

'And that's why he remembered you in his will?'

'Of course. I was the first "white" man he knew. My family have known the family from way back. I was . . .'

'Oh, don't be so daft. He was just sorry for you, you silly old fruit, and if it comes through I hope you'll remember the young fella who gave you ten of the best years of his life and stuck to yer through thick and thin!' said Patrick meaningly. But the effect was lost because their cab drew up alongside a grey Bentley and Sir Arthur cried out, 'My God, there's Chaimy, in a suit!' He waved through the open cab window.

A slight shower had given way to sunshine and the black streets glittered; it was going to be a lovely day and Sir Arthur wondered if Audrey would ask him to lunch afterwards.

Chaimy, sitting beside the driver of the Bentley, who wore a bowler, gravely lifted his Homburg in acknowledgement, and a woman in the back with a raddled face and an extraordinary hat and veil leant forward to see what was happening.

'There's going to be a tremendous turn-out,' said Sir Arthur.

'Me mother once went to a wake in Ireland. They got stuck down a muddy lane and it went on for three days,' said Paddy.

'It won't be like that at all, I assure you,' replied Sir Arthur.

Only Ezra's enormous black car – the Rolls with the long wheel-base – had been allowed to park in front of the colonnaded building which looked more like a concert hall than a place of worship. Coffin-like, the car was a symbol of his extra authority, dead but watchful. The bemedalled sergeant, his bandolier gleaming, was shooing away the other chauffeurs. And still they came.

'It's like a first night,' said Jeremy to David.

'And a sell-out. Can't you have a word with the boys about their hats?'

Joshua and Jericho, designated ushers, had taken their roles solemnly enough to kit themselves out in morning coats with black ties and waistcoats, but they wore grey toppers.

'They look as if they're off to some sort of deathly Ascot.'

'They said that only stockbrokers wore black toppers.'

'Then they could wear yarmulkas like everybody else.'

'And those were designed by God to make Jews look even uglier than they naturally are. Go and talk to Sarah,' said David resignedly. 'I give up.'

But he *had* got them out of jail, thought Jeremy.

Sarah was standing by, but not with her husband. The pig farmer was nowhere to be seen. The Brigadier was addressing an empty space.

'As I was telling Sarah, Jeremy, the proper dress for mourning is white. On Yom Kippur my father used to . . .'

'Where've yer been all these years, Jeremy?' hissed Sarah, patting his arm. 'I'm very pleased with yer. Very pleased. I always said yer'd turn out all right in the end.' Jeremy looked baffled.

'Yer commission,' added Sarah, still patting his arm and scattering ash on his sleeve. 'Now you've settled down we can have a talk.'

Typical, thought Jeremy. Now that I have some money, I am worthy to receive more.

'We're both very fond of yer and yer never come and see us.' Jeremy did not want to say that he could not abide the smell, and now perhaps also the thought of pigs.

'Don't worry, I will,' he said feebly.

'You look after *me*, boy. I'll be the next to go. Can't understand how Tattie's still alive. Should have been dead years ago . . .' She screwed up her face in anticipation of a kiss from Eva Krapf and turned away. 'Who are all these people?' he heard her mutter.

Sarah was not the only one to marvel in this way, but the celebration of the death of a great man is an attractive occasion, which draws not only the next of kin, listed in the first paragraph of *The Times*'s report on the following day, but a number who attend, armed with visiting cards, in the expectation of seeing their names in the second or, at least, third paragraph of the notices.

The sly earl, the white knights, Sir Matthew and Sir Albert, were among those of rank certain to appear in small print following H.E. the Israeli Ambassador who, the press noticed, had just arrived. He was being greeted by Mr Oscar Barnet, the new chairman of Sterling Industries. But there were scores of congregants whom nobody in the family knew. And there were some, like retired servants or remote and pensioned cousins, they almost failed to recognize. Butlers, dentists, head waiters, secretaries look so different out of uniform. One man's identity was clear: he wore a cab-driver's badge.

'Nobody,' Ezra was wont to remark, 'who can claim the faintest relationship with me has less than five hundred pounds a year.'

It is not given to every Jewish immigrant family to produce a viscount in two generations, and these faint relations represented the bulk of the statistics which appear in the *Jewish Chronicle* Year Book. They had notched up a rung or two on the social and economic scale, moving from the Yiddish ghettos of Hull and Whitechapel and Cheetham Hill, Manchester, to the sweeter purlieus of Golders Green and Didsbury, but despite the rich shirts and ties of the husbands, and the mink capes of the wives, they had a beaten, flickery, subservient air about them. When Sarah had asked, 'Who are all these people?' she had known the answer and the knowledge and her memory of the early days before the family, as she put it, 'got posh', made her shudder. The tremor was felt by the older members of the family – 'There but for the grace of Mammon, go I!'

Audrey, placed by history in a different stream of the diaspora, observed this apartheid, but was not affected. (The sons were different; emboldened by education at minor English public schools, by the Israeli success at arms, and half again as large as their parents, they looked the world straight in the eye.) They all stood in embarrassed line to pay their respects. They admired Audrey's carriage, her heavy veil and her lack of jewels. And queenlike, she re membered their names.

And still they came.

'Chuck!'

'Why, Hubert! Hello there! I don't have to ask you how you are, you look terrific!'

Hubert emanated a glow of happiness which comes only from an enriching spiritual experience or the successful launch of an Australian Unit Trust. He did not look himself.

'Honey, you remember Hubert?'

'No,' said Tattie. (Wasn't he the man who had done her beloved brother down? And Ezra had died without giving her that game of gin rummy.) But she extended her hand, the fingers squeezed into monstrous jewels. Gallantly Hubert embraced an enormous emerald as Tattie turned to receive the sympathy and reminiscences of a delegation from Leeds.

'My, Hubert, you look bright-eyed and bushy-tailed. What's cooking?'

'Well . . .' began Hubert gaily, and then, attempting sternness, 'm'yaas.'

'Well?' insisted Chuck.

'Lord Sterling, Ezra to you, put the idea into my head, as a matter of fact. He asked me, "Are you happy?" or maybe he said, "You don't look happy." And driving back from Turners . . .'

It was becoming a confession, thought Chuck, and the sort of heart-searching which burgeons in the presence of death – so he reassured himself that Tattie was otherwise, if unhappily, engaged.

'. . . So I began to hum that bit of the Sixth where Beethoven presages a storm, you know? Da da deee, dumm dee dee dumm, dee dum de dumm, diddy da,' Hubert hummed, his blue eyes shining recklessly, 'and that night I slept at the Club. I arrive at work the next morning prepared to face the senior partner with advice of my intended divorce – he's a bit po-faced about that sort of thing happening on home grounds – to be told that there was no longer a senior partner. Guess what?' cried Hubert, clapping his hands. 'The silly old bean had shot himself.'

'Oh dear.'

'No oh dear, it wasn't a scandal. An accident – he meant to shoot a pigeon. But he shot himself instead.' Hubert started to back away. 'Now I'm living in his set in Albany ... come and have a bachelor evening. Toodleoo.'

Chuck felt a hand on his shoulder. It was Oscar.

'Has he been telling you about his coup?'

'About leaving his wife?'

Oscar looked puzzled. 'No, no. He insured Ezra's life, at the last moment, as it turned out – only time for one premium. Saved the estate about a couple of million. Sun Alliance are not going to be pleased. The young Viscount should be grateful to you, Chuck, for the introduction. He gets most of it.'

'Is he here? I'm curious to see him.'

'Not a sign. Not a trace. The little shit didn't even send a cable. And Abba Eban got him out of the war. It was a close shave, I can tell you. He ...'

'Excuse me, Uncle Oscar. Excuse me, Chuck. Beginners, please!' Jericho and Joshua bowed politely. The vault-like doors of the synagogue had opened under the colonnade and music could be heard from within. Little Oscar noticed with pleasure that it seemed expected of him to lead them in, as head of the family and head of the business.

'Right, boys. Family and business on the right. The Ambassador and the goyim on the left, okay?'

'What about Madame Hélène?' asked Jericho lightly.

Little Oscar considered this seriously. He had seen Audrey kiss the Frenchwoman's cheek. 'Family,' he said.

They trooped in, the second and third paragraphs pausing to give their names, or their cards, to the reporters, the faint relations being baffled by this procedure.

'Ridiculous,' said Tattie, 'dressing a child up like that. No place for a child anyway.' Sandra had kitted out her daughter in full mourning, topped by a veil embroidered with purple flowers.

'She looks like a little Infanta,' breathed Sir Arthur. He was feeling elevated and benign. Audrey had asked him for a bite of lunch afterwards.

Jeremy had just managed to stop Sarah lighting a cigarette in the lobby of the building when he noticed an old but unfamiliar face trying to connect with his own.

'My boy, you haven't changed a bit. It must have been twenty years ago that I picked you up from the side of the road, remember? Major Bentley.' He removed his hat.

'My God,' said Jeremy.

'Tell him to put his hat on,' said Sarah anxiously. 'He's in *shul*. What does he do?' (She was aware that her habits of speech required an interpreter.)

'Sarah, may I introduce you? This is Major Bentley. My . . . er . . . Lord Sterling's sister.'

'An honour, ma'am, he was a great man. I read about this in the *Telegraph*, and I felt I had to pay my respects. I hope I don't intrude. You see, I owe him a great debt.'

'Why?' asked Sarah, wrinkling her nose.

'Your brother was good enough to advise me not to sell Sterling shares and, as a matter of fact, I moved most of my modest portfolio into Sterlings.' He coughed. 'As a result of that we were able to build a swimming pool – for the grandchildren, of course.' He coughed again. 'We call it the Sterling pool . . . er, as a matter of fact.'

'Very nice,' said Sarah, bored but gratified. 'I'll tell him.'

Slightly astonished, the major withdrew. 'I like to be near the screen,' said Sarah. 'I'm going blind.'

The body of the congregation had recognized its duty to fill the pews so that the family, obviously detached, could make their entrance. So the synagogue was full when they processed down the aisle.

'It's all right, we're probably in the front row,' said Jeremy.

They walked down the aisle and Sarah, firmly holding his arm, smiled at all who caught her eye, irrespective of whether she knew them or not. A lady with bright yellow hair, wearing an obviously American mink, appeared to be causing Joshua a problem. The expression on her face was both intransigent and uneasy. Hre jewels looked hired. Sarah halted.

"Ullo, Pat, how's Ephie? Still alive?' She turned to Joshua. 'This is your great-aunt, no, your great-great aunt. C'mon, Pat, yer'd better sit with us.' She looked sternly at Joshua who bit his lip and shrugged.

'Oh, Mrs Kind!' said the lady in mink, blushing, and then, recovering, 'Ephie couldn't make the trip, but I thought, why not? And I can combine it with some shopping in the swinging city.'

Under the lid of a slight American accent Jeremy recognized the voice of his former nanny. The eye and jaw lines had hardened, but she was still the woman he had so often hugged as a little boy. They were seated.

'Remember the movies we used to go to?' she whispered. She was grateful for his presence, and for Sarah's gesture. Nobody had recognized her, and sitting in the front row with the family she was attracting many hard, curious glances.

Jeremy nodded. She looked at him intently, then reached for her handbag.

'Here, I wanna give you a tenner.' She gave him two new notes.

'It's two tenners.'

'Never mind, never mind.'

The address was banal. The standard rabbi had never met the subject of his eulogy and had drawn upon the *Times* obituary, *Who's Who* and a clutch of press clippings sent to him by Mrs Winterbourne. This showed.

The great men of England, when they die, are better praised by the Established Church. If they are Jews they are ill-served by a rabbinate with whom, habitually, they have enjoyed no communion. As a Jew accelerates to power, he sheds his religion. Streamlining.

The modern rabbi is created, succeeds and survives in the image of the congregation which supports him. This congregation was Zionist. 'There is one member of this great family,' the rabbi intoned, 'who is unable to join in celebrating the life of its most illustrious head, for . . .' – he paused dramatically and seemed to eye the twins, somnolent and superior, in the second row – 'military

reasons. I refer, of course, to Viscount Sterling's heir, Nicholas, er
... er ...' (the surname Caspi, courtesy Israeli Embassy, in his
notes suggested an unnecessary complication) 'who will become the
second Viscount Sterling.' The rabbi inhaled reverently. 'This
young man, who could have enjoyed a life of privilege and ease in
this country, chose to live on a kibbutz in Israel.' Now the eyes of
the family were upon him in a none too friendly way, he noticed.
'... enduring the privations and dangers we all know that sort of
life entails.' The rabbi was sticking to his guns – and to his script.

'Indeed, Nicholas is one of those heroes who have recently
captured Jerusalem and reunited our holy city with our holy land.'
He raised his voice to generate the expected stir, which, at a fund-
raising dinner at the Dorchester, would have earned a round of
applause. Indeed, some of his audience were poised to clap, until
they remembered where they were. The family sat unmoved, but
Jericho dreamily (but audibly), his eyes still shut, might have
expressed their feelings when he said, 'Thank you, we gave already.'

'It is a source of immense satisfaction to many of us in the
community,' the rabbi ploughed on, 'that towards the end of his
life, Ezra Sterling, one of our great men, should have become a
supporter of Eretz Israel.' He rolled the word round his fat lips.

The religious incumbents of Jewish communities tend to reflect
the attitudes of their congregation, this one, since the cause had
become respectable, being profoundly Zionist.

'Now,' intoned the rabbi, 'he is, like Lazarus who was once poor,
in a place even more lovely than his own beautiful home in the
English countryside.'

The poor relations nodded with approving envy, but one or two
of his audience winced.

With a final glare at the twins, indicating that certainly their final
destination would be different from the first Viscount Sterling's,
the rabbi closed his notebook, which contained cuttings from *The
Times*, *Manchester Guardian* and *The Jewish Chronicle*, and the
contralto voices from behind the screen swelled piteously.

'He maketh me to lie down in green pastures.' If the words from
behind the screen were too sung to be audible, they could read them

in the programme. Lucy allowed herself the vision of a green crocheted rug, the size of a football field. Much more practical to lie down in than damp grass. She replaced it immediately with the image of a new deep-freeze.

'*He leadeth me beside the still waters.*' What, David thought crossly, is so delightful about that? Still waters were boring and stank. Better the turbulence of a North American river with rapids, danger and speed. He glanced at Oscar's rock-like face. Had he, the winner of them all, left him, David, behind, in still waters?

'*Yea, though I walk through the va'ley of the shadow of death.*' He needn't have died, thought Xavier. I should have been firmer. To much excitement. My life will be duller without him. Still, there is the widow.

'*Thy rod and thy staff they comfort me.*' She'll never marry me, thought Geoffrey. She can't exchange the title of dowager Lady Sterling for plain Mrs Nickson. It would distress the servants.

'*Thou anointest my head with oil.*' Pretty words, thought Joshua, but how horrid.

'*Surely goodness and mercy shall follow me all the days of my life.*' Madame Hélène did not know what was what, but she wept.

'I thought you had that nice blessing,' whispered Stella. ' "The Lord make his face . . ." You know, the prayer you say every night. "The Lord bless you and keep you . . .", you know. "The Lord make his face to shine upon you." '

' "*And my cup runneth over.*" '

(The choir continued the psalm which accompanies all Jews to their graves, the millionaire to his mausoleum, the gangster to the pit.)

'That is for the living,' said Chaimy, the tears running helplessly down his face and spoiling his new black tie. 'This is for the dead.'

Old City, Jerusalem